WAKE UP
AND
OPEN
YOUR EYES

ALSO BY CLAY McLEOD CHAPMAN

rest area

miss corpus

commencement

Nothing Untoward: Stories from The Pumpkin Pie Show

The Remaking

Whisper Down the Lane

Ghost Eaters

What Kind of Mother

Stay on the Line

Kill Your Darling

Children's Books

The Tribe trilogy

Graphic Novels

Self Storage

Lazaretto

Iron Fist: Phantom Limb

Typhoid Fever

Scream: Curse of Carnage vol. 1

Origins

Devil's Reign: Villains for Hire

WAKE UP AND OPEN YOUR EYES

CLAY McLEOD CHAPMAN

QUIRK BOOKS

PHILADELPHIA

Library of Congress Cataloging-in-Publication Data
Names: Chapman, Clay McLeod, author.
Title: Wake up and open your eyes : a novel / Clay McLeod Chapman.
Description: Philadelphia : Quirk Books, 2025. | Summary: "When Noah's aging
   parents stop returning his calls, he travels to their Virginia home and finds it in
   shambles. They have been violently possessed via the media they watch—and
   much of the country is succumbing, too. With his nephew—also unaffected—
   Noah tries to return home to safety"—Provided by publisher.
Identifiers: LCCN 2024033401 (print) | LCCN 2024033402 (ebook) |
   ISBN 9781683693956 (hardcover) | ISBN 9781683693963 (ebook)
Subjects: LCGFT: Horror fiction. | Novels.
Classification: LCC PS3603.H36 W35 2025 (print) | LCC PS3603.H36 (ebook) |
   DDC 813/.6—dc23/eng/20240724
LC record available at https://lccn.loc.gov/2024033401
LC ebook record available at https://lccn.loc.gov/2024033402

ISBN: 978-1-68369-395-6

Printed in the United States of America

Typeset in Bembo and Indivisible

Designed by Andie Reid
Production management by Mandy Sampson

Quirk Books
215 Church Street
Philadelphia, PA 19106
quirkbooks.com

10 9 8 7 6 5 4 3 2 1

FOR MY FAMILY

Phase One

SLEEPER CELLS

There can never be a true divergence between faith and reason, since the same God who reveals the mysteries and bestows the gift of faith has also placed in the human spirit the light of reason.

—FIDES ET RATIO, POPE JOHN PAUL II

DECEMBER 18

Get your family out of there, Noah. Please. The city isn't safe anymore. None of them are. If you'd been watching the news, you'd know this by now. Please, honey. Please. For me. For your mother. You need to leave New York before it's too late, before your family gets hurt . . .

Mom left another message.

Noah didn't even hear his phone ring this time. Her voicemails are digital mosquitoes buzzing about his ear at all hours of the day—and night—hungry for blood.

This one landed at eleven. Shouldn't she be in bed by now? Fast asleep?

Paul Tammany must've just gotten off the air.

"Everything okay?" Alicia props herself up on one elbow in their bed, sensing tension.

Noah nods, still listening to his mother.

"Is it her?"

"Yeah." The frequency of Mom's calls has really ramped up since Thanksgiving. Something's in the air. Or maybe it's the fluoride in the water. Or the cell towers, all that 5G microwaving her brain.

I just watched another news story and they said there have been more protests—these riots and I, oh God, Noah, I'm so worried for you . . . So worried about my grandbaby . . .

When Noah was just a boy, growing up in Virginia, his mom would take him to the library. She'd let him check out two books. Any two. His choice. Their deal was simple: *One for you and one for me.* Mom would read one book to Noah at bedtime while he had to read the other on his own. He'd pick a picture book to tackle—the easy reads, Sendak or Silverstein—while for his mother, he'd tug the doorstoppers off the shelf. The cinder-block books. Tolkien. Dickens. King. He can still remember the sound of her voice, a soft southern lilt gamely taking on the personas of every last character, her words filling his bedroom, his mind, his dreams.

Noah can still hear her voice now.

When I think of you up there in that god-awful city, with all those awful people around, I—I don't know. I wish you'd come home to us. You can't be safe up there. Kelsey can't be safe . . .

He doesn't recognize her at all.

It's not Mom. It can't be.

Technically, yes, that's her voice. But . . . *the words.* They don't sound like her thoughts at all. These are someone else's words in her mouth. Her mind.

It's getting worse. *She's* getting worse.

"Is it bad?" Alicia's voice is calm. Fair and balanced. Working as an admin at a nonprofit will do that—her uncanny knack for putting out fires with nothing but the serenity in her tone.

"Pretty bad."

"How bad?"

They're talking about a reckoning, son . . .

Noah stares at the ceiling, phone pressed to his ear, his mind's eye filled with his mother's distorted visions of a city on fire, of protests right outside their window, complete chaos.

I know you don't believe me and I know you think I'm overreacting, but I—I just wish you would wake up, honey, before it's too late. I wish, I wish you would open your eyes.

"Can I hear?" Alicia slides in closer. There's that curiosity of hers. That mettle. Probably the first thing Noah remembers about meeting Alicia was how she was the one to approach him at that Antibalas show in Williamsburg—what? Thirteen years ago now?—in the back room at Black Betty. She kick-started the conversation, buying the next round. They danced with their drinks held up at their shoulders, those crinkly plastic cups, spilling G&Ts all over themselves. They both carried a hint of juniper all the way back to his apartment, seeped into their skin.

"You don't want to hear this," Noah says.

"What's she saying?"

Somebody ought to do something. Somebody ought to put a stop to these people—

These people.

"Nothing." Noah deletes the message before he finishes listening to it. What Alicia hasn't said, but what Noah's sensed anyhow, is that she's starting to ebb. Pull away from him. His family. And she's pulling Kelsey away with her.

When Thanksgiving discourse shifted to immigration, who's creeping into the country, didn't his parents notice Kelsey sitting across the table? Who just passed the mashed potatoes? Didn't they realize their granddaughter is half Haitian?

An invasion, Noah's mom called it. *Why can't they all just stay in their own country?*

What about me? What about Kelsey? Alicia asked Noah's mother at the table, point-blank, in front of Ash and his whole fam, Christ, *everyone,* having held her tongue as long as the first serving of turkey. *What do you see when you look at her? Your own granddaughter?*

Mom said, *no, no,* she wasn't talking about her daughter-in-law or granddaughter. She was talking about *those other people.*

Noah hasn't picked up a call from her since; just lets Mom go to voicemail now. Lets her ramble on for as long as she wants, filling up his inbox with her endless messages. He traps them. Suffocates them, like bugs in a jar.

But it's not going away. Mom's not stopping. This has festered for far too long.

Noah needs to deal with this.

"I'm gonna call," he says, already dialing. It doesn't matter how late it is.

No answer.

Strange. Mom always picks up. No matter what she's in the middle of, she always makes time to talk to her boys. Particularly Noah. *Mr. Golden Boy,* Asher always jabs. *Pampered Prince.*

So why isn't she picking up? Why won't she answer?

"Maybe she's asleep?" Alicia suggests.

"Maybe."

Neither says anything for a breath. Alicia holds on to Noah's eyes. Really takes him in. "Plenty of people are going through this," she says, breaking the silence. "I read in *The Atlantic*—"

Noah drags his pillow over his face and releases a low groan. "Pleeeease. No more articles about deprogramming your parents . . ."

It's far too late for an intervention. That ship sailed last Thanksgiving. Noah already tried dragging Mom and Dad back from the ideological brink of their batshit conspiracy-laden crackpottery. Before packing his fam in the car and plowing through traffic to get to Grammy and Grandpa's house for Turkey Time, Noah Googled "how to deprogram your parents," like he was cramming for an exam. He clicked a couple links. Printed a few articles. He even highlighted a couple sentences.

Debate won't help. Arguing only makes matters worse. Your loved ones are lost in a conspiracy theory loophole. They are falling down their own personal rabbit holes. Only patience and understanding will pull them out. Talk to them. See their side. Find common ground.

Did the writers of these listicles even know folks like Noah's father? He's the most stubborn son of a bitch Noah's ever met. He's lived with his bullheadedness his entire life.

But Mom . . .

Not her.

Mom is still Mom, isn't she? Somewhere deep down? Trapped in her own body? There has to be a scrap of sanity left, just a glimmer of common sense buried deep beneath the calcifying wave of conspiracy theories shellacking her brain, one queasy meme after another.

"You're not alone," Alicia says. "That's all I'm saying."

Sure feels like it. This downward spiral may have started years ago, but this last month has been a wildfire of voicemails. Used to be just one a week. Now it's up to three a day. Noah has felt so isolated from his family—his own mother—ever since she tumbled down the rabbit hole.

Whatever crawled back up isn't Mom anymore.

DECEMBER 19

It's almost time. Time to wake up, son. Open your eyes. The Great Reawakening is nearly here. December 20. It's going to be a glorious, glorious day and I only hope you are ready . . .

When did she leave this message? *Christ,* four in the morning? Is his phone even ringing anymore? He left his cell on his nightstand just in case she called again. He must've slept right through it. He brings his phone to his ear, takes in a deep breath, bracing himself, aaand . . .

Listens.

Noah picks up the faintest hiss of static, an ambience in the background. Whatever room she was in when she called sounds cramped, confined, like a closet. Was she hiding? A butt dial?

One second of crackling silence, now two . . .

Three . . .

Noah is just about to delete the message, convinced Mom misdialed, when—

There's her breath. A slow, ragged inhale groans right in the receiver. Her chest sounds wet, phlegmy, as if she's coming down with the flu.

Is she choking? Asphyxiating? Is it a gas leak? Is she being strangled? *What the hell is—*

Then she speaks. Right into the receiver. Into Noah's ear.

Time to wake up, son. Open your eyes.

Noah calls his mom straightaway.

No answer.

So Noah dials Dad. No answer there, either. Dad never picks up, so it's not such a stunner. What a waste of a data plan. Dad always gripes that cellular phones are nothing but a ball and chain, tethering him to the twenty-first century. He doesn't need to be reachable *all the time*, no matter what his sons insist. Leave a message on the answering machine, if it's so important.

So Noah dials the landline. Mom and Dad aren't answering that, either.

Now *that's* a red flag.

Don't panic. Not yet.

Noah dials Mom again. It's eight in the morning. She's bound to be awake by now.

It doesn't even ring this time. Straight to voicemail. Noah leaves a message, doing his damnedest to keep his voice even. "Calling you back, Mom . . . Just wanted to see if you're okay."

Noah speed-dials Asher. It rings . . . and rings. *Does nobody pick up their phone anymore?*

He leaves a message. "Hey, it's me. Something weird's going on with Mom. Have you—"

An incoming call cuts him off. Noah glances at the caller ID.

Ash is on the other line. *Finally.* "What," he says in a flat monotone when Noah picks up.

"Hello to you, too . . ." His older brother has been royally pissed at him since Thanksgiving.

"I'm busy," Ash grunted.

And I'm not? "You talk to Mom lately?"

"All the time."

". . . And?"

Silence on the other end.

"She's leaving me these messed-up messages and—I dunno. I'm just worried about her."

"Worried."

"Could you just check up on her? See if she and Dad are okay?"

"Why."

Because you live less than an hour away, asshole. Because you're her son, too. Because I want to make sure they're not going full-on Unabomber. Because I'm worried they might be—

Might be—

Might—

"Just go over there, okay? See if they're all right?"

"Fine." Ash hangs up. No *buh-bye, love you, bro.* Not like the two of them have ever been open with their emotions with each other, but Ash has gone full-on Dad with his stoicism. It's no mystery their father favored Asher growing up. The one time—the *only* time—Noah bolstered himself, all seventeen years of himself, and confronted his father about why he always took Ash out fishing, took Ash on camping trips, took Ash to baseball games, and not Noah, Dad's stolid response was, *Ash simply has more traditional values than you, son . . .*

No arguing with that. Dad always saw himself in Asher. He never saw himself in Noah.

He doesn't see me at all.

Even Asher's own friggin' family mirrors Mom and Dad. Look at them, the Fairchild Four: Ash, his wife, Devon, and their sons, Caleb and Marcus. It's like Ash modeled his entire household after their parents. A cookie-cutter clan, complete with cookie-cutter values.

So why isn't Mr. Traditional paying attention? Can't he see what's happening?

Noah tries calling Mom again around lunchtime.

Somebody pick up the phone . . .

He leaves another message.

"Hey, Mom . . . It's me. Noah. Everything okay? Call me."

Multiple messages.

"Mom? Dad? Anyone there? Pick up if you can hear me."

Where in the hell are they? Did they go on a trip without telling anyone? Dad despises other countries, and Mom *haaaates* flying. The two rarely leave their house anymore.

Noah could call their neighbors to check in on them . . . but does he even have their contact info? Calling the police would take this all to an awkward extreme he'd never be forgiven for if it turns out they're okay. *Please let them be okay.*

Noah calls Mom at dinner. This time she'll answer, he thinks. She *has* to answer.

Pick up pick up pick up . . .

Calls Dad. Just one more time. Then the landline.

Pick up pickuppickup . . .

Calls Asher.

PICK UP PICKUPPICKUPPICKUP!

It's been a full day of radio silence. Asher not picking up is the last straw. The camel's back, snapped. Something's wrong. The anxiety settles into his stomach, takes root.

What if . . . what if they're . . .

Don't go there. Don't—

Go there.

Noah has to go down there, doesn't he? If Ash isn't going to help, he has to do it himself. Hop in the car and drive six hours—seven, if there's traffic on I-95—all the way to his parents' house in Richmond and make sure Mom and Dad are okay. That they're still—

Still—

DECEMBER 20

"Sure you don't want us to come?" Alicia asks as he packs the Prius bright and early the next morning. The fam sees him off like this is some kind of quest. *Save the parents! Vanquish the evil lurking in their hearts!*

"Probably best I do this by myself," Noah says.

Alicia takes Noah into her arms, squeezing. "Call me, okay? Whenever. Don't hesitate."

"Will do."

"Will you be back by Christmas?" Kelsey asks, unable to keep her hips from swiveling. She's roller-skating even when she's stock-still, no need to lace up, always gliding down the sidewalk on her way to school, the bodega, her friends' houses. Such a city mouse, so at home in their multicultural neighborhood, so different from the white suburb Noah grew up in. But even here, Alicia is sometimes mistaken for Kelsey's Haitian nanny. It's everywhere, even in their liberal haven. Unavoidable. Inescapable.

Noah feels this pinch in his gut. "I'll only be gone for a night. Two, tops."

He's missing her holiday recital for this. Kelsey's soloing, selected by her teacher to sing "The Greatest Love of All." She's been practicing all week, singing around the house, her voice filling their apartment. The girl's got pipes.

"Promise?" Kelsey has her mother's eyes. Plus her composure, thank Christ. What does she possess of him? What does he see of himself in her? His need to please? His corny jokes?

"Promise." Noah holds up his pinkie. Kelsey brings hers up and the two intertwine.

There it is, his word, his solemn vow, locked in with a pinkie swear.

No take-backs.

Heart attack, home invasion, gas leak, oh my!

Noah can't help himself. He imagines every worst-case scenario along the Jersey Turnpike. It's a song sung to the tune of Dorothy's panic attack along the Yellow Brick Road—

Heart attack, home invasion, gas leak, oh my!

It's the radio silence that gnaws at him. As much as Noah hates listening to Mom's messages, it's worse when they completely stop. Mom always calls, even if he doesn't pick up.

Heart attack—

He can picture it: his father keeled over at the breakfast table, Mom wailing away over Dad's dead body, too distraught to even hear the ringing, ringing, ringing of the phone.

Home invasion—

Is Noah going to find their bodies in the basement? Hands bound behind their backs? Mouths sealed in duct tape?

Gas leak—

Will he step into the house and find their bodies tucked in next to each other, as if they're just sleeping, waxen skin gone all gray?

Oh my!

Asher is closer. He could've spared a couple hours out of his *busy* friggin' life as a corporate overlord to check up on their parents, but *nope*—he couldn't be bothered.

Noah calls again—on the hour, every hour, closing in on the Mason-Dixon Line.

Mom's cell, then Dad's, then their landline.

Then Asher.

Pick up pick up SOMEBODY PICK THE FUCK UP.

Something's wrong. Very, *very* wrong.

This is all Fax's fault.

Fax News took Noah's parents away. You know their stupid slogan: *Just the Fax*—cheekily misspelled in some outdated Reagan-era wisecrack. This right-wing propaganda machine masquerading as a twenty-four-hour news network had been reprogramming his parents for years. *Years.* And Noah didn't do a goddamn thing about it. *Now they're . . .*

They're . . .

Noah's family always had an uncanny knack for repressing their politics. When he was younger, he never knew what his parents' political affiliation was. Who you voted for is better kept private. It isn't polite conversation. No ruffling of feathers at the dinner table during the holidays, that's that. Simply pass the potato rolls and keep your politics to yourself, please . . .

Then something changed.

The *channel* changed.

It all started with Dad. He was such an easy target once he retired. *Put out to pasture*, was how he put it. Thirty-five years as a regional sales rep for Chevron doesn't add up to much beyond a Walmart sheet cake. His days are now spent sprawled out in front of the television for hours on end, only getting up from his cozy recliner during commercial breaks.

Let's see what's going on in the world, he'd always say, picking up the remote. Cable news was his default, a steady stream of world events filtered through Fax. Noah wasn't around to witness his father's descent into far-right fantasyland in real time. On their rare holiday father-son chat, Dad sounded like he was rehashing poorly written conspiracy theory fan fic.

At first, it was easy to discredit his crackpot talk. *The ol' man's just getting crankier.* Noah and Alicia joked about it, miles away in Brooklyn, opining on the fate of every white man entering his golden years. "That'll be you one day," she teased Noah. "Just you wait . . ."

"Shoot me now," he begged. "If I ever start sounding like that, you have my full permission to put me out of my misery."

"Be careful. I just might."

Then Mom started to sound just like Dad.

It started off with small things. Tiny cracks in her civility. Nothing too noticeable. Definitely nothing worth pushing back on. But when they spoke on the phone, Noah began to detect buzzwords. Slogans. Batshit news headlines she must have picked up from Fax.

Mom never had a political bone in her body. A farm girl plucked up from Powhatan and planted in the suburbs, she raised two boys on her own. Their household was her world, and she rarely bothered to venture beyond it. The one exception was her volunteer work at the local library for the last twenty years, reading picture books to toddlers every Saturday.

Up until they replaced me with a transsexual, she told Noah.

Whoa, Mom . . . Noah's ribs gripped his lungs. He had to take a moment to process the words that had just oozed out from the receiver. *You don't really believe that, do you?*

It's happening everywhere now. There was a gravelly drag to her breath, every word raked over wet rocks. It could've been a cold, but this sounded phlegmier. Mom insisted she was fine. *Everywhere. Every last library. That's what they've been saying on the news.*

You mean Fax? That's not news, Mom . . .

You don't understand, son. There was the edge of belittlement in her voice, which frustrated Noah to no end. He was forty-two, married with a daughter of his own, and his mother—some twisted facsimile of her, at least—was treating him like he was still a child.

You just don't see it yet, she said. *But you will. Soon.*

Where was this sharpened edge in her voice coming from? Why was Mom so *angry?* Mom, who raised Noah to be a *thinking man,* as she always put it. Who cut the crusts off his peanut butter sandwiches. Who teared up during commercials about auto insurance.

That Mom. Noah had no idea who this woman was.

Noah flips to NPR. He needs a distraction. "Reports of protesters convening on—"

Noah turns the dial.

"A riot outside—"

On to the next station.

"Another attack at—"

Noah flips the radio off and drives in silence. Stewing; grip tightening into fists around the wheel. *I just want my parents back,* he thinks. *Back to the way they were before all . . . this.*

They were a family once. They still are. Bound by blood, even if not ideology.

Can't they be a family again?

What if they're . . .

What, exactly?

If they're . . .

＝

Dead.

Noah sits behind the wheel, staring out the windshield at the one-story, brick and vinyl box that is his childhood home. Woodmont is one of those sleepy southern subdivisions where kids ride their bikes in the middle of the street without worry of getting run over. Noah and Ash skinned their knees on this very block plenty of times, years of their blood soaked into asphalt.

"Mommmyyyy . . . Mommmmyyyyyyyy . . ."

Little Noah's in the street. His Nike is caught in the bike chain, ankle tangled into its links, while his leg folds backward. He's like a deer snagged in a bear trap, only the snare is his own Schwinn. The pain in his shin radiates through the rest of his body, throbbing up from the shattered bone. All the other kids from the neighborhood have circled around. Most still sit on their bikes, staring down at little Noah. Even Ash is among them, jaw slung open. Gawking.

"MommymommyMOMMYYYYY!"

And just like that, there she is.

Mom answers his call, pushing through the circle of kids and swooping down. She untangles Noah's broken leg, the linked teeth of the chain basted in blood, and scoops her boy into her arms, abandoning his bike. She's taking him back inside, to the safety of their home.

"I got you," Mom whispers in Noah's ear as she rushes up their lawn. "I got you, I got—"

You.

The memory's been waiting for him, right there in the middle of the street. Like it happened only yesterday.

Noah's driven seven straight hours without a single pit stop. His bladder begs for relief, but he can't bring himself to climb out of the car. Not yet.

The house seems to have shrunk. It doesn't feel like home anymore. But this is where he grew up. So much of his life was spent under that roof.

Why can't he just go inside?

Noah takes a deep breath, the air settling in his lungs, then opens the door and slips out.

The lawn is in sore need of mowing. Dad has always been a militant lawn upkeeper. The scraggly patches of grass remind Noah of when he first decided to grow his hair long back in high school. Dad wasn't all too happy about it. *Look who needs a trim.*

Dad would *never* let his lawn grow this long. Not in a million years.

Mom's flower beds have all shriveled. Scabs of chrysanthemums speckle the soil like a dozen red flags.

What's on the other side of that door?

What's waiting for him?

Noah rings the doorbell, which feels so formal. *I should just go in,* he thinks.

Heart attack . . .

He knocks. No answer. Knocks again, harder this time.

Home invasion . . .

Dad's car is in the driveway.

Gas leak . . .

No outward signs of a disturbance. No broken windows.

Oh my . . .

The spare key is where it's always been: under the terra-cotta pot on the front stoop. Whatever plant was in it is completely wilted, a husk of its former glory.

Here we go, Noah thinks as he slides the key in. The lock clicks.

The door won't budge. Something—

a body oh God it's a body

—is blocking it from the inside. Noah leans in with his shoulder and pushes, shoving the obstruction back. He pushes until there is enough space to slip his head in.

Not a body.

The console table is overturned. It was pressed up against the door like a barricade. A last stand. His fam's Alamo. Noah's throat catches. *What—who—were they trying to keep out?*

The oily smell finds him first. A rotten-apple tang hangs in the air, fecund enough to coat the back of his throat. Something organic has turned. Something that could've been living at one point but definitely isn't anymore. Whether it's food or family, Noah doesn't have a clue.

"Mom?"

There's no light. Nothing is turned on. The shades are pulled.

"Dad?" It's still a question. A plea. *Please somebody answer just answer me please—*

Nobody answers.

But *someone* is talking. Loud and clear. Defiant in his declarations, talking with a bald bravado that sounds familiar. It certainly isn't a member of the Fairchild family.

"You guys here? Helloooo?"

Noah hasn't set a foot farther in. He stands in the doorway, the sun still warming the back of his neck. Nothing but darkness waits ahead. *Turn back*, he thinks. *Just go. Leave. Now.*

"It's . . . me. Noah."

As he ventures down the hallway, step by step, he feels like he's entering a cave, spelunking deep into the earth. Even the air feels different inside, as if it hasn't moved in a month, maybe since Thanksgiving, humid and viscous. The dark is so all-encompassing, the world at his back may as well not exist. Sunlight can't reach this deep.

Everything is an inch off from where he remembers. It's as if Noah tried explaining to a drunk architect what his childhood home looked like, and then they attempted to sketch the house based on his hazy recollections. The broad strokes are all there, but the details are off.

The deeper he goes, the louder it gets.

The voices. Not just one—legion.

Their words winnow through the miasma of the house, louder now, practically shouting in synchronicity with one another. A harmonized screed. Definitely not his parents.

Chanting. That's what it sounds like. An incantation of some kind. These voices are repeating themselves, saying the exact same thing. Just how many of them are there, exactly?

Is this some kind of ritual? Noah's mind immediately leaps to a devil-worshipping cult crashing at his parents' pad. Charlie Manson sacrificing Mom and Dad on the living room couch.

Wait, Noah realizes. *Those aren't different people . . .*

It's the same voice, merely reverberating from different corners of the house. The television is still on. Not just one TV, but . . . all of them? Each and every set in the house is turned to the exact same channel, blasting its broadcast. How many sets do his parents *have*? When he was growing up, there was just the one in the living room. Now it sounds like dozens of them.

The volume is cranked up, flooding the halls with the baritone echo of—

Just the—

—Fax. Of course.

"Mom?" Noah calls out, louder now, competing with the anchor, Paul Tammany, that perpetually pissed-off pissant with a brick chin. "Dad? Anybody home? Can you answer me?"

The only reply he receives comes from the television. The news is too loud, eclipsing Noah's voice. The dim glow cast off the living room TV faintly illuminates the hall. Noah can hear another television blaring farther off, in the kitchen. The same voice swarms out from each TV, bouncing off the walls like conservative claptrap echolocation. All the Paul Tammanys talk over one another. Listening to this shit gives Noah a headache. He can't think straight.

Just the way Fax likes it.

Crrnch. There's a crumbling sensation under Noah's heel. He looks down. A light seasoning of frosted white glass is scattered across the floor. Shards of a lightbulb.

Crrnch. The brittle crackle of broken glass thickens under his feet. It's not lightbulbs anymore. He's stepping on a shattered picture frame. Photographs of himself as a child, along with the rest of the fam, no longer hang on the walls, all of them now flung across the floor.

What the hell happened here? A break-in? Were they robbed?

Noah bends down to pick up a picture.

It's a black-and-white snapshot of Mom as a dimple-cheeked corn husk of a girl. There she is—Little Miss Spat, 1968—looking just like Shirley Temple, curtsying for the camera. That satin sash is still hanging around here, somewhere, its purple hue fading into a dull lavender.

There's a photo of Noah and Asher in the backyard. Both wear cowboy outfits. Ash has a cap gun, his arm roped around Noah. He can still feel the noogie he got right after Mom snapped the picture, as if the sensation of Ash's knuckles is ingrained into the picture itself.

Noah leans over and picks up a picture of Kelsey. Four years old. She's smiling for the camera. *Beaming.* He chokes up. He can't help himself. He wasn't expecting to see her. He misses her so much.

Wants to be with her, back in Brooklyn. Not here. Anywhere but here.

Noah hangs what remains of the frame back on the wall. He doesn't want the picture of Kelsey left on the floor where someone can step on it.

"Mom? It's me . . . Noah." Why is he even talking anymore? "Dad? Where are you two?"

He can't even hear himself over the booming voice of Paul Tammany. He needs to turn off the television sets. All of them. Then he can find his parents.

Whatever's left of them.

The living room is empty. This close to the television, the volume is painful, making Noah's ears ring. Oily colors are cast across the upturned furniture. The couch is flipped over, its cushions tossed to the floor. The lamp is knocked on its side.

Dad's hallowed La-Z-Boy is pulled back into its reclining position. Its leather upholstery has been ripped open, cotton tufts plucked and flung to the floor. His empty throne. Gutted.

When they were kids, that cracked recliner was always off-limits. Asher and Noah knew never to sit in it, even when Dad wasn't around. Asher would hop in whenever they were alone, assuming the reclining position. *This is the life*, he'd sigh, pretending to watch TV. Noah never sat in that chair. Not once. The consequences of getting caught were too great. Even the name unnerved him—*La-Z-Boy*—as if the leather was the tanned hide of some good-for-nothing child, skinned for his indolence, now dressing for his father's furniture.

A break-in. Noah is certain of it now. Someone broke into the house and murdered his parents. *In Cold Suburban Blood*. He just needs to find where they are, bound and gagged and—

"We're only a couple hours away from the Great Reawakening, folks . . . Can you feel it?"

That goddamn Paul Tammany simply won't shut up.

Where's the remote? Noah glances around the floor but can't find it. Not in this mess. He'll just have to switch the TV off manually. He walks over, grabs the cord, and gives a single, sturdy tug. The screen collapses into blackness, taking Tammany and his voice into the void.

Thank God, Noah thinks, *now I can finally hear my—*

"I was watching that."

Noah shouts. He spins around and finds his father standing behind him, teetering on his feet amid the overturned furniture. Had he been hiding behind the couch this whole time? Squatting?

"Jesus, Dad . . . I've been calling for, like, the last five minutes."

Look at him. He's lost weight. A lot of weight. His button-down Hawaiian shirt sags over his shoulders, two sizes too big for his scrawny frame now. Noah knows that shirt. One of his father's favorites. It's all stained. It looks like there are extra islands rising up just next to Oahu.

When was the last time Dad slept? Shaved? *Bathed?* He's so . . . *ripe*.

Something like a smile spreads across his father's lips, but there's no mirth in it. He looks like a grinning fish. "You made it, son. Just in time."

"Time for . . . *what?*"

"It's . . ." Now he's the confused one. "It's the twentieth."

"What about it?" The date holds no value to Noah. Did he forget somebody's birthday?

"You mean . . ." Dad sounds genuinely hurt. "You're not here for . . . for . . ." He lapses deeper into himself, lost in his thoughts.

"Want to tell me where Mom is?"

No answer. Just a blank stare at the empty screen. Dad wobbles on his feet, ready to fall. *His eyes.* Noah's never seen such uncertainty in his father's eyes before. He doesn't even know where he is anymore, displaced in his own living room. A lost little boy. *What is this?*

"Here. Let me help you." Noah guides Dad back to his eviscerated throne. The dry leather crackles under his meager weight. He's diminished. He was such a giant before.

Look at him now. So small. Frail.

"Dad? *Dad.*"

Dad's eyes are still fixed on the television, even though it's un-plugged. *What's he looking at?* Noah can't help but glance at their distorted reflections in the screen's obsidian surface. He doesn't give it much thought—refuses to, forcing the notion far, far away—but he swears he sees something move behind his father's reflection, shifting across the empty screen.

"You thirsty, Dad? Can I get you some water? Some ice?"

His father barely shakes his head, eyes watering, forever focused on the blank screen.

"Dad . . . Where's Mom?"

He still won't answer.

"Stay here, 'kay? I'll be right back." If his father hears him, he doesn't acknowledge it.

Noah abandons his dad. He has to find his mother all on his own. He picks up his pace, motivated now, and heads toward his parents' bedroom.

"Mom? Mom . . . are you here?"

Noah passes through the kitchen. The fridge has been left open, its shelves pecked clean. Flies scatter with every footstep. Cooking was always Mom's currency. She showed her love through her meals. You wanted to break Mom's heart? Tell her you weren't hungry.

Noah lost ten pounds his first year at college. He had the reverse Freshman Fifteen, whittling his weight down to a svelte, sensitive intellectual physique, finally able to fit into his skinny stovepipe jeans once he was five hundred miles away from Mom's kitchen.

The glow of yet another television screen casts its dim pallor over discarded food containers and rotten vegetables. It's a tiny TV, porta-ble, the type you can heft in one hand.

Noah turns it off—and yet the news anchor's voice keeps on going, echoing from yet another room deeper in the bowels of their house. Still spouting out the Fax.

"It's December twentieth, folks!" Tammany announces. "The day we've all been waiting for . . ."

Crash! There's the sound of something sturdy falling to the floor farther down the hall.

From his parents' bedroom.

"Mom?"

No time to second-guess himself. Noah races for their room.

"Mom!"

She's standing in front of the television, stock-still, inches from the screen. She's in a nightgown, some formless floral print muumuu thing. A truly chaste affair, the hem at her ankles, long sleeves. Her Little Miss Spat sash is draped over one shoulder. It's too small for her now, practically noosing her neck. The gold-embossed date— *1968*—captures the glow from the TV.

Noah takes a quick whiff and recoils. There is a smell coming off her: Dried sweat. Urine. When's the last time she bathed herself? Those aren't all yellow daisies. *Christ, they're stains.*

"Mom?"

She sways ever-so-faintly on her feet, threatening to collapse at any moment.

"Jesus, Mom—"

Her eyes never break from the screen, never leave Paul Tammany, anchored to the anchor, even as Noah takes her by the arms and gently but firmly guides her toward the bed.

"Are you okay? Mom? Mom!"

Her lips are moving. Silently mouthing something Noah simply can't hear.

"What happened?"

What is she saying? Her lips won't stop moving, mincing invisible words.

"Mom, what's wrong?"

Then it hits Noah: *She's repeating everything Paul Tammany says.*

"Are—are you all right?"

Nothing Noah says registers. Mom's eyes remain locked on the television, lips moving faster now, breathlessly keeping up with the broadcast.

So Noah turns it off. Just a flip of the switch and—

Mom blinks.

"Noah?" She smiles. Her eyes are brimming with tears. "Oh, hon, *you made it.*"

Noah's stunned. Absolutely gobsmacked. He was not expecting . . . *this.* She seems genuinely happy to see him. Dizzy with giddiness. "Mom, what the hell hap—"

Mom's arms lift and embrace her boy. She squeezes, tighter than he expects—still got some strength to her. She nuzzles her face in the nape of his neck. "You made it, you made it . . ."

"Mom—"

"You came back to me . . ." Her breath spreads all hot down his neck. "You came *back.*"

"Are you okay? Are you—"

"I knew you'd come. Now we can all be together when the—"

"Mom. *Stop.* Please."

"—when the Great—"

"Mom."

She hesitates. Stares. A look of distrust rises up in her eyes. She senses something's not quite right. A fresh conspiracy brewing right under her own roof. "Where's . . . Where's Kelsey?"

"At home." Noah feels like he needs to add, "In Brooklyn. With Alicia."

"You didn't bring her?" She doesn't try to hide her disappointment. The heartbreak.

"No." *Hell no. Fuck no.*

"Oh," Mom says. She turns away from him.

Back to the screen.

Noah can see the desperation in her face, an addict's itch. She wants to turn it back on.

"Mom. Talk to me. What's going on?"

"Your father and I are waking up, hon." She wipes her cheek, scraping away a tear. "We're opening our eyes."

———

"It's a nightmare," Noah whispers in the front yard. He doesn't need to keep his voice down outside, but still, there's some part of him that feels compelled to speak in hushed tones.

He needed to get out of the house, to escape the suffocating space his parents have been marinating in since . . . *Thanksgiving*? How's that even possible? That was only weeks ago.

"What happened?" Alicia asks.

"I don't know." He glances back at the house. "The place is just . . . a mess. It's like a bomb went off. They haven't cleaned or . . . or . . ."

"Is your mother okay?"

"It's like she has dementia or . . . or carbon monoxide poisoning. Both of them."

"Can you call someone?"

"Who?"

"What about the police?"

"Mom says she doesn't want anyone in the house."

"Ash?"

"He's still not picking up . . ." Noah glances over his shoulder again, scanning the surrounding houses. The trees bristle behind him, reminding him how big this world truly is, how insignificant he is, how alone. "What am I supposed to do?"

"Can you call social services?"

"They don't want to leave."

"That's not their choice anymore. You might have to make that decision for them."

"Okay. I—I'll call." Noah feels his throat tightening.

"It's okay," Alicia says. "You're going to be okay. You've got this, you can do this."

He feels like a helpless little boy. He wasn't prepared to have to take care of his parents—not yet. Mom isn't even sixty-five. "I—Jesus, I need to clean up this fucking mess."

"Do you need help? Do you want me to come—"

Yes. Yes, come right now. Drop everything and save me from this nightmare. Please—

"No. No, I got it."

"You sure?" She'd have to bring Kelsey. She can't see her grandparents like this.

Please oh please help me help me—

"Yeah, no, I got it."

"You don't have to go through this alone."

"I'm probably gonna have to stay longer."

How long had he thought this would all take? A night? A couple days, at most?

"I'll be back before Christmas," he hears himself promise. Five days from now. "Maybe I can surprise Kelsey. Climb down the chimney or something. *Ho-ho-ho.*"

"Take all the time you need," Alicia said. "I've got Kelsey. Don't worry about us."

"How was the recital?"

"Good. Great. She promised she'll sing for you when you come home."

"I miss you guys." *Need you*, is what Noah really wants to say. He doesn't want to be alone with this. With *them*. "Is Kelsey there?"

"Yeah. Wanna talk to her?"

"Could I?"

Alicia switches to FaceTime, then hands the phone to their daughter.

"Hey, sprout." Noah's voice lifts an octave, suddenly sunshine. "How's your day?"

"*Fiiine*," she says with an exasperated sigh. "I got another Band-Aid."

Kelsey is obsessed with Band-Aids. It doesn't matter what the injury is, she'll demand a bandage for just about any boo-boo. It's necessitated a new family rule: *No blood, no Band-Aid.*

"Was there blood?" Noah asks.

"Yeah . . ."

"For real? What happened?"

"I got hit at school."

"*What?* Who hit you? Another student? What's his name?"

"It's a her."

A girl?

"Rachel McAuley told me it was time to wake up and then she pushed me into a desk."

The fuck? "Did a teacher see it happen?"

"Rachel said I should open my eyes."

"*Kelsey.* Did you tell an adult?"

"No . . ."

"You need to tell the teacher what happened next time . . . Promise?"

"Promise."

"You can't let people push you around. Don't let"—*the little motherfucker*—"them bully you or anyone else. That's no good, okay? Can you put your mom back on for me, please?"

Kelsey hands the phone back to Alicia.

"Did you know about this?"

"I didn't want to add to your stress."

"Who was the girl—"

"Noah? You're breaking up." Her voice fragments, splintering into digital bits.

"Can you hear me?"

"Noah? Noah, I can't—"

"Can you hear me now?"

"You're break—"

She's gone. Alicia's gone. Noah stares at his phone. He dials her again, only this time he's greeted by some other woman: *All circuits are busy right now. Please try again.*

He tries Alicia again.

All circuits are busy right now. Please try—

Tries again.

All circuits—

Noah hangs up. Turns back to the house. The nightmare of it all, nesting inside.

———

The televisions are turned on again.

Not just one. All of them, from the sound of it, switched to Fax, the volume cranked to the hilt, spewing the news throughout the house and filling every last room with its vitriol.

"What the fuuuck . . ." Noah rubs his hands over his face, moaning into his fingers. He's only been gone for a few minutes. Five minutes, at most.

Did his parents race from room to room and flip on every last TV while he was outside?

Dad's in the La-Z-Boy where Noah left him, eyes glued to the screen.

"We're only a little over an hour away, folks," Tammany says. "Can you feel it? Time to WAKE UP. OPEN OUR EYES. The masses are all gathering to make sure our voices are heard."

What the fuck is this dimpled chin in a suit talking about? Some kind of pilgrimage or protest? *Christ.* Were all the wackos coordinating their own little Million Man March?

Save the date! His parents got an invitation, apparently, RSVPing with their own sanity.

December 20.

Of all the days to pay a visit. *Just my fucking luck.* He'd laugh with half the country if his own mom and dad weren't drinking the god-damn ultraconservative Kool-Aid.

He tries Ash again. Not that he expects his big brother to pick up. He's just stalling.

At least it's ringing.

Noah leaves yet another message. "Hey. *Asshole.* Where the hell are you? I'm at Mom and Dad's and . . . *Christ.* Did you know about this? Any of this? Why didn't you tell me? Get your dick over here and help me deal with this shit because I . . . I can't do this all by myself, okay?"

He tries Alicia, but she doesn't pick up.

No more stalling.

He decides to handle Mom first. Dad can wait. He walks down the hall and hesitates outside their bedroom door, listening in. All he can hear is the Fax, Paul Tammany's oozing voice seething through: "We're counting down until THE WAKE-UP CALL . . ."

Christ, you'd think the ball was about to drop in Times Square.

More like a bomb.

Deep breath, Noah thinks. He sharply inhales through his nose, feeling the pressure mounting behind his eyeballs, then steps into his parents' bedroom. "Okay, Mom, I think we—"

Mom's naked.

The only piece of clothing on her body is the Little Miss Spat sash, barely covering her shoulder. She's inches from the screen, flesh bathed in blue and pink hues, a swirl of colors cast off from Fax News, their pastel palette soaking her pendulous breasts, her swollen stomach.

There's a moment, a mental hiccup when Noah can't help but think of the Christian Children's Fund commercials he'd seen on TV as a kid. Sally Struthers would make her tearful plea: for only seventy cents a day, the price of a cup of coffee, families just like Noah's could sponsor a child in need from some far-off corner of the world. Noah actually asked Dad once if they could support a child in Africa. He huffed, then told him to go outside and play with Asher.

The images of these children with their distended bellies come crashing back. *For just seventy cents a day, the price of a cup of coffee, you can sponsor a brainwashed mom . . .*

"Jesus." Noah races for the TV first, switching it off. "Mom, what're you—"

"NO!" The outright spite—*the rage*—that takes over his mother's face is startling. She pushes him away. The sudden outburst sends Noah stumbling back onto the bed.

"Mom!"

She turns the TV back on. *Click.* The screen bathes her body in its blue glow once more, the discordant tone of Paul Tammany's voice filling the room. She sighs, relaxed again. Lulled.

Then she begins to masturbate.

"What the *fuck* are you *doing?"*

Noah can only stare, aghast at the sight of his mother as she runs a hand over her stomach, and then—*down*—as if to rub the oily glow of the television screen into her skin.

Soaking up the news.

"Mom?"

His naked mother. Touching herself in front of the television. It's like she's . . . like she's . . .

"MOM."

To the news. To the anchorman. Fondling her left breast with her right hand as she moans over Paul Tammany's vitriolic words. Mom's eyes roll up into her sockets, hips shimmying side to side in a serpentine swivel as her other hand slides farther in—

"STOP IT."

Noah grabs her muumuu from the floor. He drapes it over his mother's shoulders. He pulls her back, away from the television, dragging her to the bed and forcing her to sit. She's stubbornly transfixed by the screen, mouth open as she continues to touch herself. Rub herself.

"Mom, please. Please, just . . . just stop it. *Stop.*"

But she won't. She won't stop. She keeps rubbing her fingers over her raw skin, winnowing across the distended flesh, the wrinkles, the coiling hairs—

"*Goddammit.*"

Noah bolts out of the bedroom. He leaves her there, barely covered. He squeezes his eyes shut, hoping to force the image out of his mind. Her pale skin and its myriad of wrinkles sear their way into his brain. All those purple veins glowing in the pastel hues of the news.

Bathing in it. Basking. Soaking it all up.

＝

What the fuck what the fuck what the ffffuuuuuuuuuck is happening to his parents?

It's like some hostile hijacking of their personalities. Jesus, their humanity. *Invasion of the Parent Snatchers.* They are GOP pod people now. This is eons beyond just some silly ideological divide between generations. This isn't about some goddamn election, who's voting for who. It has everything to do with the news. *Who* exactly his parents are getting their fax—sorry, *facts*—from. Their channel of choice has changed them from the inside out.

He barely recognizes his own mom and dad anymore.

What they are becoming.

Okay. So. Quick assessment: *What the fuck is going on?* His parents are incapable of taking care of themselves now, clearly, racist masturbating vegetables glued to the boob tube.

Okay. So . . . *What do we do now?*

Can he take them somewhere? Pack them up in the car and go to a hotel or—or—

Scratch that. His folks aren't going anywhere. Not in their condition.

Okay. So. Noah's stuck. *What next? What now?*

Clean house. Purge this place.

Or burn it the fuck down.

The temptation to call a housecleaning service—or a hazmat team—is so strong. He'd happily pay out of his own pocket for somebody, *anybody*, to go scorched earth on their home. But none of his calls are going through.

First step: fresh air.

Noah opens as many windows as he can to flush out all the foul smells. This place is in sore need of circulation. *Or an exorcism.* Can he call a priest? Spritz a bit of holy water around?

He peels back the living room curtains.

Let there be light . . .

Illuminating the mess only spotlights how much there actually is. When Noah and Ash were kids, Mom would always fuss over the smallest spills, swooping in with a damp dishrag the second one of them dropped his juice box. He remembers Mom vacuuming every night after dinner. She'd tease him by chasing after him with the hose, the nozzle sucking at his bum, *thwwwwump!*, the hem of his shirt slurped up by the vacuum's high-powered suction.

Got you now! she'd shout over the high-pitched hum of the vacuum's engine.

Food scabs the living room floor. Fluids of some kind have crusted into the carpeting. Practically every lightbulb has been shattered in its socket. Books no longer rest on the shelves. All of his father's Tom Clancy novels are ripped and fanning across the floor. Clothes are strewn about. Soiled, from the smell of it.

How in the hell did this happen? How could *Asher* have let this happen? Wasn't he checking up on Mom and Dad, stopping by every now and then, just to make sure they're okay?

How could he not have known what was going on?

Noah finds some black industrial garbage bags under the bathroom sink. He brings a broom into the living room and starts sweeping, herding the detritus into a heap in the center of the room. He has to work around his father, whose focus remains on the screen.

"Excuse me," Noah says, maneuvering around him. "Pardon me. Coming through . . ."

Dad's attention doesn't waver. It's like cleaning up in a department store after it's closed, navigating around all the mannequins.

Noah manually turns off the television as he passes by.

"Whoopsie," he says. "Guess that's it for screen time."

A barrage of sound startles him.

Noah halts. The goddamn television is on again. Somebody turned it back on.

Somebody.

Dad hasn't gotten up from his La-Z-Boy. There's no way he stood without Noah noticing. Even with his back turned, he would've heard something. Sensed it.

Dad's screwing with him. He must have the remote.

But Noah can't shake the feeling someone's watching him. There are eyes on his back, leering as he sweeps. It's just the TV, but still, it creeps the ever-living fuck out of him.

Noah turns to take in the screen. To—what, exactly? Confront the anchorman?

Paul Tammany is looking directly at Noah.

For a second, just the quickest blip, it seems to Noah as if he's hesitated. Paul pauses in his reporting, mouth open, that cocksure grin, and stares back at him.

Then he's launching into the next news story. Or what's passing as news. "Folks are gearing up for the WAKE-UP CALL. Can you feel it in the air? We're less than an hour away—"

If Dad wants to watch the news, fine, let him watch his fucking news. Noah doesn't care.

Time to tackle the kitchen.

Ants scavenge the scraps. Maggots swim through the organic stew puddling along the linoleum, their bodies a faint baby blue thanks to the glow from the tiny television screen.

Noah turns it off without paying the news anchor much mind, ready to—

The kitchen TV flips itself back on.

Noah's getting pretty pissed at this game his parents are playing. Every time he turns his back—*surprise*—the televisions turn themselves on again. He doesn't want to play along, doesn't want to dignify their weird behavior, so he tunes it all out. Acts like it's not happening.

Noah spots a sponge and decides to scrub the countertop. That feels like a good place to start, right? Got to begin somewhere. He plucks up the sponge and gently sweeps it over the—

What the hell is that?

On the wall, Noah notices these pearlescent trails weaving over the tile. Are those . . . *snail trails*? Thin veins of mother-of-pearl branch out in every direction, shimmering in the dim glow. Where did they come from? Seems like the trails all stem out from behind the television.

Noah abandons his sponge and moves to the refrigerator. The door is open, stuck on a piece of food or packaging, so there's nothing worth salvaging. He grabs a trash bag, planning to chuck it all. The food spoiled days ago. Not that it stopped his parents from eating it.

Look at that gray chicken breast. The bite marks. They've been scavenging through the scraps, foraging for food under the roof of their own home like woodland creatures in the wild.

Eating. Christ . . . Noah needs to figure out food, too, doesn't he?

Seems like the internet's still working. For now, at least.

DoorDash it is.

Mom hasn't touched her food. Her focus remains on the screen. On Paul Tammany, that slimy motherfucker. To Noah, he looks like some smarmy blend of Jay Leno and Spam, all chin, his skin as red as if his dimpled baby face had been repeatedly smacked by a Portuguese man o' war.

Eating at the kitchen table was out of the question. The surface looks like a Rorschach test of mildew stains, soaked deep into the grain. Noah tried scrubbing, but a moist shadow of mold remained. So he corralled his parents and sat them down on the couch in front of their TV trays. It took some tugging to get Mom all dressed, but now she's plopped down before the television, perfectly content, as placid as a baby transfixed by blinking Christmas tree lights.

Even with the curtains open, the corners of the living room are pitch-black puddles. What time is it? Noah checks his cell phone. *Jesus, it's not even three in the afternoon* . . . This part of the house always sank back into shadows. The only source of illumination is the television sets. Noah's got no choice but to leave them on, using their glow to light his way. He checked every closet for spare lightbulbs, but found nothing. He considered going to the store for a box of them, but he can't leave his parents alone. Not until he gets hold of some help.

Noah now sits on the floor next to Mom. He's not hungry at all. The acrid tang of the house coats his throat, even after he aired the place out. He's still breathing it in. He just needs to go through the motions of a meal. Pretend like everything's okay. But it's not. None of this is *okay. What the hell is happening here? What's wrong with them? What am I supposed to do?*

If Asher won't pick up, maybe he'll drive to his house. Ash doesn't live that far away. Close enough to deal with this shit. *It should've been him here, dealing with Dad . . .*

Asher has always been the bossy blowhard, high on his older brother status: *Let me handle it . . .*

And if Asher isn't home? What then?

Field trip to the hospital. Time for an MRI or CAT scan or anything that might peer inside their skulls and figure out if this is a stroke or botulism or some unknown airborne toxic event.

"Today's a special day for those who want to reclaim our country," Tammany intones from the TV. "We're tired of hiding in the shadows. You had your time . . . now it's our turn."

"You need to eat, guys . . ." Noah is talking to them like children. Babies refusing their food.

Oh God, he thinks. *I'm gonna have to feed them . . .*

"The time is nigh, folks," Tammany says, but Noah's not paying attention. "Time to take our country back. Who's with me? Who's ready to WAKE UP? To OPEN THEIR EYES?"

Noah kneels before Mom. Her vacant stare never breaks from the screen. The smell of her body odor mixed with the food turns his stomach. Chinese. He remembers Dad calling it "chinky-poo" as a kid. Noah didn't know any better. He just assumed that's what everybody called Chinese food. So when he casually repeated it during recess and his teacher overhead, he received one hell of a drubbing from his principal, telling him what *chink* really meant.

Those were just different times, Mom tried to explain to Noah when he came home furious at his own family. *That's just what people said back then.*

Mom's not touching her lo mein. The noodles glisten in the dull glow of the TV screen.

"Please. *Mom*. Just eat . . ." *Fresh*, he thinks. *Eat something fresh, not spoiled.*

"How about a countdown, folks?" Tammany asks at Noah's back. He's tuned Tammany out. "It's a new dawn! A new day! Let's say goodbye to the old world and welcome in the new."

Noah brings the plastic fork up to his mother's mouth—*here comes the choo-choo*—and shoves a forkful of noodles against her stubborn lips. "Open the hatch."

"Time for the WAKE-UP CALL," Tammany intones.

Mom won't open her mouth. A few noodles dangle from her chin, then slip to the floor.

"*Ten . . .*"

"Eat for me, Mom . . . Please."

"*Nine . . .*"

Noah forces the food in, jabbing the plastic fork into his mother's mouth.

"*Eight . . .*"

"Please, Mom . . . Come on." He ends up accidentally stabbing her inert tongue with the fork. One of its plastic tines snaps off. "Shit."

"*Seven . . .*"

He has to use his fingers. What other choice is there?

"*Six . . .*"

I can't believe I'm doing this . . . Noah brings his hand up to his mother's mouth and—*fuck me oh fuck this*—hesitantly presses the noodles in. *Ssssquch.* His fingers slip past her lips.

"*Five . . .*"

It's surprising how dry her tongue feels. Parched.

"*Four . . .*"

When's the last time she had any water? She's completely dehydrated . . .

"*Three . . .*"

Noah's fingers vanish up to the first knuckle, now the second, lost in his mom's mouth.

"*Two . . .*"

Mom's eyes slide across him. *On* to him. They glisten like the cold belly of a slug.

"*ONE.*"

A chill runs down Noah's neck. Freon breath. But there's no one at his back, nothing beyond the television set looming behind him—

Mom blinks back to cognition.

A switch, flipped.

She smiles.

Is that even a smile? It's a bit difficult to tell with Noah's fingers in the way. Her lips lift around his index and middle finger, the chapped vermillion rim yielding over his digits, fresh splits crackling against his skin. Even with his fingers still in her mouth, Noah knows it's a grin . . .

Just not one he's familiar with.

This is someone else's smile. Her lips undulate against his knuckles, continuing to ripple—*is she finally chewing?*—but oh, it feels wrong, all kinds of *wrong*.

Noah can't help himself. He lets out a shout, yanking his hand out just as Mom bites down—*snick!*—cutting the loose strands of noodles in half. One noodle still clings to her chin.

"*Jesus.*" Noah falls onto his ass, pressing his oily hand against his chest. "*What the fuck.*"

Mom is cognizant now. Awake from her Fax News–induced stupor. But this . . . this doesn't seem like his mother, this doesn't seem like Noah's mom at all. She's giggling at him—

tee-hee, tee-hee—

tee-veeeee

—tee-hee

"That's it." Noah stands, wiping the noodles from his shirt. "I'm done. I'm fucking done."

Mom keeps staring at him.

Giggling.

There's an eagerness in her eyes now, a dull electricity that hadn't been flowing through her body before. Her lips remain upturned but to call it a smile seems so, so very wrong.

Dad's now grinning at him, too.

What the hell?

Same lips. Same expression.

Same laugh.

teee-veeee-teeeeeee-veeeeeeeeee-teeeeeeeeeveeeeeeeeeeeteeeeeeeveeeteeveee . . .

"I've had it with this shit." Noah faces the TV. "I'm not playing anymore."

He turns the TV off. That'll get their attention. See how they like that.

"Happy? No TV for you!" *Jesus*, he's treating them like naughty children. Noah faces them, hands perched on his hips, a disgruntled kindergarten teacher about to lay down the law.

"You wanna spend your life wasting aw—"

"WAKE UP." A voice barks into his ear.

Noah shouts. Spins around. Paul Tammany is right behind him. Smirking.

"OPEN YOUR EYES."

Noah can't breathe. How did the TV turn itself back on?

How? How could it have—

Dad is holding the remote, still smiling at his son.

"Very funny." Noah grabs the remote from his dad's hand. "Hardy fucking har, guys . . ."

Noah punches the power button and the screen goes dark once more.

"I'm so sick of listening to this bull—"

The TV turns back on.

By itself.

The remote is still in Noah's hand. His grip tightens around its casing, squeezing so hard he can hear the faint crack of plastic beneath his fingers.

There's no possible way that he could've accidentally pressed the power button.

Did he?

Snickers. His parents are *snickering* at him. *Teeveeteeveeteeveee.* All day he's barely been able to get two words out of them. Now they won't shut up, acting like spoiled little brats.

Teeveeeteeeveeeteeeeveeeeetvtvtvtvtvtvtvtvtvtvveeeeeeeeee . . .

Fine. Two can fucking play at that game.

Noah reaches for the power cord, wrapping it around his hand once, twice, then yanks. *Hard.* The plug pulls free from the socket and immediately the screen snaps into blackness.

Take that, assholes. Buh-bye, Paul Tammany.

Noah faces his parents with a smugly victorious expression. "Now can the two of you—"

The TV

turns

itself

back

on.

The remote slowly slips from Noah's hand and clatters against the hardwood floor, its plastic case cracking.

He turns—*slowly*—unprepared to face the flickering images at his back. Nothing in him wants to see the screen. He doesn't want to look. He's scared. So scared. But he can't stop turning, no matter how much that petrified little boy in his brain begs him not to peek—*No, Noah!*—until he's face-to-face with the TV.

With Paul Tammany.

He's standing only a few inches away from that ghastly plasma. The swirling colors. The spectrum distorts at this angle. The image bends and disperses into pixels. Paul Tammany is composed of dots, a million tiny oscillating spheres of color. Pinks and greens and purples.

Like oil. Swirling oil. The lights. The beautiful—

gaslights

—kaleidoscope of colors.

Noah brings his hand up to his face, kneading his knuckles into his left eye, trying to rub the colors out. They're sinking into his eyes. Into his skull. His brain. Soaking in the soft matter.

It isn't possible. What's happening simply isn't possible. The TV should be—

Should be—

Should—

"WAKE UP," Paul Tammany intones. "OPEN YOUR EYES."

"Wake up," Noah's parents echo. "Open your eyes."

"WAKE UP," Tammany announces. "OPEN YOUR EYES."

"Wake up. Open your eyes."

"WAKE UP. OPEN YOUR EYES. WAKE UP. OPEN YOUR EYES. WAKE UP. OPEN YOUR EYES." Tammany just won't stop. Neither will his parents, repeating after him at full volume. "WAKE UP OPEN YOUR EYES WAKE UP OPEN YOUR EYES WAKE UP OPEN YOUR EYES WAKE—"

A switch has been flipped and now it won't shut off.

"UPOPENYOUREYESWAKEUPOPENYOUREYESWAKE UPOPENYOUREYESWAKEUPOPENYOUREYESWAKE UPOPENYOUREYESWAKEUPOPENYOUREYESWAKE UPOPENYOUREYES."

Noah can't hear himself think. Can't concentrate. His parents are laughing. Not simply snickering, but *laughing*. Braying like insane donkeys.

Listen to them laugh. Laughing at *him*. Laughing with voices that can't be his parents'.

It's only when Paul Tammany starts laughing along with them that Noah knows he is losing it. Losing his mind. *What is happening what is happening what is happening what is*—

He has to stop them. Stop them all from laughing. He can't take it anymore. The sound of it. The swirling colors. The oiliness of the screen. It's everywhere. Reaching in. His mind.

So Noah grabs the back of the television with both hands and sends the entire console crashing to the hardwood floor. The television strikes the ground, screen-first, and—

CRRRRSH!

—the glass shatters with a dull crunch, the television impacting the floor with a resonant thud. He feels the impact in the floorboards. In his feet. His toes. And it feels good. Sweet relief.

There's no light in the living room now. Nothing to illuminate the space.

It's completely dark.

And quiet.

Mom and Dad aren't laughing anymore. Aren't breathing. If Noah didn't know any better, he'd say he is the only one in the room. But that's not true. That's not true at all. His parents are right there, slouched on the couch, their food uneaten, their tray tables—

"Why would you do that, booooy?"

It's Dad.

His voice, at least. Just next to his left ear. Not on the couch. Not where his father was only seconds ago. He's so close, Noah feels the warm gust of breath spread down his neck.

"We were watching that," Dad says . . . this time in his right ear. *Surround sound.*

Noah screams. He feels his bones leap out of his body.

But where's Mom?

Where's Mom?

Where's—

Noah fumbles forward three blind steps before colliding with one of the foldout trays. Metal clatters to the floor. He tries to step over it, as if it's a track hurdle, but sets his foot down in something soft, too soft, that stomach-turning squelch splurting underneath his heel.

Please Jesus, Noah thinks in a whimper, *let that be takeout, let it be takeout, let it be—*

He slips. Of course he slips. His foot slides out from underneath him, sent on an errant skid across the floor, leaving his other leg with no other possible option but to fold back at a sharp angle and send his body toppling. Not a graceful fall by any stretch. He looks like a drunken ballerina performing a tendu before collapsing into a heap on the floor.

Nothing breaks, thank God. But nothing feels particularly pleasant, either.

Noah groans. A child's moan brought on by a boo-boo. He feels like a helpless little boy again, desperate to make sense out of the senseless.

No blood, no Band-Aid. That's always been the rule.

Where's Mom?

Where's Mom?

Where—

Mom's on top of him before he can finish a survey of his injuries. She emerges from some shadow on the floor and crawls across his body. Was she hiding behind the couch? Under it? *Where the fuck did she just come from?* One second, she's MIA—the next, Noah is on his back, flat on his ass, one leg bent painfully beneath him, and his mother is slithering on top of him, using what remains of her frail body to pin him against the floor.

"Jussssst the faaaaaax . . ."

Mom licks his face. Her flypaper tongue taps his chin and worms up the divot between his lips, cresting the tip of his nose before snaking across his cheek and veering onto his temple.

Noah freezes. His fight-or-flight response short-circuits in that moment, leaving him prostrate and panicking. Like a child. A little boy. This is his *mother.* His own mother is doing these awful, *awful* things to him. Her own *son.* He doesn't—*can't*—understand what is happening, only that it is, it is most definitely happening—*to him*—by his *mommymommyyyyy.*

Noah feels his mother's hips grind against his own. She releases a low moan right into his ear. *Pleasure.* She moans with *pleasure* as her hips pick up their locomotive momentum.

oh

God

what

is

happening

Noah pushes her with all the pent-up panic he can manifest.

There isn't much weight to his mother at this point, more kindling than flesh and bone, having wasted away these last few weeks. But there's a perverse determination to her movements. *Commitment*, you can say, and perseverance sure goes a long, long way, doesn't it? She simply won't give up on her grinding.

no mommy no

stop

please mommy

stop

Noah has no choice but to grip his mother tightly by her arms and foist her off, *wheeeeeeee*, sending her somersaulting over the floor like a tumbleweed of wizened limbs.

Noah sobs. He exhales a primal wail. The sudden release of his mother's weight from his body is just too much to deal with. To handle. His skin crawls with cool air.

"Jussst the faxxxx jussst the faaaaaaaxx just the faaaaaaaaaaaaaaxxxx."

Mom is quick to pick herself up. She hoists herself onto all fours, elbows bent, head low to the ground, more animal than suburban Grammy. A pendulum of drool swings off her lips for a few volleys before snapping and hitting the hardwood floor.

There's that grin again. Too many teeth.

Mom charges. On her hands and knees. At Noah.

"No no no noooo—"

Noah barely has time to inhale before his mother is back on top of him again, this time planting both hands on either side of his head like it's a melon ready to be cracked open.

"No no no STOP!"

She leans forward and inserts her tongue into Noah's ear. She's really rooting around in there, too. Is she cleaning out the wax? Looking for buried treasure? What is she doing?

What the fuck is she doing?

"STOOOOOP!"

Noah bucks. His body is pinned down by his mother's determined girth, giving him little choice but to shimmy like a fish out of water, writhing for release, for escape, wrestling against his mother's iron grip. He's crying now, bawling like a baby, screaming at the madness of it all.

What is happening what is happening whatishappeningtomeeeeeeeeeeee

Her tongue flickers in and out, not a mommy's tongue, but a snake's, darting sharply into the canal. Penetrating it. He wants to laugh—it tickles so much, which makes him want to cry even louder, because it's his mommy and mommies don't do these things, not to their sons.

Mamamamamamameeeeeeeeeeeeeeeeeee

Noah is able to flip onto his stomach. He attempts to crawl away, but not without his mother kneeling on his back, going along for the ride, as if her boy is some traumatized bucking bronco. *Giddy-up, horsey!* She simply won't stop. Won't give up. Won't let her son go.

"Juussst the faaaaax jusssst the faaaaaaaaaax!"

She plunges her tongue back in Noah's ear, hungry for it, greedily licking at the shell as if nothing else matters in this world, absolutely nothing, running that withered muscle through every crevice until he's squeaky clean. Spotless. She's going to scrub her son until he shimmers.

Shines.

Noah hears himself moan. He knows that the trauma of this moment will stay with him for the rest of his life. If he lives to be one hundred, one thousand, it won't matter, he'll still have to live with the memory of his mom's tongue inside his ear.

This is distilled insanity.

There's no wax left. No salt. No sweat. Just saliva. His mother's shimmering spit.

So she bites.

Hard.

It never occurs to Noah that his mother might sink her teeth into the cartilage and quickly yank her head back. Why would he ever think she'd do something as awful as that?

But she does. Of course she does. Noah feels her incisors clamp down so tightly that there's a thin click of teeth meeting, piercing the flap of tender flesh in between, and then . . .

rrrrrrrrrrrpp

Noah screams. What else can he do? What else is he physically and mentally capable of doing in that moment but releasing all his pain, all his pent-up terror, in one endless shriek?

Mom pays his screams no mind. All she does is pull.

And pull. Until—*Splk!*—off comes Noah's ear.

The lower half, at least.

"AAAAAAAH!" Noah shrieks.

The strip of flimsy flesh flaps against her chin as she grins. She looks like a dog who's just been gifted a piece of raw chicken, the skin still attached.

"MAAWWMMEEEEEEE!"

With quick efficiency, Mom slurps Noah's ear into her mouth, like sucking an oyster out of the half shell, *now you see it, now you don't,* chewing enthusiastically with a relishing smile.

MMMM-MMMM-MMMMMMM! Yummy in the tummy!

Noah presses his palm against his ear. What remains of it. Nothing but a jagged Nike swoosh of flesh attached to the side of his head. His hand comes back wet. Warm. Covered in his blood.

Mom is hungry for *more.* Second helpings of her son.

Here she is, charging on all fours.

Look! Just look! Look at her go!

"No no nooo nooooooo!" Noah whines. He has no choice but to crab-walk backward, away from his mother, clumsily making his way into the hall.

Mom is faster. Mom is more determined. Mom is more hungry.

Mom closes the gap between them in no time.

Noah's back finds the hallway wall. His head collides with a hollow *thwonk.*

Not a wall.

Wood. That sounds like cheap particle board.

A door.

A *closet* door. Look—there are the markings of faded ink, demarcating every inch, every centimeter Noah and Asher grew over the years under this very roof.

Mom is already crawling up his legs. His waist. *Here she comes!* Before there's any second-guessing—*no time, no time*—Noah's fingers find the doorknob. He grips the brass handle as best he can and twists at the wrist, but there's simply too much blood on his fingers. It's slickened the knob, skin slipping over the reddened metal. Why can't he just open the door?

His mother's breath, the reek of it, blossoms across his face.

Open the door open the door open the—

There!

Open sesame. Noah flings the closet open with one hand. Once the door swings past his shoulder, he merely lies back, as if resting himself down inside his own coffin.

Mom keeps crawling, the two seesawing over, Noah first, Mom flipping on top of him.

Tiiiiimber!

Noah thrusts upward with his pelvis, catapulting his mother into the closet. How this feat of family acrobatics works—this horrid act of Oedipal gymnastics—is really truly anybody's guess, but Mom is sent those few feet into the air, crashing into the enclosed space and landing in all those winter coats. Every last jacket rattles on its wire hanger.

Mom hits the floor, right shoulder first, then her face. She is upside down. Tangled in the coats. A crumpled spider. Her neck cricks at such a severe angle, Noah suddenly worries it might've snapped in the fall.

Time stops. All breathing halts.

Did Noah just kill his mother?

"Mom? Mom? Mo—"

Mom blinks. Her lips peel back, glistening with blood—*his* blood—teeth stained red.

"Jusssst the faaaaaaaaaaax . . ."

Mom's legs kick at the air, pumping over her severely bent head. Her body drops to the floor before she flings her torso back into an upright position. It's like watching a discarded doll spring back to life completely on its own. Something limp now alive.

She is kneeling now. Staring now.

"Jussssst . . ."

Grinning now.

". . . the . . ."

Lunging—

". . . ffffffaaaaaaaaaxxxxxxxx!"

Noah slams the door in her face. The slam is punctuated by a dull crunch of bone against particleboard. Her head, presumably. Her nose must've hit the other side as he swung it shut.

Tunk.

Then it hits again.

Tunk.

And again.

Tunk.

Over and over.

Tunk.

Tunk.

Tunk.

Mom won't stop slamming her skull against the other side of the door. Why she doesn't just grab the knob and simply open the door is anybody's guess, but Noah is grateful for the reprieve. He'll happily take it, even for a moment, to catch his breath and push his body away from the closet.

Tunk.

Tunk.

Tunk.

"What the fuck what the . . ." *Breathe.* Noah needs to breathe, but Mom's head keeps—

Tunk.

—slamming against the other side of the closet door, distracting him from the simple autonomic task of inhaling and exhaling. It's impossible for Noah not to lose himself to the—

Tunk.

—absolute madness of all this. His parents have suddenly gone from—

Tunk.

—mildly racist vegetables to—

Tunk.

—mindless monsters in a matter of seconds.

Wait.

Tunk.

His parents.

Tunk.

Plural.

Tunk.

Where's Dad?

———

Behind him.

Oh.

———

Noah's father wraps his meaty arms around his waist, sending them both tumbling forward. He knows it's his dad from all those years roughhousing as a kid, even without seeing him. Such a classic Dad move. A WWF power play, as if he's Hacksaw Jim Duggan: *Get yer opponent while their back is turned and tackle 'em from behind. They'll never see you coming . . .*

But Dad isn't wrestling anymore. This isn't play. He's crushing his son, wrapping his hand around Noah's neck and smashing his skull against the hardwood floor over and over and—

"WAKE UP!"

Noah is on his stomach, pinned beneath his father. There's no air in his lungs. He can't get the oxygen into his chest. Can't inhale. Dad still has some heft, much heavier than Mom.

Noah can't push him off. He's trapped.

"OPEN YOUR EYES!" Dad hisses into Noah's ear. His breath absolutely reeks. Drool spills from his mouth and dribbles across his son's exposed cheek and onto the floor. Noah can see hunks of partially digested insects in his spit, husks of bugs, their wings, slipping through saliva.

"WAAAKE UP."

Noah has to find a way to get his father off. Needs something to hit him with. There's so much junk strewn about the room. His fingers blindly worm over the floor, seeking a weapon.

"OPEN YOUR EEEEEEYES . . ."

Noah's fingers find a wet tangle of hair on the floor. A scalp.

Nope—scratch that.

Room-temperature noodles. A half-empty take-out container won't offer much defense, but Noah doesn't have a choice. He grabs a handful of lo mein and smacks his dad with it.

His father barely blinks.

He does eat, however, working his lips over Noah's fingers until they find the noodles dangling from his knuckles. The relish, the downright zeal, that washes over his father's face sends Noah sinking even deeper into that subconscious stronghold saved just for childhood trauma. Noah is nothing more than a little boy battling his bygone nightmares all over again.

The monster under the bed. The monster in the closet.

The monster in his father.

"*Mmmmmmm.*" Dad's eyes roll so far up into his skull there's nothing but white left in their wake as he rapturously suckles the sauce from his own son's fingers.

Dad bites down. *Hard.* His teeth clamp onto his son's fingers, trapping his hand.

Noah *waaails.* This is too much, far too fucking much, for one human being to handle. *Please,* his childhood self whimpers, *just make it all go away, make it all stop, please no more . . .*

Noah tries crawling away, bringing his free hand up front and digging his nails into the hardwood floor. He pulls with his free hand, hoping to slither out from underneath his father, but Dad only rides him like a cowboy, grinding his pelvis into his son's lower back and barking like a wild dog enamored with the full moon. But it's not the moon. His father is baying at the TV.

It just isn't human. None of this is human. Human beings don't do this sort of thing.

This is monstrous. This is *wrong.*

Noah screams again.

Louder this time.

Dad starts tickling Noah while still gnawing on his hand, digging his fingers into his son's ribs, so many worms wriggling their way into the soil, burrowing down deep.

"*Jusst the faaaaaax,*" Dad snickers. How he can talk with two of Noah's fingers still in his mouth is anybody's guess, but Dad's alarmingly adept at it.

Noah spins onto his back, miraculously without dislocating his shoulder. He twists and wriggles and bends his body until he faces the ceiling. Now he gets to stare at the hunched mess of a man that was once his father. Noah has no idea what this thing is. Chapped lips. Oil-spill eyes. A darting tongue. And drool. So much drool. An endless reservoir of saliva dribbles down his dad's chin and onto Noah. Into his mouth. His nose. He's drowning in his father's spit.

And still, Dad's fingers keep on burrowing further between his ribs. *"Just the faaaaax . . ."*

Noah screams a third time. It draws from somewhere deep, further than his lungs, down in the belly, perhaps even deeper than that, some untapped cistern within his innards.

Something rises. A self-righteous tide of bile. Moral outrage.

Rage.

That's what this is. Pure, unadulterated wrath. Noah keeps screaming, but the tenor of it shifts, lifting into an animal-like howl. A pitch reserved for wolves, not frightened children.

Not little liberal sissies. Not snowflakes.

Not Noah.

Noah's free hand searches the floor for some sort of weapon—a knife. A fireplace poker. A fucking Dan Brown novel. Something, *anything*, that he might use to bludgeon his dad with.

There. What's that? His index finger grazes against something solid.

Plastic.

Whatever it is, it slips away, pushed farther off by his own fingertips.

Fuckity fuck fuck.

Noah feels as if his shoulder is about to pop out of its socket as he stretches his arm as far as it can reach. Farther . . . *farther* . . . His fingers find the rubber nubs of a remote control.

The remote! The goddamn shattered television remote . . .

Beggars can't be choosers.

Noah's dad still hasn't let go of his hand. He licks the divots of skin between each finger, seeking more sauce. That tender webbing of skin between Noah's index and middle fingers—

spplk

—tears down the middle as Dad bites down. Noah shrieks. The flesh between his fingers is no longer connected, ripped and bleeding. The bones in Noah's thumb won't be so far behind.

"DAAAD!"

Dad pays his boy no mind, continuing to twist his son's wrist, turning it too far. Noah has no choice but to spin his body along with the rotation of his hand so his carpals won't crack.

"Fuuust neeee ffsxxxxx—"

Dad lets go, Noah's fingers slipping free. Noah yanks his hand back. Finally. *Hallelujah.*

"Jussst the faaaaaa—"

Dad's haranguing cuts itself short the second Noah rams that remote into his mouth.

"Hyuuulch!"

Rams it hard.

"Hoooork!"

Teeth clatter against plastic. A few in the front snap back. A moist hiccup squelches out from some profound depth of his father's belly, rupturing upward, muffled behind the remote.

"Yyuuuulp!"

Drool and blood funnel down the rubber buttons and lace Noah's wrist.

Still Dad hasn't let go.

Yet.

The man leans forward, pressing his full weight against his son. The only thing keeping him from completely collapsing onto Noah is the remote control. He's holding it upward like fucking Excalibur or something. Like Noah's pretending to be He-Man.

I have the poooooower . . .

Dad's eyes are livid, welling up with venom. His lips peel back in a most sickening sneer, crooked teeth biting down against the remote so hard that it cracks. He continues to talk, but the words are nothing but a wet mess of bubbles and sputters.

"jssssssst . . ."

Dad's getting too heavy.

". . . thhhh . . ."

Noah wants to roll him off, but his father's weight holds him down.

"*. . .fxxxxxxxxx . . .*"

Dad releases his wrist. Noah now has both hands at his disposal. He plants his palm against the plastic base. With all the remaining strength he can summon, he drives the remote home, all the way to the very back of his dad's throat. To the spine, even.

A hollow pop resonates through the air as the joints of Dad's jaw dislocate themselves. *PWWOP!* Noah feels it more than hears it, the two senses intertwining.

Dad's eyes widen. Is he confused? The remote is fully lodged in his mouth, jammed so far in that his cheeks bulge. *Chipmunk cheeks* is what his mother called it when they were kids. Whenever Noah or Asher crammed too much food into their mouths, looking like a pair of preadolescent Marlon Brandos, Mom would laugh and say, *Look at those chipmunk cheeks!*

Dad viciously shakes his head, struggling to shake the remote free. It simply won't dislodge itself. He pushes himself off Noah, releasing his son for the first time, and lands on his back, writhing across the floor as his face turns blue.

Noah grabs his wrist and rocks back and forth on the floor next to his flailing father.

Tunk.

Tunk.

Tunk.

Noah forgot all about Mom in the closet, but now her headbutting picks up its steady drumbeat once more. Maybe she's been headbanging this whole time but Noah simply tuned it out, his mind occupied with more pressing matters. Now that he's dealt with Dad—*oh Jesus Christ, what did I do, what did I just do*—he hears Mom pummeling her skull loud and clear.

"*Juuusssst—*"

Tunk.

"—the—"

Tunk.

"—FAAAAAXXX!"

Tunk.

The cheap particleboard cracks, splintering from the inside out. A couple more hits and she'll break free. It's utterly inexplicable why exactly his mind does this to him, lapsing back into a childhood memory right now of all fucking times—maybe to protect what's left of his fraying sanity—but the first image to pop into Noah's fragmenting brain is . . . well, it's a clip from MTV. A music video of all things, back when MTV still played videos.

Run–D.M.C.'s "Walk This Way," featuring Aerosmith.

It's such a groundbreaking moment in '80s pop culture, an olive branch between rap and rock. Hip-hop suddenly inseminated itself into suburban households across the country, thanks to the rock-'n'-roll riffs provided by Joe Perry's smoking guitar solo. Asher and Noah loved to dress up as Run–D.M.C. as kids. Ash was Run, Noah was D.M.C., while they pretended the TV was Jam Master Jay on the turntables. The boys manifested their imaginary Adidas and tracksuits, grabbing Mom's wooden spoons with the thin handles for mics, rapping along with the song whenever it came on MTV—which, at the time, was on the hour, every hour. Both brothers would fall to their knees at the sound of Steven Tyler's witch-cackling chorus the second his head burst through the wall separating their rehearsal spaces, that barrier figuratively dividing hip-hop from rock, white from Black, the projects from the suburbs.

What an immense moment. *What a coup.* When Tyler used his mic stand to—

Tunk.

—break through the wall and—

Tunk.

—lean his head through the cracked Sheetrock and shriek—

Tunk.

—WALK THIS WAAAAAAAY—

Tunk.

—something fundamentally changed for Noah's generation. Hip-hop found him in his quaint southern suburb. All the way in Virginia. In Woodmont. He wanted to walk this way.

He wanted to talk this—

Tunk.

Wait a sec. That's not Steven Tyler peering out from the wall, no—

Tunk.

It's his *mother.* She's bleeding profusely from her smashed face. Her nose. Her split lips. Her caved-in skull. She spits out what few remaining teeth she still has, white candy bits striking the floor. Mom sorta kinda *resembles* Steven Tyler now. Or maybe that's just Noah's mind playing tricks on him. He half expects his mother to start warbling JUST GIVE ME A KYUSSS.

Mom slumps over. Blacks out. The dome of her head bulges out into the hall, a tendril of hair snaking down the outer side, glued to the particleboard with a thin rivulet of blood.

Noah struggles to pick himself up, staggering to his feet. Dad won't quit shaking his head, whipping his neck to the point where Noah fears he might snap it and that will be that.

Noah takes a second. Just to catch his breath. He doesn't know what to do with his dad. His father's face has gone from blue to maroon, turning purpler by the second. He can't breathe.

The police. Call 911. Where's his fucking phone? Get an ambulance. Get help. Someone. Anyone who can just put a stop to this insanity and bring his parents back.

But let's be honest with ourselves here, okay? Mom and Dad are never coming back.

They're long gone, Noah Fairchild.

Dad locks his eyes onto his son, as if he realizes Noah is still standing over him. He quits shaking his head. The remote remains lodged in his mouth, cheeks peeled back. His jaw is crooked, at a lopsided angle, an anaconda swallowing a Honda, far too big to scarf down.

Dad's eyes tighten. His lips approximate something akin to a grimace, or a snarl.

"Jsstt—"

He tenses his abdomen.

"—tthh—"

He bolts upright.

"—fxxxx!"

The angle of it, the motion of his movement, looks like some mechanical funhouse spook popping up from a casket. It doesn't feel natural to Noah. Doesn't look human at all.

It's not his father. Not Dad. Not anymore.

So Noah brings up his foot, bending his leg at the knee, and with a rage-fueled screech drives his heel back down into his father's face. He slams the sole of his Chuck Taylor All Stars so hard, the butt of the remote control plummets even deeper, driving the plastic farther down his father's throat.

Dad's not moving. He's still. Trapped air slips past his lips, bubbling in blood.

Noah didn't mean to do that . . . Did he? That wasn't what—

What he meant to—

Whoops.

———

The truth is Noah was always a mama's boy. He feels alone without her. All he wants right now is for his mom just to be his mom again. To care for him, wrap her arms around him like when he was a child, woken by a bad dream, and tell him everything's gonna be okay.

Everything'll be fine, hon. You're okay. I've got you, I've got you.

He misses the love of his mother. To have that security taken away from him—a grown man, an adult, a parent now himself—well, he feels like a child all over again. A lost little boy.

Who can he cry to now? Who'll be there for him when he wakes from this nightmare?

No one. Absolutely no one. Noah's never felt this alone in all his life. Fax News took his mommy away, and now he has no one to protect him from all the monsters under his bed.

Mom's the monster now. Something slipped into her skin. Wears her face. Speaks with her voice. But it isn't her anymore. Isn't mommy *mommymommymommyMOMMMEEEEEEEE!*

———

Noah tries 911 for the tenth fucking time. Still nothing. Why is nobody picking up their phone anymore? Since when did everybody collectively stop answering their goddamn—

Wait. What if this isn't just his family?

What if—

The news. *Maybe there's something about all this on the news . . .*

The actual news.

Noah feels the instinctual reflex to grab the remote control, only for his fingers to freeze in midreach the second he remembers it is now lodged in his father's gullet.

Dad's lower jaw is slung at a wide angle, barely attached by his torn cheeks, the curved bit of flesh and bone resembling a horseshoe more than the bottom half of his mouth.

The living room television is totaled. No getting that one to work.

Plenty of TVs around the house, though. Just pick one.

Noah steps over his father's body and slowly shuffles to his parents' bedroom. The TV in there still works. Just about the only thing in the house that still does at this point.

The second Noah flips the television on, he's met with the grind of an electric drill. A metallic squeal worms its way in through his ears and keeps on digging.

"Aaah—" Noah winces. It's so loud. So shrill. A feedback loop. Whatever Fax News is broadcasting sounds like an industrial machine fed through a fuzzy guitar amplifier, all reverb.

The colors coming from the screen are so blinding in their hues. Noah sees purple . . .

gas

Green . . .

lights

Pink . . .

glorious

glorious

gaslights

It takes all his strength to switch the channel, but the moment he does, whatever oily fog clouded his mind quickly dissipates, there and gone in a matter of breaths.

CNN is nestled next to Fax, one channel down. Their chyron flashes *BREAKING NEWS*, but isn't news always breaking nowadays? Isn't the news all broken by now? Smashed to bits?

There's Anderson. Mr. Cooper. The Man himself. He looks . . . shaken. Ashen. It's a rare day for Anderson Cooper to lose his cool, so just what could possibly have—

ELEMENTARY SCHOOL

What's he reading? There's been another shooting. Jesus, how many is that this year?

This month?

CASUALTIES

The broadcast cuts to a school parking lot. Yellow police tape flickers in the wind. A hive of activity. Police cars and ambulances. Red and blue lights pulse as paramedics wheel one gurney out after another, each blanketed with a white sheet. Bodies too small to be adults.

The next edit cuts to a snippet of CCTV footage, a digital silhouette of a man entering the school building. It almost looks like blurry footage of Bigfoot, gray and fluctuating in and out of focus, lumbering through the front entrance.

Something about the man's gait. The face, fuzzy as it is, feels familiar.

Wait. Is that . . .

"Ash?" Noah says his name out loud, surprising even himself.

That's him, isn't it? What's his big brother doing on the news? What's he doing, running through this school's hallway, caught on camera?

Why is Anderson Cooper saying Ash had something to do with . . .

With . . .

This doesn't make sense. Noah struggles to read the words scrolling across the screen. They don't make any sense. The words slip by so fast, a fish's tail wriggling free from his mind's grip.

What did Ash do?

Noah's ears start ringing. All he sees are Cooper's lips silently moving across the screen. He watches more blurry footage of his older brother entering a school building. They play the clip again, only slowing it down and pausing, holding on Ash's grainy visage. His face.

That can't be him . . . It's not possible . . .

Cut to footage of parents huddled together, clustered behind police barricades.

No. No, this—this can't be happening . . .

Wailing mothers.

Please no noooo nooooooo . . .

All those tears.

NOOOOOO!

"We're just now receiving word," Anderson Cooper soberly intones, snapping Noah out of it, "that there has been yet another incident at a separate school located in Chesterfield County. We're learning that, only moments ago, at Greenfield High School, there was another—"

Greenfield. That's where Noah's nephew goes. *Caleb.* That's Caleb's school, isn't it?

Now Cooper is reporting on a third incident, in Winston-Salem, North Carolina.

A fourth in Minneapolis.

A fifth.

Sixth.

Christ, they're popping up everywhere. Anderson Cooper can't keep up with them all.

"It would appear that there is—there is some kind of—I don't know—some kind of mass hysteria happening. We don't know if this is a terrorist attack or—or a coordinated event—"

Not just schools. A shopping center in Binghamton. A Hooters in Orlando. A gym in Albany.

"Everywhere," Cooper says. "This seems to be happening *everywhere.*"

A coordinated event. A nexus of violence.

A great reckoning.

"It's everywhere," Cooper repeats, more to himself.

Everywhere.

Noah quickly flips the channel to MSNBC, just to see what they're covering. More footage. More wailing. He flips to the local news. To BBC.

The only channel *not* covering this carnage is—*surprise*—Fax. Their screen remains an oily void of swirling pink, green, and purple.

Everywhere.

Noah can't move. He's glued to the news. He hasn't taken a fresh breath, hasn't exhaled for what feels like minutes. He flips in a cycle, rotating through the news channels. He needs to understand what he's witnessing. Someone has to explain what's happening. *What's going on?*

He doesn't know what to do. He wants his mommy. But Mom is crammed in a closet, scratching what remains of her fingers across the wood, barely alive. Barely *human*.

He just smashed his own father's throat into a pulp.

Who can Noah turn to now?

He has spent his adult life in a liberal bubble. He has no idea what to do.

He's not equipped for this.

Any of this.

What are the odds he can reach Alicia and Kelsey? How's Noah supposed to get back to Brooklyn now? He steps away from the TV, too dazed to turn it off. He leaves it on CNN as he stumbles out of his parents' bedroom. The voice of Anderson Cooper follows him, his delivery dazed as he keeps reporting about one massacre after another after another after . . .

Fax News has gone silent on the matter. Their feed is nothing more than a pixelated oil spill.

Fax News will never go on the air ever again. Their viewership isn't at home any longer, anyhow. They have taken to the streets. Their day has come, of judgment foretold, at long last.

They have woken up. They have opened their eyes.

The Great Reawakening is finally here. Heaven help us.

Half of us, at least.

Phase Two

RECRUITS

Perhaps in sequential order of severity and often of progression, demonic activity takes these forms: (1) demonic impression, often through expression; (2) demonic repression, both the putting down, the hindering of good, and the forcing of ideas or impulses into the subconscious; (3) demonic obsession, whereby the victim is greatly preoccupied with the unholy and/or unwholesome and, in some cases, with the Evil One himself; (4) demonic depression; (5) demonic oppression, just short of (6) demonic possession.

—*THE COSMOCRATS: DIABOLISM IN MODERN LITERATURE*, D. G. KEHL

Baby Ghost, boo-boo, boo-boo
Baby Ghost, boo-boo, boo-boo
Baby Ghost, boo-boo, boo-boo
Baby Ghost . . .
Boo!

Mommy Ghost, boo-boo, boo-boo
Mommy Ghost, boo-boo, boo-boo
Mommy Ghost, boo-boo, boo-boo
Mommy Ghost . . .
Boo!

Daddy Ghost, boo-boo, boo-boo
Daddy Ghost, boo-boo, boo-boo
Daddy Ghost, boo-boo, boo-boo
Daddy Ghost . . .
Boo!

Grandma Ghost, boo-boo, boo-boo
Grandma Ghost, boo-boo, boo-boo
Grandma Ghost, boo-boo, boo-boo
Grandma Ghost . . .
Boo!

Grandpa Ghost, boo-boo, boo-boo
Grandpa Ghost, boo-boo, boo-boo
Grandpa Ghost, boo-boo, boo-boo
Grandpa Ghost . . .
Boo!

Let's go haunt, boo-boo, boo-boo
Let's go haunt, boo-boo, boo-boo
Let's go haunt, boo-boo, boo-boo
Let's go haunt . . .
Boo!

NOVEMBER 15

stage one: *impression/expression*

DEVON

I'm burning. Oh God, I'm on fire.

A searing heat reached deep into Devon Fairchild's body, all the way down to her tissues, the tendons, spreading across the musculature that strapped itself to her very bones.

Make it stop, she pleaded to herself. *Please make the flames stop . . .*

"Feel that burn, everybody."

Devon felt the fire enveloping her. Her limbs twisted backward like kindling threatening to snap. Arms bent behind her spine. Legs tangled together. Nothing more than a knotted mass on the floor. Still, she kept contorting. Her appendages found fresh angles to twist and twist.

"Now . . . let's go deeper. Deeper."

How much farther could she bend before snapping completely in half? Devon felt the strain in her back, every vertebra singing along in this hollow aria—*Pop! Pop! Pop!* She wanted to scream:

Hurts it hurts oh God it hurts it huuuuuuuurts . . .

"Keep going, keep going . . . That's it."

Her body was now a crescent moon. A prostrate salutation to the sun. A fiery offering.

Hurtshuurtshuuuurts . . .

"Good," her instructor, Claudio, said as he gently pressed his palm against her lower back and pushed, adjusting her position on the mat ever so slightly. "Don't forget to exhale."

Devon felt a relenting in her tendons, the stubborn muscles giving a bit more, *just a bit more*, stretching even farther into the burn, the flames rippling along her blazing body.

"There. Do you feel it?"

She did. Her pain slowly ebbed into pleasure. The ecstasy of martyrs burning at the stake. Devon swore she saw God hovering above her yoga mat . . . and he had a man bun. She was surrounded by sweating angels, all of them striking a beatific pose like an Italian fresco.

There it is. The agony, the ecstasy. The absolute burning bliss. *God, it hurts so gooood* . . .

Devon exhaled.

ASHER

Asher Fairchild reached out and touched the man's face. Stroked his cheek. It didn't feel like flesh, the skin stiff. The man didn't flinch at Ash's touch, continuing to talk, never hesitating.

"Violence broke out yet again today when police clashed with so-called protesters . . ."

Asher pressed his finger into the man's cheek, barricaded behind this plastic membrane. Oily colors radiated out from around his fingertip.

"This marks the third day in a row where clashes between city police and rioters . . ."

Their new plasma screen television took up most of the wall. Eighty-five inches in width, thirty-three in height. 4K HD resolution. Dolby surround sound speakers. Mounted like a trophy.

Asher had sunk more money into this baby than he'd budgeted, but that's okay. He was already imagining the movie nights the family was going to have, sitting here in the living room.

But the motion smoothing . . .

Something was off.

Everyone on-screen looked uncannily flat. Ugly. Actors looked just like normal people—like him. Every imperfection—their tan lines, their wrinkles, their acne—was on full display.

The motion smoothing took that magic away.

Most shows are shot at twenty-four frames per second. Asher's new plasma screen TV operated at one hundred twenty FPS. With the motion-smoothing settings on, his television inserted extra frames into his viewing experience to artificially pad the frame rate. He'd need to figure out how to fix that—navigate the controls and switch the motion interpolation off. The instructions were bound to be around here somewhere. Had he tossed them out already? Oh well, he'd figure it out. Just wing it. How hard could it be?

"Police have reported in an uptick in looting as more protests around the country . . ."

Asher dragged his hand across the screen one last time, the faintest wake of his fingertips trailing across the plastic, as if he'd scratched the anchorman's face. The plasma resettled, the colors calibrating back to their proper levels, Paul Tammany's cheek healing again.

CALEB

The creamy stem corkscrewed out from Caleb Fairchild's face. It looked, to him, like a pale pig's microscopic tail emerging from his skin, wriggling about in the air. *Here piggy, piggy* . . .

No—not a tail. Greasy grubs. Earthworms during a storm. The rain summons them up, luring these pale, burrowing invertebrates out from their muddy slumber.

Caleb leaned into the bathroom mirror, inches from his own reflection, and imagined himself bidding these oily worms to rise up from the pores along the bridge of his nose. *Rise!*

The doxycycline hadn't kicked in yet. The doctor swore up and down his new prescription would take a while, but still. Wasn't his skin supposed to have dried out by now?

Where was all this oil coming from?

Caleb held his breath and started to imagine himself squeezing all these zits with nothing but the power of his own will. His mind. *Look, Ma, no hands!* Could he really do that?

I call upon thee . . .

His cheeks turned red. Then purple. His lungs began to burn, the air fizzling within.

I call . . . upon . . . theeee . . .

A particular pressure mounted at the very back of his skull.

I CALL—

His brain stem was about to snap.

—UPON THEE—

Just as an aneurysm threatened to burst in his brain, seconds away from blacking out . . .

—RIIIIIISE!

There they were. Over his nose. Across his cheeks. Every last pore throughout his face yawned open and out wriggled the oily worms, curling and flickering and shimmying free.

He summoned them, all pale and slippery, from his skin—*Rise! Rise! RISE!*

At least it was fun to pretend he could. In Caleb's world, he had the power to beckon his whiteheads. Make them *rise, rise, RISE!*

What power. What utter control Caleb was capable of.

RISE, WHITEHEADS, RISE!

FAMILY NIGHT

Wednesday nights were Pizza Night.

They'd mix it up each week. Dad preferred Domino's. Marcus

loved Papa John's—they had the dipping sauces. Caleb always picked Little Caesars. Mom didn't really mind where they ordered from, as long as she could get a side salad, defaulting her vote to one of the boys.

Two pies. One regular, the other meat.

If it was Caleb's call, they'd go pepperoni, but Marcus wasn't a big fan of spicy stuff, so he'd beg for bacon or sweet sausage. One time they ordered a Hawaiian pizza, which . . . *yuck.*

Papa John's was the best. Their cheese wasn't too gooey. Didn't stretch into a stringy mess. Marcus liked to peel the spongy mozzarella off his pizza and roll it all up and eat it like a cheese wrap.

"Either of you put any thought into what you're asking Santa for?" Dad wanted to know.

Marcus put down his pizza. "A Pi-Pi." This was what their family called an iPad. When Marcus was a baby, he'd reach for his mother's tablet, saying, "Pi-Pi, Pi-Pi!" The name stuck.

"We'll see what Santa says," Mom said. Marcus didn't like the sound of that. Everybody else in the family had their own screen. Couldn't he have one? He was seven years old now.

When will it be my turn?

"Slices down, gang. Time for a family powwow." Dad drum-rolled his fingers against the kitchen counter. "Christmas break's coming up. Your mom and I have been discussing it for a bit and, well, we thought it might be fun to . . ." He grinned, nodding to Mom to deliver the payload.

"Go on a cruise," she said, unable to contain her own giddiness.

No. Way. A cruise? Marcus had never been on a boat before!

When was the last time they'd gone on a trip together? Marcus could barely remember some hazy vacation from when he was little, years ago now. A ski trip. They fastened a balloon to his beanie when he went down the bunny slope so the other skiers could keep tabs on him.

A vacation. A real vacation!

"This ship's got *everything*," Dad said. He talked with his hands whenever he got excited about something, waving them through the air like he was performing a magic trick. "We're talking water slides. Pools. An arcade. Even a movie theater. We booked it for right after Christmas. Five nights. We'll ring in the New Year in the Bahamas, boys . . . How's that sound?"

Umm, it sounded *awesome*. It sounded butt-kickingly cool. It sounded—

"Okay," Caleb grunted, gnawing on the drawstring of his hoodie. It definitely sounded like he *didn't* think it was actually okay.

"It'll be fun, hon," Mom offered. "An adventure for the family."

Family. That word sure kept coming up a lot. Marcus heard it more often nowadays. His parents kept talking about what was best for the *family*. How they needed to consider the *family*. How this or that might affect the *family*. What about the *family*?

Like Dad's new TV. When he installed it, taking down the family portrait from the living room wall and hanging the screen in its place, Marcus heard Mom ask, *Is that for the family?*

That portrait now hung in the hallway leading to the kitchen. Marcus had still been a baby when the family sat for the picture, barely even one year old. They were all wearing matching Christmas outfits, nothing but reds and greens. Even Marcus's onesie matched, topped with a red bow on his head, like *he* was the present. Dad stood in the center, draping his arms around Mom and Caleb. Caleb was barely ten back then. Not even a teenager yet. No acne on his face. No hoodie to hide his head.

Look. Just *look* at them all. Smiling. *Beaming.* A perfect picture for a picture-perfect family.

"Everybody bring it in." Dad brought his hand in. He always did this. His big rallying cry for their clan. Mom was next, resting hers on top of his. Marcus planted his palm on Mom's. Caleb hesitated, considering it for a second, before plopping his hand on top of everybody else's.

"On the count of three, the Fairchild family say GO," Dad called out. "One, two, three—"

"GO!"

NOVEMBER 22
stage two: *repression*

DEVON

TIME TO WAKE UP.

Devon shouldn't have clicked. She sensed it the very second she tapped the touchpad, regretting her decision even before her fingertip lifted from the pressure-sensitive tablet.

Devon, don't!

It was somewhere in the midst of the double click, that valley between taps, when her common sense piped up—*I probably shouldn't be clicking on this, should I?*

Too late. A door opened, a portal between her pastel-accented world and theirs.

TIME TO WAKE UP TO A HEALTHIER, HAPPIER YOU.

It didn't even sound like a human being had written it—or at least one with a firm grasp of English. Was this a bot or some Bangladeshi? Who can tell the difference nowadays?

That was a little racist, wasn't it? Devon questioned herself. *Shit, it was . . . Shit, shit, shit.*

The email came from a friend. Well, someone she'd like to consider a friend.

Larissa.

The two had met at yoga, unrolling their mats next to each other. During their salutations to the sun, Devon couldn't help but dwell on her neighbor's lithe limbs. Her svelte figure. Sweat pebbled her toned body, Ayurvedic gemstones washing up along the beach. A bronze goddess.

Devon felt like a bloated sponge compared to her. *SpongeMom YogaPants.*

Was that a bit of envy in her heart?

Jealousy?

The class was a gift to herself, an early birthday present meant to recenter herself, root Devon back inside her body, but looking around the studio at all the lovely young things twisting and twining only pushed her further outside herself. She wanted back in.

Ever since she turned forty-five, Devon had felt progressively further and further outside her own body, an astronaut cast off into deep space, unable to tow herself back into her skin. Two kids will do that to you—blast your sense of self into the stratosphere, abandoning your body altogether. How could she get back to herself? Climb into the cockpit of her body?

"You feel torn open as I do?"

Devon didn't know who said it at first, but then she turned to find Larissa staring back. Smiling. Wiping the oily sheen of sweat from her skin.

"Sorry?"

"Your muscles," Larissa said. "I feel absolutely ripped apart."

"Oh. Absolutely." Devon let out a light laugh. "To pieces."

Devon and Larissa got to chatting after class. Harmless stuff. A compliment from Devon regarding Larissa's featherweight twist-out tee led to a convo about Claudio, their instructor, escaping their kids and husbands, diets—standard yoga class banter, all done with an eye roll and a laugh. During a natural lag in conversation, Larissa suggested they get tea sometime.

"That'd be great," Devon said. Perhaps a little too quickly. She was ready to grab a frappé right then and there, ditch her mommy duties for the rest of the day and play hooky with her new friend—

but they were running low on frozen chicken nuggets. Plus she needed to pick up a refill on Caleb's prescription at the pharmacy. Plus
Asher had asked her to grab him a—

No. Today was chock-a-block full.

"How about next week?"

"You got it," Devon said.

The two exchanged email addresses—not numbers—and that
was that. No set plans, nothing on the calendar, nothing more than
the vague promise of a future afternoon chat.

Devon was pleasantly surprised Larissa had reached out so quickly. It was her email address all right, even if it didn't exactly *sound* like
her—or what Devon assumed Larissa would've sounded like. This
felt more like a press release. It had an automated sales pitch vibe,
like something your senile grandma might forward to you: *Saw this.
Thought of you . . .*

WAKE UP.

Devon skimmed. Nothing but bland platitudes. *Do you feel re-
moved from the rest of your body? Has life left you behind? It is time to
reconnect with your sense of self again.*

Time to WAKE UP. OPEN YOUR EYES.

Who writes this stuff? Devon wondered. Clearly it couldn't be a
human being. Was it AI?

*A great REAWAKENING is coming. People all across the country are
OPENING THEIR EYES and embracing their selfhood once again! Want
to join them? All you have to do is . . .*

There was a hyperlink embedded into the words—

CLICK HERE

—which, obviously, no one in their right mind would ever do.
That was simply an invitation to empty Pandora's box onto your hard
drive. It was digital VD just waiting to happen.

Devon knew better than to—

CLICK

—but who doesn't want to feel better about themself? Who

doesn't want to be a healthier, happier you? Happiness was on the other side of that hyperlink. Healthiness was only a simple tap away.

Devon wanted to—

WAKE

UP

—so she aligned her cursor over the cerulean-tinted letters and—

click

(I probably shouldn't be clicking on this, should I?)

click

—that was all it took. A tiny aperture. A digital window.

A gateway, now open.

Devon welcomed them in. A willing submission: *Yes, I accept. Come in. Enter.*

It wasn't long before Devon was receiving texts from friends. A fellow mother from Marcus's school reached out, suggesting she change her password.

You just sent me an email asking if I wanted to buy some supplements. Was that you?

Sorry, Devon immediately texted back. *What are we talking about here?*

Check your email.

That's odd . . . I swear I didn't send anything.

Hate to say it buuuut . . .

What? What is it? What's wrong?

You've been hacked, hon.

Sure enough, every last contact Devon had in her email account had received the exact same piece of spam. She had circulated the curse even further, to over two hundred friends and family.

A HEALTHIER HAPPIER YOU.

She reached out to as many friends as she could, begging them not to click on the link. *Sooo . . . this is a little embarrassing,* she wrote once, then copy-and-pasted ad infinitum. *If you received an email from me, please PLEASE don't click on it. My account got hacked. AAH! Sorry!!*

In the header of her email, she wrote in all caps—DON'T CLICK! DISREGARD!!!!

No amount of exclamation points would suffice. No emojis could save her now.

This was really embarrassing.

Anyone with common sense would have taken one glance at that email and known not to click. How had she fallen for it so easily? How could Devon have clicked?

What the hell was I thinking?

Larissa, that's what. *Larissa,* who looked so stunning as she twisted her limbs into some fleshy pretzel. Larissa, whose sweat rolled right off her smooth skin with such perfection.

This was all her fault.

Devon went straight to the source. Just a simple email. She didn't want to come off too antagonistic: *Hey, gal!! Um, don't know if you know this or not buuut . . . I think your email might've been hacked? I should know cause I got hacked, too! AAH! Hope you caught it in time!!*

Larissa never responded.

Devon gave her until that evening before checking her inbox to see if she got a reply.

Nothing.

Devon refreshed her browser once, then twice, waiting for an answer that never came.

Devon should've checked her bank account straight away. She should've canceled every credit card linked to her email before she received a call from their bank alerting her to *suspicious purchasing patterns.* Nearly four thousand dollars of mysterious orders had been made online, all in her name, all with the family's Amex, all within the first three hours of clicking that godforsaken email. Someone pretending to be her was buying all this junk, not her! They were still out there, right now, buying all kinds of expensive crap under her name.

What the hell was happening? *Why* was this happening? To her?

What had she done—

WAKE UP

—to deserve this? This was an absolute fucking nightmare. All she wanted was to—

OPEN YOUR EYES

—make it stop. Make *them* stop. Make them all go away.

Just leave me alone!

Asher would never let her live this down. She avoided the topic all day, all through dinner, waiting until the absolute last minute—last second—when they were both in bed. Ash had already assumed his sleeping position for the night, facing away—from her. It wasn't until she clicked off the lamp after checking her phone one last time, Ash breathing deeply, at the very brink of sleep, that Devon decided to finally spill the beans.

"You got *hacked*?" He sat upright, suddenly very awake. "You're kidding me. When?"

"This morning . . ."

"You waited *all day* to tell me? *Christ*, Devon . . . They've probably bought a boat by now."

"I didn't think it'd be this bad . . ."

"What was the email?"

"What?"

"The email. The spam. What did it say?"

HEALTHIER.

"Oh, it was . . ."

HAPPIER.

"Just some silly thing . . ."

YOU.

"How could you?" he asked, crushing her with just one simple question.

How could she?

How could you? Something about the way Asher had asked it, the tone of his voice, rattled about Devon's head. *How could you how could you how . . .* She spent the rest of the night answering Asher's question over and over again in bed, wide awake, staring up at the ceiling.

How could you?

Because you barely look at me anymore . . .

How could you?

Because we barely talk to each other . . .

How could you?

Because I want to . . . want to . . .

WAKE UP

Devon spent the following morning calling the credit card company and canceling every last one. Reordering new ones. Changing her password on nearly all of her subscribed websites.

Who were *they*, anyway? Who was on the other side of that email? Traipsing around online with her virtual identity draped over their own ugly fucking face?

Devon felt so cheapened. So *used*. Her virtual profile, her very sense of self . . . *gone*.

All because she clicked.

You let them in, she thought, examining herself in the bathroom mirror. Getting in real close to her own reflection, too.

Just look at yourself, she thought. Twenty years ago, she had the fresh face of an ingenue. Two kids later, that tender expression had ebbed into jowly suburban mom naïveté.

Resting chump face.

I want my face back . . .

The errant purchases finally stopped, thank God. Those friends who received the spam accepted her apology and moved on. *Water under the digital bridge! Happens to the best of us!*

Not to Devon.

The whole experience had completely shaken her. Every time her index finger hovered above her touchpad, ready to click, her breath caught.

Should she click? What was waiting on the other side of that link?

HEALTHIER

HAPPIER

YOU

She'd never felt so violated in all her life. These faceless attackers took over her life from the inside out. Her identity was theirs now. They became her. They possessed her online presence and she was powerless to stop them.

That's not me. I'm not doing this. This isn't who I am.

Who am I, then?

Devon had welcomed them in. Even now, they were now in her laptop. In her house.

Inside her.

ASHER

Blame Alex P. Keaton.

Michael J. Fox's iconic character from the seminal sitcom *Family Ties*, which ran for seven seasons until its grand finale in 1989, had indirectly influenced—groomed, some might say—an entire generation of future Republicans.

Growing up, Asher Fairchild wanted to be like Alex P. Keaton.

Not just *be like* him, but *be* him.

Since Keaton idolized Ronald Reagan, so did all the boys and girls watching at home. It wasn't like little Ash actually *understood* what Reagan proselytized. He'd heard something about our fortieth president having something to do with *Star Wars*, which was pretty awesome, but that's about it. But if Alex P. Keaton thought Ronnie was cool, well . . . so did Ash. So did an entire generation of easily influenced kids. His wiseacre character made conservativism cool.

Who did Asher's children have to look up to? Where was Alex P. Keaton when you needed him? Who were the role models for kids today? Online influencers? TikTok stars?

Screw that.

"Discontinue cable," Asher overenunciated into the phone, breaking the words down into a phonetic hopscotch, *dis-con-tin-ue-ca-ble*, hoping against hope that he'd be understood.

Okay, the chipper automated bot replied. *Let me see if I can help you with that . . .*

That Asher still watched cable was something of a running joke in their family. *Nobody* watched television in real time anymore. What TV show, what sitcom or premium cable program, necessitated tuning in at a specific hour on a specific day? None. Nada.

Except for the news. The news was happening *now*. And right . . . *now*. And . . . *now*.

Now now now.

News needed to be experienced in real time. It unfolded faster than you could keep up, unspooling like a chyron ticker-taping away, that endless centipede of information squirming over the screen. Asher needed to stay informed. Up-to-date. In the present tense. Just in case there was any late-breaking news, a global catastrophe or a school shooting nearby or . . . who knows what. There was always *something* happening out there, wasn't there?

News was always breaking. Wasn't that reason enough to keep the cable connected?

Devon always complained that they were throwing three hundred bucks out each month for channels nobody else ever watched. Time to trim a little excess financial fat.

How can I help you today?

"I want to discontinue my cable."

Let me see if I can help you with that. In as few words as possible, tell me your issue.

"I want to discontinue cable."

I'm sorry. I didn't get that—

"Discontinue cable."

I'm sorry. I didn't get that. Did you say—

"DIS-con-TIN-ue-CAB-le."

Asher had promised Devon he'd cancel their subscription after the last election. Once the world settled back into some state of normalcy, it wouldn't be necessary to maintain a constant vigil over the news. He could read about it the following morning and not miss a beat.

Severing ties was tough. Asher was having a hard time letting go. What if there was a terrorist attack? An earthquake? Tsunami? He needed to stay connected for his family's sake. For their safety.

Besides, these cable companies made it practically *impossible* to unsubscribe, didn't they? Asher had already wasted half his day on the phone with their provider, stranded for hours—and still counting—with no solution in sight.

Okay. Do you want help with your cable?

"Yes! Yes, I want to discont—"

Okay. Press one for technical help, press two for accounting, or stay on the line to speak with a customer services associate.

"Speak with a customer services associate!" It didn't matter what country they were calling from, it didn't matter what their mother tongue was, he just wanted a living, breathing fucking flesh-and-blood *human being* on the other end of the line to talk to.

Okay. Let me see if I can help you with that. In order to better serve you, please tell me—

"For fuck's sake, I just—I just want to stop my cable."

Okay. Let me see if I can help you with that.

"STOP CABLE."

Okay—

"STOP—THE FUCKING—CABLE."

Are you sure you want to do that, Mr. Fairchild?

His name. The automated voice on the other end of the line just said his name.

How did it know . . .

He hung up.

Asher wasn't an angry person per se. He always liked to think of himself as an easygoing guy. A good dad. His temper rarely flared. He took care of himself. Ate right. Exercised. His cholesterol kept at an even keel. He didn't smoke. Barely ever drank. No heart attack for this fella. Sure, Asher worried over what kind of world his children were inheriting just as much as the next dad, but he certainly didn't *diatribe* over it. He wasn't a proselytizer of the world's woes. There were plenty of times when he felt his blood pressure rise after reading a particular headline, of course, whose didn't, but you'd never find him frothing at the mouth over it.

Asher wasn't *that* guy.

So where was all this bile suddenly coming from? He felt it slowly climbing his throat most days now, this gradually mounting volcano of indigestion working its way up his stomach.

Maybe it had something to do with the news.

Just the Fax.

Even their tagline was an insufferable pun custom-built for boomers, their target audience. Asher fell well below that key demo's age range.

Everybody knew Fax News was raw red meat for its Republican viewers. Asher wasn't one of those gun-toting, bumper-sticker-boasting, baseball-cap-wearing types. *Socially liberal, fiscally conservative.* That was where he landed on the political spectrum. He slept well at night—used to, at least—knowing that he and his wife were raising their children to be decent people. Good, law-abiding, taxpaying people. With a little common sense. He was—

keeeaton

—intelligent enough to know when he was being pandered to by TV programming.

CNN had been his channel of choice for years. Back then. You know when. The *Before* Times. It seems inconceivable that any Republican in their right mind would watch CNN now, but there had been a time when civic-minded conservatives considered it the balanced channel. Their programming felt more even-keeled when it came to delivering the bad news. After a while, though, all of the anchors at CNN took on the same whiny, condescending tone. Snide little comments about our slimy president-elect slipped into their coverage that made them sound like . . . well, a bunch of know-it-alls. Stuck-up, coastal elite jerk-offs.

Even if Asher agreed with them—in theory—the absolute cringe of liberal snobbery was grating. It wasn't enough to be on the right side of history, *no*, these journalists just had to nag.

There goes your country! Told you so! Hope y'all are happy . . .

It was exhausting, to be honest. This hand-wringing intermingled with the smug attitude of being correct. The world was on fire—*Rome's burning, folks! Sure was fun while it lasted!*—and here were these highbrow news anchors rubbing it in, nearly reveling in it.

Don't blame us for the floods and famines. We tried to warn you, didn't we?

It started with a bit of rubbernecking. Asher wanted to peek at what was happening on the other news channels. It was wise—healthy, even—to take in a range of reporting. He was well aware of how social media siloed people into echo chambers of recycled misinformation. He saw it in his own family. All the scrolling. His wife got her news from Facebook, of all places. That wasn't news, that was simply an algorithmic force-feeding of bullshit masking itself as info.

Ash wasn't about to get duped. Not like Devon. He couldn't hide in his own ideological bubble. He needed to bear witness to what else was out there.

His father had been a Fax convert. The ol' man's channel of choice. *What if I'm becoming just like him?* Ash laughed. *Always shouting at the TV. Arguing with the anchorman . . .* Wouldn't that be a gas? All he needed was his own La-Z-Boy.

He'd clicked over a few times before, but never for long. Tiny doses of diatribe. Just *listen* to these guys. It was a bit rich, even for his blood. Pissed-off pigs wallowing in their own shitty discourse. Asher felt like he needed a bath if he stayed on the channel for more than a few minutes. The absolute oiliness of their banter. Unapologetic xenophobia. Blond-haired bigotry getting passed off as news. Who did Fax think they were they kidding with this crap?

Half the country, apparently.

Asher decided to perform a little thought experiment: Watch Fax News for one evening. One night, that's it. He could always come crawling back to CNN whenever he wanted.

"What're we watching tonight?" Devon asked from her love seat. Her tablet was open in her lap. She barely watched what was on television anymore, focusing on her own screen.

"How about the news?"

"Isn't there something funny we can watch? What's that one show? What's it called?"

"I have no idea what you're talking about."

"You know . . . The one. The funny one."

I'm not a mind reader, he wanted to say, a candlewick flicker of his temper flaring up.

"How about *Family Ties*?"

Asher sat up. "I'm sorry, what?"

"I don't remember the name of—"

"No. After that. You said . . ."

"The show? I don't remember . . ."

"Just now!" His voice was rising. "You said *Family Ties*."

"I don't think that one's on the air anymore." Devon picked herself up with a sigh, taking her tablet with her. "I'll be in bed. Don't stay up too late, okay?"

"Night . . ."

"Night." She could've kissed his forehead as she walked by, but nope. Away she went.

Alone, Asher clicked over to the other side.

The second he changed channels, Asher was met with the network-English accent of an Aryan anchorwoman. Her hair was frosted into a bulletproof bouffant. Her spray tan took on a leathery texture under the spotlights, no thanks to the motion smoothing on his new plasma screen TV. She had this whole *Real Housewives of the GOP* vibe going on. Her male co-anchor was no better—a poreless Ken doll with irradiated teeth, blindingly white. His hair was a shining Plasticine black, the spotlights bouncing off his stiff helmet. The two were bantering on about something or other. It was so hard to tell. There was no shape to the discourse, no structure.

Was there a script to all this? Were they reading off a teleprompter or just winging it? Asher had been watching for a full ten minutes and he still had yet to hear any actual news. All these two seemed interested in chatting about was the degraded state of the country.

The absolute end of times. Hell in a handbasket.

Just listen to these two . . .

Asher felt as if he had switched over into an alternate reality. Watching Fax News was like living in an upside-down world. What bizzarro bubble was this?

Had nobody seen *Network*? Had nobody learned anything?

It was kind of entertaining, if Asher was being completely honest. It was enjoyable in a holy-shit-is-this-horror-show-for-real kinda way. You just had to see it to believe it.

See it to believe.

Asher rolled that phrase over in his head: *See it to believe.* In order to understand, to believe, one had to bear witness.

So here he was. Seeing.

Believing.

He wished Devon were here. They could hate-watch together. Poke fun at the anchors and their awful spray tans. He could turn to her and ask, *Who's buying this BS?*

But Ash watched alone.

He flipped back to CNN and was greeted by the somber, stately coverage of the war in—well, wherever the war was right now. Poised, composed, regal reporting. *Boooooring.*

He flipped to MSNBC. Same coverage, same war, same prim posturing. *Kill me now.*

He switched back to Fax.

No war at all. Just aimless anger. Anger at what they're doing in the public schools. Anger at the libraries. Anger at vaccination mandates. Anger at—at—

Jesus, anger at just about *everything.*

He felt it at the back of his throat, the bile of it all, slowly mounting. It started deep in his stomach and began its slow ascension, funneling up his esophagus. Burning every inch of it.

The motion smoothing was giving Asher a migraine. The longer he stared at the screen, the deeper that drill bit skewered his temples, grinding against his skull.

Asher could've changed channels. He could've gone crying back to Anderson Cooper and his liberal clique would take him back, wouldn't they? Of course. And what would they say?

Told you so.

Anderson Cooper made him feel stupid. Fax didn't make him feel stupid.

Fax just made him *feel.*

Doesn't the loudest person in the room always draw the most focus? Isn't it the biggest, brassiest, most booming voice that wins an argument? It didn't matter who was *right.* It was all about who had your *attention.* Fax News had had Asher's undivided attention for fifteen minutes now.

Then twenty. He hadn't changed the channel in over thirty minutes. Forty . . .

Fifty . . .

Before Asher knew what the hell had happened, it was well after midnight.

Where did all that time go?

Asher turned off the television. His eyes hurt, dry from watching the screen. This lingering buzz settled into his chest as he slipped into bed. He hadn't felt this floored in a while. His pulse picked up, a rabbit thumping its hind legs against his ribs. He felt alive.

He had a secret now. Almost like he'd done something dirty. Naughty.

What a ride . . .

Asher couldn't wait to watch again tomorrow night.

CALEB

I want to be someone who matters

Caleb should delete the tweet. Thinking about it now, an hour after posting it, still sent a flush of blood through his cheeks, warm with fresh embarrassment. It was so stupid. So needy.

Benjamin Pendleton had pushed him in the hallway. Again. He played it off like it was an accident, *oops*, but this was the fifth time this week Ben's shoulder had rammed into Caleb's back.

"Sorry," Ben said. "Didn't see you there."

Didn't see you there.

Didn't see you there.

Didn't see—

Caleb was tired of being invisible. He wanted to be someone people saw. Heard.

I want to be someone who matters

Who tweets stuff like that? People who want attention, obviously. People who are so desperate for approval, they'll end up tweeting their *actual* feelings. Bad call. Nobody likes Sincere Tweets. Anytime somebody goes earnest, they're torn to pieces. Kiss of death, dude.

Rule #1: Never expose yourself.

Not that anyone would actually read it. Caleb's Twitter account never broke two hundred followers. Mostly bots, but still. He found himself in an echo chamber of faceless profiles. Anime avatars. Mountain Dew–drenched selfies. Cartoon frogs.

Caleb pulled out his phone for the third time at dinner and cast off into The Scroll.

The Scroll . . .

Caleb slipped into that endless stream of unfiltered id like he was tubing downriver and paddling off with his thumb, swiping and swiping and swiping. The private thoughts of his peers bounced off one another, some in harmony, others pinballing against each other. He'd occasionally type a tidbit of anxiety and send it downstream with all the self-conscious flotsam.

Sometimes a follower might *like* it. Most days no one did.

That was okay. Tweeting these deep-seated feelings tended to re-linquish them, expunge them, even for just a moment. All he had to do was press *POST*. Let the thought go. Release it.

testing testing one two three microphone check one two

Not deep thoughts by any stretch. Just impulsive missives.

another night at home with the fam oh joy lol

Caged feelings, now free.

saw her she didn't see me

Exorcised.

hellooo . . . ? is this tweet even on?

Ever since Caleb's acne cropped up sophomore year, his hoodie had become a second skin for him. He adopted a slouching posture, much to his mother's chagrin, chin dipped to his chest, hood up to hide the coral reef of his complexion. He had a habit of chewing on the drawstrings, gnawing on the knot until it was soaked in spit, which miffed Mom to no end. She was always telling him to *take that out of your mouth*. She'd even reach for it if she was close enough, yanking on the drawstring at the dinner table, almost taking his teeth with it.

The Accutane was helping kill the coral reef, but *holy sheeyet*, did it ever dry him up from the inside out. No amount of water could rehydrate him, his throat constantly parched.

No selfies for this guy. It'd be a long, *long* time before he snapped off a pic of him—

Ding!

The instant Caleb heard his phone's digital trill, he pulled it from his pocket.

XAPHAN2001 now follows you.

Whatever dopamine rush he felt quickly dissipated as soon as he glanced at their profile. No photo. No mutuals. XAPHAN2001 had no other followers at all. Not a single tweet.

So . . . a bot.

Obviously.

The best thing to do was pay no attention to him. Or her. Or . . . *it*? Whatever they were. A digital mosquito, really, buzzing about his profile, trying to get him to click on something. It wouldn't be long before XAPHAN2001 shared a link:

Click here for a brand new iPad!

Caleb did not need that crap in his life. His mom—oh, man, his mom had totally fallen for some hacker's trap and clicked on a phishing scheme, hijacking her whole account. She didn't realize it for almost, like, a whole *day* before all her friends and family told her they'd gotten some suspicious emails from her.

Dad would never let her live that one down. It was the closest thing to a private joke between him and Caleb, at Mom's expense, just a little father-son bonding over her misfortune.

"So she, like, clicked on the link?"

Dad nodded. "Yup."

"Holy shit, Mom!" Caleb couldn't help but scold her, his own mother. "Never click!"

"How was I supposed to know?"

Dad and Caleb had laughed away, harmoniously doubling up on his mother.

"Go ahead." Mom was clearly stung. "Laugh it up. See who eats tonight."

"Oh, come on . . . Why the thin skin, hon?" Dad asked. "We're only teasing . . ."

Caleb hadn't stopped guffawing, wiping the tears away. "Yeah, Ma . . . We're just teasing."

"I'm so glad you two can have a bonding experience at your mother's expense."

It felt good to share a moment with his father. When was the last time the two of them had something like that? Little League? There had been a few disastrous fishing expeditions when Caleb was, like, ten, but Dad gave up and Caleb never picked up a fishing rod again.

Mom's fallout from this phishing fiasco brought Caleb and Dad back together again, even for just a little bit. She got snagged, hook, line, and stinker.

Caleb even tweeted about it: *mom totally got catphished ooops!*

Ping!

XAPHAN2001 turned out to be a constant liker. Every time Caleb posted a stray thought—*barely survived chem today*—the first follower to click *Like* on his post would be none other than him. No comments, no DMs. Just a simple digital nod of approval. *Thumbs up!* XAPHAN2001 always hovered over his profile, waiting for Caleb to post something. *Anything.*

Should Caleb block him? It would be such a cinch. Just report this creeper and then let the social media police deal with him. He'd be gone in no time. *Buh-bye,* XAPHAN2001 . . .

What was the harm, though? It's not like XAPHAN2001 was actually *doing* anything. He just liked all of Caleb's tweets. Weird, for sure. Creepy, even . . . But if XAPHAN2001's support got Twitter's algorithm to pay attention to his posts and boost them, leading to more followers . . .

What could it hurt? A bot's just a bot. Everybody had them.

XAPHAN2001 was Caleb's.

Learn to live with your parasites, Caleb decided. Theirs was a mutually beneficial social media symbiosis. Caleb needed a sense of approval and XAPHAN2001 needed him, apparently.

Win-win.

How long had Caleb felt uncomfortable in his own skin? The self-doubt always came in waves of whispers, sudden and persistent, his own voice washing over his mind at any moment:

I don't belong here . . . I don't fit in with my own family . . . I don't have any friends . . . I don't have anyone . . . I wish I was somebody else . . . Anybody else . . .

Caleb never shared these feelings with anyone. Not out here in the real world, anyway. Not with his parents or anyone at school. Calling his classmates "friends" was a definite stretch.

Only on Twitter. Only to his bots. His personal parasites.

Only XAPHAN2001 seemed to notice.

Like.

Like.

Like.

When Mom had her second glass of white wine at the dinner table, she might opine over the loss of her eldest son. "Whatever happened to my beautiful little boy?"

That boy was buried beneath a crust of acne.

"I miss my baby . . ."

Caleb hated it when Mom got this way.

"Remember how happy you used to be? You always used to laugh and laugh . . ."

"Mom. Stop."

"Can't I miss my little guy? You used to love it when I—"

"*Mom!*" He was sixteen now. He was no longer that gap-toothed kid.

He was nobody.

All anyone ever saw was the surface. If they saw anything of him at all. Did anybody really look? His GPA was average. In middle school he used to run cross-country because Dad made him. Now he was just one of the managers of the team, and the only reason he was doing that was because Dad promised to buy him a brand-new laptop as long as Caleb did something, *anything*, outdoors. In the sun.

Cross-country used to keep his anxiety in check. He could exhaust his thoughts. For a few years, he literally ran himself into the ground. He outpaced his own self-loathing. The second he stopped, his insecurity caught up with him—his shadow at his shoulder, wearing his smile, his teeth, reaching out to grab him, take him down and sink.

None of it mattered. His grades didn't matter. Life didn't matter. *I just don't matter . . .*

I'm nothing . . .

I'm—

PING!

The family had a no-phones rule at the dinner table.

Ping!

Most nights Caleb could abide by it—but tonight, whenever the digital trill of his cell chirruped from his pocket, he felt the burning urge to pull his phone out and check.

Ping!

He needed to be covert about it. Not that Dad would notice. He was lost in his own thoughts most nights now, anyhow, barely looking up from his plate.

Ping!

Ping!

Ping!

Mom had the same Pavlovian response to her own phone whenever it chirruped. If her phone dinged—*ping!*—she'd have to fight off her own burning urge to sneak a peek.

Hypocrite.

Who would be reaching out to Mom, anyway? She was on her own social media sites, which was hilarious. The quickest indication that it was high time to cancel your account on any app was the moment your mother signed up for it. She was on Facebook. Instagram. Ancient apps that were flooded with far-off family members. Nobody under the age of forty was on Facebook anymore. That was where all the dinosaurs socialized. Caleb wouldn't be caught dead on there. He kept his profile, sure, but he hadn't actually checked it in months.

The second his mother sent him a friend request on Facebook, Caleb was officially out.

See ya . . .

Caleb preferred Twitter, to be honest. It was like going to the beach and sitting in the sand, water rushing over your feet. He could relax and bask in the gentle flow of info as it drifted by. Thoughts washed over him, these tiny waves of digital information lapping at his brain. A tweet would rush across his screen and then it was gone, replaced by the next wave of 280 characters. *So sooooothing . . .*

Ping!

Ping!

Ping!

Not tonight. For some reason, Caleb's Twitter account felt like a bird in a cage, struggling to break free, constantly fluttering in circles around the wire spokes of its own prison.

Ping!

Ping!

PING!

It just wouldn't stop. Why was Caleb suddenly blowing up?

I want to be someone who matters

Oh shit.

Caleb had never put himself out there like that before. It wasn't like a cry for help or anything. Not really. He wasn't suicidal or having any self-destructive ideation. It was just a stupid thought that popped into his head. That wanted out. Just a blip escaping from his brain and then making its way out into the world.

Caleb pulled up the list of interactions on the tweet. XA-PHAN2001 had liked it. As always. No surprise there.

Then he retweeted it.

Okaaay, now *that's* weird . . . XAPHAN2001 had never done anything like *that* before. Why would he? The tweet didn't *mean* anything. What was the point of retwee—

Ping.

Somebody else—SARIS—liked it.

They retweeted it, too.

Who the fuck was SARIS? There were no mutuals between them. Not even XAPHAN2001. Just another bot.

Then KLOTHOD retweeted it. Then TRACHI.

Who the fuck were these guys? Why were they retweeting him?

What the hell's going on?

A fresh wave of embarrassment rushed up Caleb's chest. He could feel the blood in his face, his acne seething. He set his phone to vibrate. Even with his ringer off, the abrupt vibrations sent a subtle hum throughout the dining room. *ZZZT!* He kept his phone in his pocket, the fabric pressed tightly against his skin. *ZZZT!* It sent a steady jolt through his leg, all the way down to his bones. *ZZZT!* An electrical shock raced up his femur and along his spine, vertebra by vertebra, until it tapped the root of his brain to release a rush of dopamine into his blood.

"Turn it off," Mom said.

"Sorry."

Instead of powering it down, Caleb simply wedged his phone deeper into his pocket, hoping the tight confines of denim would muffle the vibrations . . . but it just wouldn't stop.

ZZT! More likes. *ZZZT!* More retweets. *ZZZZZT!* Caleb's skeleton rattled with every last notification, a tuning fork constantly struck. *ZZZZZZZZZT!*

"Do you want me to take your phone away?"

"Sorry . . ."

Mom held out her hand, palm up. "Give it to me."

"I'll turn it off."

"Nope, too late, hand it over."

"I'm turning it off!"

WHO THE FUK R U?

Caleb was the first to break down. He'd been waiting for XA-PHAN2001 to DM him. Tweet at him. Send him a sketchy link or dick pic. Something. *Anything.*

But XAPHAN2001 never did. The two were playing social media chicken, staring each other's avatar down, just to see who would crumble and reach out to the other first.

Clearly this wasn't a real person. It had to be a bot . . . right?

What else could they be?

The constant likes. The instant hit of gratification. XAPHAN2001 was always there, waiting for Caleb to tweet something, and then he'd swoop in and cheer him on.

Caleb didn't want this. *Any* of this. He just wanted XAPHAN2001 to stop.

Stop looking at me!

Caleb tried to find any other social connective tissue to this weirdo, but there simply wasn't one. Their profile was a siloed island all to itself. XAPHAN2001 never tweeted their own stuff or liked anyone else's tweets or did anything but obsess over him. His own stalker-bot.

Caleb sat in bed, under the covers, phone in hand. He opened Twitter and scrolled through the hundreds—oooh shit, *thousands*—of likes and retweets he'd received just over the course of dinner, gobsmacked at the amount of attention he was getting, still getting, for just one simple missive that meant nothing, absolutely nothing. What the hell was happening?

XAPHAN2001. This was all their fault. His tweet was now being volleyed between bots.

So he DMed him: *WHO THE FUK R U?*

A second after pressing send, he received a reply:

We believe in you.

Whoooa, now that's *super* creepy. Caleb did not need this shit in his life. *Block this pedo.* He hopped through reporting protocols, swiftly clicking through the quick-and-easy survey:

Are you being harassed?

Yup.

Is this profile harmful to you and others?

Abso-fucking-lutely.

Are they sending you suspicious links that appear to be phishing schemes?

Yeah, sure, why not . . .

Reported.

Blocked.

Buh-bye, XAPHAN2001 . . . Been nice knowing you, meatwad. It was fun while it lasted.

Caleb shut down his phone. Everything felt so quiet. So . . . still. He turned his phone back on and peeked, double-checking that he'd actually gone through with blocking XAPHAN2001.

They weren't there. Their profile had vanished, wiped clean. All that remained was the faceless avatar every new profile has before users upload their own photo, a blank silhouette of someone's head and shoulders, dark gray against light gray.

A ghost.

Caleb lay there in bed, still wearing his hoodie. Staring up at the ceiling, he tugged on the drawstrings, cinching his face within the cozy confines of the red cotton hood.

Sealing him inside his cloth cocoon.

Even with his phone off, he swore he could still hear the digital trill of his phone notifications, alerting him of another like—*Ping!*—but of course that was just his imagination.

He was just hearing things.

Ping!

FAMILY NIGHT

No more Pizza Night. Wednesday nights were now officially re-
named . . .

Family Night.

"I don't want to hear any huffing or puffing," Mom announced.
"No matter how busy we all are, no matter what else you've got
going on, every member of the Fairchild family will block off their
Wednesday evenings for dinner together. No exceptions."

To Dad, she added, "That goes for you, too."

"I didn't say anything . . . Did I say anything?"

"This is for all of us. To connect. Got it?"

"You got it, Mom," Marcus said with his best can-do attitude.

"Fine," Caleb muttered.

Mom explained how she watched a video that talked about making time for family. "*Sit together. Break bread. Share quality time with one
another, engage, learn something new about each other over a home-cooked,
healthy, organic meal. No delivery!*"

"This was one of your social media sages, wasn't it?" Dad asked.
"Which one is it now?"

Caleb coughed but it kind of sounded like a laugh. Mom didn't
say anything.

Marcus didn't mind. He kind of liked the idea.

Most days, Marcus felt like his whole family forgot about him.
They were always too busy. Not on Wednesday nights. *No screens at
the dinner table.* That's Mom's #1 rule.

"I want to see the whites of your eyes," she said. "Flip your phones
to silent mode and keep them out of sight."

Everyone had a tough time with this rule. Even Mom. Everyone
except for Marcus. He still didn't have his own Pi-Pi. Or iPhone.
Or smartwatch. Plenty of friends at school had screens of their own
already, rubbing it in at recess. Not Marcus. No matter how much he
begged, Mom wouldn't budge. *Your brain is still developing*, she'd say.
But every now and then she let Marcus borrow her tablet, whenever

"Mommy needs some quiet time," she always said.

But only for thirty minutes. Just enough time for Marcus to watch his favorite video—*Baby Ghost*, clocking in at two minutes and sixteen seconds—approximately 13.8888889 times.

Baby Ghost, boo-boo, boo-boo
Baby Ghost, boo-boo, boo-boo
Baby Ghost, boo-boo, boo-boo
Baby Ghost
Boo!

The last *boo* was the best. A cartoon ghost leapt right out at Marcus from the screen:

BOO!

Marcus played the video so many times, the rest of his family would groan and leave the room whenever they heard the first notes of the song starting up again.

Caleb hated it. "Turn that shit off."

Dad would crank the volume up on his brand-new super-big-screen TV, letting the sound of the news drown out *Baby Ghost*.

Mom would simply take her tablet back after half an hour. "That's enough screen time for today, dear . . ."

"Can I watch it just one more time?"

"Your eyeballs need a break."

"Pleeeeease?"

"Go outside. Get some sun. Dinner will be ready in an hour."

The Fairchilds had become guinea pigs for Mom's culinary experiments. Living test subjects for new recipes that she'd found online. Marcus never quite knew what they were going to eat.

"Where's the pizza?" Caleb asked.

"I'm testing out a new recipe tonight," Mom said. "Pull your hood down, hon."

Caleb pretended like he hadn't heard.

"Hood. Down. *Now.*"

Caleb sighed, pinching the hood and pulling it back.

"*Bon appétit*," Mom said.

Marcus examined his meal. *What the heck is this? Broccoli? And what's this squishy thing? Pumpkin?*

Dad glanced at Caleb and Marcus from across the table, silently signaling to both brothers that they should eat what was in front of them before they hurt their mother's feelings.

Caleb missed the message. "What's this supposed to be?"

"Quinoa." Mom's voice sounded hopeful.

Caleb raked his fork across the tiny pellets, its tines scraping the plate. "It's dry."

"Add some soy sauce."

The days of hot dogs and tater tots felt like a long-forgotten memory. Now they ate lentils and something called *tempeh*. "It's really good," Marcus lied. "*Mmm.* I like it a lot."

"Thank you, hon," Mom replied, eyes crinkling as she smiled.

Caleb shot him a look, puckering his lips and silently pecking at the air: *Kiss-ass.*

Marcus wanted to clean his plate just for her. The chicken was dry. There's always ketchup for that. But the squishy squash was impossible. Simply nibbling it made him gag. Marcus couldn't do it. He tried—several times—but it was too much. Even for Mom's sake, there was no swallowing that squash. How was he going to get a *happy plate*, as Mom called it? Marcus needed to get rid of his leftovers. Luckily no one was paying any attention to him.

Where are you, Rufus? Marcus tried to summon the family dog with his mind. *I need your help, boy! Ruuuuffffuuuuuuusssss!*

"How was work?" Mom asked.

"Another day," Dad said.

"That's it? Anything interesting happen?"

"At *work*?"

Marcus didn't exactly know what his father did for a living. Sometimes he wasn't sure Dad knew either. He never answered Mom's questions about it.

"How about you, hon?" she asked Caleb. "Anything interesting happen at school?"

"No."

"Nothing? Nothing at all? What were you learning in—"

"Nothing, Mom." Caleb's voice was so flat. Like a pancake.

"Well, my day was lovely," she said to everyone and no one. "Thank you all for asking."

Mom had the conversation all to herself. "I read this article that spoke a lot about . . ."

Marcus's focus drifted.

Grown-up talk.

Suddenly, he felt a cold, wet nose on his leg.

Rufus to the rescue!

Marcus didn't have a single memory that didn't include his closest, bestest friend. Rufus may have belonged to the family, but Marcus was definitely his favorite human. He slept at the foot of his bed and waited with him at the bus stop every day before school.

It was unclear how old their mangy mutt was. Twelve, maybe? *Old.* They adopted sweet, shaggy Rufus, who was already pretty worn down to begin with, when Marcus was only three. Streaks of matted fur covered Rufus from head to toe. The only part of Rufus that wasn't covered in hair was his tongue, dangling out with each slightly stinky pant of air.

Marcus pinched some burnt squash and cupped it in his palm. He quickly slipped his hand under the table. Rufus didn't mind that the vegetables were burnt. He'd eat anything.

"How about you, hon?" Mom asked, snapping Marcus back. Was he caught? "How was school? Anything special happen?"

"We played soccer on the playground today," Marcus said.

Mom smiled encouragingly. Everyone else ignored him.

"I got hit with a soccer ball," Marcus said. He lifted his arm up to show them his bruise.

"Eat your dinner," Mom said, nodding at his squash.

"Pass the butter," Dad said.

"Less cholesterol, hon."

"Then why bring it to the table? Why put it out if you're not going to let me—"

"I'm just telling you what your doctor said—"

"Thanks, thank you for reminding me."

Marcus moved his vegetables across his plate, but it was impossible to hide them.

He felt that familiar wet nudge against his hand. Rufus nuzzled Marcus's thumb, licking his fingers. Marcus giggled, it tickled so much. He sneaked the dog another hunk of squash.

"Marcus." Mom stared at him from across the table. "Stop feeding the dog."

Uh-oh. Caught red-handed. "I wasn't . . ."

"People food can make dogs sick."

"It's making *me* sick," Caleb mumbled.

The words hurt Mom's feelings. Why didn't Caleb see that? Mom took a sharp breath through her nose and lifted her chin, pretending like she hadn't heard.

"Go on," she said. "Eat your veggies."

There were still three slices of squash left on his plate. Marcus was trapped.

He had to eat. Mom was giving him that look. If Caleb wouldn't eat his squash, Marcus had to. He only wanted to make her happy.

Be brave. Be strong. For Mommy.

Marcus took a deep breath through his nose and took the teeniest bite. The type of bite that doesn't taste like anything. But it was still too much. The slippery sliver of cold, squishy mush slid down, down, down his throat. He felt like he was going to—going to—to—

Marcus barfed. Orange squash-mush splattered all over his favorite purple T-shirt.

Caleb laughed. "Hooooly shit . . ."

"Welp," Dad said as he dropped his napkin onto his plate, covering what remained of his own meal. "I'd say this Family Night sure was a raging success, wouldn't you, hon?"

Mom didn't say a word. She held herself perfectly still—and for a moment, just a moment, Marcus couldn't help but wonder if it was his mom at all, or a robot of some kind.

Something else had taken her place. Just for a moment.

Mommy? Where are you?

"I just . . ." she started, eyes elsewhere. "I just want to wake up."

And then Mom blinked back. Smiling at him.

"I'm sorry," she said, all sun. "Did you say something, hon?"

Marcus slowly shook his head.

"Oh. Huh. I thought I heard you . . . call my name. Are you sure?"

Marcus shook his head once more. It hadn't been him. So if it hadn't been him . . .

Who was talking to Mommy?

NOVEMBER 29
stage three: *obsession*

DEVON

The first package arrived two days after the hacking: a tissue-box-sized white cardboard container. No fancy logo, no brand name. Just a tiny corrugated box with a PO box for a return address.

I didn't order this, Devon thought as she picked it up. *I didn't order any—*

Oh.

Oh no no . . . Not another purchase made by her digital doppelgänger. Devon was positive she'd put a stop to them all. The bank told her they'd canceled every last unauthorized order. Then . . . where did this package come from? Why was it on her doorstep?

Devon didn't want to touch the box. She stood there on the front porch, taking in the rest of her cul-de-sac, eyeing the neighboring homes.

Is Mr. Deliveryman still here? Can I return it? Tell him to take it back, wherever it came from?

Devon brought the box through the double front doors with stained-glass insets, carrying the container at arm's length, as if it were an explosive device in need of dismantling.

She plopped the box on the kitchen counter. The slightest scent of earth seeped out from the cardboard, drifting up through the packaging. Was that cardamom she smelled?

Devon shook it. Gently. The faintest crumple of tissue paper sounded from within.

Might as well peek, right? Technically speaking, she'd already bought whatever it was . . .

Devon went about dissecting the box. She sliced through the packing tape with a pair of kitchen shears, digging her fingers into the cardboard chest cavity and cracking the flaps back. Beneath the musculature of bubble wrap, she discovered a swath of pink pastel tissue paper.

Within, a glass heart: a four-ounce jar with a suction-sealed lid. No plastic casing with a pre-perforated tear, no logo, no list of ingredients. A print-at-home sticker on its broadside said:

AWAKEN

What was that grit inside? Dirt? Protein powder? Must be a supplement of some kind . . .

There were no FDA regulations printed on the bottle—no calorie intake guidelines. Asher would be furious if he found out there were fraudulent purchases coming to their home.

Devon needed to hide it. Bury it. Burn it. So she stored it in the pantry.

There. Crisis averted. Out of sight, out of mind.

Devon had woken up with yet another crippling migraine that morning—third day in a row. All week, this searing headache lingered throughout her day, making it nearly impossible to concentrate. She had things to do. Groceries to buy. Meals to make. A very, very busy day.

I'm sick, I know I'm sick . . . She couldn't diagnose it on her own. She needed help.

She had already visited their family physician the day before.

"What seems to be the problem?" he'd asked.

"How long have you got?" Devon half laughed at her own joke. Even then, her skull throbbed, the fluorescent lights microwaving her head, set to slow cook.

"You quit caffeine recently?" he asked without looking at her.

"Should I?"

"Your diet change at all? Have you been dehydrated?"

"No, not really, I don't—"

"It's probably nothing. Pick up some extra-strength Tylenol and see if that doesn't help."

"But I've already tried—"

The doctor placed his hand on Devon's knee and squeezed, effectively silencing her. "Don't you worry. I bet you won't even notice it tomorrow morning."

Devon yearned for better medical attention. She wished there were someone in her life who spoke to her personal beliefs rather than just her body. She needed healing.

Spiritual healing.

It was her soul that needed cleansing. What else could this ailment possibly be? She'd tried every over-the-counter remedy, and none of it helped a bit.

Devon had always considered herself a spiritual person. Not religious per se, simply . . .

Well, you know. *Spiritual.*

She came from a family of lapsed Catholics. She was sympathetic to the notion of a higher power—not that she actually believed in a bearded fellow hanging out in the clouds. If He was up there, well, yeah, sure . . . she'd totally be down with Him.

But those beliefs had never felt like her own. She wanted something else. Something more in tune with what she felt in her own heart.

Who knows? Maybe there was higher power within *her* . . .

It was possible, wasn't it? She felt it, a nebulous presence, whatever it was. Something *special*. Something that could make sense out of this cruel, uncaring world she was stuck in.

In order to make sense of that chaos, Devon needed to make sense of herself first. Look inward. Seek her inner peace. Become the best rendition of herself.

Time to reconnect. To awaken. To open her eyes.

Devon was ready and willing to rediscover the identity that had been taken away from her. A piece of her had gone missing among their Crate and Barrel and Pottery Barn accents, lost within the cozy confines of their Benjamin Moore White Dove walls.

She had to find herself again. Reclaim herself. Salvage her inner goddess.

Where better to look for spiritual guidance than on Instagram?

Devon's feed was full of beaming faces. Pristine features. Perfectly poised expressions.

Just look at all those smiles . . . The piercing eyes. Their pouting lips.

The sirens of Instagram.

These lovely ladies struck a pose as the sun set behind them, casting their tanned, toned skin in the gloaming glow. They pranced across the sand as a wave splashed their smooth legs, laughing as they ran. They huddled in an oversized sweater that rolled softly off their bare shoulders, curled on the couch with a coffee mug, wearing a pair of glasses, their luscious locks pulled up in a bun. They ate freshly picked blackberries from the farmer's market with their feet kicked up as they read a new book.

Each photo was captioned with daily affirmations in flowery font, words to live by: *Live your life to the fullest. Always reach deeper into your personal core. Find the goddess within. Let her breathe . . .*

Pilgrims, every last one, all on their own personal journey toward self-enlightenment. All with something very special to share. A story to tell. A wealth of wellness.

This particular type of spirituality made sense to Devon. Rather than pack the fam in the car and head to church every Sunday, her services were right here, in her feed.

I just felt like I'd been asleep standing up, ya know?

I was auto-piloting through my life . . .

It was high time to WAKE UP. To OPEN MY EYES and see the world around me.

Devon wanted to join them. Be one of them. Swim in their stream. She yearned to crawl through her tablet's screen and be a part of that photo-filtered existence. Crema. Perpetua. Valencia. So many filters to pick and choose from. She was spending more time online, scrolling through her tablet. It was so easy to lose herself in the endless outcropping of profiles, the tea-drinking, sweater-wearing, mountain-hiking, parasailing beauties. Smiling back at her. Winking.

Calling out to her—*Join ussss . . .*

Not every profile had perfected their inner Paltrow, though. You had to find the right guru for you-you, so Devon surfed through a few profiles. She followed a few influencers:

MRS_INNER_PEACE.

HEALTHY.LIVING.LADY.

GO.GODDES.GO!

One daily affirmation became ten, all preaching their own carefully crafted brand of wellness: *Be the woman u want to be! Stand up for ur truth! Be loud + be heard!*

Then she found her.

Her. The One she'd been looking for. Her sage suburban guru.

Her . . . *suburu?*

YOGAMAMA.

There was just something so . . . downright iridescent about her, something that separated her from all the others. Something that shimmered. Her profile pic shone in pearlescent hues.

Devon squinted. Leaned into the screen. Is that . . .

Larissa?

That was her, wasn't it? How did she find her?

Maybe she found me, Devon thought.

Hey there, y'all . . . Yogamama here! Just wanted to reach out and see how all of my beautiful soul sisters are doing! Me, I'm hanging in there . . . Last night, I had a thought that I wanted to share with y'all . . . It came to me in the middle of the night, almost like a dream . . .

Sometimes her videos discussed healing stones. Sometimes they were about the newest gloop. But there was always a story behind her journey—Larissa's particular path to wellness. Her quest to becoming YOGAMAMA. *We're all on this voyage together. We're going on an adventure of self-exploration and when we come out the other end, we will REAWAKEN as different women . . . We will emerge as something better . . . Something new. You ready?*

It would be difficult, YOGAMAMA warned. Painful, perhaps. The best quests are. You have to hurt in order to return triumphant. You need to bleed, just a bit, to be reborn.

Imagine the butterfly you want to become, she preached. *Picture the pupa you must emerge from. Crawl out from that cocoon, gurrl . . . Be a new woman. A healthier, happier YOU.*

Devon was ready. She needed this. This connection. She curled up with her tablet and ran her index finger across the screen, grazing YOGAMAMA's tanned skin. Touching her body. It was like Larissa was encased in glass, hidden behind a picture frame. Close, she was so close . . .

If only Devon could break through that window. Crawl in.

All these sirens offered private glimpses into their homes, snapshots into the lives of women just like her, mothers *just like her.* The same struggles. The same endless search for soul sustenance. The same uphill battles with their health.

But Devon liked Larissa's—sorry, YOGAMAMA's—life best. She spoke to her the most.

Aren't you just tired of . . . being tired?

Yes, as a matter of fact, she was.

Well, it's time to WAKE UP, hon!

A holy war was being waged within her body, YOGAMAMA said. Devon needed to fortify the front line. She began to meditate. The sirens of Instagram would teach her how to do it—how to dig into the core of her true self. How to reach for a higher sense of well-being.

How to pray. To eat. To love.

Sure, you can pay out the wazoo for a yoga class full of twenty-year-olds . . . or, you and me can have a little gurrrl time, just us gal pals, taking it slow, at our own pace. Whaddya say?

Yes. Devon said yes to that.

I didn't hear ya, gurl!

"Yes," Devon said. Out loud this time.

A little louder, hon!

"Yes!"

Can I get a hell yes this time?

"Hell yes!"

That's what I'm talking about!

Devon unrolled her yoga mat across the floor and assumed the lotus position, perching her iPad at her feet. She scrolled through the pics and clips until she found today's sermon.

YOGAMAMA sat on a balsa-wood mat, overlooking the beach, the gentle rush of waves in the distance. Devon wasn't sure if it was real or white noise in the background.

Gooooood morning, gals! Y'all ready to WAKE UP with me?

Where was she? In the Bahamas? Hadn't she just been in their yoga workshop? Maybe that's why she hadn't been answering her emails. Of course. Fam vacay. There, mystery solved.

Devon felt like it was just the two of them sitting on the beach. Everyone else was off to work or school. Devon and YOGAMAMA had the house all to themselves. Alone, at last.

Let's all go on a journey together . . . What do you say? Can I hear a "hell yeah," guurls?

"Hell yeah!" Devon said.

You and me, we've got a lot of work to do. But we can do it together. We're warriors. We truly, truly are. But when you're on the front line, you got to trust the folks you're in the trenches with . . . We rely on one another. Do you trust me? Are you gonna open yourself up? Let me in?

Yes, Devon thought. Yes, she would let YOGAMAMA in.

Good. Then let's get to work, y'all . . . It's time for us to WAKE UP. Time to OPEN YOUR EYES. The GREAT REAWAKENING is on its way and we want to be at the front of the line . . .

The Great Rea—whatnow?

Trust me, gals, YOGAMAMA said, as if she sensed Devon's apprehension. *The Great Reawakening is gonna be a day like no other. A Woodstock for Wellness! We gotta be ready!*

Well, that certainly sounded like fun . . .

First up, and this is important, ladies . . . Don't be a doom-scroller . . . Be a bliss-skimmer!

There was so much negativity in the world, YOGAMAMA explained. It was in the news. In her feed. The very airwaves, thanks to the 5G cell towers not five miles from their home, were transmitting their toxic technology into the atmosphere. Into her house. Devon was breathing all these noxious contaminants into her lungs. They were seeping into her bloodstream, infecting her very soul. She needed to cleanse herself. Purge all the pollutants.

That began with her timeline.

I want you to carefully curate your feed. Weed your garden so that it luxuriates in nothing but inner beauty. That means saying buh-bye to family members who don't understand, fake friends you've had in your life for years. They're only dragging you down . . . Cut! Them! OUT!

Prune the pessimism. That absolutely made sense. Let the algorithm of the soul cleanse her timeline of any negativity. Block the bad guys. Unfollow the phony friends. This was about self-preservation, about blossoming in positivity.

It was liberating, in a way, letting go of all the naysayers. Devon didn't need to hear from any Negative Nancies cluttering her feed. She deserved to be happy. To be encouraged.

Unfriend.

Unfriend.

Unfriend.

There. Devon was breathing easier already. It felt like a weight had been lifted off her tablet. Things were so quiet. She may have less friends, less family, but that didn't matter.

She was still connected to YOGAMAMA.

Let's be honest: YOGAMAMA was . . . stunning. A naturally blond naturopath. She had been hot in person, but here—online, in her Instagram stories—she was an absolute revelation.

An angel. There was just no other word for it. YOGAMAMA was a goddess. She glowed.

Devon no longer thought of her as Larissa. That name felt like a far-off memory. Maybe they'd met at yoga or maybe they hadn't. Devon hadn't been to class for a couple weeks now.

Wait. When was the last time she left the house? Devon couldn't quite remember.

A few days, maybe? A week?

Did it really matter?

Devon and YOGAMAMA were bound to be around the same age, both somewhere in their early forties. Early-ish. Okay, maybe YOGAMAMA was a bit younger. She had whole posts about her beauty regimen—not a makeup tutorial, mind you. YOGAMAMA was all about beauty from the inside out. It wasn't about putting the right products on your face, but about putting the right food in your body. Taking care of your skin. Purging yourself of toxins.

They had so much in common. They were both mothers, for starters. YOGAMAMA's angels were younger than Devon's. She and Ash had Caleb when they were practically kids themselves—a whole lifetime ago. Devon couldn't help but wonder who she could have been if she'd never had kids so young. What could she have become?

YOGAMAMA paraded her two towheaded, blue-eyed beauties online every day.

Picking up these ragamuffins from schoooool! Just had to take a Cupcake Break!

Had Devon really taken the easy route? The conventional domestic life?

Sipping some hot chocolate around the campfire! YUUUMMM.

Had she slipped into a preordained flight pattern?

Snow day! Who wants to play?

YOGAMAMA lived everywhere and nowhere all at once. Every other pic seemed to be snapped in a different location: a rustic ski chalet or a beach house or a yurt in the middle of the rain forest. It was impossible to nail her down to one location longer than a single photo.

Devon was dying to go on a vacation. She'd begged—literally *begged*—Asher to take the fam somewhere, *anywhere*, for the holidays. They settled on a Caribbean cruise this Christmas.

That's still the plan . . . right? It felt like forever since she and Ash had last chatted about it.

Just imagine all the snapshots Devon could take of herself. On the beach. At sunset.

She would be a siren on Instagram soon. *Soon.*

There might have been about ten—okay, fifteen—pounds between the two women that Devon wasn't particularly proud of. She wanted to narrow that gap—*stat*. She'd pinch the inch of flesh around her waist while poring over photos of YOGAMAMA wearing her pastel Lycra workout gear.

"What's wrong?" Asher asked that night—*where did the day go?*—catching Devon examining her waist before the mirror. "You keep poking yourself."

"It's nothing." Couldn't he see? The rolls? The squishy pinch of flab gathering at her hip?

"You sure you're okay?"

"Why wouldn't I be okay?"

"You've been . . . absent."

"I'm right here." *Like always. Right in front of you.*

Why was Asher suddenly so suspicious? What was he sniffing around for? He never looked twice at her when they got ready for bed—if he came to bed at all. Most nights he fell asleep in the living room in front of the television. Watching the stupid news.

That allowed Devon and YOGAMAMA to have their time together. Devon brought her tablet to bed and scrolled through her profile, catching up with YOGAMAMA's recent exploits.

Date night!! Got a babysitter. Got a loving husband. Got a rez at the best reztaurant in town. What else can a gal want??? DREAM COME TRU!!!

Something wet nuzzled her hip. A nose.

Rufus. Their dog.

Devon hated it when Rufus crawled into bed with her. "Down," she muttered, using her leg to push their pooch off the mattress. "Go. Get. Scootch."

Devon kept scrolling and scrolling, diving deep into her stream. She'd reach the end eventually, right? All profiles begin somewhere, with one snapshot, but this well of wellness never stopped. Her feed went on for hundreds of pictures. Years of travel. Of saluting the sun on the beach. Of sipping yummy lattes from mugs that said *HEALTHY MAMA = HEALTHY FAM.*

All with the same smile. The same sense of rootedness. Of happiness. An abyss of bliss.

YOGAMAMA's flesh was constantly on display: Smooth. Supple. Toned. She wasn't into bodybuilding—goddess, no. Her muscles weren't a bunch of icky, veiny lumps. She wasn't some rippling hulk of a woman. But she had definition. Her physique was sculpted by a few hours in the gym and a special juice blend made with vegetables from her very own garden.

Devon's mouth watered as she looked at a pic of YOGAMAMA posing with a green smoothie. She was thirsty. Downright parched, actually. She hadn't realized how dry her throat was. She didn't want water. What could quench this thirst?

The doorbell rang. Another delivery. Another package arrived, just for Devon . . .

And another.

A blitzkrieg of boxes bombarded Devon's doorstep all week. The same nondescript cardboard container that read *AWAKEN*. Same font on each one.

Who'd bought them all?

When was this going to stop? There had to be someone she could turn to for answers.

Someone online.

YOGAMAMA.

The impulse to scroll wormed its way into Devon's brain by eight every morning. Everyone else was gone by then—Asher off to work, the kids off to school. That left the house all to herself. Some days Devon didn't know what to do with herself. *What can I do? What am I capable of doing?* This was more than mere boredom. This was soul fatigue.

She was sick. She knew she was sick. She had to be, right? Why hadn't her family seen the symptoms? Why did Devon feel so alone in her illness? So ignored and scorned by doctors?

Only YOGAMAMA noticed.

Do your research, gurlz. Don't let the hackquacks tell you what they tell all their patients. You need to listen to your body, not let some medical mal-practitioner manhandle you! Here are some handy-dandy links that'll lead you to THE TRUTH about your body. Just click here, y'all!

It dawned on Devon that she desperately needed more than just an alternative lifestyle. She needed *salvation*. Her body begged to heal itself naturally, on its own, far from Big Pharma. From vaccines. From GMOs. Her body, her soul, yearned for a holistic approach to well-being.

"Help me," she said to her screen.

"You say something?" Asher mumbled in bed just next to her.

Shit, shit. Where did he come from? Devon had no idea Asher was listening. That he was even there. Hadn't he just left for work? What were they doing in bed? "Nothing."

"You doing okay?"

"I'm fine."

"You sure?"

"I'm fine."

Devon needed help. Look. Just *look*. The truth was all there. Right at her fingertips. It was online, ready and waiting for her, as long as she was willing to dig. But . . . how? Where could she click? There was too much truth online. An ocean of information. Devon didn't know where to begin. She was lost, adrift in a sea of links.

YOGAMAMA would guide her. She was the only one willing to listen to Devon. *These docs will prescribe you another pill to pop, but that only perpetuates the problem. These medical monsters want to exacerbate the underlying illness rather than relieve it. Know why? Becuz that's how they make their munny, hunny! Off your illness. They want you to stay sick 4-evaaah!*

YOGAMAMA was right. They *wanted* her to be sick . . . conspired to *keep* her sick. "Those bastards . . ."

"What was that?"

Devon glanced up from her screen, freezing. She was in the living room. On the couch. Since when? What day was it again? Ash had turned away from the television, staring over his shoulder while the screen flickered in purple and green. His eyes looked bloodshot.

"I didn't say anything."

"You keep talking to your tablet."

"No, I'm not." Devon barely paid attention to the television anymore. Ash tuned to the news most nights now, so she focused on the smaller screen settled between her legs.

"I just heard you—"

"I'm not." Devon didn't offer any more, so Ash shrugged and turned back to the TV.

Christ, that was close.

Asher wouldn't understand. He never understood. He'd say what he always said when Devon came to him with an enigmatic ache: *Call the doctor. Schedule a checkup.*

Was Asher in on it, too? Did *he* want Devon to stay sick?

Who could she trust?

YOGAMAMA. Her guide. Her mentor. Her suburu. Devon felt like she could tell her anything, and she would respond: *Don't let the haters get you down. Your inner beauty is more powerful, more STRONG than all of their voices combined. You're in control of WHO YOU ARE.*

"Yes." That's right. Devon was in control. She wasn't about to let those haters get to her.

You gotta tap that inner self, YOGAMAMA preached. *Let your inner lion roar, you know?*

"Yes . . ."

Don't be afraid to be HEARD. You are a woman who deserves to be WORSHIPPED.

"Hell yes!" What did she need to do? How could she unlock her inner self? Her lion?

Your body's a temple. A vessel. We need to clean it first. Purify it. So let's get cleansing!

"With . . . what? How?"

Don't you worry, hon. You've already got the ingredients . . .

The Vitamix blender arrived right on cue, as if her smart devices had read her mind. Its sixty-four-ounce container was perfect for making smoothies for the whole family. It had preset blending programs, variable speed control, and "pulse" features to manually fine-tune the texture of any recipe: Purée. Chunky. Silky smooth. Its blades were laser-cut stainless steel.

What was she going to blend?

Then she remembered . . .

Devon peered into the kitchen pantry. A whiff of cardamom drifted out. Waiting for her was a stack of tiny corrugated boxes. Dozens of them.

The cure had been right there under her nose all along, just waiting for Devon to wake up. To open her eyes. She had to get ready. Prepare. The Great Reawakening was on its way.

ASHER

The box was bigger than a friggin' refrigerator. He could've climbed inside the cardboard, built himself a cool fort, just like the ones he and his baby brother used to make.

Who ordered this?

Devon, of course. She hadn't mentioned any deliveries. What in the hell had she bought now?

When he tore open the cardboard, there it was:

A La-Z-Boy. A goddamn recliner, just for him.

A throne of your own . . . Love, D.

That was all the preprinted card said inside. Not handwritten, mind you: typed and printed. That little minx never said anything about getting Asher his own leather recliner.

We're talking top of the line: single-needle topstitching, adjustable three-position leg rest with a side-mounted handle, double-picked blown fiberfill for maximized shape retention.

A lifetime guarantee of comfort. What a beaut.

Devon was getting a little too trigger-happy with the credit card. Ash would have to talk to her. They were doing fine, financially speaking, but still. Money doesn't grow on trees. Just last night, he'd watched a report on Fax about how the economy was gearing up for another recession, all thanks to the dumbasses in Washington. If families like Ash's wanted to survive the next economic crisis, they'd better think hard about who to vote for this next election. Maybe another recession is what it would take for this country to finally wake the hell up. Open their eyes.

Not that he was going to look this gift horse in the mouth. Ash slid into the seat and eased back, feeling the chilled leather against his skin. It warmed to his touch, cradling his body.

The chair fit. It felt *right*.

His throne—just like his father's. The old man had been on to something. Ash picked up the remote and turned on his television: *Let's take this baby for a little test drive . . .*

All Asher needed was a guide: a man to help explain the news, to contextualize how he should feel. Simply having the information wasn't enough. He needed a helping hand.

A conservative sherpa. An anchorman.

Asher needed Paul Tammany.

Paul Tammany was Fax News's bright, shining silver fox. He had the chiseled features of an all-American linebacker and the chin of Superman. A thicker, meatier George Clooney. All beefcake, no weak-chinned liberal sissy here. He wasn't ropy like that pipsqueak Anderson.

Tammany could mop the floor with Mr. Cooper, no doubt about it.

You could tell he worked out—not jogged or biked. *Worked out.* Bench-pressing, bitches. This guy was in the gym power-lifting. Playing touch football on Saturday.

But it wasn't all machismo, no . . . Tammany had a pair of bedroom eyes that pierced the plasma of Ash's TV screen. A soothing, smoky voice. Heart *and* balls, that's what Tammany had.

Tammany Hall, hosted by Paul Tammany, showcases his candid, take-no-prisoners style and no-holds-barred conservative commentary on politics, aiming to right wrongs from the left.

Paul was fighting for America, night after night, one episode at a time. Every evening, Tammany would look to the day's headlines and bemoan our country's slow descent into hell.

Can't you see what's happening right under your nose? You gotta WAKE UP, people! You gotta OPEN YOUR EYES before your country's no longer yours . . .

Asher's pulse always picked up and stayed high for the whole hour. Watching Paul take his guests down a peg was such a jolt—*Save those tears for someone who gives a rat's ass. Next guest!* Nothing pressed the gas pedal on Ash's heart rate like *Tammany Hall.* He felt *alive* watching this show.

What? You're just gonna sit in your La-Z-Boy and do nothing? Tammany spoke right through the plasma. *You and me, pal. We're saving this country, come hell or high water.*

Funny. He just got a La-Z-Boy. It was like Tammany was talking directly to him.

Only him.

Asher kept the television on in the background even after *Tammany Hall* wrapped—the whitest of white noise. The night's episodes of *Tammany Hall* and *Crosshairs with Cullen Dunn* repeated at midnight for those who didn't catch it the first time around.

Asher always watched for a second time. The words really sank in on a second viewing.

Went deeper.

Did you know that the public schools have been quietly revising their history textbooks to reflect a "more contemporary viewpoint" on Christopher Columbus? What the hell does that even mean? They're phasing the motherfucker out! Did Asher really care about Columbus? Not particularly . . . But doesn't that seem *wrong* to you?

That the school board would do something like that and not even tell parents about it? What else were they doing behind our backs?

Tammany hammered this point home on the air nearly every night: *If you don't look, you'll never see. You'll be blind to what's really happening around you. So OPEN YOUR EYES.*

Tammany was on to something, wasn't he?

That's how our country gets undermined right under your runny nose, folks! It doesn't happen overnight. It's not a coup. It's gradual. Insidious. Our country is slowly bleeding out from a million and one paper cuts and we're not doing a goddamn thing about it . . . so WAKE UP!

Asher always set a time limit for himself: no more than three hours a night. Otherwise he ran the risk of staying awake all night and he didn't want to be groggy the following morning and stumble through his job. Waking up after a night of Fax News felt like a hangover. He'd be all headachy and parched, need to rehydrate himself, drinking glass after glass of water.

Three hours. That's more than enough.

Four, tops.

Five if there was something *really* important on. Five was the line. There, he'd drawn it.

Five hours.

Tops.

Most nights he had to wait his wife out. He couldn't watch while Devon was in the room. If she went to bed now, there would be just enough time to catch the first airing of *Tammany*. If he missed it, he'd have to wait and watch the show when it re-aired at midnight.

Devon was taking her precious time tonight, that's for goddamn sure, scrolling and scrolling on her damn tablet. *Come on, get it over with already . . . Come on, come on, come on.*

"Want to watch something together?" she asked. "Something other than the news?"

Shit. Fuck. Balls. "Like what?"

"What's that—that one show? The funny one?"

"Can you try to be a bit more specific?"

"You know . . . the funny one. With that actor."

"Are you kidding?"

"Don't snap at me." For some reason wholly unknown to Ash, Devon pivoted the conversation toward their family vacation. "Have we booked our flight yet?"

"I don't know how many days I can take off from work. I can look, but . . ."

"I thought we were all set."

It's true. The ball had been in his court to book their flights, get everything squared away with the cruise line. But he'd just watched a story about yet another norovirus outbreak on a luxury liner, stranding passengers in international waters for weeks on end, shitting themselves to death in their cabins with no rescue from the Coast Guard in sight and, well . . .

"Now's really just not a good time, hon."

"What do you mean *now*? We've been planning this trip for—for—" Devon blanked.

How long *had* they been talking about it? Asher couldn't remember either.

"I've just been really busy with"—*opening my eyes* —"work. I can't leave just now."

"What's gotten into you?"

Into? What did that even mean? Did she think something else, some foreign presence, had invaded his body? What the fuck was she saying? "I'm fine," he said.

"Are you mad at me about something?"

"I'm not mad."

"I didn't mean for it to sound like I was implying—"

"Yes, you did. You *implied* I'm mad, even after I told you I'm not."

"You don't have to be such a jerk about it."

"Then stop prodding."

"Fine," Devon said, springing up from the couch, dragging her tablet with her.

"Where are you going?"

"Bed."

Never go to bed angry. That had always been his mother's advice. *If something is sticking in your craw during the day, hon, you better get rid of it before you fall asleep.*

That anger embeds itself into your very soul, his mom always said. A spiteful seed.

It will grow inside you, if you're not careful. Take root. Before you know it, whatever that anger is, it'll become a part of you . . . and then it just gets harder to uproot. Anger is a weed.

Sage advice. Asher had watched it happen with his old man. Whenever his parents got into an argument at the dinner table, his father would slink off to his La-Z-Boy, muttering to himself for the rest of the night. By the time he woke the next morning, that kernel of resentment had sprouted in his father's subconscious. And once it was in his system, it grew roots. One day's anger became the soil for the next day's petty resentments, and the next, choking out his arteries. That root of rage only reached deeper into his dad, until there was no ripping it out. He never lifted a hand to his wife or sons, but there was always this simmering bitterness just below the surface. He'd come home grumpy and go to bed grumpy and wake up grumpier.

Asher needed an outlet for his anger.

Fax felt like a good fit.

He shouldn't have to hide his viewing habits. It wasn't porn, for fuck's sake. It was the *news.* He could watch the news any goddamn time he pleased. So he flipped on the television.

Already he could feel the rage oozing from his pores, sweating it out. That was sweat, wasn't it? Something about his skin . . . He felt slimy. Oily, almost. His skin stuck to the warm leather of his La-Z-Boy, softer now, flesh clinging to flesh. Holding him. Cradling him.

It was all the other hours out of the day, when he wasn't watching Fax, that his frustration had nowhere to go. At least here he knew what to be angry *about*, because Paul Tammany told him so. Like tonight. Did you hear what's happening in Topeka? It's unbeliev- able. Their libraries let kids—*kids*, for Christ's sake—check out books about gay relationships. Whatever people want to do in the privacy of their own homes, behind closed doors, hey, that's their business, as far as Asher was concerned. But even he had to draw the line some- where.

Somebody ought to do something about it, he thought. *Someone should go and—*

Asher hesitated. Should do . . . *what*, exactly? Where was he going with all of this?

Where had that thought even come from?

He should apologize to Devon. He hadn't meant to take it out on her. He should just slip under the covers and spoon her, hold her in his arms and kiss her shoulder and tell her he loved her and that everything would be—

Another news segment started. Prescription drugs were being doled out to kindergartners. Babies on meds.

"What the hell's happening to this fucking country?" he said out loud to the TV.

You said it, Paul Tammany answered back.

Asher froze.

Paul Tammany always—*always*—directly addressed the viewer. That was just his personal presentational style. His delivery made it feel as if there wasn't anybody else watching. None of the other mil- lion viewers sitting in their own homes mattered. They may as well have not existed. It was just Asher and Paul, shooting the shit, getting down to brass tacks.

But Asher could have sworn Paul Tammany was staring right at him. Things had gone silent. Tammany wasn't talking anymore. The dead air was in Asher's chest. He hadn't exhaled.

Tammany was waiting for him to respond.

"Are you, uh . . . Are you talking to me?"

Asher had never talked to his TV before. He felt like he'd just crossed a line. This was uncharted territory—grumpy ol' Dad territory, griping at the world today. *Get off my lawn* territory. He wasn't becoming his father, was he? Was he going to start talking back—

Damn straight, pal, Paul Tammany shot back. *The real question is: What do we do now?*

"We, ah . . . we . . ."

I'm just fucking with you, Tammany chuckled. *Don't worry, my man. I got you covered.*

Relief. Ash felt it. The tension ebbed from his shoulders. He breathed freely, exhaling for what felt like the first time in a long while. It felt so good to know that someone finally had his back.

≡

Ash?

He heard a voice. A woman's voice. Calling for him.

Ash . . .

He dragged himself out from his sleep.

Ash.

"Devon?" He felt her skin. Or *someone's* skin. It slid beneath him, shifting around. Had he fallen asleep on top of his wife? There was a moment, barely a breath, where he assumed it was Devon. But the tone of her voice felt off. That determined tenor didn't sound like Devon.

Aaash . . .

He had no idea where he was. This wasn't his bed. A thin paste of sleep crusted his tongue to the roof of his mouth. His back was sore from falling asleep in an upright position.

Christ, he was still in the living room. He'd fallen asleep in his recliner. The leather upholstery absorbed his body temperature, trapping the heat until he was covered in sweat.

It was dark outside. The television was still on, the faint fishbowl glow of the plasma screen pulsing across the walls.

What happened? He'd been watching the news, when . . .

When . . .

Asher had never drifted off in front of the TV before. *Never.* No matter how late he surfed the channels, he'd always been able to turn off the TV, pick himself up, and head to bed.

This wasn't like him. This wasn't like him at all. What the hell was happening?

I need to get to bed, he thought. *Before Devon wonders where I am.*

If she ever glanced up from her tablet, that is.

Fax News kept pumping out its reportage. The air felt oppressively muggy, as if the broadcast itself was polluting the atmosphere, far too thick to breathe.

He was so sweaty. This felt worse than sweat, actually. He felt like he was basted in some kind of cooking oil. He rubbed his face and it felt filmy. When he glanced at his own palms, he noticed they shimmered in the dull glow of the television. *What the fuck is this stuff?*

He should take a shower. Wash this shit off.

The chyron at the bottom of the screen said it wasn't even four o'clock yet. Nobody else would be awake for at least a couple more hours.

The news anchor wasn't someone Asher recognized. He'd never seen her before, this blond-coiffed newscaster. Gorgeous—if that airbrushed, booth-tanned look was your thing.

Was it Asher's thing?

It hadn't been before. Devon definitely didn't look like her—she wouldn't be getting hired by Fax News anytime soon. There was an obvious mandate that all their female anchors fit into a narrow physical mold. They weren't all blond, sure, but that one brunette seemed handpicked to show just a smidge of variety. *Ethnicity.* But who did Fax think they were fooling?

Startling news from Wall Street today, she said. *If the Nasdaq continues this disturbing trend for the remainder of the year, forecasters fear we may be looking at another recession . . .*

What was this anchor's name?

Julia. Julia Turin.

She had a harder edge to her. She was sharp. She definitely wasn't one of the bubblier anchors from the morning programming that kicked in around seven a.m., nor was she one of the headliners from their prime-time evening block. She was the closest thing to an actual newscaster that Asher had seen on Fax, and yet . . . well, just look at her. Her green eyes. Her lips.

Investors continue to prove skittish with their money, a grim sign for the year to come . . .

They locked eyes. Julia was looking right at him—staring. The digital gulf between them suddenly narrowed. Asher swore he could feel her breath spread across his skin.

What are you gonna do about it, Asher?

"Me?" Asher felt a sudden stirring in his boxers.

What're you gonna do about your investments, Asher? How are you going to protect them? Everything you've saved, that you've worked so hard for . . .

So hard.

What are you going to do now, Asher?

Asher leaned in. He realized he was standing only a few inches from the screen. He didn't know how he got there, when he approached the television, came nose to nose with Julia.

"What do you, uh . . . what do you want me to do?"

Anything, Asher.

"Anything?"

Anything.

Asher did something he'd never done before—never imagined himself doing in all his years as a sexually active adult. As a teen, even. He gripped the upper corner of their wall-mounted plasma television to steady himself. Then he spread his legs like he was being arrested by this blond police officer—*Assume the position, sir*—and began to stroke. His eyes never left Julia Turin as she spouted off about the Dow Jones. Something about the proximity to her, something about the way her lips moved. Plump, pixelated, pink. Asher couldn't control himself.

Julia Turin was there, *right there*, her pink blouse emblazoned on the other side of the screen, sitting behind her news desk, reading off the financial reports. "You want the Fax?"

Yeah. Yeah, gimme the fax, Ash. Just the fax . . .

"Yeah? Like that?"

Yeah . . . Yeah, give them to me. Give them.

"I'll give 'em to you."

Just the fax . . . Just the fax . . . just the . . . the . . .

"Yeah. Yeah."

That's it, that's it, right there, put the fax right there, yeah, yeah—

Asher glanced up and realized he wasn't alone. There, standing just behind Julia, was . . .

"Paul?"

Paul Tammany winked back, giving Asher his patented cocksure grin.

You got this, pal.

Asher nearly sprang back from the TV, but Paul took hold of his free hand before he leapt.

You with me?

"Yeah, okay." The two were in a Julia Turin sandwich.

You ready, buddy? Asher and Paul found a particular rhythm together.

"Yeah."

Asher stood to the side of the news desk, pressed against Julia, against Paul, feeling the electricity gather within the atmosphere, the space between them crackling with a current of galvanized air, increasing in its wattage, intensifying so much that Julia Turin's body began to lose shape, the pixels that composed her flesh rippling, distorting in bands of color, of—

gaslights

—wondrous light, a million dots barely held together anymore, bursting all over Asher.

"Oh—"

His knees buckled.

"Oh shit—"

A spasm racked his backbone, his spine like a whip cracking toward the screen, his pelvis thrusting at the plasma.

"Oh. Oh."

That was *intense*. Asher stepped back and looked at his mess. Pearls of semen glistened in the television's glow, a drag race of snail trails, the floorboards slick with shimmering rivulets.

What in the ever-living fuck just happened?

Asher ran his hand over the television as he gathered his breath, tracing his fingers across the screen, leaving a trail of oily fingerprints in his wake. He pressed his palm flat against the plasma. The screen sank under the pressure of his fingertips, like a thin layer of gelatin.

Well, that's certainly a first . . .

Ash glanced at his feet. For a second, he swore he saw his own semen slither away. The pearly, serpentine strings began worming over the floor, reaching the walls and climbing upward, snaking over the ceiling and leaving behind their shimmering translucent trails.

He squeezed his eyes shut. Forced the image out.

Asher quickly cleaned up his mess. This was embarrassing. What if Devon walked in? *Jesus*, what if one of his kids saw? They would never forget something like that. *Never.* They'd treat him differently. Think of him differently. But . . . that was the point, wasn't it? The danger? The risk of getting caught? He wanted to tempt fate. He wanted to stare Julia Turin in the eyes again and risk everything, risk it all for a—for—*what*, exactly? A wank?

To be a man, Julia cooed.

Yes. For a moment, the briefest flicker, Asher Fairchild felt alive. Felt like a man. A beast in the wilderness, roaring through the plains.

Ready to pounce on his prey. To eat raw meat.

Something's coming, Paul pillow-talked him. *Something big, bud. You feel it, don't you? It'll be here before you know it . . . Time to WAKE UP, Ash. Time to OPEN YOUR EYES. You ready?*

"Yes," he said, his voice barely above a whisper.

Are you ready for the Great Reawakening? To lead the charge?

"Damn straight."

I knew I could count on you . . . You're going to be the WAKE-UP CALL this world needs.

Asher crept back into his own bedroom, slipping under the covers without waking his wife. He wondered whether he should take a shower, wash any incriminating scent from his skin. Would Devon notice? Would she sense that he'd done something? Something naughty?

Jesus, what was he? Twelve? He was a man. *The Man!* He lay on his back, staring up at the blank expanse of the ceiling. His thoughts drifted back to the news. To the broadcast. To . . .

"Paul," he whispered as he smelled his fingers.

CALEB

ELZEGAN911 was now following him.

So was PROMAKOS.

And ZAINAEL.

By the time Caleb woke the following morning, he discovered he had over three thousand more followers then when he fell asleep the night before, barely six hours ago.

What—*the actual*—fuck?

Bots. They had to be. A swarm of virtual mosquitoes, clinging to his skin. Piercing him.

Clicking: *Like. Like. Like.*

What was he supposed to do? Could he block all the bots? Report them? They'd just come back as different profiles, different names, all creeping the ever-living fuck out of him.

Should he delete his account? Go DEFCON 1 on his profile and start all over again?

This all started with XAPHAN2001. It was his fault. Could he find him? Ask him to stop? But he was long gone. Reported and blocked. Who could he run to now?

ELZEGAN911.

Caleb didn't know if he was dealing with a thousand trolls . . . or just one.

Got to start somewhere, right?

WTF?? WHO ARE U?

Nothing.

Nothing.

Noth—

Three pulsing dots materialized on his screen, rippling in shades of gray. Then:

We see you.

Caleb felt every vein in his body constrict, tightening around his frame and squeezing. He didn't realize he hadn't exhaled until a dizzy spell enveloped his mind, pixelating his eyesight.

What the—

The dots materialized again. ELZEGAN911 was writing more.

You might not see yourself, but we do.

Who the fuck was this? What did they want from him? Why were they—

We believe in you, Caleb.

Caleb did his best to collect himself. Attempt to control his breathing. He needed to write back. Say something. *Anything.* But what? How could he take control over the situation?

Finally, he typed:

what do u want

Those three fluctuating dots rippled across the screen in a hypnotic rhythm that felt like something tubular was pumping thick, black liquid into his brain.

A ghost penis. That's what those dots belonged to. Their rhythmic rippling made Caleb think of a ghost's invisible dick spurting invisible ghost spunk all over his phone.

A phantom dick pic.

Gross. Stop thinking of cocks. But now that he'd thought it, he couldn't unthink it.

Caleb waited. Held his breath for the message to pop up and then . . .

Nothing. The DMs stopped. That phantom dick ghosted him.

Caleb stared at his screen, rereading the exchange. No matter how many times he read and reread it, the words never changed. The dots never came back. Not a single invisible ripple.

A fresh flame of shame seethed through his bones, a burning sense of frustration. How could they *see* him? *Believe* in him? They didn't know the first fucking thing *about* him. They didn't know him at all! Caleb didn't even know himself, so how could these jerk-offs?

What exactly was it that they saw in him? It was a simple question, wasn't it?

Caleb wrote back:

tell me what u see

The dots materialized. Pulsing. Throbbing.

We see a little boy who is afraid.

More black dots, digitalized ejaculations pumping, rhythmically punctuating the screen . . .

We see a boy who does not know his true potential.

Potential? For what? What kind of *potential* could Caleb possibly have?

We see you. See everything. We believe you can make a difference, Caleb.

He wanted to shut down his laptop. He wanted to throw it across the room, smash it against the bedroom wall, let it shatter into shards of plastic and glass.

Just get it away from me. Get it as fucking far away from me as—

The dots reared their pinheads again.

You are so special, Caleb.

Caleb slammed his laptop shut. The heat from the computer seeped into his legs, burning his thighs. He sat in the stillness of his room, keenly aware of the enveloping silence.

Potential. True potential.

Caleb flipped open his laptop and powered it down this time. Something about the notion of it remaining in sleep mode, dormant but still alive, still connected, made him anxious.

What if they were watching? Listening in? Could they really do that?

Caleb placed his laptop on the floor next to his bed, then slipped under the covers, resting his head on his pillow and staring out at the wall before him.

Potential.

Potential.

Poten—

Caleb's phone vibrated from the nightstand. He lifted his head, startled by the abrupt rumble. He reached for his cell. Without even looking at the screen, he powered that down too.

Caleb runs along the narrow wooded paths that surround his school.

He is alone.

It feels like the early morning, those liminal hours just before school begins. The air is cool against his exposed skin, even though he is covered in a thin layer of sweat.

He's not wearing his hoodie. He always wears his hoodie.

A dream, then. Obviously. Cool, okay . . .

How long has he been running? One moment he was in bed, the next he was . . .

Out here. In the woods.

He's out of breath. Out of practice. Utterly out of shape. It's been so long since he's run cross-country. Run at all. His body's not used to moving anymore. His legs are cramping.

The sun barely penetrates the dense canopy of branches overhead, casting thin shafts of hazy light through the morning mist. Even if he quit cross-country years ago, he still knows the route like the back of his hand. The bends in the path are ingrained into his body.

He knows he is alone, but he can't help but get the sense someone is following him. Someone else is on the path, running right behind him. Caleb glances over his shoulder.

No one.

But this persistent feeling won't go away. Someone is watching. There are eyes in the woods. So Caleb picks up his pace. Runs faster. He can hear the crackle of dried leaves under his shoes. His own panting picks up. The sound of birds chirruping from the trees grows louder.

Wait. Those aren't birds. It's his alert notifications. A cell phone emitting the tiniest trill.

A phone. Not his own. Someone else's.

There it is again. Louder this time.

And again. The alerts are everywhere.

There's more than just one phone.

The woods are full of alerts, this discordant chorus of digital warbles. There have to be hundreds, thousands of chimes going off all throughout the forest, tweeting at him.

They're only getting louder. Where are they all coming from?

The branches. They're in the branches.

In the trees.

Watching from above. From behind. He can't escape. No matter how fast Caleb runs, picking up his pace, racing faster, faster, the alert notifications clamor all around, mounting in their chiming, millions of birds in the darkness, their wings now flapping, taking flight, swarming him.

He's wheezing. So out of breath. The air can't reach his lungs, locked out by his throat.

A sharp jab at his neck jolts his shoulder.

Ah! *He screams.* AH!

Pecking. They're pecking his shoulders, his head, his neck, his cheeks. Taking bits and pieces, tugging him away. All the meat. Whittled down to the bone. Nothing but a screaming skeleton—

===

Caleb woke with a start in bed, out of breath. Covered in sweat.

That's sweat, isn't it?

But it felt thicker.

Oilier.

Caleb ran his hand across the slope of his forearm and it came back filmy. He wasn't certain, but in the dark, his skin seemed to shimmer like mother-of-pearl.

What is this stuff?

The dream felt so real. He could've sworn he'd been running. He even felt the burn of muscle tissue, like after a long race, legs searing with the strain. How could he be cramping in bed?

His alarm clock glared in the darkness with its red numbers. 3:20.

He felt thirsty. Completely dehydrated. One of the side effects of his acne medication was that it dried him out. He needed to drink, like, three times the amount of water most other people did just to keep himself from crumbling to dust. But this felt different. He was a husk. Even his eyes felt dried out, as if he'd been staring at his screen for too long.

But he'd been sleeping, hadn't he?

Caleb kept a water bottle next to his bed. He reached for it and—

It was gone. No water bottle on his nightstand table.

Where was it?

Caleb climbed out of bed and made his way down the hall. The stillness of their house had a density to it. Nobody was awake at this hour. It was the type of quiet that only comes when—

Caleb halted. There was a light on in the kitchen.

Not a light.

A *glow*. Someone's screen cast its dim aquamarine hue across the cabinets. Had someone left their phone in the kitchen?

"Hello?" Caleb took a step forward, then waited, expecting to hear someone.

Nothing.

He slowly made his way to the kitchen, ready to find Dad raiding the fridge.

His mother's tablet was on the counter, awake. *Okay, well, that's weird.* Aren't devices supposed to slip into sleep mode after a minute of inactivity? How could hers still be on?

The screen was unlocked, allowing Caleb to peer into his mom's personal life. Her Instagram app was open. Caleb glanced over his shoulder. It felt wrong to peek at her profile.

Not that that stopped him.

The rest of the house seemed to recede. The enveloping darkness pushed the parameters of their home back even further. The kitchen simply wasn't there anymore.

All there was to see was the screen, emitting its dull glow.

Caleb scrolled through his mom's pictures: selfies in silly poses, drinking her awful dietary concoctions that tasted like ass. Look. Just look at her posed smiles. Those awkward life affirmations nobody was buying. Just look at how unhappy she appeared behind those smiles.

Caleb laughed. He hadn't expected to, the sound of his guffaw surprising even himself. He didn't mean to be cruel, but *holeeee shit*, just look at all the selfies Mom had snapped!

Look at the desperation on her face! The awkward poses! The unnatural angles!

What the hell's she thinking? Just look at—

Something shifted behind Caleb.

He lifted his head, met by darkness. "Who's there?"

Caleb waited for someone to answer.

No one did.

"Mom?"

The tablet faded into sleep mode on its own, abandoning Caleb to the pitch-blackness of the kitchen. Locked out for good now. His eyes couldn't adjust to the dark. His depth perception was off. He couldn't tell where the noise had come from, whether it was only a few steps away or farther down the—

Mom's brand-new blender turned itself on.

The fuck?

Caleb practically jumped out of his skin as its rotary blades whirred to life, grinding away at the air in a shrill-pitched shriek of gears.

Caleb raced to the screaming contraption and searched for the switch. It simply wouldn't turn off. He kept futzing with the controls, but the empty container kept blending.

The fuck the fuck the fuck—

Caleb had no choice but to yank the power cord. The blades immediately whirred to a halt, silence taking over the kitchen once more. *Jesus, that was—*

In the living room, the television turned itself on. A roar of static crashed through the hall. Caleb quickly beelined for it, peeking in before entering, just to see if Dad was watching.

"Dad . . . ?"

The room was empty. Nobody on the La-Z-Boy. Then who turned on the—

The channel changed. All on its own.

Was someone else here? Hiding behind the couch with the remote, fucking with him?

Marcus? That little shit wouldn't be doing this, would he? Caleb would kill him . . .

The channel landed on Fax News.

Why they even had cable anymore was anyone's guess. Dad still hadn't canceled this crap even though he'd promised Mom up and down that he would. They were probably, like, the last family in the entire country who still subscribed to cable TV, subsidizing the whole industry.

Some airbrushed dipshit pundit was griping about the price of gas. His blowhard voice sounded like Dad. Or maybe Dad sounded like this guy. Who knows. All that mattered was finding out who was messing with him and turning this shit off before his parents woke—

Then the channel switched again.

On its own.

Static. Digitized bands of color bent and warped over the plasma. Caleb couldn't help but wince at the brightness of it all, the sheer blast of—

gaslights

—flickering colors causing him to shield his eyes. The channels kept switching, climbing higher and higher until the TV eventually landed on a forbidden destination.

On pay-per-view.

On porn. *Sheeee-iiit.* The stuff Caleb would never in a million years order through their cable provider, knowing fully well that *BIG MILF JUGS* would show up on their monthly bill.

Everybody knew that's what the internet was for. *Duh.* What dumbass would ever order porn through their cable television? Not Caleb. Then who the hell was—

Moaning. So much moaning.

A woman—a MILF, apparently—was fondling a pool boy's penis on the plasma screen. Their television was so big, it was like they were in the room with Caleb. Dad had yet to master the motion-smoothing controls, taking the magical filter of cinema away from the actors. They looked like normal people with blemishes and acne—just like him. Disgusting.

The volume cranked up.

On its own.

Caleb spotted the green volume bars increasing across the screen, the sound of this MILF's moans intensifying. Filling the living room. Flooding the halls. Reaching the bedrooms.

Fuck oh fuck where's the remote where's the goddamn remote—

Moaning. So much moaning. *How do I turn this off before—*

"Caleb?"

Caleb spun around, his back now to the screen—to the high-def porno—only to discover his own mother standing in the hall. The glow of the screen was on her, the oily sheen of those pounding bodies, the shift in colors hitting a hypnotic rhythm—*pink now purple now blue now red, pink now purple now blue now red*—punctuated with so many moans.

"It's not—I'm not—"

"What are you . . ." Mom couldn't finish her own thought, her attention drifting to the sexual act unfolding behind Caleb, the soft padding of flesh against flesh, the moaning.

"I—I didn't." He wanted to say more: *I didn't do this. It turned on by itself. It flipped to this channel by itself. It wasn't me. I would never do this, honestly, hand to fucking God—*

But the moans were too much. The moans filled up the silence between them.

"Why . . . why would you do something like this?" Mom asked, sounding truly confused.

"I didn't! It wasn't me, Mom. I swear!"

"You used to be such a good boy . . ."

"That's a good boy," the MILF wailed right behind Caleb's shoulder. "Such a good boy. That's it, that's it. Yeah. Oh yeah. Such a good boy. Wake up, hon. Wake up and open your—"

FAMILY NIGHT

The noise came from the kitchen. The high-pitched whine of blades grinding away filled the house. It wouldn't stop. Had Mom left the blender on?

What's she making?

Mom usually set the table with such precision. With care. Tonight it felt like she was in a hurry, tossing everything onto the table and rushing back into the kitchen to continue cooking.

What was that smell coming from the oven? Something about it was off. A bit burnt.

It's Wednesday night, isn't it? Family night? So . . . where is everybody? Why was Marcus the only one at the dinner table? Didn't they know the rules?

The blender—*juicer*, Mom called it—screamed even louder as its blades hit something they couldn't chop up. It sounded like Mom was weed-whacking in the kitchen.

Dad hadn't budged from the couch all afternoon. Wasn't he supposed to go to work? Even now, Marcus could hear the news blaring from the living room. Lately Dad would turn the volume up as loud as it would go, the voice of the anchorman booming throughout the house like the voice of Marcus's principal droning on during the morning announcements.

Caleb never left his room. The door had been shut all day, but Marcus could hear a hollow *pop pop pop* sound when he put his ear to the door. What was he doing in there? Playing video games? It kinda sorta sounded like when Dad cracked his back. *Pop! Pop! Pop!*

Mom sure was making a mess in the kitchen. Pans clattered. Pots toppled into the sink. Whatever she was cooking, it required a whole lot of banging. And a whole lot of blending.

Marcus's stomach grumbled. Hopefully it was something good. Lately her meals tasted like chalk.

Marcus waited in his seat. Nobody joined him.

Minutes passed. Time was a sludge. Time was a smoothie.

Should he say something? Should he call out for—

"Dinner bell, *ring-a-ding-ding!*"

Mom shuffled in from the kitchen carrying a pot that she plopped onto the table in front of Marcus. There was something funny about her eyes. She looked tired. Really tired. Usually, she pushed back her unhappiness—hid it behind a smile that even Marcus knew wasn't true. But tonight Mom seemed downright exhausted.

"Dinner's ready," she called as she headed back into the kitchen. "Marcus, get your brother."

Marcus did as he was told, even if he didn't want to.

Was afraid to.

On his way to Caleb's room, he looked at all the family portraits on the wall. He could see himself growing through the photos as he climbed the stairs, starting off as a swaddled newborn and slowly turning into the boy he'd become today.

Look at his family. Just look. They were all smiling so big in the photos. He wished it were like that in real life. Weren't they supposed to take this year's Christmas card picture soon? Mom had never missed a year. Maybe everyone was sick? It happened all the time: Marcus would catch a cold at school, bring it home, and before you knew it, Mom had it, then Caleb, then Dad. Everybody would be coughing and sneezing and lying in bed. He hoped that was it.

Sick days! No school!

Marcus stood outside his brother's door. He could hear the *pop-pop-pop* noise from within. Were those video game sounds? Marcus couldn't tell. Something didn't sound right.

He pressed his ear to the door. Was that panting? Was Caleb breathing really fast?

Marcus knocked. "Caleb? It's dinner time."

Pop pop pop.

"Caleb?" Marcus called, a little louder. "You in there?"

Of course he was in there. What a silly question. Why wouldn't his brother just answer? The panting picked up on the other side of the door. It sounded like a woman. Several women.

"Caleb?" Marcus got down on his knees and peered through the gap under the door. He tried to spy his brother on the other side, but there were too many socks blocking his view. The blue glow of Caleb's computer was the only light to see by. The dull glow flickered and pulsed in random patterns, casting shadows across the bedroom walls. Just looking at the parade of flickering colors—pink now purple now green—made Marcus's head hurt.

Marcus could hear Caleb panting: *huh huh huh huh huh* . . .

But he couldn't see where his big brother was. Was he hiding?

Huh huh huh huh huh . . .

"Caleb?" Marcus whispered into the chasm. "Mom said it's time for—"

The door swung open.

Caleb towered over Marcus, catching him crouched on the floor. He had his hoodie pulled over his head. Marcus couldn't see his eyes. Caleb stepped over his little brother without so much as a single word, storming toward the dining room.

Marcus picked himself up and trailed after.

Dad was already sitting at the dinner table. The news had been left on in the living room, the volume turned up high enough that the anchorman's voice traveled down the hall.

Caleb slumped into his seat.

"Hood down," Mom said.

Caleb slowly peeled his hoodie back from his head. It took some effort, from the pained expression on his face. He winced. Marcus could've sworn he heard the slightest crackle as Caleb shook loose his greasy hair.

Mom dropped a pan in front of Marcus's seat, startling him. "Serve yourself."

"What is it," Caleb asked, but it sounded like he forgot to add a question mark.

"Chickpea crust pizza."

Caleb leaned in and examined it with a look of disgust before slumping back in his seat.

Marcus took a whiff. It *almost* smelled like pizza.

"Where's the cheese?" he asked, hoping to keep his voice as innocent as possible. He didn't want to sound critical of Mom's cooking. He definitely didn't want to hurt her feelings.

"We need to cut down our dairy" was all Mom said. *Okay, so no cheese pizza, then.* Instead of sauce, there were specks of wilted vegetables on top. No pepperoni. No sausage.

Dad grabbed a puck of pizza. He must've been starving, because he ate it in three bites. *Nom nom nom.* He chewed with his mouth open, sending a dusting of chickpeas over the table.

Mom carried the blender jar into the dining room, filled to the brim with some foul-smelling green gunk. It looked like she had scooped it out of a fish pond.

Mom picked up Marcus's empty glass and poured him his own helping of algae. "Drink."

"What is it?"

"Just drink," Mom said. "It's good for you."

It didn't *smell* good, it definitely didn't *look* good, so Marcus didn't think that it would taste good, either. A bubble of eggy-smelling gas rose up from the depths of his glass and burst over the surface—*plaaap*—turning Marcus's stomach.

Dad had no problem drinking it. He practically downed the entire smoothie in one gulp, wiping his wet lips with his sleeve before releasing a belch.

"I was watching this video," Mom said as she whipped out a circular pizza slicer, "and it was this woman talking about how she cut out all the excess dairy from her life and all of a sudden she felt a hundred times better. A million times better. All that dairy had been settling into her gut, her intestines, clogging her up. Constipating her soul. All it took was cutting it out of her life. No milk, no cheese, no ice cream. *Cut, cut, cut . . .*"

Each *cut* was punctuated with a swing of the pizza slicer through the air.

Snk—

Snk—

Snk!

Mom took a deep breath for the first time since she'd started talking. She laughed at herself, just a little. The clarity came back to her eyes and settled on Marcus. She stared at him.

Was he supposed to say something?

She was waiting. "Eat," she said.

Marcus did as he was told and lifted a sliver of the burnt pizza. It immediately fell apart, the chickpea crust crumbling between his fingers.

"Oh" was all Mom said.

"Did you hear about what happened in Pittsburgh?" Dad asked no one in particular.

Nobody answered. Dad didn't wait for a response, barreling straight ahead. "A kindergarten teacher brought in a porno film for the class to watch. A goddamn porno. Just slipped the DVD in and pressed play. *Time to watch a movie, kids . . .*"

Was Marcus supposed to respond? What should he say?

What *could* he say?

"What's a porno?" he asked, but nobody answered. They simply stared.

"Apparently"—Dad kept going—"the class watched for ten minutes before another teacher walked down the hall, heard the sounds, and alerted the principal. *Ten minutes.* You believe that? A *kindergarten* teacher, for Christ's sake. If it'd been my kid's teacher, I would—"

Dad cut himself off. His eyes were caught on some far-off point along the wall. He suddenly wasn't there, his mind elsewhere. He hiccupped. His breath smelled like rotten veggies.

Nobody said anything to fill up the silence. They all simply sat in the awkwardness.

Caleb hadn't looked up once. He kept poking his pizza with his fork, the tines cracking the chickpea crust into smaller and smaller powdery chunks.

Marcus suddenly felt something cold and wet nuzzle his fingers from under the table.

Rufus to the rescue!

Not a moment too soon. He was beginning to feel alone at dinner, even with his family all around him. Marcus pinched off a shard of burnt crust and slipped it underneath the table.

Nobody seemed to notice. Or care.

Rufus dug his muzzle into Marcus's palm, licking away the crumbs. The boy reached for another hunk of pizza from his plate. He was trying to be sneaky about it, even though it didn't seem like anyone was paying attention to him. As usual.

The coast was clear.

Just as Marcus was lowering his hand beneath the table—

Mom seized his wrist.

"*Marcus.*" Her grip tightened, her fingers squeezing. She was staring right at him. Staring in a way that made Marcus feel nervous. Not just nervous. *Scared.*

Mom had never looked at him like that before. Her eyes were . . . wrong. They were flickering, moving in and out of focus. Changing color. Pink, purple, green.

What was wrong with Mom? With his whole family?

"How many times have I told you"—Mom leaned in—"not to feed the dog?"

Her breath stank. He could see flecks of green caught between her teeth—kale or some other dead leafy vegetably thing. Her grip tightened even more, squeezing so hard that what remained of the chickpea crust in his hand crumbled into a dust that sprinkled all over his lap.

"I'm sorry . . ." He didn't know what else to say.

"*Sorry?*" Mom held Marcus's gaze, staring back with such spiteful eyes. "You're *sorry*? Sorry just doesn't *cut* it anymore, hon . . ."

The pizza slicer. It was still in her hand. She waved it around. *Snk.* Through the air. *Snk.*

"You're hurting me . . ."

"*You're hurting me*," Caleb mimicked in a high pitch.

"What am I supposed to do with you?" Mom demanded. "How am I supposed to *feed* you?" *Snk.* "You need to eat *healthily.*" *Snk.* "Take *care* of your body." *Snk.* "Keep it *clean.*"

Marcus pulled back on his arm, trying to free himself from his mother's grip.

But Mom wouldn't let him. She only squeezed tighter, waving the pizza cutter more wildly through the air the louder her voice rose. "I made avocado brownies just for *you*." *Snk.* "If you want dessert, I need to see a clean plate." *Snk.* "A *happy* plate." *Snk.* "Do you understand?"

"Please." Marcus pulled harder. He felt as if his shoulder might pop out from its socket.

"When are you going to WAKE UP, Marcus?" his mother shouted, nearly shrieking. "When are you going to OPEN YOUR EYES? No dessert until I see a happy plate!"

Marcus's hand finally slipped out from his mother's fingers, freeing him so fast he lost his balance and fell onto the floor. He let out a startled cry.

Mom snapped out of her stupor. She blinked back to the dining room. To Marcus.

The pizza cutter slipped from her grip, clattering across the table.

"Hon? Honey, are you okay?"

Marcus didn't know what to say. Didn't know what to do. He simply froze in place as his mother crouched down and put her hands all over his body, checking and rechecking to see where he might have been hurt. Were there any broken bones? Any bruises? Any blood?

"I'm sorry," she said. Was she crying? "I'm so sorry. I . . ."

Mom pressed Marcus against her chest.

"I—I don't know what's happening."

Marcus kept very still, letting his mother hold him.

"What's happening," she repeated, crying into his hair. "What's happening to me . . ."

DECEMBER 6
stage four: *depression*

DEVON

Can I be real with y'all? YOGAMAMA asked Devon in her most recent video testimonial.

"Absolutely," she replied.

You have to choose to awaken. Only you can OPEN YOUR EYES. No one else will do it for you. It's up to you to pull the wool away . . . Where once I was blind, guuurl, now I can see.

"You're right. You're absolutely right."

Your body is a temple. A ripe vessel. We want to make sure that it's ready for receiving.

"Receiving . . . what?"

A gift, gurl.

The juice cleanse was step one in Devon's spiritual awakening. YOGAMAMA insisted she scrub the plumbing. *You gotta purge yourself of any toxins polluting your body, hon. Flush—it—all—out! Make your vessel pure again. Then—and only then—can we welcome in the Wellness.*

The Wellness. Devon wanted it so desperately. Her body ached for that healing feeling.

She wanted to wake up.

To open her eyes.

Hot water. Lemon juice. Cayenne pepper. Ginger. Turmeric. That was her diet for the next few days. Devon scheduled her cleanse for the weekend, but before she could begin, she needed to fast first. She had never cut out food altogether. Diets, sure, but never fasting. It seemed extreme, but it certainly worked for the women in her feed. The sirens all swore by it, testified to its impact on their bodies, their very souls. Look! Just look at how pure they were!

Devon was already imagining the selfie she'd snap, her own posed portrait of the new, healthy her. That's what she wanted, didn't she? To be one of them? To have her own profile in the pantheon of bronzed goddesses? Devon was desperate to enter that endless current of photos on her feed, to swim with the women of wellness, a siren herself. She imagined them all as mermaids. Every last lady. Beautiful mermaids. The scales on their tails were thousands of tiny smartphone screens, shimmering with that familiar pixelated mother-of-pearl, a swirling rainbow hue, purples and pinks and greens, an oil spill of glistening electricity.

She wanted—*needed*—to be clean. To cleanse her temple, just like YOGAMAMA said.

So she had to fast.

To purify.

The fast wouldn't be easy, but she had her support system. Whenever Devon felt a hunger pang, she could simply click to Instagram and pore over the sirens cheering her on:

You got this, gurl!

You're on your way to achieving your dreams, just like we all have!

Join usssss!

YOGAMAMA's 3 Day Juice Cleanse Powder Detox was one hundred percent natural—no additives, no chemicals. All organic ingredients, made from the earth's finest elements: dandelion root extract, turmeric root extract, ginger root, milk thistle, and monk fruit for a little sweetener. *Mmm-mmmm!* All blended in a pea-protein-and-brown-rice base. All Devon needed to do was simply add water and crank up her Vitamix to a low setting, blending the ingredients *aaaaand . . .*

Drink Me.

Wasn't that what the bottle said to Alice? Devon nearly giggled at the recollection, giddy with light-headedness, thanks to her fast. It had been so long since she'd read *Alice in Wonderland*, but here she was, taking the plunge down her own personal rabbit hole.

She unscrewed the lid, brought the jar to her nose, and took a whiff.

It smelled like burnt earth. Compost. Devon gagged, dry-heaving in the kitchen. The aroma permeated the entire house—there was no airing it out.

There was no way, no *possible* way, YOGAMAMA expected her to drink this stuff.

Was there?

Three times a day, for seventy-two hours. It would take all of her strength to swallow it down, but she had to. It was just a simple cleanse to purge the foulness from her body once and for all. She needed to let her temple heal. When she emerged on the other end of this cleanse, Devon would have a boost in energy, reduced bloat, and a soft-focus aura.

She could do it.

She had to.

If Devon thought the powder mix smelled awful, it tasted even worse.

Here's what the selfies never showed Devon: *This shit is like drinking gasoline. What the hell is in this stuff?* Should there have been some kind of warning label on the jar? An FDA advisory? Every breath singed her throat. It burned to breathe. She felt the sizzling liquid flood her gut, swell within her intestines, a flush of fire in her stomach that sent her pitching forward.

It hurts. Oh God, it hurts so much. Only two more doses to go . . . today.

Devon had diarrhea for the next ten hours.

Then came the headaches.

The dizzy spells.

Mood swings.

Irritability.

"Hey, hon," Ash started in on her. "What're you thinking for dinner to—"

"Why don't *you* cook?"

"*Whoa.* Easy, tiger."

"Why am I always the one who has to feed you? Ever think about feeding yourself?"

"The hell's gotten into you?"

"Here's an idea," she growled. "Fix your own damn dinner."

Asher turned back to his television, sinking into silence. Devon had her screen nestled in her lap, like a cat, if they had a pet—*Hold on. Didn't they? A dog, or . . . or . . .*

Their dog—*what's its name*—started sniffing her leg.

Rufus! Just another mouth to feed.

"Go. Get. Scootch." Devon punted it away. Just a slight kick in the ribs. The fucking mutt whimpered off.

Delirium set in by day two. It made it hard for her to focus on her family. Basic chores around the house were no longer doable. She spent most of the day in bed, leaving the rest of the fam to fend for themselves. That's okay. Let them cook dinner for a change. They'll live.

Live. Devon wanted to live, live her own life, spread those wings and finally take flight.

I felt sorry for my family, YOGAMAMA shared in a video testimonial. *Their way of thinking is getting in the way of my own healing. Of WAKING UP and OPENING MY EYES . . .*

Devon could relate.

It was almost like . . . they wanted me to stay sick. My own family. My husband. My kids.

Devon felt that way, too. It made so much sense. Her heart skipped a beat when she realized she was in the same predicament YOGAMAMA had been in, just a few phases before.

What if . . . ? No, it couldn't be . . .

Could it? Oh God, what if Devon's family was a part of the problem? What if they preferred her to be in servitude to her sickness? Enslaved by her inability to heal? To wake up?

To open her eyes?

"Mommy?" Someone was calling her. She could just barely hear a faint voice. "Mom . . . ?"

Devon turned to find a child.

Her child. *Marcus.* That's right, that was his name. "What."

"I . . . I'm hungry . . ."

Why was everyone always coming to her to tell her they were *hungry?* What was she supposed to do about it? If they were so fucking hungry, then they should—

"Go get something to eat," Devon said. "Knock yourself out."

YOGAMAMA never mentioned the nightmares. Were they a part of the cleanse, too? Hallucinating in the middle of the night?

Devon was thrust out of her sleep somewhere around two in the morning, covered in sweat—but thicker somehow, almost oilier— buckling under the intense cramps in her stomach. It felt like something was crawling around inside her intestines, worming through her organs.

Ow ow ow. Devon's mind turned. *What's happening to meeee . . .*

She rolled around in bed, moaning. She was afraid she'd disturb Ash, so she curled up into a ball, bringing her knees to her chest and wrapping her arms tightly around her shins, biting her bottom lip and silently praying for the pain to go away. *Please, just make it all stop . . .*

Wait a minute. Where was Ash? Devon had the whole bed to herself.

But she wasn't alone.

Devon stared at a spot where shadows were cast along the far wall of their bedroom, barely making out the silhouette of some runty thing crouched in the corner.

Two shimmering scales. Screens the size of fingernails.

They looked like eyes. Oil-spill eyes. Such wonderous—

gaslights

—colors, first pink, now purple and green, staring back at her.
They blinked.

Devon didn't move. Didn't scream. She could barely breathe as
this runty thing lurched closer toward her, hobbled on its hands, sim-
ian-like, an ape made of shadows, dragging its legs.

No—wait. Devon caught another shimmer as its body unfolded.
Scales.

The lower portion of its torso tapered off into a tail: a mermaid
of glistening mother-of-pearl. A thousand tiny screens shone in the
darkness of their bedroom, so mesmerizing.

The siren reached the edge of the bed and climbed in.

It crawled toward Devon.

Squatted on top of her.

The mermaid's pendulous breasts shuddered above Devon as she
marveled at this beast. She was in awe of it—terrified and tantalized.
It looked like YOGAMAMA—like Larissa—but some wizened old
hag version of her Instagram self, no longer young and beautiful.

The heat of its fecund breath spread over Devon's face. Compost
rot. She smelled the ocean depths, the muck and mire of a million
years pouring forth.

The siren's eyes swirled in such lustrous colors and all Devon
could think was—

gaslights

—how stunning they were, a rainbowed tornado in each socket,
swirling, swirling, swirling. Devon lost herself in those hypnotic colors,
those wondrous oil-spill eyes, trapped like a pelican wrestling against
the icky effusion of the *Exxon Valdez*. The grease oozed out from the
siren's sockets and over Devon's body, coating her skin. She opened
her mouth to scream and the—

gaslights

—oil poured down her throat. It filled her stomach, *no, no, not possible, it's not real, please,* her belly swelling into a rippling womb before bursting all over the bedroom walls.

The siren licked Devon's cheek, the scrape of her tongue like sandpaper against skin.

scrape-scraaape-scraaaape

Not sandpaper. This felt like a cracked iPhone screen. Its tongue had the texture of fractured glass, a shattered cell phone grating across her skin.

Devon abruptly woke in bed, realizing she was raking her iPhone over her face. Her right cheek was flayed from having scratched her face over and over again with her broken phone.

Did I do that . . . ?

———

Gooooood morning, guurlzzz! Who's ready to make some smoothies with me today?

Devon absolutely loved her new juicer. When no one else was in the kitchen, she'd bring the blender in between her legs, straddling it, and flip the switch. She'd set the blades at a low speed to start with— something for a heartier recipe, like chunky pasta sauce—feeling the low wattage throb begin in her thighs and work its way up her body and down her legs.

vvvvvvvvvvvvvvvvrrrrrrrrrrrrrrrrrrr . . .

When the whir of the blades met her pulse, she'd crank it up a notch, making the blades go faster, *faster,* slipping past the whips and spreads setting all the way to frozen dessert, *faster,* until the steel blades between her legs created a tornado coursing through her bones.

VVVVVVVVVVVVVRRRRRRRRRRRR!

Nothing says yummmmy in the tuuummmy quite like a kale cleanse, am I right, gaaalz?

Rapture set in by day three.

Colors. Devon was now seeing liquid colors in broad daylight: swells of pastels swirling at the corners of her eyes. Everything had a lens-flare quality to it now, cinematic in its luster. Sunbursts of amber bloomed all around, blinding in their golden glow. It was like looking through the filter of her Instagram app, the soft-focus haze of her iPhone's camera cast across everything. She was living in a selfie. Beautiful. The world looked so fucking beautiful.

Devon had never felt so euphoric. So alive. *It's working! YOGA-MAMA's cleanse is working!* At first, she had felt like she was dying, but here she was, merely three days later, emerging from the sweat-soaked sheets on her bed like a cicada crawling out from its cocoon.

Triumphant. Enlightened. *Healed.*

Devon was on a religious pilgrimage right here in the cozy confines of her own home. Her trip to Mecca was underway. Spiritual enlightenment was just a few clicks away.

Devon's cell vibrated. She glanced at the caller ID, irked that her bubble was bursting.

Who the fuck is ruining Mommy's healing moment? This is my selfie time, goddammit—

Caleb's school. Caleb's school was calling.

"What?" she answered straightaway.

"Yes, um, hi," the voice—a woman's—chirped on the other end of the line. "This is the attendance office? Sorry to bother you, but . . . well. I'm calling about Caleb."

Devon didn't know how to respond. "Yes?"

"He's been absent for . . . oh, four days now, and we're just wondering if he's okay."

"What are you talking about?"

Now it was the woman on the other end of the line who was quiet. Finally, she spoke again, this time in a measured tone. "If Caleb's sick, we'll need to see a note from his doctor."

"No doctors," Devon blurted. *No more misdiagnoses. No more malpractice. No more—*

"I'm sorry?"

"He's got a fever thank you bye." Devon forced the words from her mouth before ending the call. She stared at the cracked screen of her phone, afraid it might ring again.

Please don't call back please.

Caleb's door was closed. She pressed her ear against it, listening. She heard noises—

pop pop pop

—seeping through the wood. *So he is home. The sniveling shit's been skipping school.*

pop pop pop

Had he been hiding in his room all this time? For four days? *What's he doing in there?*

"Caleb!" Devon knocked.

No answer. Devon swore she heard Caleb panting or gasping or—*something.* Choking?

huh huh huh huh

So she opened the door. Any concerned mother would. She had every right to.

"Caleb, what the hell is—"

Devon cut herself off. What she saw confused her. It took her a moment to process.

Caleb was hunched over his computer.

The oily flicker on the screen.

The images of—

gaslights

—writhing bodies. Moaning from the speakers.

"Mom!" Caleb shouted. He was facing away from her, hood up. He turned just enough that she could see the right side of his face peering out from beneath his hoodie. His laptop cast its glow over his skin, spotlighting his patches of acne in pinks, purples, and greens. "Get out!"

"I . . . I knocked . . ."

He slammed his laptop shut—and just like that, the moaning ceased. *Thank God*. The blue glow of Caleb's computer screen snapped off, abandoning them both in blackness.

"What do you want?"

"I . . ." Devon could just barely make out the silhouette of her son, hunched forward. She couldn't say for certain, not in the dark, but she could have sworn she saw—but *how?*—the cotton contours of his hoodie rippling along his back. Shifting, almost, as if his spine was—

pop pop pop

—contorting beneath his skin, all on its own. Devon merely blinked the image away, forcing it from her mind. "School called," she said. "They said you've been absent."

"I haven't been feeling well."

"Then why didn't you—"

"Can we talk about this later, Mom? Can you just go? *Now? Please?*"

"At least open a window," Devon said. The room smelled awful. The air hadn't moved in here for days, from the odor of it. "Get some sun in—"

"Get OUT, Mom! GO!"

All she could do was step back into the hallway, doing as she was told, and close the door. Devon lingered there for a moment, speechless. She didn't know what to do. What to say. All she could do was listen, waiting for something to happen.

huh pop huh pop huh pop huh

She was losing her family. Her grip was slipping. She didn't know who to talk to.

She needed help.

Needed—

YOGAMAMA. She'd know what to do. She'd probably dealt with this plenty of times before. So Devon sat down, right there in the hall, opened Instagram, and started scrolling.

Scrolling . . .

Scrolling.

She was trying to focus on YOGAMAMA's missives, but the words were out of focus, the font too fuzzy. She couldn't latch onto the maxims. The words . . . *wriggled*. Squirmed. They wouldn't stay in one place, worming about the screen, a platter of maggots, slipping and falling from her tablet, tumbling all over the floor. *What's going on?*

Trails of glistening residue branched out from her screen, as if a dozen slugs had been gliding along the tablet.

The words. The words were worming their way out.

Close your eyes. Deep breath. Just let the room settle.

When she opened her eyes again, the slugs were gone. Just words on the screen.

There. Much better.

Hey there, gurl! YOGAMAMA here. How's it hanging? Today I want to get real with y'all. Get ready for some hard truths. You ready for some tough love, ladies? Buckle up now . . .

"Yes," Devon said to no one. To herself. To the sirens in her stream.

I think of all the hard work you've done for yourself. The self-reflection. The spiritual rebuilding. The homeopathic rebranding. I look at how far you've come, gurl, and . . . well, Devon, hon, sometimes I gotta wonder if your own family is holding you back.

"My . . . family?"

Your husband, your children . . . they want you to stay exactly the same, stuck in a rut, so they'll always have someone to tend to them.

Devon nodded.

I know you love your husband. You love your kids. But . . . you're on a different path now.

"Yes."

You're almost there, gurl. Look at you grow! Now it's time to WAKE UP. To OPEN YOUR EYES! We want our bodies all pure and ready to pledge for THE GREAT REAWAKENING, right?

"Yes. Goddess, yes . . ."

Perfect. Then let's begin the next phase . . . Time to testify.

"How?"

I'll show you! Just follow me . . . This part's gonna be tough, but we can do it. Together.

"But I . . . I'm scared."

Don't be! Look how far you've come! Opening your eyes takes strength. To see the world for what it really is takes courage. You can do it, Devon. I know you can . . . Are you ready?

Devon hesitated. Was she? "I . . . I'm ready."

That's what I like to hear, gurrrl. Say it again.

"I'm ready."

A little louder now . . .

"I'm ready!"

Great. Now take my hand. We're going on a deeeep dive today.

Devon tightened her grip around her tablet.

And awaaaaaaay we go . . .

Devon felt the world tip. The floor pitched. Even though she was sitting, squeezing her tablet, her balance teetered and she fell forward, into her iPad. Her head hit the screen and—

down

down

—down she went. Into the rabbit hole. All the way to the bottom of the well of wellness.

Splash.

ASHER

"So you're probably aware we've been hit with some tough times," the HR guy began.

Ken. That was his name. The color of his tie—shale—reminded Ash of his plasma screen before he powered it up.

"Redundancies," HR Ken called it. "Less of a layoff, more of a furlough? Time to tighten our belts, until we get over this financial hump. We might even be able to hire you back . . ."

What had Asher's job been here, exactly? Did he even remember?

HR Ken was waiting for Ash to say something, but to be honest, he was having a hard time focusing. Ken's face kept blurring. His features weren't in the right resolution.

Someone must've futzed with the motion smoothing.

All he wanted to do was go home to his La-Z-Boy. His back was killing him. If he could go home and pull on the hand crank, ease into his lounging position, he'd be fine. Better than fine.

There was a severance package. Not much, but enough to coast for a couple months—plenty of time to find something new. To get back on his feet again.

Asher knew he should tell his wife about the layoff. He had absolutely every intention of telling her. He just hadn't. *Yet.* The right opportunity simply hadn't presented itself.

How could he tell Devon he'd been rendered redundant? All he wanted was to collapse into her arms and bawl his eyes out. He wanted Devon to hold him and say it was all going to be okay, *everything's going to work out, don't worry, you'll be fine, we'll be fine, I love you . . .*

That wasn't entirely true. What Asher *really* wanted was his job back. He wanted to sit behind his desk and log in and pretend like the meeting with HR Ken had never happened.

That wasn't entirely true, either. What he *really* wanted, down deep, more than anything else in this world, was to march into his office with a sawed-off twelve-gauge and—

Okay, let's stick with Devon.

If she only knew how lost, how *redundant* he felt. The word echoed through his head.

Asher the Redundant. The Useless. He felt himself making a fist. He squeezed his fingers, nails digging into his palm, until a little bit of that rage was released into the meat.

Respect. Just a little fucking respect. That wasn't too much to ask for, now was it?

Apparently it was.

Paul Tammany laid it all out for Asher with his trademark no-nonsense, just-calling-it-like-it-is swagger. *Some underqualified succubus half your age is getting your job because they'll work for less, settle for less, and take it all . . . A new dawn is on its way, my friend. Just you wait.*

A new dawn. Asher liked the sound of that.

Time to WAKE UP, people. Time to OPEN THOSE EYES and see what's coming our way . . .

Asher now watched Fax News in the mornings. Afternoons, too. He suddenly had a lot more time on his hands.

He would have loved to crack open a cold one, if there were anything left in the fridge. But all there was to drink these days was Devon's rank-tasting smoothies—like slurping diarrhea straight out of a vegan's asshole. But beggars sure can't be choosers, can they? Not in this economy. Time to tighten the belt. And it's not like Devon's healthy concoctions were all that bad, once you drank enough of them. It burned at first, sure, but Asher got used to them.

Down the hatch.

"Honey?" A voice. Someone was talking to him.

Ash turned away from the TV.

Devon had caught him. "What're you doing home?"

"Watching the news." *Clearly.* Couldn't she see he was busy?

"Should you be at work?" She broached the subject gingerly—like he was a piece of porcelain. Always with the kiddie gloves, lately. What the fuck happened to her cheek? He decided not to ask.

"I took the day off." Ash turned back to the screen.

"We need to talk about Marcus."

Marcus? Who the hell is—

Oh. Their son. The little one. Right. "What about him."

"School called. They're concerned."

"About."

"He's been telling his classmates . . . *things*. About his family. Do you think that . . . maybe you could talk to him?" Asher could hear the sharpened edge of accusation slicing at his ears.

"You want me to talk to him."

"Can you?" If Devon kept prodding him with her incessant questioning, well . . . it wouldn't be long before this dog was bound to bark. Was that what she wanted? A fight?

Respect. Just the teeniest, tiniest scrap of respect. That was all he wanted. If that was too much to ask for, well . . . then just maybe the country really was going to hell in a handbasket.

Maybe the world deserved to burn down.

"I'll talk to him," he finally said, just to get her to drop the subject. Asher was sick and tired of trying. He tried *so hard* and still it wasn't good enough. What else was there to do but—

But . . . *what*, exactly? What could he do?

Paul will know. Tammany always had an answer. *Let's see what he says . . .*

Asher needed the news on all the time. Everywhere. In every room. He set up a television set in their bedroom; installed one in the kitchen. The news was on during dinner. At night. It would stay on while he drifted off to sleep. The news followed him through the house, the assured voice of the anchor drifting down the hall, echoing through each and every room.

It was unavoidable now. Everywhere now.

If there were twenty-four hours in a day, that meant the twenty-four-hour news needed to remain on. Ash needed to stay updated. He needed to know what was happening in the world.

Out there.

It's when you turned off the television that you let your guard down. That's when the attacks happened—that's when they got you. Whoever *they* were was anybody's guess: Terrorists. Transsexuals. The government. The world was full of degenerate people wanting to slither into his house and corrupt his defenseless wife and innocent children.

Asher needed to protect his family. Keep vigil. The news needed to stay on. If Devon or either of the kids ever reached for the remote, Asher batted their hand away—"*Don't touch.*"

Asher wasn't sleeping. There simply wasn't time to rest. This was not the moment to lower his guard. If anyone asked him what was wrong, he'd snap at them. If anyone tried talking over the television, he'd bark. Didn't his family see what he was trying to do here?

Look! Just *look* outside!

Asher no longer recognized the world around him. Nobody looked *human* anymore. Had someone messed with the motion smoothing? Had one of the kids fucked up the adjustments on his TV? He'd just calibrated it, for Christ's sake! Something was always slithering under their skin—their faces. They walked on two legs, yes. But their humanity was missing, their smiles askew.

Look. Just *look* at their blurry faces! Everybody was out of focus. Their faces wouldn't sharpen, completely pixelated. Someone need-ed to fix the motion smoothing on them all.

"Dad?" There it was again. A voice. This one smaller. A child's. "Daddy?"

Asher pulled his eyes away from the TV.

A boy. His boy. His . . . son.

Marcus.

"Come here, kiddo." He held out his hand to the child and brought him closer, sat the boy on his knee. There. Just like his father had done for him when he was his age. "What's up?"

"Are you sick?"

What a loaded question. Of course he was sick. Sick and *tired.* People were changing—their faces blurring. Asher had to fix the motion smoothing—*pronto.*

"Your mom wanted us to have a little father-son chat," Ash started. What were they supposed to talk about again? He couldn't quite remember. The words were at the tip of his tongue, but he just couldn't articulate them. So many wires were getting crossed in his mind.

If only he had a script for this sort of thing. A teleprompter to read from.

Oh, well . . . Ash would simply have to wing it.

"You're probably beginning to notice your body's going through some changes."

"Dad?"

"Don't worry about it. It's perfectly normal. Every boy goes through it."

The birds and the bees. That's what he was supposed to be talking about, right? Isn't that what Devon wanted from him? To give the spiel about how every child changes?

Transforms into something new?

"You might find yourself feeling a little curious about the *opposite sex*."

Ash's dad delivered the same speech to him when he was his son's age. He had Ash sit with him in his La-Z-Boy—the one time he got invited to sit in his father's leather throne.

Now it was his turn. How old was this kid again?

"What you've got to understand is what you're feeling is perfect-ly natural," Ash continued, trying to get the story straight. "There are gonna be some people out there who tell you that those feelings are dirty. There's gonna be a whole rainbow coalition of folks who—"

"Dad." The kid was squirming in Asher's grip.

So he squeezed. Just a bit. Just enough to keep him in place. Keep him listening.

Can't you see I'm trying to help here? Ash thought. *Can't you see I'm doing this for you?* He fucking *loved* his kids. He'd do anything to protect them. Keep them safe.

Didn't Marcus *understand* that?

"I don't know what they're teaching you in school about your body, but you—"

"Dad, you're hurting me—"

"—can't be afraid of these changes. They're natural. Perfectly natural. Your body is—"

"Let go!"

"—just telling you it's ready to wake up. To become something special. Something—"

"DAD."

New. Those were just the fax of life. "You just—have to—open your eyes, son—"

The boy wriggled free from Asher's hands and fell to the floor. Asher didn't move from his seat at first, still in front of the TV. He merely watched this kid—his son—crab-walk away from him, flipping over onto his hands and knees before scurrying out of the living room.

Don't let him go, Tammany said from the screen. *Get him.*

"Marcus!" Ash clumsily stumbled after his son. "I'm talking to you, young man!"

Marcus had made his way back to his bedroom, slamming the door in his father's face. The latch clicked from inside. Ash tried opening it. Locked.

"Marcus!" He banged his fist against the door. "Open up right now!"

Ash pummeled the paneling with his fist. When that didn't seem to do the trick, he lunged for the door, ramming his shoulder into the wood until it rattled on its hinges.

"Open—"

BANG!

"—your—"

BANG!

"—goddamn—"

BANG!

"—EYES!"

Nothing. Ash waited outside the door, spent and panting, straining to hear movement within. "There's so much out there, son. So much to be afraid of. But you won't have to."

Ash pressed his ear against the paneling, listening in.

"Marcus? Can you hear me? I'll protect you, I promise . . . You'll see."

He kept still.

"Marcus? The Great Reawakening is almost here."

Very, very still.

"Marcus?"

Fuck. That didn't go well. What should he do?

Kids are too soft these days, Tammany said, luring Ash back to the living room.

Soft. His son's skin. So tender. Only seconds ago, he'd had his son in his hands.

You know what they're teaching kids in school now?

Asher glanced up at the television.

To be afraid of their own bodies. To hate themselves. They want to shame our sons. You think that's right of them? Making them feel like they don't belong? Do you think that's fair?

"No . . ."

Somebody's gotta take a stand, Tammany said. *I'm looking for a few good men out there to lead the charge. You wouldn't happen to know any bulls who fit that bill, do you, Asher?*

"I do."

Oh?

"Me." That Asher had started talking back to the television shouldn't have come as a shock to anyone. It was a rite of passage for most middle-aged men. *Happens to the best of us.*

His dad did it all the time. Now it was simply his turn.

Tammany huffed. *And what makes you think you're qualified?*

"I have a very specific skill set and over twelve years in the professional—"

Blah blah blah. Are you even listening to yourself? I didn't ask you to regurgitate your résumé. I asked you what makes you think you're qualified to lead my Tammany Army?

"Because . . . because I . . ."

Yeah? What?

"I'm a man."

Really, now? Says who?

"Me."

You seem pretty sure of yourself all of a sudden. You wanna double-check?

"No."

Wanna bring in your wife and see if she can—

"NO."

You're not a man . . . You know what you are? You're lazy. Just another lazyboy.

"Am not."

Just one big LA-Z-BOY.

"I am not!"

What are you then?

"A LA-Z-MAN!"

That so?

"I am a LA-Z-MAN!"

Then get off your fat ass and prove it!

"I'M A LA-Z-MAAAN!"

Not just anybody can lead the charge. When the Great Reawakening arrives, it's gonna be like the Rapture on Red Bull. People aren't gonna know what hit them. You ready to wake up?

"Yes."

I'm sorry, what was that? I couldn't hear you—

"YES."

Well, then . . . I want to hear you say it. Say the words.

"What words?"

Here. I'll show you—

Suddenly, the world tipped. The room itself seemed to turn on itself—a shoebox in God's hands—and here He goes, tilting it to one side.

Asher slipped. He was no longer on the La-Z-Boy. He was in the air, falling forward, tumbling toward the television.

Asher was hurtling through the air. He felt the gravitational drag of the screen. The smooth black surface was suddenly undulating—an opaque infinity pool.

Asher swung his arms through the air, but there was nothing for him to grab hold of, nothing that could stop him from plummeting straight into that lopsided vat of boiling oil.

Asher belly flopped into the screen, and almost immediately its roiling black plasma singed his skin, melting flesh right off the bone, pain searing every last nerve ending.

Asher cracked open his mouth to release a scream, but the plasma poured down his throat, the oil funneling its way through his insides, scorching everything in its wake.

It all went black. Into the rabbit hole he went.

Down . . .

Down . . .

Down.

CALEB

"Sorry," Benjamin Pendleton said after colliding with Caleb in the hall. "Didn't see you."

On any other day, any other run-in with Benjamin, he'd let it get under his skin. Let the anger sink in. Not today. Nah. Caleb felt a bit more solid lately. He walked with purpose.

They just don't know, he thought. *None of them do.*

Not yet. But they would.

Soon.

Everybody would know who Caleb Fairchild was, he could feel it in his—

pop

—bones. Caleb existed within two separate worlds: There was the world his family inhabited, the world of school. His nonexistent friends. The Chads and Beckys. The breeders.

Then there was E.

He and Elzegan had carved out a world just for the two of them. Caleb yearned for his virtual existence more and more. The longer he was away, the more he pined to slip back in.

Mom made him go to school. He'd missed way too many days these last couple weeks. Mom called the principal and she begged him to give Caleb another chance. *Just one more chance.* She dragged his ass back to school and now here he was, wasting away in English class.

Look. Just look at these clueless kids. They just don't get it.

The world where E was from was unlike Caleb's suburban bubble. It wasn't a life of Starbucks mango dragonfruit lemonades or Taylor Swift serenades. That world felt so flimsy.

So *empty.* Look. Just *look* at them all, going about their empty lives.

Had he really been like them before?

He was no longer alone. He felt like he belonged. He was a part of something greater than himself. There was more to his life than the trivial vapidity of his suburban existence.

E said he had plans for Caleb.

Big plans.

Caleb could wake others. Shake the world's foundations. Send the pillars of this trivial society crumbling. He could do something drastic. *Huge.* Something they'd never see coming.

CALEB_RUNS: mom tried taking my phone away

CALEB_RUNS: shes cutting me off the fam plan if she catches me on it at dinner

CALEB_RUNS: mom thinks I'm on drugs

CALEB_RUNS: like I'd actually do drugs

CALEB_RUNS: she doesnt know anything about me its like itd be easier for her to believe I wuz on drugs because then shed be able to cry boohoo my baby boy . . .

CALEB_RUNS: I hate her

CALEB_RUNS: so empty

CALEB_RUNS: everything is just so pointless

ELZEGAN911: What do your parents want from you?

CALEB_RUNS: be like them I guess

ELZEGAN911: Do you not see? Their way of life is atrophying.

ELZEGAN911: Their existence offers nothing but emptiness.

ELZEGAN911: We want to give you a sense of purpose, Caleb.

ELZEGAN911: A place to belong.

CALEB_RUNS: what can I do?

CALEB_RUNS: Im nobody

ELZEGAN911: It only takes one person to topple an entire empire.

ELZEGAN911: You are capable of so much, Caleb.

CALEB_RUNS: yeah right

ELZEGAN911: The life your parents have to offer you is hollow.

ELZEGAN911: The future they see for you is an echo of their own.

ELZEGAN911: They lack the vision to see beyond their own failure.

ELZEGAN911: The world needs to WAKE UP.

ELZEGAN911: It needs to OPEN ITS EYES and see what is coming.

ELZEGAN911: The Great Reawakening will be here soon enough.

ELZEGAN911: Will you be ready, Caleb?

CALEB_RUNS: wutz the great reawakening???

ELZEGAN911: A storm on the horizon. The clouds are already gathering.

ELZEGAN911: You will soon see for yourself.

ELZEGAN911: We will call for you on that day. You will be put to the test, Caleb.

ELZEGAN911: Your parents cannot see you for who you truly are.

ELZEGAN911: The girls at your school cannot see you for who you truly are.

ELZEGAN911: You are such a strong soul, Caleb.

ELZEGAN911: Others see only the surface, what is before their eyes, but we see so much more. We see YOU. The real YOU.

The true YOU.

CALEB_RUNS: how

ELZEGAN911: You radiate strength. You burn so bright. Such wonderful light.

CALEB_RUNS: yeah right

ELZEGAN911: Just because you cannot see it in yourself does not mean that it is not there.

ELZEGAN911: We see what you cannot see in yourself.

CALEB_RUNS: I want 2 see

ELZEGAN911: Then WAKE UP, Caleb.

ELZEGAN911: OPEN YOUR EYES.

CALEB_RUNS: How???

ELZEGAN911: Let us show you.

E told him about a messaging platform that made texting untraceable. The two of them could keep their conversation private, away from Caleb's parents and off their data plan.

You should not be afraid to speak your mind, E said. *To say what you really think.*

So E sent Caleb a fresh link.

CLICK HERE.

Caleb considered it. For the longest time, Caleb had felt safe DMing E within the confines of his Twitter messages. Whether it was true or not, he at least knew his profile was contained behind the firewalls of his social media account. Clicking on videos was one thing, but to completely abandon the parameters of Twitter for another, shadier platform felt . . .

Felt like *what*? What was Caleb afraid of?

Did he truly trust Elzegan?

Caleb had never "talked" to E, but the way he wrote things sounded like English wasn't his first language. It was almost like an AI bot attempting human conversation.

What if E wasn't American? What if E wasn't human? Could he be a bot?

Trust us, E wrote. *Believe in us . . . as we believe in you.*

Us.

There was that word again.

We.

It was never just *him*. Never just E. E spoke as if there was a whole army hiding behind the screen. Just how many people were *us*, exactly? Who was Caleb talking to? Did he know?

Did it matter? Look at what E was offering him: Confidence. A manly morale boost. A *purpose*. He kept saying he saw Caleb for who he truly was, which, shit, felt pretty good.

Somebody out there saw him the way he wanted to see himself. At long last, someone saw his potential. His *true* potential—none of that aspirational guidance counselor BS. This was the real-deal-we-don't-say-this-kinda-stuff-in-public-for-fear-of-being-canceled stuff.

E wasn't afraid. He didn't give a fuck what people thought, so neither should Caleb.

So Caleb signed up.

Just like a dam breaking, drowning everything else out, the conversation flowed between Caleb and Elzegan. They overloaded computer servers with hours' worth of chats. The threads of their communication intertwined until the early hours of the morning. He would stay awake in bed, sharing his most private thoughts. Things he'd never shared with anyone before.

He talked about the girls at his school. How they never looked at him. They were so focused on the athletic Chads, primping and dolling themselves up for breedability, that they never once glanced his way. But that was okay, E said. Caleb had something else to offer.

What did Caleb have that made him so special in E's eyes? What did E see in him?

E's answer was always the same: *In time. Soon. You will see.*

Caleb spent all of his time in his room. The door was always closed—lights off. The only source of illumination came from his computer screen.

E sent Caleb links. Usually it was these hilarious videos—things they watched together online. Stupid stuff. Totally harmless, like videos of police body cam footage or CCTV footage of car accidents. Snuff films. Fakes, no doubt. Caleb would watch the clip on his laptop and then DM E about it.

Caleb asked for a photo. E was nothing but words on a screen. He wanted more. He wanted to see E's face. His real face.

But E never shared one.

You will see. Soon.

Caleb ran his fingers across the screen. He couldn't help but wonder if E was pressing his fingers against the other side. He imagined E looking back across the virtual gulf between them. No matter how many miles separated them, he felt that chasm closing, drawing E near.

CALEB_RUNS: where are u?

ELZEGAN911: Here, with you.

CALEB_RUNS: no I mean like where do u live

ELZEGAN911: Paradise.

CALEB_RUNS: umm ok

ELZEGAN911: It is unlike anywhere you have ever been. It is wonderful.

ELZEGAN911: When you are ready, we will show you.

CALEB_RUNS: when Im ready???

ELZEGAN911: Not everyone is capable of offering themselves. You have to prove yourself.

ELZEGAN911: We believe you can, Caleb. We see you for what you truly are.

CALEB_RUNS: what do u see?

ELZEGAN911: Someone who is strong. A capable vessel for making great change.

CALEB_RUNS: tell that to my dad

ELZEGAN911: They will never understand. They cannot see you the way we do.

ELZEGAN911: You are strong, Caleb.

CALEB_RUNS: nobodys said that to me before

ELZEGAN911: Listen, Caleb, and understand:

ELZEGAN911: YOU ARE A GOD HERE.

ELZEGAN911: All you need to do is purify yourself.

ELZEGAN911: Sanctify yourself.

CALEB_RUNS: what does that mean

ELZEGAN911: Your body is a temple.

ELZEGAN911: You must cleanse it.

CALEB_RUNS: You mean like with food or something??

ELZEGAN911: We must anoint you with oils.

CALEB_RUNS: umm ok

ELZEGAN911: There is one very important thing that we must know.

ELZEGAN911: Are you pure?

CALEB_RUNS: pure?????

ELZEGAN911: Are you pure, Caleb?

ELZEGAN911: Is your body unsullied?

ELZEGAN911: Have you kept yourself unblemished?

ELZEGAN911: Untouched?

CALEB_RUNS: u mean like a virgin????

ELZEGAN911: YES.

ELZEGAN911: A virgin.

ELZEGAN911: We need to know.

ELZEGAN911: It is very important.

ELZEGAN911: Caleb?

ELZEGAN911: Caleb?

ELZEGAN911: Are you still there?

ELZEGAN911: We know it is a personal question. A private matter.

ELZEGAN911: But look how close we are.

ELZEGAN911: We feel so connected to you.

ELZEGAN911: Do you feel it? That power? The energy flowing through you?

ELZEGAN911: We feel it.

ELZEGAN911: We sense it in you.

ELZEGAN911: So strong.

ELZEGAN911: That is why we chose you.

ELZEGAN911: That is why we need you.

ELZEGAN911: We need you, Caleb.

CALEB_RUNS: yeah

ELZEGAN911: Tell us the truth.

CALEB_RUNS: yeah I am

ELZEGAN911: Say it.

CALEB_RUNS: Im a virgin

ELZEGAN911: You cannot lie. It is important that you be truthful with us.

CALEB_RUNS: its the truth

ELZEGAN911: Do you swear?

CALEB_RUNS: yeah

ELZEGAN911: Say it. Swear it.

CALEB_RUNS: Im celibate.

CALEB_RUNS: a virgin

CALEB_RUNS: I swear

ELZEGAN911: How wonderful, Caleb.

ELZEGAN911: Thank you for protecting your most sacred offering.

ELZEGAN911: There are a few steps that you must take in order to prepare.

CALEB_RUNS: What steps?

ELZEGAN911: Your body must be clean. Purified.

CALEB_RUNS: I already told you I was

ELZEGAN911: Before we are to be together you need to adhere to a special diet.

ELZEGAN911: Our union requires certain preparations.

ELZEGAN911: Are you willing to do these things for us?

CALEB_RUNS: yeah

ELZEGAN911: That is wonderful. So wonderful to hear.

CALEB_RUNS: What do I need 2 do?

ELZEGAN911: You must cleanse your body of all pollutants.

ELZEGAN911: No poisons must sully your flesh.

ELZEGAN911: We will choose the proper foods for you. Are you willing to let us?

CALEB_RUNS: ok

ELZEGAN911: Wonderful.

ELZEGAN911: You are so strong, Caleb.

ELZEGAN911: Soon you will be rewarded for your strength.

ELZEGAN911: There is a Great Reawakening approaching.

ELZEGAN911: Soon it will be time to WAKE UP and OPEN YOUR EYES.

ELZEGAN911: Will you be ready for that day of reckoning, Caleb?

ELZEGAN911: Will you join us?

CALEB_RUNS: ok

ELZEGAN911: We have been watching you, Caleb, for so long now.

ELZEGAN911: We have seen what your classmates have done to you.

ELZEGAN911: How they have made you feel.

ELZEGAN911: They will never understand you.

ELZEGAN911: They are afraid of what they do not understand.

ELZEGAN911: They are afraid of you.

ELZEGAN911: People will always scorn those who do not abide by their narrow-minded standards. But you are better than them. Stronger than them.

ELZEGAN911: You have much to offer this world, even if they do not accept your gifts.

ELZEGAN911: We do, Caleb.

ELZEGAN911: We want to nurture your strength.

ELZEGAN911: In order to do that, we must prepare your body. Sanctify it.

ELZEGAN911: You are THE WAKE-UP CALL, Caleb.

ELZEGAN911: You are exactly what we have been looking for.

The Wake-Up Call challenge was simple enough. All Caleb had to do was cleanse himself in front of the camera. He'd have to repeat a few words, pre-scripted by E.

Mom kept her juice cleanse crap in the pantry. There were dozens and dozens of jars—more jars than cans of actual food.

All Caleb had to do was grab a jar, take it back to his room, ingest a spoonful of his mother's awful juice cleanse powder for the camera, and repeat some stupid words. That's it.

Then he'd upload his pledge online for the rest of the world to see.

Easy peasy, right?

Caleb set up his iPhone to record his pledge video in his room. He made sure to align the lens, getting the angle just right. He took a deep breath, letting the oxygen settle in his lungs.

Then he pressed record.

"Hi. Um . . . my name is Caleb. Today, I'll be doing the Wake-Up Call challenge. Okay, here we go." He had never done one of these dumb meme challenges before. He'd seen plenty of others fall flat on their faces trying to climb a pyramid of milk crates or dumping a bucket of freezing water over their heads. There were a million and one challenge videos to scroll through.

But to make one of his own? To contribute to a trend? Fuuuuck that noise.

But E convinced him this was different from all those other dumbass challenges. This was a way to show his allegiance. His devotion. *If you are willing to cleanse your body, to testify to the world that you are willing to make this simple sacrifice, then you are one of the chosen.*

Caleb didn't see why it was such a big deal. But E was adamant about him going through with it. He wanted—*needed*—Caleb to testify before the rest of the world.

He was willing to submit his body. To purify.

CALEB_RUNS: wuts so special about that juice cleanse crap

ELZEGAN911: It is a sacred anointment. It is used for brides before their wedding ceremony.

ELZEGAN911: Boys entering into puberty must cleanse their bodies of all poison.

ELZEGAN911: We need you to be clean. To be pure.

CALEB_RUNS: But why do I need to record it?

ELZEGAN911: It is a testament.

CALEB_RUNS: I can just do that on FaceTime . . . why do I need to post it?

ELZEGAN911: To show others. To let them see. Then they will join.

ELZEGAN911: Others will follow your example. More will purify themselves.

CALEB_RUNS: U want others to do it too?

ELZEGAN911: Of course. We need more, Caleb. More.

CALEB_RUNS: More . . . wut?

ELZEGAN911: Followers.

ELZEGAN911: Believers.

CALEB_RUNS: For wut?

ELZEGAN911: To join us. Help us. Our cause.

CALEB_RUNS: But u said I was special

ELZEGAN911: You are!

ELZEGAN911: You are so very special, Caleb . . . So brave.

ELZEGAN911: You are a leader.

ELZEGAN911: Others will follow your example.

CALEB_RUNS: I dunno . . .

ELZEGAN911: Someone needs to be the first.

ELZEGAN911: Someone needs to show others how it is done.

ELZEGAN911: The Great Reawakening is drawing near. Can you feel it?

ELZEGAN911: Who will be leading the charge on that day?

ELZEGAN911: Who will be the fist that shatters the screen to let us through?

CALEB_RUNS: Me?

ELZEGAN911: You, Caleb.

ELZEGAN911: YOU.

ELZEGAN911: You are THE WAKE-UP CALL. You will deliver our message.

A leader. Caleb was one of the chosen few. E kept calling him their guiding light.

Others would follow in his footsteps.

Wake them up, E had said. *Open their eyes.*

A holy war was being waged within his home. So many children like him were born into privilege, but their blindness to the truth left them wanting. *Yearning.* They were all alone, disconnected from their bodies—their souls. They had everything they could ever want and yet they still had *nothing.* The emptiness of their existence was a gift given to them by their parents, born under the same curse. This generational chain was their prison sentence.

Slaves. All were suburban slaves.

Not Caleb. His eyes were now opening, thanks to E. He was waking up. All he wanted was to leave this privileged life behind, step out of his sheltered existence and escape.

He fasted for three days, just as E had instructed. No one in his house even noticed that he was skipping meals, simply sipping water throughout dinner.

Nobody was talking to each other, anyhow. Not anymore. Dinners slipped by in excruciating silence. All Caleb wanted was to pull his phone out and see if E had written—*You can do it, Caleb!*—but his mom was always watching over him, hawk-eyed, mouth puckered, just waiting for the moment when Caleb would pull out his phone and she'd take it away.

None of that mattered. His parents didn't matter.

Now he had E.

Showtime.

First up: Anoint himself with oils. He had to strip down to his tighty-whities.

Fuck me, this is so embarrassing . . . The patches of acne across his chest were exposed. His pale skin somehow looked even paler on camera, washed out on the screen.

Caleb had pilfered a bottle of olive oil from the pantry and now he poured it all over his shoulders, rubbed it across his arms. The smell of cooking oil filled his bedroom, obscuring the dense funk of teenage boy—of crusty socks and abandoned pizza boxes and farts.

He couldn't believe he was doing this. If anyone at school were to watch this video, he'd never hear the end of it. "What am I doing," he muttered under his breath, "what am I doing . . ."

He was a leader. E said so. Caleb's testimony would lead more to follow in his footsteps.

So, with the spoonful of powder at his lips, he dizzily repeated the pre-scripted words E had given him to recite: "I offer up my body to purify. I am unsullied. Undefiled."

Because what girl would ever want to fuck him, right?

"I offer my virtuous flesh. I offer my sinless skin. I offer my inviolate body."

Down the hatch . . .

Caleb opened his mouth and swallowed the golden-hued powder before his gag reflex kicked in—*hork, hooork*—his stomach rebelling against the pungent powder.

It was disgusting. Absolutely awful. He had a water bottle by his nightstand table. He grabbed it, twisting the cap and guzzling a stomach full of water.

Caleb retched again—*hork, hork, hork*—struggling to keep it down.

Please don't puke please don't puke please—

A golden tide of water spilled from his mouth. It dribbled down his chin and onto the front of his shirt, splashing over the carpet and his feet.

His bedroom smelled of turmeric now. An acidic hint of bile lingered in the air. He needed to open a window before he vomited again.

His phone was still recording. Caleb simply stood there, struggling to catch his breath. He could see himself on his iPhone's screen, a golden tendril of saliva dangling from his chin.

"Peace out, y'all . . ." Caleb stopped recording. Then he posted the vid on all of his socials.

#WakeUpChallenge

FAMILY NIGHT

Marcus smelled meat. Maybe it was the hunger making him imagine things, but he could've sworn he smelled the aroma of steak wafting down the halls, filling up his bedroom and reviving him. The boy slowly came to under his bed—not in it—and lifted his head.

When was the last time Mom cooked meat? Cooked *anything*?

Felt like forever.

Marcus's mouth watered. He was so hungry. *Starving.* Lately, their dinners didn't include much dinner. Mom might scrounge together some scraps from the pantry and toss them onto the table: A box of uncooked pasta. A jar of dill pickles past its sell-by date.

Mom never stopped making her gross-smelling smoothies, though. The blender was on at all hours of the night, its blades grinding away. A few nights ago, Marcus came upon his mother in the kitchen, hoping she might have a snack for him. He was so hungry. She couldn't hear Marcus over the whir of the juicer chewing through whatever she'd just forced into the container, smashing it to a pulp.

Mom finally turned, the blender still grinding, laying her eyes on Marcus.

She smiled.

The blender kept grinding, even as her lips moved. She was saying something to him.

"What?"

She kept talking but Marcus couldn't hear what she said. Not above the blades.

"What are you saying? I can't hear you . . ."

Just what exactly was she blending, anyway? What was left in their house to eat? It looked pink. Purple. Red. The colors of something raw and bleeding. What was it?

Mom finally turned off the juicer. Even so, it took a second or two for the echo to dissipate in the boy's head.

"What can I help you with, honey bun? You all right? Hungry?"

He was absolutely famished.

"Would you like a smoothie, hon?" She lifted the container off the blender's base and held it up to him. "It's fresh."

It smelled . . . *awful.* Bubbling and stinky. Purple and pink. The color of beets. Nothing in him wanted to taste it. Marcus shook his head without a word, crinkling his nose.

"Suit yourself," Mom said, bringing the blender's vat up to her lips and drinking directly out of it. Once she started, she just didn't stop—*glup, glup, glup*—guzzling the pink and purple contents down. *Chug-a-lug.* It spilled down her cheeks and chin, wetting the front of her shirt, but Mom didn't stop drinking, tilting her head back farther and farther and farther—*glup, glup, glup*—until it was all gone, every last drop, Mom gasping for air.

"*Aaaah,* yummy in the tummy!" She released a victorious belch, lips smacking. The front of her shirt was drenched in red. "Better already! *Healthier.* Don't you wanna be *healthy*, hon?"

Marcus stepped away, putting enough distance between him and his mother before turning and running back to his room. "Din-din will be ready in a minute," she shouted.

For most other meals, Marcus fended for himself, sneaking into the kitchen when no one was around to see if he could dig himself up a snack. The cabinets were pretty bare by now.

When was the last time Mom had gone to the grocery store?

Marcus missed Pizza Nights. So much. There was a lot that he missed about his family these days.

Marcus knew where Dad was. Always in the living room. Always watching television.

Caleb was in his bedroom, door shut, music blaring. Guns blazing. *Pop pop pop!* Playing video games or whatever it was he was doing.

Mom was the one Marcus worried about the most. She was hard to pin down around the house if the blender wasn't blending. She could've been anywhere. *Hiding* anywhere.

Marcus holed up in his own room. Sometimes he even locked the door. He didn't come out unless he absolutely had to, mainly for food or the bathroom—and even then, he had perfected his ability to pee in a cup and toss the urine out the bedroom window.

Rufus stayed with him most nights, but it was getting harder for them both to find food.

Now it was Wednesday.

Family Night.

That must've been why the house smelled so good. Marcus hadn't realized how dizzy he was, delirious with hunger. He cracked open his door. Peered down the hall.

Nothing.

Just the sound of the news blaring from the living room. All the lights in the house were off except for the television, its blue-green glow flickering across the walls.

Marcus took a deep breath, steeling himself, and stepped out from the safety of his bedroom. He tiptoed his way past the living room, terrified his father might spot him.

No table settings tonight. The dining room table was bare except for the scraps of their previous meal. A housefly hovered over the crumbs, landing for a moment before taking flight again, buzzing about the room. Marcus swatted the fly away from his face.

A candle stood at the center of the table, lit, a warm beacon.

A crash from the kitchen.

Marcus turned, gasping.

Mom must have been rummaging through the cabinets. "Dinner bell, *ring, ring, ring!*"

The flame on the candle flickered. A gasp of wind.

Somebody's coming—

Dad appeared at the doorway. He grabbed the back of his seat and dragged it across the floor, legs scraping. He plopped down, landing in the chair like a bag of cement hitting the floor—*Whuump!*

Caleb scurried into the dining room next, hood over his head, a pimple-ridden grim reaper, brushing against Marcus's shoulder. He sat in his usual chair and slumped down, arms crossed.

Everybody was *changing*. His parents were *changing*. His brother . . . *changing*.

What's happening to them?

"Dinner is served," Mom announced as she shuffled in, her feet bare, carrying a covered casserole dish. The sides were caked in a brown-red crust, boiled over and baked against the edges of the dish. Whatever was inside smelled amazing.

Mom held the dish with her bare hands. Marcus could see how pink her fingers were.

"Sit, sit," she chided him. "Butts in seats." She released the casserole dish before it reached the table. It skidded a few inches toward Marcus before coming to a halt.

"Hood down, hon," Mom instructed Caleb.

Caleb had to grip his hood's lip and tug hard. The cloth wouldn't give easily, crackling as he peeled it back, *crrrrrk!*, almost as if he were scalping himself with his own hands. The crusts along his temples glimmered, his face covered in gleaming trails of oil.

"Aaand . . ." Mom grabbed the knob on the lid and lifted. "*Voilà.*"

Meaty steam wafted up from the dish.

Marcus peered in. What he saw was ribbed—a slab of baby-backs. The skin was crispy. Mom had even seasoned the meat, basting it in some kind of sweet-smelling sauce.

Was that BBQ? Teriyaki? Marcus couldn't tell, but his mouth flooded with saliva.

He wasn't the only one who was starving. His father leaned in to take a closer look at what Mommy had cooked. A string of drool dribbled down his chin. "Mmmmm . . ."

"Help yourself," Mom singsonged.

So they did. Dad dug his hand in, grabbing a rib and ripping it off from the rest.

Caleb went next.

Then Mom.

They all used their bare hands, tearing into the slab of beef or pork or . . . *whatever* it was.

Only Marcus held off. He sat in his seat, hands below the table, fingers worrying themselves. He was hungry. So hungry. But something felt . . . *off.*

This is all wrong, he thought. Marcus couldn't comprehend what was going on, but he knew something was very, *very* wrong with his family.

"How was everybody's day?" Mom asked the table. "Anything *exciting* happen?"

"Almost time," Dad said between swallows. "Time to wake up."

"Open your eyes," Caleb mumbled.

Mom tore off a bite from her rib. The ripping motion sent her neck swiveling in his direction. As soon as her eyes rested on Marcus, her mouth open, the bite of glistening meat dangling from between her teeth, she halted. She looked at him—*stared*—still chewing.

"You haven't touched your dinner." She almost sounded hurt. Stung.

Marcus chose his words carefully. "What . . . is it?"

Mom swallowed. Smiled. Marcus could see the mouthful of meat sliding down her gullet. "Just a li'l something I scrounged up."

Caleb snorted. Clearly there was a joke here that Marcus wasn't privy to.

Was he the butt of it?

A thought pinged at the back of the boy's mind: *Where's Rufus?*

Just when an even more disturbing question began to form—

Are . . . are they eating . . .

—right on cue, from under the table, Marcus felt the familiar lick against his fingers.

Rufus!

There he was, *Rufus to the rescue*, doing what that dog always did: *lick lick lick . . .*

Wheeew . . . The boy could feel the relief, the breath coming back to his lungs, as he exhaled that awful, awful question away. How could he ever think they were—

The tongue scraped against his skin. More forceful than before. This tongue was rougher, far more coarse than normal, almost like sandpaper. Cracked glass. Rufus must've been parched.

That tongue wound its way around Marcus's fingers, the muscle weaving between his knuckles like a dry, thorny vine. It tightened. *Squeezed.* He couldn't help but let out a cry of surprise—of pain. Everyone's head swiveled his way. His mom, dad, and brother all stopped chewing in unison, their blank-eyed focus fully on him, sending a chill down the boy's back.

Rufus hadn't stopped his licking. The dog forced his face deeper between the boy's legs.

What was Rufus doing? What was he looking for?

Marcus had no choice but to scootch back, push the dog's head away, distance himself from his own . . . his . . .

Dog.

Dogs have fur. Rufus had lots of fur. So . . . why did his face feel so bare? So . . . slimy?

Rufus kept nuzzling. Marcus had always been his provider, his under-the-table dealer in human food he didn't want to eat himself. The two of them had an agreement. His dog—

notadog

—depended on him. Sure, Rufus could be persistent sometimes. Annoying, even. But he never acted this forceful. He kept licking, licking, licking, scraping the salt from Marcus's skin.

Marcus had to look. He needed to see his—

dognotadognotadognota

—friend. Marcus leaned over, peering under the table.

Nothing was there.

All Marcus saw were his family's feet. Then who—

notadognotnotnot

—had been licking his fingers? He brought his hand up, examining the slime trail still glistening across his skin. It swirled with oily pinks and purples and greens, thick and gloopy.

"Rufus?" Marcus called out his best friend's name, turning to look over his shoulder.

"Better clean your plate, hon," Mom said.

"I . . . I'm not hungry" was all the boy could muster. It was a lie. A big fat lie.

"Do what your mother says," Dad said.

"If you want dessert," Mom chided, "you're going to have a *happy plate.*"

He couldn't. Never.

Mom's expression puckered into a pout. Not a sincere one, but an exaggerated look of wounded self-pity. "You don't like my cooking anymore, hon? You used to *love* my cooking . . ."

"Clean your plate, kiddo."

Mom leaned forward, inches away from Marcus. Her breath stank. That compost rot. "Maybe we could get your pal to help?" She started laughing. It wasn't her normal laugh. Not a natural laugh at all. It started deep in her chest, then rose into a shriek, like a teakettle that had been left on the stove for far too long. Her laughter only grew louder. Raspier.

"Ruuuufus!" Mom wiped the tears of laughter from her eyes. She took a bite from her rib, tearing a bit of burnt meat free. They all joined her. Laughing. Eating. His family—his own parents—were teasing him. Making fun of him. Why were they being so mean?

"Here, boy!" Dad whistled, but Rufus never came. "Come, Rufus! Here, boy! Here!"

"Rufus?" Mom cackled. "Oh, Ruuuufus, where are yoooooou?"

Marcus pushed his chair back, away from—

not

—his mother. He stumbled backward, away from the table, from—

not

—his family. Their laughter followed him out of the dining room, all the way down the hall, even into his bedroom after he slammed the door shut. He only muffled the sound of their cackling after he crawled under his bed and padded his ears with pillows, burying himself. He grabbed the closest stuffed animal—Baby Ghost—and squeezed it tight, staring at the inch of space between his door and the floor. Looking for movement. After a while, Marcus started humming to himself. A lullaby to help him sleep. "*Baby Ghost, boo-boo, boo-boo . . .*"

What had happened to his family? This wasn't his mommy and daddy and brother anymore.

Changing. They were changing.

Into what?

DECEMBER 13
stage five: *oppression*

DEVON

Why did it always fall on Devon to go to the grocery store? Because that's what *mommies* do? Go shopping? Cook meals? Change diapers? What did her family ever do for *her*?

They were part of the conspiracy. The doctors, the food companies, *her fucking family*, all of them wanted her to remain in a docile state of infirmity in order to keep prescribing her more. More medicine. More processed foods. More poison. *More, more, more . . .*

They were intentionally making her sick. How long had this been going on? *Years?*

Christ, her whole *life?*

It shouldn't have come as such a surprise that Devon skipped her annual checkup that morning. Why shouldn't she? What was her doctor going to tell her that she didn't already know? *Lies, lies, lies . . .*

They just want to keep me sick, she realized. *Sick, sick, sick . . .*

For too long she'd been held hostage by her doctor. Shackled to his prescriptions.

Not anymore. She was free at last, free at last . . .

Devon had forwarded a few pertinent emails about the fallacy—*phallusy?*—of the health care system to her closest friends. Well, people who used to be, at least. Back when she was blind to all this. For those old acquaintances who deigned to respond offered curt concerns: *Are you okay, Devon? This doesn't sound like you . . . It's a little disconcerting. I'm worried about you. Do you want to grab a cup of—*

They're worried about *her*? She was worried about *them*! They were still blind to it all, sick with it all, filled with dose after dose of poisons masquerading as medicine, vaccinated into their own submissiveness. All they needed to do was click on the link Devon had sent and READ THE DAMN ARTICLE and they would see for themselves. They'd know what was really going down.

But noooope, sorry, can't do it.

That's what truly frightened Devon more than anything. These women, these mothers, they all wanted to remain sick. How repulsive was that? To actually *want* this blinded life?

Who was going to put a stop to all this?

Devon, that's who.

This was a holy war waged upon the bodies of women. The sirens of her Instagram feed were the true warriors here. Freedom fighters of the finest order. They were sent to save us all.

Protect our temples.

Save our children.

But first—sandwich fixings. The plan had been to pull into Walmart or Costco or wherever was closest, run in real quick, and grab a few toiletries. Some food might be nice.

Everything felt brighter outside their house. The low-grade hum of fluorescents reached deep into her loose molars, a power drill to her jaw. She wondered if there was a conductive infusion of cell phones somewhere in the store. All that 5G—no wonder she had a migraine.

Devon needed to get out of here. *Fast.* Before the nearest cell tower seared its insidious electrical tentacles into her skull and she could no longer think for herself.

There were eyes on her. She felt them staring. *Leering*—all the other customers. Couldn't they see what was going on right in front of them? People were willing to let go of their personal freedoms to be herded along.

Not her. Not anymore. She could *see.* Finally *see.*

WAKE UP, people!

OPEN YOUR EYES!

Devon hadn't dressed to go shopping, still wearing her yoga outfit. When had she slipped it on? Yesterday? The week before that?

Days tended to blend together. The Lycra itched against her skin, chafed under her armpits, so she *scratch-scratch-scratched.*

Too many eyes followed her down the aisle. Heads turned as she picked up her pace. Did she recognize that woman? Was that a parent from Caleb's school? Why was she staring?

Devon had to get out of here. *Now.* Too many sheeple. Too many eyes. Too many haters who wanted to keep her down. The doubters and the naysayers lockstepping right along to their own demise. Look at them all. Just *look.* Always *tsk-tsk*ing. Always sucking—

Pssst.

Devon halted, her attention locked onto a brightly colored array of plasma televisions.

Hey, guurl . . .

Devon was drawn deeper into the electronics aisle.

Is that . . . ?

YOGAMAMA was on the television. Just the one. She was laughing on the beach, pirouetting through the sand, waves splashing against her tan legs, her screen surrounded by dozens of flatscreens, all the others tuned to a football game. She halted and locked eyes with Devon.

You are strong, child. That's why we chose you. You are THE WAKE-UP CALL. The first!

"First?"

Devon stepped up to the screen, taking in her sage's pixelated face. She pressed her hand against the plasma, fingers sinking in. It felt warm, electric, like jellyfish nettles.

We need to send a message. You need to go viral. To testify and spread our word. The world needs an example. To show everyone it's time to WAKE UP. To OPEN THEIR EYES.

"Me?"

Your testimony will kick off the Great Reawakening. Are you ready to show the world?

"Yes," Devon said to the television screen, her eyes full of tears.

She'd never been chosen for anything her whole entire life. She'd never been the first. It was almost too much.

Show them it's time to WAKE UP.

"Yes," Devon said.

Open their EYES.

"Yes," Devon said.

Suddenly YOGAMAMA was on all the televisions, her beaming face magnified a hundredfold, pushing those quarterbacks off the screens and taking over.

Hey, laaaaaadieeeeeeeeees . . .

YOGAMAMA's voice boomed through the speaker systems of every last flatscreen, shouting so loud Devon had to press her palms to her ears and cower.

We're counting down the days to THE GREAT REAWAKENING, guuurls! I want each and every one of you to tune in to this very channel on December twentieth at exactly three p.m., Eastern Standard Time. I'll be livestreaming during the big day and y'all better believe me when I say you don't wanna miss this . . . We're talking the biggest health summit this country's ever seen!

Was anyone else watching? Was Devon the only one paying attention?

No more lies! No more vaccines! No more people telling us how to take care of our bodies. This is our day, ladies. Get ready to WAKE UP and OPEN YOUR EYES! I'll have a special guest . . .

Devon felt her pulse pick up from the electronics aisle.

You all know her as Devon Fairchild, but guurrls, let me tell you . . . Once Devon testifies, you'll forget all about ol' Mrs. Fairchild. From December twentieth on, you'll know her as . . .

Devon held her breath.

NOMAMADRAMA.

It rolled right off the tongue, didn't it?

NOMAMADRAMA.

Devon kept repeating it, muttering her new name just under her breath.

NOMAMADRAMANOMAMADRAMANOMAMADRA-
MAAAAAH . . .

She now had her very own social media nom de plume, re-christened in honor of those wellness pioneers who forged a digital path before her, the Lewis and Clarks of the feminine era, bravely trailblazing their way online, all in the name of opening others' eyes.

You're THE WAKE-UP CALL, gurl, YOGAMAMA cooed. *They'll never see you coming, hon . . .*

"I am the wake-up call," Devon echoed.

What's your name?

"I . . . I am NOMAMADRAMA."

Say it again.

"I am NOMAMADRAMA."

Louder.

"NOMAMADRAMA!"

Louder!

"NOMAMADRAMANOMAMADRAMA!"

"Ma'am?" A voice—a man's—cut through Devon's revery, snapping her back to the aisle. To Walmart. Or Target. Costco. Whatever box store this was. She couldn't remember.

"Are you . . . uh, you okay?" A boy Caleb's age crept up on her, hands held up in the air, as if to say he meant no harm. *CHAD,* his name tag said.

The wall of TV screens glitched. The channel changed, the same laundry detergent ad broadcasting across each plasma screen. YOGA-MAMA was gone, replaced by a sheeplemommy.

"Do you want me to get you some help?"

Devon felt helpless, cornered. She didn't know what to do. She needed YOGAMAMA. Why had she left her here, all alone, when Devon needed her the most?

"Do you want me to call someone or . . . ?" Chad started to ask, his voice fading. Devon didn't hear the rest, bolting off down the aisle before he could finish. "Hey! Ma'am? Ma'am!"

Maybe this was a test. Was that it? What was she supposed to do?

Maybe a better question to ask was: WWYMD?

What . . .

Would . . .

Yoga . . .

Mama . . .

Do?

There. Devon skidded to a halt, heels squeaking over the linoleum. *Right there.*

There was her answer.

The pharmacy aisle: hundreds of over-the-counter medicines, lined up row upon row. It made Devon sick simply looking at it all.

Don't just stand idly by, YOGAMAMA whispered into her ear. She was no longer trapped behind the television screen, captured in plasma, she was in Devon's head. *Do something. Show these sheep it's time to WAKE UP!*

She was ready to testify. To bear witness. She had been waiting for the right moment—*her moment*—to become one of them. To finally enter that pantheon of Instagram crusaders. She felt dizzy with giddiness as she fished through her purse.

Her iPhone in hand, Devon swiped the camera to video mode, flipping the lens around to face herself.

Suddenly she saw herself on the screen. Sunken eyes. Gray gumlines. Flayed cheek.

Is that . . . Is that really me?

What was happening to her?

How could—

It was a trick. The lights, that's all—the fluorescents overhead were sapping the life right out of her. She needed to get out of this hellhole before they sucked her soul dry.

But first, Devon needed to testify.

"Hey, y'aaaall," she said directly into her camera phone. "It's your guuuurl here . . . NOMAMADRAMA. I'm coming to you live at the local Costco and ladies, you have just *got* to see the poison they're passing off as medicine right here on the aisles. It makes me absolutely *sick*."

She panned her camera phone over the aisle of multivitamins.

"Look. Just take a look at this! These corporations are shackling our kids with these poison-placebos, calling them multivitamins . . . but we know what they really are, don't we?"

A crowd had begun to form farther down the aisle, lured in by the shrill sound of her voice, the other shoppers gawking at Devon's impromptu video testimonial.

"Look," she shouted. "Just look! Don't you see what's happening here, people?"

Nobody answered. Everyone merely stared.

Lemmings, every last one of them. Lambs to the goddamn slaughter.

"Don't you see?" She lunged, swiping an entire row of pain relievers off the shelf. Cardboard cartons tumbled to the linoleum. "Don't you see what they're doing to us?"

She sent a row of flu medicines cascading to the floor, boxes toppling everywhere.

"Are you just going to stand by and let them do this?"

Another row came crashing down—gummy vitamins this time.

"Who's going to take a stand? Who's going to fight for our children? Who—"

She saw the security guard coming up from behind her on her iPhone's screen. She saw his hand reach out before it seized her shoulder, watching her own arrest play out in real time.

The other customers now had their own phones held up, taking aim at her, recording. One snapped a picture, the flash flaring up and momentarily blinding her. She winced.

"When are you people gonna wake up?" she shouted. "When are you going to open your eyes! There's a reckoning heading our way! Don't you see the clouds gathering? There's a storm coming! The Great Reawakening! Will you be ready? Will you be ready? Will you be—"

ASHER

Asher is in his dad's La-Z-Boy. He knows it's his father's chair because of the way it crinkles. The old, dry leather always crackled under his old man's body whenever he shifted.

Asher and his baby brother, Noah, were never allowed to sit in Dad's chair. Even when he wasn't around, the La-Z-Boy was always off-limits. Somehow, their father would know if they'd sat in it. Even for just a second. And boy, would their dad ever be pissed if he found out . . .

So how come Asher's sitting in it now?

Wait a second . . . This is his living room. What's his father's La-Z-Boy doing in his home?

He glances down at the recliner, squeezes the armrests with boy hands— small and smooth again—until the leather crackles within his grip.

Strange—the color of the chair is different from how he remembered it.

Asher glances over his shoulder to the headrest behind him. He sees his father's face. No eyes. Just the skin—nose, ears, and chin protruding, and empty holes where his eyes should be.

"Dad . . . ?" His father is stitched into the recliner.

Not just the headrest—the whole chair. It's made from his father's flesh. The leather—it's him. Dad. The La-Z-Boy is a La-Z-Man. Asher has been reclining against his father's rawhide. The stitchwork along the headrest runs across what had been his dad's chest. He can just barely make out the birthmark his father had on his left leg, just above his knee, now an armrest.

It's been his father this whole time.

"Dad . . ." He's crying now. When did Asher start crying? He presses his cheek against the chair's cushioning, upholstered with his father's face, and wails. "Daddy . . ."

"Hey, son," his father's skin replies. "Comfy?"

"What happened to you?"

"Oh, you know. Put out to pasture. What happens to all dads one day."

"Did it . . ." Asher swallows. ". . . hurt?"

"Not gonna lie," his father's rawhide recliner says. "A little. But don't worry, son . . . You've still got some time before you become a La-Z-Man. So just sit back, relax, and enjoy the show."

"No, Dad, please . . ." The second Asher tries to move, to get up, leap out of the seat—

He can't.

The chair won't let him. It's holding him down. His father's hide, the husk of him, clings to his own skin. It's so sticky, like the glue from a humane mousetrap, gummy and gelatinous.

Asher realizes his TV is on. White snow fills the screen, roiling with black and white static.

Not static.

Maggots.

They're spilling out from the screen as Dad's La-Z-Man reclines farther back and the chair gets closer to that churning waterfall of maggots cascading down from the television oh God all of those maggots are pouring across Asher, scattering over his legs, his chest.

The chair's scootching too close, too close, those maggots are going to go in his mouth—

Don't scream don't scream don't—

Too late. Asher's lips split and he releases a low wail that just won't stop. Now that his mouth is wide open, those crackling staticky maggots pour right down his—

═══

GAAASP.

Asher jolted upright in front of the television, alone in the living room. The sun was long gone, his clothes covered in—what was that? Some kind of thick film. He was basted in it.

Asher glanced at the clock.

2:30 a.m.

His skull throbbed. A jackhammer hangover, although he hadn't touched a drop of alcohol. His tongue clung to the roof of his mouth. So parched. *I'll get one of Devon's smoothies.*

Something was wrong with the screen.

Paul was on the air. It was a rerun of that night's show. He was sitting behind his desk, spouting off about school shootings—*When's the last time we saw any real footage? Actual news coverage? CCTV footage? A cell phone video? Anything?*—when his face began to break down. The feed kept glitching, freezing. The pixels fragmented into digital shards, a stained-glass window shattering onscreen. Paul's pores went mother-of-pearl, skin swirling with colors.

His voice was still there, emanating from the mess of his pixelated face, but the image was all off. The tones of his suit seethed across the screen, the color of his tie distorting every few seconds, red to blue to purple to green. It looked like an oil spill rippling in the sun, something you might see forming in the grocery store parking lot.

That's 'cause it's not real, Tammany intoned on TV. *Ever think of that? These shootings, these victims . . . it's all just made up. All a part of some elaborate plan to pass gun reform laws.*

There was a hypnotizing quality to it—the colors, so alive. Pearlescent rings of Saturn. They warped and rippled off Tammany's body, rainbow heat waves radiating off his shoulders.

Too bright. Too close. The colors. The bright—

gaslights the glorious

glorious

gas

—lights flashing across the screen caused Asher to wince. Was he about to slip into an epileptic fit? Fall to the floor and start flopping about like a fish?

But he couldn't look away. Instead, he leaned in toward the screen. That ghastly plasma. It leaked out from the TV, dribbling down the wall, bleeding.

Tammany kept talking on air. *You think it's any wonder why they've had to resort to elementary schools? Because high schools weren't cutting it anymore. They're cranking up the volume on the ol' waterworks, tugging at the heartstrings . . . but it's not real. None of it's real.*

More shimmering, glittering plasma poured forth from the screen.

Down the walls.

Up the walls.

To the side.

Not plasma.

Slugs.

Slugs crawled out from the screen, heading in every which direction, the pearly chemtrails of their escape shimmering across the living room wall—everywhere. So many pulsing slugs, pushing their gray bodies along the plaster.

None of it is real, Paul Tammany said. *These people are not real. They're not human.*

Asher picked a slug from the wall. Simply plucked it up like a berry off the bush and—

Ate it.

Hmm, Asher thought. *Not bad. Not bad at all . . .*

So he went back for another.

Salty.

Now that he was on his feet, he stood eye-to-eye with this melted mass of Paul Tammany. Just when there was a moment of clarity—of seeing Paul reassembled—a wave of pixelated distortion rushed over the screen and the substantiality of his body was gone again.

It reminded Asher of when he was a child trying to catch the late-night Skinamax movies. Soft-core smut. Tepid stuff in comparison to the pay-per-view porn a few channels away. Asher's parents didn't actually subscribe to any of the premium cable channels, so the screen was always a distorted mess of toxic colors, a box of Crayolas in the microwave. There were these fleeting moments of bodies on-screen, there and gone in a blink, but young Asher still heard the moans of pleasure buried behind waves of warped color. If he was lucky, he might catch a glimpse of a pair of breasts or lips, stockpiling the forbidden image in the back of his brain. Save for later.

Paul Tammany melted across the screen, his flesh and suit swirling together in one molten mass. The image simply wouldn't hold.

Wake up, Asher. Open your eyes.

But his words. His words were still there.

There's a reckoning coming. The Great Reawakening is on its way . . .

Asher leaned into the television, mere inches from Paul Tammany's distorted self. He could smell Tammany's breath. The stink of his last meal—red meat. A rusted-penny tang.

Will you be ready, Ash?

"Yes . . ."

Will you?

"Yes."

Asher brought his hand up to the screen and pressed his palm against it. The plasma softened under his skin. There was a warmth to it, emitting a dull electrical radiance that coursed through his fingertips and deep into his wrist. It hummed. His bones vibrated with Paul Tammany's voice. Asher could feel him inside, the very timbre of his words reaching into his body and resonating throughout the rest of himself. Reaching down deep. To the very core.

His heart.

You're ready, Ash. You're a natural-born leader, bud . . . You are my WAKE-UP CALL.

When Asher pulled his hand back, the screen came with it. The plasma was attached to his skin—gelatinous, like tar. Thin strands snapped as he pulled free, lashing back at the screen.

Asher examined his fingers. He still felt the slightest electrical current coursing through the tips, stinging, like he'd just run his fingers through the nettles of a jellyfish. It burned.

He looked back to the screen, at the whirling mass of Paul Tammany's face. Someone else's melted form was on-screen now. He could just barely make out Julia Turin. That was her, wasn't it? It was so hard to tell. Asher couldn't be sure, but he swore Julia and Paul were now copulating on top of Tammany's news desk. The image would never settle long enough to be certain, but Asher caught flickers of flesh pressed against flesh. That could have been a breast. Maybe it was a hand—arms intertwining. Thrusting. Thighs fusing into one liquid body.

Julia's breath picked up on-screen, panting like a sled dog in the middle of a winter sprint. Paul kept on script, speaking his mind, thrusting himself against Julia.

Crisis actors. Fabricated kids. None of it's real. They aren't real people. Aren't human.

Asher wanted to join them.

You know how you can tell the difference? The motion smoothing. That's how you know. You can see who's human and who's just another crisis lizard because the motion smoothing shows you what their skin looks like without the cinematic filters. Exposes what's underneath.

Asher pressed his hands against the screen again, this time forcing them as deep into the plasma as they would go. First it swallowed up his fingers, then his hand, all the way to his wrist. The throbbing wattage of electricity singed his skin, but he didn't care. It felt good.

We need the motion smoothing, you see? The motion smoothing is the only way you can tell who's human and who's just another blurry lizard person pretending to be human . . .

Ash pressed his face against the screen. He felt a singe on his nose. The pain spread to his cheeks.

Asher kept pushing.

Pushing.

His face mashed against the plasma. The screen was stiff at first, but eventually gave way, pulling back like electrified taffy, letting Asher squirm inside.

Through.

Asher gasped for air. He stumbled forward, the pressure suddenly gone. There was no resistance, sending his body into a free fall down . . .

Down . . .

Down.

He was in the newsroom now. Stumbling onto the soundstage. No one else was around. No Paul, no Julia. No crew members, no camera operators.

Where had everyone gone?

Asher slowly stepped up to the desk and glanced around, taking in the world as Paul Tammany saw it. The glare of the spotlights was blinding at first, but Asher got used to it.

His eyes adjusted to the—

gaslights

—Fresnel lamps overhead, their bulbs swirling in oil-spill hues, pink now purple now green. Asher had to force himself not to stare directly into the—

glorious glorious

gaslights

—tungstens because they could burn a hole right through his retina.

There was a teleprompter just a few yards away. The pre-scripted spiel for that evening's broadcast kept scrolling on its own, directly below the camera's looming eye.

The words were there, right there, waiting for someone to give them voice.

To testify.

Asher sat himself down in Paul's seat. He adjusted his clothes, smoothing them out.

He cleared his throat and began to read.

"Another thing they won't tell you is these kids"—it wasn't Asher's voice, it was Tammany, Paul Tammany's voice spilling out from his mouth—"these kids that they've got crying on camera—they're not even kids. They're too old to be in kindergarten. Anyone with a pair of eyes in their head can see that. They're nothing but actors. Crisis actors. But do we talk about that? No, of course not. That would be considered disrespectful. Impolite. So where are these kids four months from now? Why can't we get any one of these students on our show?"

It felt good, saying the words. He felt his bones expand within his body—*pop pop pop*—as if his skeleton itself were growing. He was filling out. Becoming stronger. A soldier. A righteous warrior.

He was becoming Paul Tammany.

"I'll tell you why. They're not real. Not human. They sob for the news and then they just disappear. Onto the next pimple commercial . . . It's all for show, folks!"

The words on the teleprompter flickered—faded. But Asher didn't need to read them anymore. He knew the words by heart, as if they were coming straight from him. Unscripted.

"The day is nearly upon us, people. The day we've all been waiting for . . . You got that right, folks. The Great Reawakening. That glorious day of reckoning. Which side are you standing on? It's time to WAKE UP. Time to OPEN YOUR EYES and see what's coming our way."

Will you be ready?

Will you be ready?

Will you—

Asher cut himself off.

There, standing behind the camera, hidden in silhouette, was a blackened shape.

It stood on two feet.

It looked like a man, but there was nothing human about it. It could've been a cameraman, or Paul Tammany playing peek-a-boo, but the first word to pop into his mind—

demon

—was there and gone before Asher could even finish the thought.

This swarthy thing leaned over to one side, sliding out from its hiding spot behind the camera, still obscured within the intense glare of the spotlights overhead. Its skin undulated within the shadows, an inky blackness that possessed substance—possessed mass.

It grinned. Its teeth cut through its own radiating darkness. Without moving its lips, it said—

Smile for the camera.

CALEB

Caleb couldn't pull his hoodie off anymore. The cloth stuck to his skin. He'd fallen asleep with his hood pulled over his head, but when he woke up the following morning, it had somehow adhered itself to his face. He tugged and felt—*heard*—his skin pull away from muscle.

He had to tug harder. *Harder.* Just a bit more pressure aaaaand . . .

Ow owie ow ow.

His cheek peeled. There was pain, lots of pain, but just underneath it was something sweet—soothing. There was relief in the cool air funneling across his fresh flesh.

So he tugged even harder.

Harder.

He felt his hair ripping from its roots. This crusty stuff had gotten into his scalp.

Crusty socks. Crusty hoodie. Crusty clothes. Crusty everything.

A crusty cocoon.

Caleb's entire body was sheathed in an amber-hued carapace. He needed to break free, crack out from his outer shell, emerge.

pop

He felt his backbone stretch, expand.

pop

Another vertebra extending his spine.

pop

He never left his bedroom anymore. The muggy air never moved in here, a million exhales trapped within. The walls were lacerated with pearlescent strings. Snail trails ran up the walls, along the ceiling, painting the room in a slimy glimmer.

Come on, Caleb, he said to himself. *You can do it. Crawl free.*

The itch was everywhere. His skin seethed with dry heat. Caleb scratched at his arms, raking his nails across his skin, digging red trenches of irritated flesh. He just couldn't stop.

Scratch scratch scratch scratch scraaaaaaaatch—

A scab pried free under his fingernail.

Wait a sec . . .

A pimple flaked off. Then another. *That's not possible . . .*

Is it?

Caleb pinched the amber crust and brought it up for a closer look. There was the faintest iridescent sheen to it, a snake's scale, swirling in pinks and purples and greens.

No, not a scale. It was more like a—

A screen.

The crust had a similar oily swirl as his cell phone. Its colors fluctuated when he held it up to the light, shimmering in his laptop's glow.

Did that just come from my body?

His pimples were shedding. *He* was shedding. *Holy shit, the purity challenge worked . . .* Actually *worked!* Look—*just look*—at him! Caleb's pubescent shell was peeling away. He was a butterfly emerging from its pimply cocoon.

Just like E promised.

ELZEGAN911: We always saw you for what you truly are.

ELZEGAN911: The beautiful boy hiding underneath.

ELZEGAN911: Now others will see. The world will see.

ELZEGAN911: You, our glorious creation. You, our beautiful butterfly.

ELZEGAN911: It is too late for your classmates. They are lost. You have transcended them.

CALEB_RUNS: somebody should teach them a lesson

CALEB_RUNS: teach them all

ELZEGAN911: Perhaps you are the one to teach them.

CALEB_RUNS: for real?

ELZEGAN911: Be their teacher, Caleb. Open their eyes.

ELZEGAN911: Show others. Testify. Lead them.

ELZEGAN911: You are THE WAKE-UP CALL.

ELZEGAN911: You are so beautiful, Caleb.

ELZEGAN911: We love you, child.

CALEB_RUNS: love u 2

The soldering tools were simple to purchase at the hardware store. The clerk didn't bat an eye when Caleb bought a surplus of nails, barely glancing from the register as he rang him up.

Assembling the device was a challenge, but E sent links to You-

Tube videos on how to build your own explosive device at home in three simple steps, all the way down to the wiring.

Just watch and follow the instructions. This was just another high school science project, like a potato-powered battery or baking soda volcano.

Caleb brought his hand up and wiped away a thin trickle along his upper lip. He stared at his fingers. Blood sank into the creases of his skin, branching out in a red root system.

Weird. He noticed on-screen that his nose was bleeding—thicker now, rustier. He wiped the blood from his upper lip with the back of his hand, smearing a red streak across his cheek.

Something was plugged in his left nasal cavity.

Caleb felt it wriggle.

He pinched. Whatever was up there tried to squirm out from his grip, but Caleb had enough of a hold to tug. It took some wrestling, but eventually the slug slid free from his nostril, glistening between his fingers. It writhed, frantically flexing back and forth, covered in mother-of-pearl mucus. Those oily hues swirled over its body as it continued to squirm.

Caleb popped the slug in his mouth and swallowed.

Salty.

Time to go to school. Caleb switched his camera to selfie mode. He brought the phone up, extending his arm as far as he could, and posed, smiling wide enough to show his jaundiced gums. Mom's juice cleanse powder, the turmeric, had turned his teeth yellow. His gums looked like lemon rinds. His fingers were stained with it, too. His sallow complexion took him by surprise every time he glanced at himself on-screen, but he'd never felt better. More *clean.*

He lifted a pair of bony fingers and made a peace sign.

Click.

Look. Just look at him now. His acne was *gone.* The pimples had all flaked away.

He thought back to the frightened little kid he used to be, who didn't know where he fit in, who felt so alone even when he was surrounded by so-called *friends* and *family*, who never belonged to this hollow suburban life. What a sad child he'd been. Couldn't anyone see that he'd been crying out for help? But Caleb would never be that unhappy child anymore.

That kid was gone.

Deleted.

Now Caleb belonged to something larger than himself. He was a warrior.

A messenger. The Wake-Up Call.

And you damn well better believe he was going to make himself be heard.

Loud and clear.

FAMILY NIGHT

Marcus woke up to his stomach seizing. The pain—the pain was unbearable. He couldn't think straight anymore. Delirious and dizzy, his throat dry. He needed to eat. Needed food.

The sun had gone down—at least he thought it had. Everything was so dark in the house. His dad had shattered all the lightbulbs in their sockets. Marcus had seen him do it, his face illuminated by the warm glow of the lamp, squeezing the bulb with his bare hand until it shattered with a brittle *pop*. There was a brief flash of electricity and everything went dark.

He had to get to the kitchen. That meant making it down the hall. Past Caleb's bedroom.

Past Dad.

Marcus unlocked his door as quietly as he could. He stepped out into the hall, using the wall to hold him up. The darkness made it difficult to see how far he had to go, so he took his steps slowly. Very *slowly*. He didn't want to step on anything that might make a sound.

Marcus picked up his pace as he slipped past the door to Caleb's room. He could hear wet sounds from inside. *Pop.* Sounds that made no sense. *Pop.* He didn't understand what could be making them—*what's so wet*—but he felt it was better not to know. Not to see. *Pop.*

So Marcus kept going.

Glass cracked under his foot. A searing pain spread through Marcus's heel. He held his foot in place, gritting his teeth, then slowly lifted his leg up. Beneath his foot was a shattered picture frame. He bent down to see it. It was one of their Christmas card portraits. Look at his family—the matching plaid flannels, the matching smiles. Look at how happy they used to be.

He stepped over the photograph and continued on, limping now.

Dad was in the living room. He stood before the plasma TV, watching the news. His face was only a few inches away from the screen. Mom scolded Marcus for sitting too close to the television, but even he never got as close as Dad was just now. His eyes were out of focus, jaw hanging open. Drooling. Taking the whirling images in.

Nobody was in the kitchen.

Where was Mom? She had to be around here somewhere.

Hiding.

Marcus had to act fast if he was going to grab something and take it back to his bedroom before she caught him sneaking a snack before dinnertime.

It was Wednesday, after all. Wasn't it?

Family Night?

Mom had made the rule: no matter what was going on in their lives, no matter how busy they were, they must—*they must*—come together as a family and break bread.

The kitchen looked as if it had exploded. Cabinet doors were flung wide open. Drawers had been yanked out of their place and tossed to the floor, sending silverware everywhere. Cereal boxes were torn open, their contents crunching beneath Marcus's feet. All kinds of cartons and containers were smashed or ripped. Food was flung against the walls, the floor, even the ceiling. It smelled terrible—like something had died.

Something had.

The oven door was open. What remained of Rufus was caked to the oven rack. Marcus knew it was his dog because there were tufts of his fur clinging to the wires. The smell of burnt hair was unmistakable. They had all eaten their dog for dinner. For last week's Family Night.

Marcus had to eat *something*, no matter how sick to his stomach he felt. He had to forage for scraps. Anything other than Rufus. He refused to eat that.

The refrigerator door was swung open. The bulb inside cast a yolky yellow hue over the mess. Someone had yanked out the shelving units, sending perishables all over the floor. Now the door wouldn't shut anymore, the white metal grating half in and half out.

Marcus kneeled before the fridge to rummage through the soft mess. A cold breath of chilled air drifted out from the open door. It felt good against Marcus's skin. The fruit had gone bad. Slimy vegetables formed a puddle. There was an inch of curdled milk left in the carton that he forced himself to drink, then keep down. There was soft butter that tasted okay. Salty. Marcus sipped from a bottle of soy sauce.

He needed to hurry. *Hurry.* Before Mom came back. Before she found him and—

And—

There. Buried below the puddled mess. *What's that?* Something hidden at the back of the fridge. Marcus reached his hand in and pulled a jar free from the cesspool of moldy veggies.

Pickled kumquats—still sealed.

It was a miracle the jar hadn't been shattered. He remembered his mom making cocktails with these once, way back when. A whole lifetime ago. When they were still a family.

Still human.

Marcus quickly twisted the lid and plucked a kumquat out from inside, swallowing it. It was so sweet. *So goood*. He brought the whole jar up to his lips and drank the sweet brine as if it were fruit juice. It tasted so good. So sweet. Too sweet. All that sugar. But he couldn't stop—

Marcus retched. He'd swallowed too much, too quickly. His empty stomach couldn't handle that much sweetness all at once. He tried to keep it down, but kumquats came back up.

Splsh.

Marcus tried to catch his breath. He wiped the syrup from his lips. He felt so lost, so unbelievably alone. He couldn't stop himself from crying, there on the kitchen floor, kneeling in a puddle of rotten vegetables and vomit. He knew his father would scold him for crying, for acting like a baby. *Buck up, kiddo. Stop acting like a little whiny crybaby and act like a real—*

Someone was behind him. In the kitchen.

"Baby Ghost . . . boo-boo . . . boo-boo . . ."

Marcus heard her breath. Wet. Labored. Raspy and far too shallow.

"Baby Ghost . . . boo-boo, boo-boo . . ."

Marcus slowly turned his head. He knew who it was, but he still needed to see.

"Baby Ghost, boo-boo, boo-boo . . . Baby . . . Ghost . . ."

There was Mom, perched directly above him on the island's counter. She was crouched on her feet, looming over him like a granite gargoyle.

Mom sniffed the air.

"Mommy Ghost . . . boo-boo . . . boo-boo . . ."

A slender thread of drool escaped her mouth, dribbling down her chin and reaching for the floor below. For Marcus. All he could do was keep still, very still, and not make a sound.

"Mommy . . . Ghost . . . boo . . . boo . . ."

Mom hadn't noticed him, blind to the boy, even though he was on the floor below her.

"Mommy Ghost . . . boo boooo booo boooo . . ."

Mom grabbed a torn box of Cap'n Crunch and scooped a handful of cereal into her fist. She brought her hand up and shoved the cereal into her mouth. Most didn't make it in, bits of cereal slipping through her fingers and falling to the floor. Into Marcus's hair.

"Mommy . . ."

Mom crunched. And crunched. Then sniffed again.

"Ghost . . ."

She caught the scent of something.

Her son.

"Boo."

Mom glanced down and found Marcus trembling in the cesspool of moldering kale and fuzzy tangerines. He wished he could have slipped his head below the surface of that puddle.

"There yooou are." Soggy bits of Cap'n Crunch slipped out of her mouth, tumbling down her chin as she grinned. "I've been looking everywheeere for you . . ."

Mom leapt off the countertop and landed on the floor next to him, only a few inches away. Her sunken eyes were glassed over. Her gray gums had receded around her teeth, exposing the roots. Her nose had collapsed, as if the cartilage itself had shriveled, leaving behind the crater of her skull. Her skin had a waxy pallor. Purple veins laced her face.

She looked sick. *Very* sick.

"It's Wednesday night . . . *Familyyyyyy Night.*"

Mom leaned forward. Her shriveled nose prodded his cheek, a loving, primal gesture.

"Let me get a good look at my baby boooy," she whispered. "My little angel."

Mom sniffed her son. She took in the aroma of him.

She licked the side of Marcus's face, beginning at his chin, moving up his cheek, over his ear, and through his hair. Wet flecks of Cap'n Crunch crusted the side of his head. Yellow scabs.

"Give me a hug."

Marcus whimpered as his mother brought him in closer, tighter, pressing him against her chest, her sunken, withered breasts clinging to his arm.

"That's my baby. My baby ghost boo boooo booooo boooobooboobooooobooooo . . ."

Mom pulled Marcus away and held him at arm's length, smiling.

"Let's whip you up some dinner," she said. "Something special, just for yooooou."

Mom reached for her juicer. She tucked the blender under her arm and brought it down to the floor with them, much like a mother cradling a newborn. The power cord snaked across the counter, still plugged in. Then Mom took her bare hand and grabbed hold of the closest scrap of food moldering on the floor. Whether it was a fruit or vegetable, Marcus couldn't tell, but Mom swiftly scooped it up, rotten bits dribbling through her fingers, and plopped it into the juicer's container. Mom repeated this sloppy motion, scraping up random chunks of food that had spilled out from the fridge and haphazardly tossing them into the blender.

Blue-and-white fuzzed tomatoes.

Splat.

A sunken and soggy green pepper.

Splat.

A hunk of crusted cheese.

Splat.

The lukewarm dregs of bottled kombucha tea.

Splat.

Mom flipped the Vitamix's switch. The blades rumbled to life, set at a low and steady grind that slowly whipped the soggy contents into a chunky salsa.

Marcus wanted to run. To escape. To cry. Mom must've sensed his plan because she suddenly clutched his forearm with a smile. "What else are we going to add to the mix?"

Mom glanced down at her hand that held his arm. Marcus's hand hovered above the open blender.

His tiny fingers.

Mom tugged.

Just a bit.

It drew Marcus in, his hand now uncomfortably close to the blender's open mouth.

Mom tugged again.

Harder this time.

A smile played upon her lips as she forced Marcus's hand even closer to the humming blades. *Deeper.* He balled his fingers into a fist, simply to keep them from touching the spinning cesspool of rotten food swirling below. And beneath that . . .

Mom tugged again. Harder. Lips peeling farther back.

Smiling she's smiling . . .

Marcus pulled on his own arm, struggling to free himself from his mother's vise-like grip. Her fingers tightened, cutting off the circulation to his hand. His fist was growing purple.

"Mom—"

She only forced his hand farther down. His knuckles dipped into the swirling pool.

"Mom, stop—"

His fingers sank below the spiraling surface. Deeper . . .

"Please, Mom—"

His hand was now wet, the pungent puddle splashing against his wrist. Deeper . . .

"PLEEEEASE!"

Marcus's slickened forearm slid out from between her fingers. He yanked his hand back, sending the blender over onto its side. A flood of rotten soup spread across the floor while the juicer's blades continued to spin, now bare, greedily whining their high-pitched shriek.

Marcus fell back onto his butt. He crab-walked backward, away from his mother. She let the blender continue to spin on its own, eclipsing all other sound, as she leaned her face over the floor and lapped up the purple puddle, making quick work of the mess he'd just made.

"*Mmm*," Mom said, licking her lips. "Yummy in the tummy, honey bunny . . ."

Marcus huddled into himself. He wanted to run, but his limbs refused to move.

Mom noticed him crying. Her grin flipped to a frown, sad, so sad, as if she were suddenly crestfallen by her youngest son's sobs.

"Poor baby ghost . . ."

Then her eyes widened. A look of joy. An epiphany.

"I have something for yooooou," she said. "A gift."

Mom brought her index finger up to her chapped, bleeding lips.

"*Sssh*. Don't tell your brother, mmkay?"

Mom climbed up the counter. Rummaged through the pots and pans. When she dropped to the floor, she had something in her hands. Something just for Marcus.

"An early Christmas present, just for yooooou . . ."

Mom held it out to him with both hands, the giddy grin returning to her lips.

His very own tablet. Brand new.

"Your father and I feel it's time you finally have your very own screeeeeen . . ."

DECEMBER 20
stage six: *possession*

DEVON

Today's the big day, ladies! YOGAMAMA announced from her live-cast. *The Great Reawakening is finally here! Who's ready to testify? Y'all with me?*

Devon Fairchild was so ready. She had reached peak immuno-logical radiance. She had scraped out the toxins until her intestines sparkled within. Now it was time to reawaken.

To testify.

She felt the energy resonate deep within her bones, humming with a delirious electricity. She'd worked so hard for this: prepping her body, maintaining her frame of mind.

And *waiting*. God, the wait had been endless . . .

No longer. YOGAMAMA had given her the green light for her own enlightenment. *Time to WAKE UP, gals! It's a new dawn! A new day! Time to OPEN YOUR EYES once and for all!*

This video testimonial was the final step in Devon becoming THE WAKE-UP CALL. Not only did she need to testify, she needed to offer something of herself up to the sirens.

A sacrifice.

You need to leave your flesh behind, YOGAMAMA instructed. *Give us your body and enter the warm digital stream of selfies. Give yourself over to the virtual tide and simply . . . drift.*

All Devon ever wanted was to belong to this echelon of well-ness women. They were her friends. Her mentors. She had learned so much from them, painstakingly studying their video testimonials until she could recite every last maxim, knowing each and every video by heart.

Now it was time.

She could feel herself breaking away from her body. This fleshy frame was only holding her down, weighing her to this world. All she wanted was to dig her fingers into her chest and crack her rib cage open, let the butterfly of her soul breathe freely and emerge triumphant.

Something great awaits you, YOGAMAMA promised. *Something . . . miraculous. Feel it?*

Yes, Devon felt it.

The kitchen was all hers. It was difficult to tell what time of day it was. The shades were pulled but Devon didn't feel like peeking. It could've been night. Or morning. It didn't matter.

Outside the world was burning. She could nearly feel herself choking on the smoke.

I am ready for my close-up, Mr. DeMille, she thought with a giddy, dizzy grin.

She didn't have a ring light for perfectly balanced luminosity. Her phone's flashlight would have to do. She would've preferred something a little softer on her features, but beggars can't be choosers. She set up her cell on the counter, propping it against her Vitamix. She flipped the camera to selfie mode, framing the angle perfectly, and took herself in.

Look at her. Just look . . . The sirens of Instagram may have all been natural beauties, but Devon recognized she needed a bit more upkeep.

Just a little foundation to conceal the gray sagging bags of skin under the eyes . . .

A little blush on her hollow, flayed cheeks . . .

There, that's better. Good as new. Better than new. Devon was . . . reborn. No!

Reawakened.

She could barely contain her excitement, mounting with every sandpaper rasp that dragged across her throat. She could hardly keep her eyes open, on the cusp of passing out from the anticipation. The nervousness of it all. What would she become? Who would she be?

What would she see now that her eyes were open?

Devon tugged out her tablet and rested it on the countertop so its screen faced the ceiling. She swiped, unlocking it. The screen awakened, casting a cool blue glow over her face that made her gums look gray. She'd recently lost a lower incisor, but that was okay.

Two screens.

Two portals.

Devon composed herself. She cleared her throat. Deep breath. Her finger wormed its way toward her iPhone's screen, pressed record, aaaaand . . .

Showtime.

"Hey, y'all . . . It's me, NOMAMADRAMA, coming to you live . . ." Devon coughed up something wet. Spat it out. Whatever it was, the thick globule hit the kitchen floor with a *splkk!*

Devon started over again. "Hey y'all. It's NOMAMADRAMA. I'm coming to you live and in the flesh today, on this very special day . . . The Great Reawakening! Are y'all as excited as I am?"

There was a tickle at the back of her throat. That's okay. A little huskiness was sexy. Like Kathleen Turner. Remember her? Devon didn't mind a cigarettes-and-whiskey tinge to her voice.

"I just wanted to thank you all for following me these last few weeks. Your support has been such a blessing. I couldn't have gone on this journey without all of you cheering me on."

Devon glanced down at her open tablet. The dull glow flickered, its dim—

gaslights the

glorious

glorious

gas

—light fading, distracting Devon for a moment, almost as if the Wi-Fi had momentarily disconnected. But just as quickly as she'd lost her train of thought, the glow on her tablet brightened, back up to its full power, and Devon snapped back.

"I want to give a special shout-out to YogaMama. You've been my bright, shining star . . . I couldn't have woken up without you. You helped me . . . open my eyes once and for all . . ."

Devon stared down at her tablet.

Her holy healing tablet.

Devon couldn't help but think of Moses for a moment, just a brief fleeting thought of him and his stone tablets, the Ten Commandments, inscribed by the very finger of God.

Or something like that.

It had been so long since she'd seen the Charlton Heston movie. *How did it go again?* She barely remembered. *Didn't Moses smash those tablets? Something about a golden calf?*

Before she could second-guess herself, Devon quickly reared back her hand and—

CRNCH

—brought her fist down, punching her tablet's screen so hard it crackled.

aaaah

Devon hissed through her teeth, feeling the dull crumble of glass under her knuckles. A fine dusting of aluminum silicate now covered her skin, digging its little teeth in.

ow ow ow

The tablet's screen was made of tougher material than Moses's stone. It wasn't like a window or plate glass. This was a thinner substance, the shards clinging together even after Devon repeatedly brought her fist down and down and down, over and over again.

"It's time to—"

crnch

"—wake up."

crnch

"Time to—"

crnch

"—open our—"

crnch

"—eyes."

It took five strikes for the glow to finally futz out. Now all that was left was a spider's web of fractures and cracks spun across the screen.

Devon's knuckles were lanced with cuts. She could feel minuscule flecks of glass powdering the back of her hand, embedded into her fingers, like a light dusting of sugar.

"Are y'all ready . . . out there? Ready for . . . the Great Reawakening? I know I . . . sure am . . ."

Something caught Devon's attention.

There. On the counter.

An oily shimmer.

A thin pearlescent trail of dried slime extended across the countertop. She ran her finger over it. The tackiness stung, like static electricity. The trail began at her tablet's cracked screen.

What . . . is that? She leaned over the counter, following the trail, until she spotted it.

A slug.

Or at least something that moved like one. So slimy. So . . . *shiny*. Pink and purple and green. Oil-spill hues rippled and spiraled across its glimmering skin. This determined worm inched its way down the other end of the counter, patiently working its way toward the floor.

Where did you come from, little fella?

Devon quickly pinched it between her fingers. The slug squirmed against her skin. It was cold. Slippery. It flexed backward, bringing its writhing lips across her cuticles.

Now there was a trail of slime across Devon's fingernail. It shimmered. A tiny screen on her index finger. It looked like she'd given herself a new manicure, lacquering her nails in a swirling polish of oil.

Devon brought the slug up to her nose. She took a whiff, then popped it into her mouth.

It crunched.

Aaah . . . Devon wasn't expecting that. It wasn't soft and squishy at all, but brittle. Like glass. The shards dug into her gums and sliced at the inside of her cheek's lining.

But she couldn't stop now.

Look at those pesky li'l buggers go! *Come back!* Devon had to catch them before they got away. She picked up another wriggling shard and tossed it into her mouth like popcorn.

Crnch crnch crnch.

Then another.

Crnch crnch.

Swallowing the glass was tough, but at least the blood gave her something to help wash it down. With each strained gulp, the shards slicing at the lining of her throat, she took a moment to regain her composure, spit out some of the blood pooling in her mouth . . . and smile.

Smile for the camera.

"I want to thank . . . *hyooorch* . . . all my . . . followers . . . for—"

Something came back up.

A slender tendril of pink glass and drool trickled down her chin and hit the countertop.

But Devon didn't stop. She couldn't stop now.

"Thanks for . . . sticking . . . *hyuulp* . . . with me. We're . . . all in . . . this . . . together."

Devon had never felt better. Never felt healthier, happier in all her life. She felt *well*. Her well of wellness was absolutely brimming, overflowing with healthiness. Happiness. Joy.

"You can find your—*hyulch*—inner goddess, too . . . You just have to . . . to let her free."

Her throat was in tatters. Her teeth spilled out from her mouth and tumbled across the counter. But she kept smiling for the camera.

She needed something to drink. Something fresh to wash this all down.

Her Vitamix.

Of course.

Devon dragged her splendid blender across the counter, making sure it was in frame. She tossed the container's lid away, then the flipped the switch and cranked it all the way up to purée.

The blades instantly sang their high-pitched whine, blurrily whirring to life.

vrrrrrrrmmmm

Devon couldn't help but feel a bit mesmerized by the ring of stainless-steel teeth spinning just inches away, *round and round and round they go, where they stop . . .*

Devon plunged her fist into the blender.

VRRRRRRRRRRRRM!

The pitch of the blades immediately shifted into a higher octave as Devon pressed her knuckles farther in. The flesh sprayed away first, sending a red mist up the sides of the container.

Since there was no lid, Devon got a bit of an eyeful of her own warm soup. When the blades reached bone, the tone lowered even further, grinding against her metacarpals.

SSSSSKRRRRRRRRKKKKRRRRRKRRRRRRRM!

By the time Devon pulled her hand out, well, there wasn't much of a hand left. Everything above her wrist flipped and flopped in a spongy, stringy tangle. Flecks of flesh draped over Vitamixed shards of bone. Fresh blood pumped freely from the pulpy suet.

But look how fresh that smoothie was!

Devon drank right out of the container, bringing it up to her lips and tilting her head back, guzzling the warm purée as if it were salty gazpacho. She'd never tasted anything like it.

"This is my testament." Devon belched, wiping the blood from her lips with her bare arm. "I am ready . . . to wake up. I'm ready to . . . to open my . . . eyes."

She took another swig, tilting her neck back until the fluid spilled down her cheeks.

"I am the Wake-Up Call! I am the messenger sent to—"

Devon cut herself off, her attention now drawn toward the refrigerator.

Someone was standing behind the open door.

Hiding.

At least she thought it was someone. It was too dark to see. The
bulb inside the fridge cast a lens flare of warmth, a faint spotlight.
Devon had to shield her eyes, bringing her hand up and holding back
the light, *the gaslight*, the blinding burning light . . .

Blackened fingers gripped the door.

Whoever—*whatever*—they were, now leaned to one side, peering
out. They were wrapped in shadows—no, they *were* the shadows—
skin burnt to a crisp.

YOGAMAMA. It was Larissa. Her cindered flesh. Eyes shimmering like fish scales. The first thought to pop into Devon's head
was—

demon

—but just as quickly as she thought it, the word itself was gone.
Washed downstream.

Are you ready to awaken, gurl?

"Goddess, yes . . ."

Well, then, all you need to do is—

CLICK HERE

ASHER

"How's Marcus feeling?" The tone of the woman's voice held too
much sunshine. Far too buoyant for Asher's ears at this hour. He
focused all of his attention on the oversized button pinned to her
shawl-collared cardigan's lapel. It was a picture of a cat precariously
dangling from a shelf.

Hang in there!

When Asher didn't reply straightaway, the woman behind the

desk said, "We called Mrs. Fairchild a few times, just to check in, once we realized he'd been absent for a few days."

"He's, uh . . . he's been sick."

This seemed to sate the woman. She leaned back in her rolly chair, nodding. "There's definitely something going around. Nearly half the kids are out. Never seen anything like it."

Asher just stood there, in the main office. The walls were covered with artwork. Children's drawings. Collages. Squiggly pictures that seemed to wriggle in the corner of his eye.

He glanced at his watch. What time did Tammany say? The Great Reawakening was kick-starting any minute now, and that meant Asher needed to act fast. Open people's eyes.

He was the Wake-Up Call, after all.

"Any big Christmas plans?"

Asher snapped back. "Sorry?"

"Christmas. Got any plans with the fam?"

Did Asher even know it was Christmas?

"A cruise," he said.

"Ooooh, I'm jealous. Where to?"

"Bahamas." He coughed. Something was stuck in his throat. He coughed again, dislodging whatever phlegmy tumor was lodged in his chest. Now he had to swallow it down.

"Was there something you needed help with today?" the woman asked, still polite as ever, but Asher could sense her chipperness was chipping around the edges. Her smile wavered just a bit. "Did you want to pick up some of Marcus's schoolbooks?"

Asher nodded, coughing again. He was so parched. So dry.

"Let me see if I can get his teacher to come down. If you don't mind just waiting here . . ."

No. No, he couldn't wait here. The teachers were hiding.

Hiding *them*.

Asher was certain of it. He just had to find out where. Which room. He hadn't come with a particular plan other than to walk in and find them, expose them to the rest of the world.

Prove none of this is real.

He needed to reach the classrooms—the special ones—where they kept the crisis actors. They were probably practicing a new scene even now.

That's probably why this beam of bubbling sunshine with the double-fucking-chin wouldn't let him go any farther. She didn't want him to see what was hiding in the classrooms.

Asher had to go. *Now.* Catch these lizards in the act before it was too late.

The woman was on the phone, calling up Marcus's teacher. *More like warning her,* Tammany whispered into his ear. *Better hurry, big man . . . They're probably on to you by now.*

Asher glanced over his shoulder, hoping not to look too suspicious. The main office was walled off with windows, an aquarium for the administrative staff. Asher had a vantage point of the school's central thoroughfare, a straight shot that stretched on for several classrooms.

Clock's ticking, big man . . . Now's your chance.

Asher bolted for the door.

"Mr. Fairchild?" the woman behind the main desk called out, but Asher was already out of the office by then, racing down the hall. "Mr. Fairchild—wait!"

No turning back now. He had to hurry.

Which room?

The classrooms all looked the same. Where the fuck did they keep them? The crisis students? The test tube kids? These lizard children had to be here somewhere. Hiding.

They looked like normal kids—but they weren't. They weren't real children at all. You just had to look closely enough. Adjust the motion smoothing. Then you'd know the difference.

Then you'd see.

If Asher could just prove to the people at home, prove to Paul

Tammany's audience, that it was all an act, just for show, then he'd prove himself to Paul. Show him that he was worthy.

This was it. His moment. The Wake-Up Call. He had a message to deliver today.

But where? Where in the hell were they hiding?

Which room which room which—

Asher stumbled into a classroom.

The students—third graders, maybe?—were sitting in a circle where their teacher read to them from a book about transsexuals. All heads turned toward him with wide-open eyes.

Nope, not these kids. They were real. "Sorry," Asher mumbled, ducking out into the hall.

Time. He didn't have enough time. They'd be after him soon.

Which room which room which room . . .

His heart pounded.

Which room which room which . . .

Skull throbbed.

. . . room which room which room?

Asher spotted a collage Scotch-taped to the door of another classroom. Bits and pieces of photos clipped from glossy magazines had been reassembled into new images. He saw body parts. Plump lips. Oversized eyes that didn't match. These weren't people. They were pixelated.

Here. This must be them.

Asher burst through the door, out of breath. The room looked like any other room—

that's what they want you to believe

—complete with student-drawn artwork. There was a bunny in a cage in the far corner. Someone had scribbled its name on a sheet of construction paper: *PROFESSOR HOWDY.*

The students. The students were all at their tiny desks. So young. First graders, maybe?

Marcus's age.

Twenty children total, from the quick head count Asher did. They all turned, staring back at him with bovine eyes. Empty of expression. They were all hollow. But just under their skin . . .

Below their cheeks . . .

Another face hid. Blurry features in sore need of some motion smoothing.

Bingo. Found them.

Look. Just *look* at them all . . . These weren't children. They just looked like them. Anyone could see that these—these *things* were mere approximations of people, of children, made to look like our kids. But they weren't. They had no parents. No family. They weren't even human.

"Can I help you?" The teacher—a young woman with cropped hair, a lesbian maybe, in her late twenties—stood up from her desk, quickly making her way toward Asher.

"It," Asher started, struggling to catch his breath, "it's not—not real—"

"Is there something that I can—"

Asher struck her.

Hard.

Several students screamed as their teacher hit the floor. A shriek of chairs scraping over linoleum filled the room. Kids leapt out of their seats, clustering in the far corner as Ash stomped his heel down on her head, feeling her skull eventually split like a melon. A special effect.

Look. Just look at their exaggerated terror. These students had been trained for this. Rehearsed for this very moment.

See? Tammany was right. Had always been right. *All a part of the show, folks . . .*

Asher locked the door.

"It's not real," he said as he stepped toward the cluster of cowering children. He wasn't looking where he was going, accidentally knocking into a tiny desk and sending it toppling over.

"None of this is real. Here," Asher said as he closed in. "I'll show you."

The bunny was pacing its cage, unable to escape.

"It's okay," Asher said. "It's okay, I am the Wake-Up Call. I'm supposed to show you."

He hadn't brought anything to help. What tool could he use to expose their lies? Peel their masks back and show the world what was hiding underneath? There were so many school supplies lying around. Would a pencil work? A stapler?

Ash spotted a pair of scissors resting on the teacher's desk.

There. That'll do the trick.

A funny thought popped into his head: *How is Tammany going to talk about me?*

There would be cameras. The local news was probably on their way already. The coverage would feed their reporting to the national affiliates, and from there the cable networks would pick it up. Get in on this while the getting was good. CNN. MSNBC. FAX.

They would squeeze this story dry, down to the last drop of blood. Asher's blood.

He knew how CNN would report on it. He could nearly hear the *tsk-tsk*ing coming from Anderson Cooper's mouth before they'd even scripted it.

But what about Paul? What about his people? His core demo? Would the Tammany Army see Ash as an ally? An emissary of their truth? Would they bow their heads and take a moment of silence on the air to honor one of their own fallen comrades?

This was for them. Asher was doing this for their sake. Wouldn't they see that?

They would tell his story the right way. The *dignified* way.

Everyone's eyes would be opened. Time for everyone to wake up.

The Great Reawakening was finally upon them.

"*Just the fax*," he said, stepping forward and doing what had to be done.

CALEB

Caleb stood in front of his English class. He didn't look so well, to be honest. Both nostrils were crusted in rusty scabs. He was wearing his cross-country team's sweatsuit, stained and stiff, hood pulled over his head, sweatpants swallowing the contours of his withered body. The bags under his eyes testified to several sleepless nights. His hair was greasy, auburn tentacles reaching out from beneath his hood.

He hadn't showed up to school in days. Weeks, now. His GPA was at risk of deep-sixing itself completely. At this rate, he'd be forced to repeat the eleventh grade.

Well, look who decided to show up, he could imagine everyone thinking. *When was the last time he showered?* He didn't know himself. The funk lifting off his body seemed to suggest it had been days. Jeez, weeks. *What is up with him? Is he actually sick? On drugs?*

Twenty students sat at their desks, their attention drifting in all directions. Some slumped deeper into their seats. Some doodled along the margins of their notebooks.

He hadn't commanded their complete attention.

Yet.

"I—" Caleb cleared his throat. Tried to, at least. It was a wet hack at the back of his esophagus, congested with something phlegmy. "I have something to say."

A few students glanced up, then dropped their eyes, back in their own personal worlds.

Worlds that didn't involve Caleb.

"Caleb?" his teacher, Mrs. Meader, asked. "You okay, hon? Do you need to go to the nurse's office?"

After another moment of uneasy silence, this standoff between Caleb and his class, his chapped lips finally split and he spoke. "Today I'd like to talk about . . . talk about . . ."

What was he supposed to talk about?

Sylvia Plath's *The Bell Jar*. His report had been due a week ago, but Mrs. Meader was willing to let it slide, as long as Caleb finished the oral portion before the end of the semester.

"I want . . ." Caleb's nose began to bleed again. He didn't wipe the blood away, letting it trickle down his lips this time, over his chin. "I want to talk . . ."

Eyes dropped. Some rolled. Nobody was paying attention. His voice barely carried to the front row, let alone the back. He was a nonentity. A mealy-mouthed absence.

Until he smashed his head against the whiteboard.

Caleb simply turned from his class, facing the vast expanse of white behind him and—

Thwonk!

—slammed his face straight against its flat surface.

That certainly seized everyone's attention.

One girl gasped. Samantha Havemeyer sat in the front row and watched it happen. Benjamin Pendleton, far in the back, caught it too, more by mistake, but still. He couldn't help but guffaw, stupefied by it all. Nobody moved, though, suddenly frozen within their seats.

So Caleb did it again.

Thwonk!

"Caleb!" Mrs. Meader stepped forward, then halted the second Caleb turned around.

A purple welt had already begun to blossom along his forehead. Both nostrils were bleeding, two red rivers converging into a thickened rivulet of blood that ran into his mouth.

"I have a message." When Caleb smiled, his teeth were red. "You're not gonna like it."

Benjamin Pendleton was the first to pull out his cell phone. He held it up and recorded Caleb. Another student pulled out their camera as well, recording. It was such a knee-jerk reaction, Caleb thought with contempt—capturing the moment on camera. Rather than stand up from their seats and help, see if he was all right, they videotaped him. Livestreamed it. The lens put enough distance between Caleb and themselves that they could pretend this moment wasn't happening to them, too. As if they weren't even there. It was more pressing to share this slice of life than to participate in it. The moment needed to be spread rather than resolved.

Good. Caleb had everyone's undivided attention now. He waited until there were at least five cameras recording him. He peeled back his hoodie, flesh ripping free along with it.

"Today's the Great Reawakening," he said with a sudden sense of self-assuredness, his voice sturdier. Deeper, even. It dropped to an octave that didn't sound natural. It couldn't have come from a boy's throat. It sounded like someone else. A ventriloquist. "Time to wake up."

Caleb Fairchild was the Wake-Up Call.

"Time to open your—"

One moment, he was standing before his class, arms held out. The next, he was . . . *gone.*

Evaporated.

Poof.

Pink mist. Uploaded to the cloud. From his classmates' perspective, the videos they livestreamed, it simply looked as if Caleb's body had disintegrated in a bloody eruption.

The homemade explosive he had been wearing underneath his hoodie detonated in a red flash. He had strapped the device around his chest. It took an entire roll of duct tape to secure the bomb in place, his baggy sweats softening any remaining awkward angles or bulges.

The cinder-block walls contained the blast itself, but the sound of the explosion reverberated through the hallways. Neighboring classrooms could even feel the vibrations of it.

The blast wave sent the contents of the classroom toppling back. The overpressure thrust Mrs. Meader against the far wall, slamming her skull and rendering her unconscious.

The physiological composition of his classmates was completely disrupted by the explosion. There was the rupturing of organs.

Hemorrhaging. Think of soft-boiled eggs. The yolk rent asunder by a sudden jolt, now oozing out from the tender intestinal casing.

Caleb's body parts dispersed in the blast wind. He was now shrapnel. His own bone fragments embedded themselves inside his classmates. Those sitting in the front row suffered the brunt of the explosion, shards of bone digging through their soft tissue. Their faces.

His blood basted the walls, but his message was sent. Caleb made a meme of himself, and with the help of his classmates, he was able to reach a wider audience.

There was the immediate blast radius, the damage done within the classroom, but what about the secondary blast? The tertiary? Quaternary?

Caleb's internet challenge would soon be everywhere. How long before other kids picked up where he left off?

What Caleb understood, thanks to the teachings of ELZE-GAN911, is this: there is the immediate pain you can inflict, the immediate impact you can have, but there is an even *greater* impact that goes well beyond the reach of one person, one body, one moment in time. There is the world at large, the global stage, the spread, the sprawl. Those are the real targets. The true aim. To reach them, you need to leave your body behind.

If you really want to wake people up, you need to go viral.

To spread into a million glimmering fragments.

FAMILY NIGHT

It's Wednesday night.

Family night.

WAKEUPOPENYOUREYESWAKEUPOPEN YOUREYESWAKEUPOPENYOUREYESWAKEUPOPEN YOUREYESWAKEUPOPENYOUREYESWAKEUPOPEN YOUREYESWAKEUPOPENYOUREYESWAKEUPOPEN YOUREYESWAKEUPOPENYOUREYESWAKEUPOPEN

YOUREYESWAKEUPOPENYOUREYESWAKEUPOPEN
YOUREYESWAKEUPOPENYOUREYESWAKEUPOPEN
YOUREYESWAKEUPOPENYOUREYESWAKEUPOPEN
YOUREYESWAKEUPOPENYOUREYESWAKEUPOPEN
YOUREYESWAKEUPOPENYOUREYESWAKEUPOPEN
YOUREYESWAKEUPOPENYOUREYESWAKEUPOPEN
YOUREYESWAKEUPOPENYOUREYESWAKEUPOPEN
YOUREYESWAKEUPOPENYOUREYESWAKEUPOPEN
YOUREYESWAKEUPOPENYOUREYESWAKEUPOPEN
YOUREYESWAKEUPOPENYOUREYESWAKEUPOPEN
YOUREYESWAKEUPOPENYOUREYESWAKEUPOPEN
YOUREYESWAKEUPOPENYOUREYESWAKEUPOPEN
YOUREYESWAKEUPOPENYOUREYESWAKEUPOPEN
YOUREYESWAKEUPOPENYOUREYESWAKEUPOPEN
YOUREYESWAKEUPOPENYOUREYESWAKEUPOPEN
YOUREYESWAKEUPOPENYOUREYESWAKEUPOPEN
YOUREYESWAKEUPOPENYOUREYESWAKEUPOPEN
YOUREYESWAKEUPOPENYOUREYESWAKEUPOPEN
YOUREYESWAKEUPOPENYOUREYESWAKEUPOPEN
YOUREYESWAKEUPOPENYOUREYESWAKEUPOPEN
YOUREYESWAKEUPOPENYOUREYESWAKEUPOPEN
YOUREYESWAKEUPOPENYOUREYESWAKEUPOPEN
YOUREYESWAKEUPOPENYOUREYESWAKEUPOPEN
YOUREYESWAKEUPOPENYOUREYESWAKEUPOPEN
YOUREYESWAKEUPOPENYOUREYESWAKEUPOPEN
YOUREYESWAKEUPOPENYOUREYESWAKEUPOPEN
YOUREYESWAKEUPOPENYOUREYESWAKEUPOPEN
YOUREYESWAKEUPOPENYOUREYESWAKEUPOPEN
YOUREYESWAKEUPOPENYOUREYESWAKEUPOPEN
YOUREYESWAKEUPOPENYOUREYESWAKEUPOPEN
YOUREYESWAKEUPOPENYOUREYESWAKEUPOPEN
YOUREYESWAKEUPOPENYOUREYESWAKEUPOPEN

YOUREYESWAKEUPOPENYOUREYESWAKEUPOPEN
YOUREYESWAKEUPOPENYOUREYESWAKEUPOPEN
YOUREYESWAKEUPOPENYOUREYESWAKEUPOPEN
YOUREYESWAKEUPOPENYOUREYESWAKEUPOPEN
YOUREYESWAKEUPOPENYOUREYESWAKEUPOPEN
YOUREYESWAKEUPOPENYOUREYESWAKEUPOPEN
YOUREYESWAKEUPOPENYOUREYESWAKEUPOPEN
YOUREYESWAKEUPOPENYOUREYESWAKEUPOPEN
YOUREYESWAKEUPOPENYOUREYESWAKEUPOPEN
YOUREYESWAKEUPOPENYOUREYESWAKEUPOPEN
YOUREYESWAKEUPOPENYOUREYESWAKEUPOPEN
YOUREYESWAKEUPOPENYOUREYESWAKEUPOPEN
YOUREYESWAKEUPOPENYOUREYESWAKEUPOPEN
YOUREYESWAKEUPOPENYOUREYESWAKEUPOPEN
YOUREYESWAKEUPOPENYOUREYESWAKEUPOPEN
YOUREYESWAKEUPOPENYOUREYESWAKEUPOPEN
YOUREYESWAKEUPOPENYOUREYESWAKEUPOPEN
YOUREYESWAKEUPOPENYOUREYESWAKEUPOPEN
YOUREYESWAKEUPOPENYOUREYESWAKEUPOPEN
YOUREYESWAKEUPOPENYOUREYESWAKEUPOPEN
YOUREYESWAKEUPOPENYOUREYESWAKEUPOPEN
YOUREYESWAKEUPOPENYOUREYESWAKEUPOPEN
YOUREYESWAKEUPOPENYOUREYESWAKEUPOPEN
YOUREYESWAKEUPOPENYOUREYESWAKEUPOPEN
YOUREYESWAKEUPOPENYOUREYESWAKEUPOPEN
YOUREYESWAKEUPOPENYOUREYESWAKEUPOPEN
YOUREYESWAKEUPOPENYOUREYESWAKEUPOPEN
YOUREYESWAKEUPOPENYOUREYESWAKEUPOPEN
YOUREYESWAKEUPOPENYOUREYESWAKEUPOPEN
YOUREYES . . .

Phase Three

HOLY WAR

And he asked him, "What is thy name?" And he answered, saying, "My name is Legion: for we are many." And he begged Jesus again and again not to send them out of the area.

A large herd of pigs was feeding on the nearby hillside. The demons begged Jesus, "Send us among the pigs; allow us to go into them." He gave them permission, and the impure spirits came out and went into the pigs. The herd, about two thousand in number, rushed down the steep bank into the lake and were drowned.

—MARK 5:9–13

VIDEO #1: 12/20 at 2:58 p.m. EST/Savannah, Georgia

(Personal cell phone footage recorded by Adam Davidson [32], deceased.)

DAVIDSON: Yeah, we're recording now. Somebody's got to document the Big Day. If you know, you know—know what I'm saying? And if you don't know, well . . . you will pretty soon, won't you? There's a storm coming, folks. See those clouds?

(Davidson turns camera away from himself, records a blue sky.)

DAVIDSON: The Great Reawakening's finally here, bitches! We got the TV turned on to our main man Tammany, just like he said. The boys are standing by until we get the signal. The Wake-Up Call's a-coming. Then we take this country back.

(Davidson trains camera on a Diamondback DB15 5.56 NATO Semi-Automatic Rifle AR-15. Davidson turns camera back onto himself. Smiles.)

DAVIDSON: Say hello to my little friend . . . He might not be exactly legal in our fair state, but I think once we get the go-ahead, it won't matter much what the law says. First order of business is going to be to—going to—to—to—to—

(Pause.)

DAVIDSON: Wake up.

(Pause.)

DAVIDSON: First order of business is . . . is going to be . . . to . . . to wake up.

(Pause.)

DAVIDSON: Wake up. Wake up. Wake up. Wake up. Wake up. Wake up wake up wake up wake up wake up wake up wake up and open your eeeeeeeeeeeeyes.

(Camera drops. Sounds of movement. Recording continues in silence.)

VIDEO #4: 12/20 at 2:59 p.m. EST/Westport, Connecticut
(Rachel LaRocca's TikTok ["deserveUReyes"] livestream.)

LAROCCA: Hi, everybody . . . My name is Rachel and, um . . . today I'm doing the Wake-Up Call challenge. It's almost three o'clock and I—uh, I think all I'm supposed to do is, like, connect with the rest and . . . say the words. Deep breaths. Okay, here we go . . . Wish me luck!

(Pause.)

LAROCCA: I offer up my body to purify. I am unsullied. Undefiled. I offer my virtuous flesh. I offer my sinless skin. I offer my inviolate body. Time to, um . . . wake up. Open my eyes.

(Pause.)

LAROCCA: I said . . . it's time to wake up. Open my eyes.

(Pause.)

LAROCCA: Wake up. Wake up!

(Pause.)

LAROCCA: Shit. Shit. Nothing happened. Why did nothing happen? Why didn't—

(LaRocca hits herself in the forehead with her phone as it continues to record.)

LAROCCA: —it work why—

(Hits herself with phone.)

LAROCCA: —didn't it work why—

(Hits herself with phone.)

LAROCCA: —why why why—

(Hits herself with phone.)

LAROCCA: I want to wake up—

(Hits herself with phone.)

LAROCCA: Wake up—

(Hits herself with phone.)

LAROCCA: Wake up—

(Hits herself with phone.)

LAROCCA: Wake up—

(Hits herself with phone.)

LAROCCA: Wake—

(Livestream ends.)

VIDEO #9: 12/20 at 2:59 p.m. EST/Tampa Bay, Florida
(Livestream recording from Karina Harrison's phone, including Jenna Knighton [deceased], Lindsay Hearst [deceased], and Felicia Camp [deceased].)

HARRISON: *Margaritamommies!* Cheers, everyone! To the Great Reawakening!

ALL: To the Great Reawakening!

HEARST: I forgot to salt my rim.

CAMP: What is that? There's a little kick to it . . . Is that cayenne pepper?

HARRISON: Guess again. You'll never get it. It's Old Bay seasoning.

CAMP: Oooh, I love it.

HARRISON: I know, right? I read about it online . . .

KNIGHTON: Is it time?

HARRISON: Lean in, ladies. Good. To all our soul-sustenance sisters out there—

(Everyone lifts their glasses to the camera.)

HEARST: Heeeey . . .

HARRISON: We thought it would be a fun to share this moment with all of you . . .

CAMP: Hiyeeeee . . .

HARRISON: So if you got the Facebook invite, welcome. Hope you got a glass of something bubbly to sip. We're only—oh—a minute away from the big day!

HEARST: I told our nanny to turn the TV on for the kids. Let them watch at home.

CAMP: What about Bill?

HEARST: What about him?

CAMP: *(Laughing.)* You are so bad, Lindsay!

HEARST: I told him I was at yoga. I don't know if he even knows—

HARRISON: Oh! Oh! Quiet down, shh! Shh! It's time, everybody. It's time!

HEARST: Let's do a countdown!

CAMP: Great idea! Glasses up, girls! Raise those glasses!

HARRISON: Ten seconds . . .

ALL: Nine . . . eight . . . seven . . .

CAMP: Eeeek, I'm so excited!

ALL: Six . . . five . . . four . . .

HEARST: Here's to a new era, ladies!

ALL: Three . . .

HARRISON: A new dawn—

ALL: Two . . .

HARRISON: —for a new woman!

ALL: One!

(Pause.)

CAMP: Is . . . ? Is that it? Did it happen?

HEARST: Are you sure you got the time right?

HARRISON: The Facebook invite said three o'clock. It's three o'clock on the—

(Knighton drives her glass into Harrison's face, shattering it against her eyes.)

KNIGHTON: Wake up.

(Harrison bites down on Knighton's glass, crunching on it as she speaks.)

HARRISON: Open—your—eyes.

(Harrison drives her glass into Knighton's neck, shattering, slicing her throat.)

HARRISON: Wake up—and open—your eyes.

(Hearst drives her glass into Harrison's head three times.)

HEARST: Open—

(First stab.)

HEARST: —your—

(Second stab.)

HEARST: —eyes.

(Third stab. The glass's stem remains lodged in Harrison's head.)

CAMP: Wake up.

(Camp drives her glass into Hearst's lower jaw, cutting her throat.)

CAMP: Time to—

(Camp removes the remnants of her shattered glass from Hearst's lower jaw.)

CAMP: Open your—

(Camp drives the stem of her shattered glass into her left eye.)

(Livestream continues for thirty-seven additional minutes in silence.)

VIDEO #6: 12/20 at 2:01 p.m. CST/Minneapolis, Minnesota
(Body-worn camera footage from Metro Police Department depicts assault on Officer Tony Malinenko [deceased] by unknown assailant.)

(Officer Malinenko approaches Assailant #1 (unknown)—female, Caucasian, 30s—in street.)

MALINENKO: Ma'am? Excuse me, ma'am? You mind stepping out of the street?

(No response.)

MALINENKO: Ma'am, I'm going to ask you again. Step out of the street, please.

(Indecipherable muttering.)

MALINENKO: Ma'am, are you under the influence of alcohol or any controlled substance? We been having ourselves a little too much fun? Pretty early in the—

ASSAILANT #1 (UNKNOWN): Bliss-skimmer.

MALINENKO: Okay, I think we've had enough fun for one—

ASSAILANT #1 (UNKNOWN): Be a wealth of wellness.

(Assailant #1 charges at Officer Malinenko.)

MALINENKO: Whoa, whoa—

(Assailant #1 scratches Officer Malinenko's face.)

MALINENKO: Goddamn it. My—my fucking eye—

ASSAILANT #1 (UNKNOWN): Your body, your temple.

(Assailant #1 pounces upon Officer Malinenko.)

ASSAILANT #1 (UNKNOWN): Healthy body—

MALINENKO: Get off me—

ASSAILANT #1 (UNKNOWN): —healthy mind, healthy body, healthy mind—

(Shot fired.)

ASSAILANT #1 (UNKNOWN): —healthy body, body, bod—

MALINENKO: Jesus—

(Multiple shots fired.)

MALINENKO: Oh. Oh Jesus. Jesus Christ. What the—what the fuck. What the . . .

(Pause.)

MALINENKO: Dispatch. 10-47. Repeat 10—

(Officer Malinenko is assaulted by three unknown assailants.)

MALINENKO: Holy—

ASSAILANT #2 (UNKNOWN): Just the facts.

(Officer Malinenko is dragged across the pavement by his arms.)

MALINENKO: Help! Help me! Help—

ASSAILANT #2 (UNKNOWN): Just the facts.

ASSAILANT #3 (UNKNOWN): Just the facts.

ASSAILANT #4 (UNKNOWN): Just the facts.

(Video cuts out.)

VIDEO #72: 12/20 at 3:03 p.m. EST/Bronx, New York
(Cell phone footage at wedding ceremony for Kelsey and Tyrell Rumfit.)

(Hotel ballroom. Several individuals (unknown) dance. Indistinct chatter.)

MALE #1: "Do the humpty hump! Do the humpty hump!"

MALE #2: Holy shit, check it out.

MALE #1: What kind of dance is that, Gram? You a breakdancer now?

MALE #2: Go, wela! Go, wela! Go—

MALE #1: Oh my God, is she wasted? Grandma's been drinking too much punch—

MALE #2: Hey—hey, Grandma. Be careful. You're going to break a hip if you're—

MALE #1: Whoa!

MALE #2: You okay? You okay, Grandma?

MALE #1: Jesus, look at her knee—

MALE #2: Gram! Don't move, don't move. Here, let me get some help—

MALE #1: The fuck—her fucking knee is bent backward—

MALE #2: Put the camera down and help me—

FEMALE: E is coming.

MALE #2: Grandma, Grandma—you can't move—

FEMALE: E is here.

MALE #2: Grandma, get off me—

MALE #1: The fuck—

(Screams.)

MALE #2: My ear—my fucking ear—

FEMALE: E is with me and I am E.

VIDEO #28: 12/20 at 12:03 p.m. PST/Olympic Valley, California
(Taken from Mobile Video Audio Recording System from Tahoe Valley Police squad car #1034. Officers on duty: Jermaine Nichols and Jennifer Choi.)

NICHOLS: —responding to a call about a riot. We know what they're protesting?

CHOI: Nope. News to fucking me.

NICHOLS: Dispatch—what's the number on the crowd? We got eyes on—

CHOI: Look out! Look—

(Assailant #1—female, Caucasian, 70s—runs into traffic. Squad car veers abruptly to the left in order to avoid contact.)

NICHOLS: She—she was running right for us. What in the hell was she doing in—

CHOI: Jermaine!

(Squad car makes impact with Assailant #2—male, Caucasian, 20s.)

NICHOLS: What the fuck—

(Squad car brakes, comes to a stop.)

NICHOLS: Where—where did he—

(Assailants #3, #4, #5 and #6 climb onto squad car and pound on its windows.)

CHOI: Holy shit!

ASSAILANTS (MULTIPLE): Just the facts, just the facts, just the facts.

NICHOLS: Dispatch—10-15 in process. We're—we're in the middle of the—

(Windshield breaks.)

NICHOLS: Shit! Shit! They're trying to get inside—they're trying to—

ASSAILANTS (MULTIPLE): Just the facts, just the facts, just the facts.

CHOI: Let go! Let go of me!

(Assailants #5 and #6 drag Officer Choi out from windshield.)

NICHOLS: Jenn! Let her go!

ASSAILANTS (MULTIPLE): Just the facts, just the facts, just the facts.

(Officer Choi screams, pulled outside squad car.)

NICHOLS: Jenn! Jenn! Jenn!

VIDEO #19: 12/20 at 1:04 p.m. MST/Denver, Colorado
*(Taken from body-worn camera footage from Metro
Police Department depicts assault on MPD Officers
Frank Nazareth [deceased], Carlos Siguencia [deceased],
and Allison Hopkins [deceased] by multiple assailants.)*

NAZARETH: Got some activity on the east side.

SIGUENCIA: What is it?

NAZARETH: Crowd's gathering.

SIGUENCIA: Call it in.

HOPKINS: How many?

NAZARETH: Ten? No—scratch that. Twenty. Shit, hold up. They keep coming.

SIGUENCIA: Just call it in already.

HOPKINS: I'm not reaching out for a few—

NAZARETH: Whoa. There's more now.

SIGUENCIA: Just radio it in, all right?

NAZARETH: Fifty or sixty or—

HOPKINS: Dispatch, got a small crowd gathering. Please advise.

NAZARETH: They just—they're coming out of nowhere—

HOPKINS: Dispatch, come in. Please advise, over.

NAZARETH: There's bound to be—shit, a hundred. Where in the hell are they all coming from?

(Unintelligible sounds, loud chanting.)

SIGUENCIA: You hear that?

HOPKINS: What is that? What're they saying?

SIGUENCIA: Things are getting heated over here. What are we supposed to do?

HOPKINS: Are they still behind the barrier?

SIGUENCIA: They're trying to climb over.

HOPKINS: It'll hold.

SUGUENCIA: The fence isn't going to hold.

HOPKINS: It'll hold.

NAZARETH: What the hell are they—

SIGUENCIA: Call it in. Hurry.

HOPKINS: I just did—

SIGUENCIA: Call it in again!

(Unintelligible sounds, loud chanting.)

NAZARETH: One's over! Three! We've got three—fuck, five—over the barrier.

SIGUENCIA: Fuck. Fuck me.

NAZARETH: Ten—

SIGUENCIA: What do we do? What're we supposed to do?

HOPKINS: Dispatch, please advise. Dispatch? Answer!

NAZARETH: They just keep coming, they—just keep coming—

HOPKINS: Dispatch, what the fuck are we supposed to do?

ALL HELL BREAKS LOOSE
Day One. 0 miles.

Good afternoon. Anderson Cooper reporting to you live. Startling news today as reports of multiple incidents of random violence erupting across the country continue to pour in.

We have some disturbing footage . . . We want to warn everyone at home about its unnerving nature . . . Please, if there are children watching, parental discretion is advised.

What you are seeing seems to be happening . . . *everywhere.* All across the country. These riots have no reason. If these are in fact protests, we have yet to be told what they are for.

There is simply too much conflicting information at this point for us to say with any certainty what the cause of these heinous acts might be. We simply do not know.

We are still waiting to hear from our nation's leaders on what is happening.

For those watching at home, please, we encourage you to stay inside, lock your doors, and shelter in place. Do not—we repeat, *do not*—engage with anyone else. This includes your neighbors, perhaps even members of your own family. I just don't know what else to say . . .

How'd that sound? Good?

Did I get it right?

Suffice to say, Noah Fairchild, the Great Reawakening is finally here and you are nowhere near prepared for it, you soft-skinned, sniveling li'l snowflake . . . This is what happens when you spend your adult life in a blissfully ignorant liberal bubble, sheltered from any shit hitting the fan. *La-di-da-libtard* . . . Look at you now. Standing in a shitstorm without an umbrella.

You are simply not equipped for this.

Any of this.

Dad is dead. You did that, pal. *You.* Shoved a fucking remote down his throat. Who does that? To their own father, for Christ's sake? What kind of son are you?

Let's not even talk about Mom. You just abandoned her—the woman who gave *birth* to you, *raised* you, *loved* you—in a closet, after banging her head against the door like she was some kind of kick drum in a speed metal band, Lars Ulrich–ing her skull into a pulpy oblivion.

It was only when you turned on the TV and realized this was happening all across the country that your mind shattered. Pretty commendable you held on to your sanity that long.

Kudos to you, kiddo.

Really.

Your brain needs to break. Let's let your mental faculties take a breather. How about we hand over the controls to the professionals, okay? Who can pilot us through the apocalypse?

Anderson Motherfucking Cooper, that's who.

In the face of every horror happening, your mind decides to adopt a cloyingly liberal coping technique. You now have my calm, collected voice to guide you through the carnage.

I'm sitting at the news desk in your head, broadcasting from your brain, reporting on this late-breaking chaos as it unspools before you. My nuanced tone allows you to take in the madness. Process it. That's what ol' Coop does, right? When shit hits the fan, I'm there, keeping it cool, keeping it calm, keeping it together, and telling you what in the ever-living fuck is going on.

I'm your trusted news source in the midst of the world going to shit. I'm honored, frankly, that your fragmented mind would pick me.

Thanks, Noah.

Just you and me, pal. We'll get through this mess together. Simply sit back and try to survive, okay? Because let's be honest with ourselves . . .

You're so fucked right now. How in the hell are we going to

skedaddle back to Brooklyn? How are we supposed to get back to Alicia and Kelsey? How in the hell do we return to our little liberal enclave in Park Slope, where we can breathlessly expound to our fellow turtleneck-sweater-wearing brethren about how awful conditions are out there in the red states? How are you going to regale your elite pals with your horror story at the next dinner party—*I did my damnedest to deprogram my parents, but by the time I got down there, it was too late. They were already monsters. Possessed by their programming. I barely got out of there alive . . .*

How, Noah?

Just get home. Try. You can cross the Mason-Dixon, alive and in one piece.

I've got all the faith in you, pal. You got this, you can do it.

Shall we start?

Deep breaths.

On your mark . . .

Get set . . .

GO!

You stumble out the front door of your childhood home, gasping for air. You instantly wince as the late-afternoon sun strikes your eyes. You haven't been outside since you first arrived. Your knee-jerk reaction is to howl. Let it all out. All the pent-up panic. The downright dread of it all comes spilling out of your mouth, chest relenting, unraveling in a drawn-out wail.

Others answer back. The neighborhood is alive with screams.

You go silent.

What the . . . ?

You have entered a world you no longer recognize. The life you knew before? The one held together by a social contract and laws? Held together with a paper-thin skin of morality? Of humanity?

Yeah, that world no longer exists. Not anymore.

It's theirs now.

All theirs.

Who are *they*? Who the hell knows. We certainly don't. I know just as much as you do . . .

You hear screams. Not just one shriek, but several. Too many to pinpoint. Neighbors are yelling. High-pitched howls rise up from all around, pouring out from shattered windows.

Women's voices. Men's. All of them pleading. Crying. Wetly bellowing bloody murder.

None of this makes sense. What the hell is happening here?

What the fuck is going on?

I'm trying to tell you, Noah. Listen to your ol' pal Coop, okay?

People are panicking. Losing their shit.

Everywhere.

A discordant chorus seeps out from the suburbs and you're still trying to make sense of it all, rationalize this somehow . . . But you can't. Abandon all rational thought. *Now.* Hurry.

You just left the insanity inside your parents' house and now you're waltzing into—

Screeeeeeech! Squealing tires seize your attention.

An Audi weaves over the road.

A drunk driver, most likely. Jesus, they can't drive straight! They're speeding far too fast for a residential neighborhood . . . Kids play in these streets! Children, for Christ's sake!

Look. There's a man—some jogger, maybe?—running down the road right now. Seems like a strange time to be out for some exercise, what with the world ending, but okay.

If Mr. Driver doesn't pump his brakes, and fast, he's going to run right into—

Oh! Holy shit!

The jogger just folded under the fender! His right leg got swallowed up by the Audi's wheel. You watch his ankle fold in on itself at such a painfully severe angle, it leaves his leg looking like a hairy question mark. Now the rest of his body curls under the car.

You watch the jogger—*why was he in the middle of the street?*—hit

the pavement, *whomp*, face first, arms splayed and disappearing beneath the wheels.

Hit-and-run. Holy shit, you've just witnessed a hit-and-run.
What should you do?

What should you do, Noah? Think. *Think.*

Call 911.

911? *Really?* Don't you think we're already beyond 911 by now?
You're slowly—too slowly—catching on to the fact that all these systems are collapsing at this very second. In real time. Your brain keeps
insisting the safety nets of society are still here, still holding you up
from utter failure, still protecting you . . . but it's just now dawning
on you that that's simply not true, yeah? At least some distant part
of you, some lingering scrap of your liberal lizard brain, is screaming
there is no safety net, not anymore, not ever again. *Wake up! Get your
ass moving!*

Run, rabbit! RUUUUUN!

The Audi weaves, leaving trails of blood on the pavement as it
keeps going, going, going. It's not going to slow down. Not for you,
not for anyone.

What do you do? What the hell are you supposed to do?

No time to *think*. Just react. *Do* something.

Move.

The car veers into the far lane. The driver is obviously blitzed
beyond any Breathalyzer test when all of a sudden—

Oh! What the fuck—

Another car!

Where in the flying fuck did that Hyundai come from? What the
fuck is happening?!

The rending of metal tears the air open.

Glass shatters. Our drunken Audi driver emerges from his windshield, a butterfly quickly crawling out from its cocoon. He's in the
air, look at him go, look at him soar freely into the—

Whoops, now he's down.

The driver lands on your parents' lawn, skull first, his face finding the ground and skidding across the uncut grass for a few yards before halting right before your feet.

what

the

fuuuuuuck

You haven't moved. Nothing in your body works. You simply stand there, holding your breath like it's the last bit of oxygen you'll ever have, ass cheeks clenched in a panicked pucker.

You can't believe what you just witnessed. This personalized horror movie was made for an audience of one—you, Noah Fairchild, it's all for you—playing out in such immersive detail, your brain can't fire off a single command. Your fight-or-flight has failed. All systems, *down*.

The driver's not moving. Bald and bloody.

Is he dead . . . ?

Are you asking *me*? This is new info to me, too. I'm watching this unfold alongside you . . .

He's dead. Bound to be dead.

Go check. I'll wait right here.

Just give him a little kick. Go on. Just a tap.

You stare at his inert body. By the time your mind suggests that you lean over to see if the driver is still breathing—

Oh, shit!

—he gasps. He flops over onto his back, sputtering. You're too close, still leaning in.

Wet. Your face feels wet.

Blood. He's coughing up blood. On you. In your eyes. You feel it dribble down your nose.

You think Ebola.

You think hep C.

You think COVID.

You imagine some new kind of virus. Something that doesn't

even have a name yet. The CDC hasn't whipped up a kick-ass code word for what this guy has and now it's seeping into your skin, into your bloodstream. You're done for, you just fucking know it. Zombified before it even began, because *of course* you wouldn't last that long in the apocalypse. Fucking *of course*.

So you just close your eyes and stand there.

And whimper.

And wait.

Aaaand . . . wait a little bit more.

You're bracing for the moment you turn into one of *them*, saying farewell to your privileged existence once and for all, your cells rotting into a soup of soulless pus.

But nothing happens. Nothing at all.

You're fine. *You're alive.*

For now.

You crack open your eyes, slowly, slowly, and take in the world around you.

Mr. Audi is still alive. Barely. He's bald in a Friar Tuck kind of way. Purple sweatsuit. He's spitting blackened blood in these hacking, arcing spurts. The blood falls back onto his own face and it reminds you of some neglected water fountain, its spigots gummed up with algae.

You can help this man. You can! Hold on to a little bit of your humanity. Snap out of it and assist your fellow brother in need. All you have to do is reach down and take his hand—

Oh!

A woman launches out from the front door of her house directly across the street, screaming her head off. She's wearing a silk bathrobe and not much else, untied and open and fanning at her shoulders like a silken cape. *Super Soccer Mom* or . . . or *the Caped Carpooler*.

She's coming straight at you, breasts swinging. Mouth foaming. Her eyes hold the exact same distorted stare your parents had. What's wrong with her? Is she sick, too?

Why is she charging at you?

Why is she—

Why—

You instinctively step back, forgetting all about the broken man bleeding at your feet. You're reversing course, hands in the air in a placating gesture, *hold it, hold it*, as you backpedal up the porch steps of your parents' house, suddenly wondering if maybe it's actually safer inside. Perhaps it would be best to lock the doors and hide. Let this all simply blow over.

This woman—middle-aged, with a close-cropped haircut, frosted blond—crosses the street, scaling the fresh wreckage of the car crash on all fours. She leaps into the air and—

Oh!

—pounces upon Mr. Audi. You let out a sputter of indignation as the woman seizes his head with both hands and examines it, much like one would scrutinize a melon before buying. This woman clearly doesn't care for the condition of this particular piece of fruit. She slams it against the ground, smashing the man's head further and further into the earth, until—*Oh!*—the rind cracks—*Oh, Jesus!*—the nose breaks—*Fuck!*—the jaw snaps and now there's melon gunk all over the grass. Now, *now* that she's broken open this man's skull, *now* that there's fruity pulp pouring freely fourth from his cranium, *now* this woman dives in and starts eating.

You watch in mortified silence as she digs her face into the man's face. She's really rooting around his brain matter with her bare teeth. She runs her tongue along the fresh fissure, and when she rears her head back, she tears off a hunk of the man's nose.

This elicits another shout from you. Just a short retort—"Oh!"— as if all you can do is let out these abrupt outbursts of exasperation as you clutch your self-righteous pearls. Typical liberal distress response from someone who can only stand there and watch as the world goes to shit around them without lifting a damn finger.

Super Soccer Mom spits at you. Sorry, spits *it*—a mouthful of flesh—at you. A chunk of nose lands at your feet, as if she wants to share. She barks in staccato bursts like a rabid seal:

Arf!

"Just—" Blood splatters the grass.

Arf!

"—the—" This is definitely not sanitary.

Aaaaarf!

"—faaaaax!"

Oh . . . Oh, okaaaaay now. So this is interesting. This just in: We are receiving new information here and it, uh . . . well, it seems to suggest we're dealing with some fucked-up shit.

Fax News Brain. It's spreading. It's communicable. Mad cow disease for conservatives.

Totally makes sense.

So this isn't simply isolated to your mother and father. One glance at the half-naked woman drenching herself in a dying man's crushed cranium, as if she were bathing in your lawn sprinkler, and it's starting to dawn on you, thanks to me, that this is happening *ev-er-ee-where.*

The whole country . . . or, well, at least half of it.

Time to go. Time to say *buh-bye* to our neighbor. Let's go back inside, shall we? Lock all the doors and wait for this all to blow over, yeah? Sounds good to you? Sounds good to me.

But you're not looking where you're walking, backstepping up the porch to your parents' house. There's one last step that you don't sense underfoot and end up falling.

Now you're on your ass.

Super Soccer Mom has got you dead to rights, barreling hand over foot for you, when—

Oh! Fuck me!

She's tackled—plowed into from the side, linebacker-style—by a—a—a swarm or a herd or a horde or whatever the hell is the appropriate term for a mass of manic neighbors. All of them rabidly charge across your lawn with no regard for whatever or whoever may be in their way, landing on top of the woman and what remains of the dead Friar Tuck on your lawn.

At first, you assume the horde is tearing her to pieces . . . Ripping her limb from limb . . .

But . . . no, nope-nope, it's just her clothes.

And their clothes.

Suddenly there's a pale tangle of limbs on your parents' front lawn. One elderly woman begins to nibble another woman's earlobe. An overweight man burrows his face in another's butt. Really digs in, a pig at the trough. They start pounding away at one another. Five—no, make that six—bodies knot into one tapestry of desperate sexual intercourse. An impromptu orgy right here, out in the open. On your parents' goddamn lawn, for fuck's sake.

What is this? What the hell is going on here?

I don't know about you, Noah, but . . . I personally am not finding this particularly arousing. Their moaning holds no pleasure. It's craven. Gluttonous. They're going to devour each other when they're through. Already you see them tearing with their teeth, taking bits of flesh with every greedy kiss, slathering themselves up in each other's blood as they hump away.

"Your—bod—eee—is—a—tem—ple," they all shout with each subsequent thrust, sounding like pounding seals barking out platitudes. "Be—a—wealth—of—well—ness!"

Oh boy. Oh dear. Oh shit. Oh God. This is some kind of . . . of . . .

What the fuck is this? A social plague? An STD outbreak?

A zombie orgy?

That's where your mind goes when the shit hits the fan? *Zombies?* No wonder you're as good as dead. Your brain is too full of movies right now and it's not helping. You think of zombie films. Pandemic narratives. Disaster movies. You can't keep thinking like this, Noah. It's casting you as the protagonist—but there are no protagonists in plagues. You're a bit player, at best. A glorified extra. All you have is what you've seen on TV to guide you through this absolute chaos.

TV.

Bingo. Lightbulb moment. This all started with Fax News. Your parents were stuck at home, feeding their minds on a steady diet of conservative cable news and now they are . . .

Whatever this is.

A switch flipped inside their heads. Your father had a name for it when you were a kid.

Boob-Tube Charlie.

That's what he called you and your brother if he ever caught you two sitting too close to the television screen. *Looks like we've got a bunch of Boob-Tube Charlies on our hands here . . .*

That's what these people remind you of. The glassy-eyed stares. The inability to focus. The snail trails of drool. The dulling of the mind. Nothing but a bunch of Boob-Tube Charlies.

Dad was right.

If there's any justice left in this world—cosmic justice—you would be dead already, but no, nope, you've lived longer than a lot of other people, still chugging dumbly along, for some asinine reason, a hell of a lot longer than people far more equipped to handle this shit.

To survive.

You—you're on borrowed time. A sitting liberal duck.

Quack-quack.

Oh well. Won't be long now before you're attacked and your skull is cracked and your brains are bleeding out all over the pavement like that guy. Or that gal. Or . . .

Or what about that man walking his dog? Nope, sorry, *eating* his dog. Definitely eating.

Or what about the lovely couple across the street, holding hands as they—

Nope, scratch that. He just ripped her arm from its socket.

Let's take a quick pause, can we? *Time out?* Can we just, you know, pull the camera back a bit, as it were, and get a bird's-eye view of the immediate scene playing out in front of you?

Already you see the columns of smoke rising on the horizon. Buildings are burning. Homes are on fire. Whatever's happening here, right in front of you, on this street . . . seems to be happening farther out. Jesus, it really is everywhere. Like *everywhere*-everywhere.

You know this because you can hear it. Faint screams from blocks away. Behind closed doors. In other houses. Trumpet blasts of screeching tires. Hollow pops that may as well be party favors, but no, nope, that's not what that is. Those are gunshots. Lots and lots of gunfire.

And who are you, Noah Fairchild? I, Anderson Cooper, want to know. *What kind of person will you be when the apocalypse comes? Will you make it through the next five minutes?*

The next thirty seconds?

Of course not.

You're not built to survive. To fight. You simply don't know how. These are the sad fax.

Sorry, *facts*.

After years of Instacart and Uber rides, you do not have the tools to survive. Your liberal values aren't going to save you now that the world has gone to total shit.

Come on. Let's be honest with ourselves, Noah. What are the odds of you reaching your family, all the way back in Brooklyn, alive? Sane? In one piece?

Zero. Zilch. Nada.

That's when it hits you. Truly hits you, like a ton of bricks made of shit: *I'm fucked.*

Yup. So fucked. Sorry, Noah. I really am.

VIDEO #33: 12/20 at 3:16 p.m. EST/Baltimore, Maryland
(Local news affiliate, eyewitness news, Jenny Pohlig [deceased] reporting.)

POHLIG: Thanks, Jim. Confusion and panic run rampant in the streets this afternoon as several instances of spontaneous protests erupt throughout the area. It's unclear what these demonstrations are for, though one eyewitness—

(Cameraman Tom Henderson is attacked by unknown assailants.)

POHLIG: Tom! Tom—

(Camera falls to the ground.)

POHLIG: Get off! Let—let me go! Tom! Tom, help—

ASSAILANT #1 (UNKNOWN) *(Speaking into microphone)*: Wake up! Wake up!

POHLIG: Tom!

(Assailant #1—male, Caucasian, 40s—bludgeons Pohlig with microphone.)

ASSAILANT #1 (UNKNOWN): Time to—

(Assailant #1 bludgeons Pohlig with microphone.)

ASSAILANT #1 (UNKNOWN): Open your—

(Live video feed cuts out.)

VIDEO #51: 12/20 at 3:23 p.m. EST/Philadelphia, Pennsylvania

(Video clip taken from phone footage recorded by Daniel Silliman [deceased].)

SILLIMAN: Yeah—smash that shit! Smash it!

(Silliman runs to catch up with crowd.)

SILLIMAN: Hey—what're we protesting? What're we protesting? What's—what's this all about? Hey! Hey, you—

(Runs for several seconds in silence.)

SILLIMAN: Black Lives Matter? Hey—is this Black Lives Matter? What're we—

(Stops running.)

SILLIMAN: What the fuck's going on, guys? What're we angry at?

VIDEO #24: 12/20 at 3:06 p.m. EST/Washington, D.C.

(Body-worn camera footage from Metro Police Department depicts assault of Officer Carl August [deceased] by unknown assailants.)

RADIO: Please be advised that there is a group of a hundred civilians charging the southern lawn of the White House.

AUGUST: Multiple law enforcement injuries! Repeat: Multiple injuries!

RADIO: Pull back resources.

AUGUST: Where? Where am I supposed to go? We're surrounded!

RADIO: Pull back. Repeat: pull back.

AUGUST: Jesus, I see them coming. It's—it's just a sea of people. So many people.

VIDEO #57: 12/20 at 3:20 p.m. EST/Richmond, Virginia

(WWBT/NBC 12 News "Eye in the Sky" traffic report with Grant Burgess.)

BURGESS: Hello, everybody—it's Grant Burgess with your eye-in-the-sky afternoon traffic report. Sure seems like a lot of folks are getting a head start on their holiday traffic here! Expect a fair amount of congestion on both the north- and southbound lanes of I-95, as well as heading out of Richmond on I-64. There have been reports of multiple lane closures along . . . along . . .

(Pause.)

BURGESS: You seeing this?

(Pause.)

BURGESS: There. Over there. Can you get in closer? Do you—do you see that?

(Pause.)

BURGESS: Sorry, Megan. We seem to be witnessing . . .

(Indistinct chatter from pilot.)

BURGESS: Zoom in on that. Closer. Tighten up on it. What the heck's going on . . .

(Indistinct chatter from pilot.)

BURGESS: Are we—are we still live? Are we on the air? What am I supposed to—

(Pause.)

BURGESS: I, uh . . . Well, Megan, it appears that there is a . . . a pack or . . . a herd of . . . of people moving across the northbound lane of I-95. They seem to be . . . they are moving together. I don't know if it's a riot or a group of—of protesters or—

(Shouts.)

BURGESS: Oh! Holy—

(Shouts.)

BURGESS: They're running right into traffic! Right into the south-bound lane! Jesus, I—I just saw three people run straight into the same semi and—oh, Jesus—they didn't stop—they just—just aimed straight at that sixteen-wheeler and—

(Shouts.)

BURGESS: Oh! Oh my God—they're about—I'd say about two, maybe three—yeah, three dozen people. Just—just pouring into all six lanes now. Both north and south corridors of I-95 have come to a—a complete standstill. They're climbing on top of cars and—and—oh God, I've never seen anything like this—they don't care if they get hit or—so many bodies—so many people on the road—the cars—the cars are swerving around them, but there's too many—just so many—so many—

(Shouts.)

BURGESS: They're using their hands—their fists—to break through the windows and—and now they're pulling passengers out from—from inside the cars.

(Indistinct chatter from pilot.)

BURGESS: No—no we've got to stay. We've got to keep filming. We're on the air—

(Indistinct chatter from pilot.)

BURGESS: They're grabbing these passengers and pulling. Pulling in different—oh, Jesus! They're tearing them apart. Just ripping these people to pieces!

(Shouts.)

BURGESS: Now they're raising—oh oh, my—they're raising those limbs in the air—over their heads and—and they're using them to—to beat the bodies.

(Pause.)

BURGESS: Wait . . . Wait, are they? Are they . . . ? Oh, Jesus. Oh God, what are they . . .

(Indistinct chatter from pilot.)

BURGESS: Yes, I can see! I see that they're fornicating!

(Indistinct chatter from pilot.)

BURGESS: We're still on? They haven't cut the feed? This is going out live?

(Indistinct chatter from pilot.)

BURGESS: I—I'm going to be sick. I can't look anymore. Just get out of here. Go.

(Indistinct chatter from pilot.)

BURGESS: I don't know where! Just go!

(Indistinct chatter from pilot.)

BURGESS: This has been your eye-in-the-sky traffic report. Back to you, Megan—

(Indistinct chatter from pilot.)

BURGESS: What? What did you say—

(Indistinct chatter from pilot.)

BURGESS: What're you doing? What're you—

(Indistinct chatter from pilot.)

BURGESS: Oh—oh—hold on—hold—

(Indistinct chatter from pilot.)

BURGESS: Going down! We're going—

(Feed cuts.)

HOUSECALL
Day One. 11 miles.

The highways are hell. Traffic is at an absolute standstill on I-95, an endless stretch of cars clotting up both north- and southbound lanes. I-64 is no clearer, completely blocked.

Hopping onto 301 isn't happening, unless you have a tank.

Or a monster truck.

Richmond just had a heart attack. A citywide coronary has halted the flow of traffic. Most folks abandoned their cars and started running. Some left their doors wide open, keys still in the ignition, that persistent door-ajar *ding-ding* chiming for miles.

Other cars still have families trapped inside.

You've been on this road trip before: Dad's stubbornly strapped behind the wheel. The kids are in back. Mom sinks into the passenger seat, praying this nightmare ends soon. They're waiting for traffic to clear. *Just a little bottlenecking, that's all. This will smooth out in no time . . .*

Because how is this any different from all the other dismal trips you've taken on I-95?

Uh-oh. Here they come . . .

You sense the rumble of metal. Hands and feet clamber over cars, leaping from one hood to the next, an endless flow of disturbed citizens, charging through the lanes.

A stampede.

Even then, this father is staying put. *Everybody just calm down*, he says, *it's all right, don't you fret, this will all blow over before you know it* . . . The whole fam cowers and cries as the Boob-Tube Charlies pound on their windows, shattering the glass, grabbing at their trembling bodies and yanking them out, raking their teeth over flesh and pulling it free.

That family never stood a chance. Dad still believed in a system. That father put his faith in the idea that his family was protected by the time-honored safeguards of the old world.

He hadn't woken up to this new world yet. He hadn't opened his eyes. He never will.

Now there is only chaos.

This is hell on earth.

If you'd left ten minutes earlier—Christ, *five*—you could've had a head start. Instead, you dillydallied at Mom and Dad's, trying to figure out what to pack, what to grab, when what you should've been doing was *go go GOOOO*. But nope, you needed to get your clothes. Like you'll ever wear any of these linen pants again. As if there will ever come another day on this planet when donning some Banana Republic duds will be a necessity.

You are still assuming this will all blow over. You are convincing yourself this is a simple blip in the routine of civic-minded citizens such as yourself. It's a minor inconvenience that will come and go and then you'll simply get back to the blissful existence you had before.

You've got to stop thinking like this, Noah, and listen to me. Listen to your ol' pal Andy.

It has yet to dawn on you that you're dead already.

Shut the fuck up, Anderson Cooper, you think.

Hey, now! I'm just calling it like it is . . . You're still thinking like a sniveling liberal, and liberals are not going to inherit this earth. You are not entitled to this planet, pal. Sorry.

You have heard their screams eclipse all other sounds. You have seen the soft-skinned suffer with your own eyes, attacked with ravenous rage by their neighbors. Their own family.

Family.

Asher would know what to do. He was always better at these sorts of things. When shit hit the fan, Ash had a plan. You used to tease him for being paranoid. *Who's laughing now?*

But he's gone. You saw him on television, remember? You watched me solemnly dole out the bad news: your brother walked into an elementary school and . . . well, he's gone.

What about Devon? Could she help? Their house is in NoVa, so it's sorta on your way.

Worth a shot, right?

Why it hasn't occurred to you to go to your sister-in-law before now is anybody's guess.

You are going about this apocalypse all wrong.

When you were a kid, Ash loved reading those Choose Your Own Adventure books from the Scholastic Book Fairs: slim paperbacks with knights and wizards on the cover. Each novel offered options on how to navigate the narrative. Simple decisions were posed throughout the book. *Do you turn left? Or right? This path or that?* You were so eager to read them, begging your older brother to borrow his copies. One story had something to do with you being a squire for a knight and being tasked with seeking some magical herb for a wizard.

Do you pick the plant?

Turn to page 78.

Or do you hide behind a tree and wait and see what happens?

Turn to page 23.

Pick the plant. Obviously. You quickly flip to page seventy-eight, and when your fingers finally land on the page, you read the first—

the only—sentence: *The plant is poison and you've been tricked by an evil wizard, sent to the Otherside on a foggy haze of nightshade!*

That's . . . it? That's all there is? But . . . you just started reading! The book can't end that quickly. You can't be dead, right? Not *actually* dead. Just what kind of cruel cosmic joke is this?

So you start at the beginning again.

Twenty pages later and you're dead a second time. So you try again and the same thing happens yet again. No matter how many times you begin at the beginning, you never seem to choose the right path or take the correct turn, always dying unceremoniously upon reaching The End.

No *Happily Ever After* for you. No victorious win or knighting by the king.

You just die, over and over again.

This book sucks.

You can't help but remember those annoying novels now, in the very moment when you should be focusing on the back roads before you. Life has presented its own apocalyptic *Choose Your Own Adventure for Fragile Democrats*, and if you don't start making better choices, dare we say *conservative* choices, you're going to flip to the next page and realize your narrative has come to an abrupt end before it even starts.

So what's it going to be, young squire? Do you . . .

A) Take the back roads between here and your (dead) brother's house in NoVa or . . .

B) Stay on I-95 and see if you can navigate around the aneurysm of traffic through D.C.?

The back roads it is.

Driving fifteen miles an hour through the winding suburbs of Northern Virginia—behind a slow-moving convoy of like-minded travelers—extends your endless trek. That and the fact that you have to plow through a few possessed people. The less you think about this, the better.

But your ol' pal Coop isn't about to let you forget, hitting the airwaves in your head and announcing each hit-and-run as if it were the latest, most-breakingest news.

This just in: We have received word there has been another hit-and-run on Shoreham Drive. Noah Fairchild has been plowing through possessed pedestrians and doesn't appear to be stopping his assault. He's going to mow down just about anyone who gets in his way, folks . . .

Slow news day.

≡

You knock on Devon's—no longer Ash's—door. Politely. As if decorum still exists.

Ding-dong, surprise! Hey, sis . . . I was in the neighborhood and I just thought I'd pop my head in and say howdy. See how you're holding up. Saw Ash on the news. Yikes . . . Sorry.

You're covered in blood because you had a little run-in with a young woman who could've been in college, but something in your gut says she was probably only in high school.

Your car broke down about a mile back. You had to hoof it the rest of the way to Asher's after grinding the gears so badly that the transmission crapped out.

You shouldn't have hit those people. You should've just stopped the car and shut off the engine and ducked down and waited for them to pass, but no, nope, you panicked and pressed down on the accelerator the second you saw them zeroing in on you and—and—and—

Thwump.

Thwump.

Thwump.

When the first wave of bodies hit, you squeezed your eyes shut. But to be honest, all those bodies on the windshield did a pretty good job of eclipsing your field of vision anyway.

You would've never have seen that telephone pole, no matter what. Smashing into the wooden post at fifty-seven miles an hour definitely sends several bodies a-flyin'.

People. They are still people.

Even now, after plowing through these lunatics, you're still seeking out some common ground—trying to understand them. As if pinpointing where these people are coming from, their class background, their economic anxieties, is going to be the solution to all your woes.

You sat behind the wheel for a bit, disoriented by what just happened. What you have done. What you are.

A killer.

You're holding on to your humanity like it's the last bread crumbs left to eat before starvation sweeps through. You cling to these concepts of *compassion* and *empathy* and *goodwill*, but they're all slipping through your fingers, they are burning up before your very eyes, they are evaporating faster than you can breathe the fumes of human kindness into your lungs for one last hit of brotherly love. These notions are dead as the dodo and you'll be dying with them if you don't unbuckle your fucking seat belt and move your ass before the next wave comes.

So. Here you are. *Ding-dong.*

Nobody answers.

The surrounding houses all look like sherbet sundaes to you, each painted in a different pastel hue, peach or pineapple or pomegranate. It's Easter every day in this neighborhood.

He has risen, you can't help but think.

Good one.

Thanks.

Devon's car is still parked in the driveway. She's probably hiding. After everything you've seen on the news? You wouldn't answer the door, either. You'd lock the doors, close the curtains, and hunker down in whatever room is farthest from the street, avoiding the world.

"Devon? It's Noah. Can you hear me? Please just—just open the door."

You don't want to be outside any longer than you absolutely have to. You want to be inside, doors locked, window shades pulled, curtains drawn, thumb in mouth, sucking yourself into some catatonic state where you revert back to that infantile phase all feeble-minded Democrats go to when shit gets real. You want to hide. Go cry to Mommy, you pansy ass.

You try the door.

Unlocked.

Oh.

You open the door. Slowly. Quietly. You peer your head inside.

"Devon? Hello? Anyone home?"

It smells . . . *funky*, to say the least, but you slip inside anyway.

"Hello?"

A mausoleum-like calm permeates every last molecule of air. This is not the feeling of an empty home. There's a palpable presence inside. Someone is here. You know it. Feel it with every fiber. The question is whether they're dead or alive or whatever the hell is in between.

Asher's house is in even worse condition than your parents' place, if such a thing were possible. Food has had a bit longer to fester, from the smell of it.

At least this house has the air-conditioning on. It's really been pumping too, from the chill of it. That Freon breeze thickens the atmosphere. Still, there's an oiliness to the air. All the smells simply suspend themselves, too thick to dissipate.

"Devon?"

Clearly no one is going to answer. You need to stop. Conserve your energy. Hold your—

Something moves down the hall.

A pale shape. Tiny, gangly limbs.

What the hell was that?

It crawls farther down the hall, hunched down low to the floor, on all fours, racing away from you. Into the kitchen of all places. You can hear the faint crunch of food under their hands and knees.

Where did they go?

That had to be a human, right? Didn't Ash have a dog? They did, didn't they? Maybe it's just their pup. Yeah, sure, *maybe*. Even as you attempt to rationalize it away, file your fear in the cabinet at the back of your mind and go investigate, you know this is the wrong call.

I'm sorry, I've got to ask: *The hell are you doing, Big Guy? We should be going thataway.*

Of course you shouldn't follow it—him, her, whoever they are. That would be silly. Not just silly—absolutely stupid. Have the last few hours taught you nothing? Turn the fuck around!

But this is family, you rationalize. This is someone bound by blood. They could be hurt. They could be in trouble. You're here to help, you smug, dunderheaded, ineffectual intellectual.

You won't listen to me. To common sense. To your inner Anderson Cooper.

Bad call, dude. Stunningly bad.

"Hello?"

You head into the kitchen. There's food everywhere. The floor is tacky with the fluids of abandoned juice boxes. The soles of your shoes cling to the floor before peeling away. The air-conditioning is counteracting the smell of decay, but it's a losing battle.

The fridge is open. The dim light from within spills over a cornucopia of moldy food. The air is alive with flies—so many, it's almost like looking at television static. You sense the kinetic energy of their wings in your teeth. All that buzzing, it hums. It's electric.

You wave your hand before your face—to do what, exactly? Sweep the smell away? Wipe away the flies? They dissipate and just as quickly regroup on a mass in the open oven.

Oops—you found the family dog. What's left of it.

Something crunches.

Behind you.

Spinning around, you see the door to the pantry close on its own.

Someone is inside.

Hiding. From you.

Okay. You've been here before. Let's not be a complete idiot about this. Find something—*anything*—that you can use to protect yourself. A knife or a tenderizer or a—

A pizza slicer?

Red sauce and a scab of dried cheese—please, let that be cheese—cling to its circular blade. It's the best you can do at the moment, so you grab it. The wheel spins like a spur on a cowboy boot. Not the sharpest blade, but it's the only option we've got. We can work with this.

Now. To the pantry.

You take your steps slow. Obscenely slow. It's not helping with your heartbeat. Your feet stick to the tackiness of the floor, and you have to rip them away with each step.

rrrp . . .

rrrp . . .

rrrp . . .

When you reach the pantry door, sweating, your pulse is thrumming like a beehive.

"Hello?"

Take a deep breath. Tighten your grip on your pizza slicer. Grab hold of the doorknob.

Open-sez-a-meeeeee . . .

The shelves are full of tiny white boxes. There's also a nest. The floor is covered with empty packaging, torn open. Then you see the emaciated child nestled within.

Marcus.

Your nephew. Good God, what's happened to him? His eyes have sunk back into his sockets. There are smudges of chocolate across his cheeks. Please let that be chocolate.

This kid hasn't taken a bath in days. Weeks?

He's clutching a tablet with both hands. Its screen casts an aquamarine sheen across his sallow cheeks. His eyes look up at you, dulled by days of sheltering in this pantry.

"Marcus?" You hear your own voice crumble.

The boy doesn't speak.

"It's . . . Uncle Noah."

Your voice doesn't penetrate the trauma. You can't reach him, wherever he is.

"Remember me?"

His mind is at the bottom of some deep well in his subconscious.

"Where is everybody? Where's . . . your mother?"

A flare of recognition flashes in the boy's dull eyes.

"Maa . . ." It merely comes out as a squeak. His parched voice cracks.

The boy swallows. He tries again. Whispers this time, to preserve what little voice he has. "Mommy went down a rabbit hole . . . What crawled back up isn't Mommy anymore."

Okaaaaay . . . So that's not exactly what you had expected to hear. But, all right, fine. You're going to simply let that statement settle for a spell, marinate on it, before you respond.

"Do you think your mommy might—"

Marcus brings a bony finger up to his chapped lips. He doesn't give the command any vocalization. No breath. Just the mere display of "shush" is enough to deliver its message:

Shut. The fuck. Up. You dingbat.

Or . . . what, exactly?

Someone will hear you, this kid tries to convey. *Duh.*

But . . . who, exactly?

Kitchenware falls to the floor behind you. Someone just sent it all toppling, a cacophony of utensils, a cymbal-crash of spatulas and whisks and other cooking implements.

The hairs on the back of your neck rise. Your spine hums.

Someone is right behind you. Like, *right behind you* behind you.

Marcus grabs your wrist and yanks you into the pantry. You turn just enough to close the door behind you both, barely catching a glimpse of the crouched gargoyle on the center island.

You see stringy hair covering a face.

You see bare, bleeding knees, up around their shoulders as they crouch.

You hear gurgles.

But you don't see anything else because you've slammed the pantry door and now you're both standing stock-still in the dark. Holding your breath. Trying hard not to make a sound. The tablet pressed against Marcus's chest casts a blue-green glow over his throat, a tiny sliver of light illuminating the boy's face, giving his chin and sharpened cheeks a dim contrast, as if he were holding a flashlight under his face to tell a *spoooooooky* story around the campfire.

The crumble and crackle of empty potato chip bags crinkles under your feet, giving your whereabouts away, and it's enough to get you wincing at your own doltishness.

You're dead. So goddamn dead.

It's amazing how quickly you fall into familiar childlike patterns. You're forty-two years old, and yet your body still has a sense memory of how to hide. How to go on emotional lockdown. How to hold your breath and keep still, very, very still.

But it's too late. You've been caught.

crrnch

Bare feet on the center island.

crrnch

Bare feet hit the floor.

crrnch

Bare feet making their way through the mess of empty food containers.

ccrr—

Bare feet halt just on the other side of the door.

Everything is still. The absence of movement, of breath, makes you question whether there's anyone actually on the other side of door or maybe you're just imagin—

The door swings open.

What you see makes no sense. Nothing should surprise you at this point, but still you find fresh opportunities for brand-new what-the-fuckery.

The remnants of Devon are hunched before you. That is most certainly her standing on two feet. But possession hasn't been so kind to her body. First, there's her face. Her throat. Her lips. She looks as if she's been bleeding from the inside out, drooling blood.

Then there is the matter of her hand. The right one appears to have been . . . gnawed off? There's nothing beyond the wrist but gnarled bone. A bloody stump.

You feel Marcus's arms tighten around your waist. He's trembling like an airplane hitting turbulence. His entire body rocks with a series of shudders that reach into your own bones.

"Devon?" you ask. Why is it a question? Of course it's her. Her body, at least. But what about the rest of her? Is she still there? What is this thing standing before you?

Devon grins, unspooling a tongue that you wish had stayed inside her mouth.

"Noo mamaaa draamaaaaah . . ."

She lunges first. You want to be clear on that point. In the court of cosmic law, your sister-in-law made the first move. This harkens back to that age-old argument you and Asher used to have as kids, nearly every day of your life for years: *Who shot first? Han Solo or Greedo?*

Devon lunges at you, spurring your reflexes into action.

All you wanted was something between you two.

It just so happened to be a pizza slicer.

The circular blade meets Devon's belly. It isn't nearly sharp enough to cut through her soiled yoga outfit, but impact sends the wheel on its own journey upward, a unicycle rolling across the plane of her stained Lycra shirt before finding the tender flesh along her chest.

Now we're slicing.

The terrain softens just enough for the blade to embed itself, the tiniest blood trail forging its northern sojourn across your sister-in-law's neck.

Your arm simply trails *up, up, and awaaaaaay*, sending the pizza slicer aloft in some sort of violent rendition of the Statue of Liberty, torch held over your head.

The blade slices through Devon's throat in a vertical slit. You nick the bone of her chin. A shallow cut. The angle is too awkward to reach any deeper than a centimeter or so.

But there's blood. It soaks through the front of her shirt and onto you.

"Oh," you start. "I'm so sorry—"

Why are you apologizing?

Devon grabs you by your shirt with both hands—no, just one. Her right hand is simply gone. Streamers of flesh flip and twist against your chest as she presses the bone to your throat and yanks you out of the pantry and flings you down. There's no countermeasure, no defensive move to perform. You simply spin, an awkward ballet move sending you twirling to the floor.

You hit the ground, right shoulder first, and it knocks the air out of your lungs.

Devon pounces. She's on top of you, straddling you, her lips at your ear.

"Nomamadramanomamadrama—"

"Devon!"

"—mamamamadramamamadramaaaamaaamaaaadraaaaamaaaaaa."

You've got just enough wiggle room to turn onto your back, the two of you face-to-face.

This is Devon. Devon, your sister-in-law. Your brother's wife. You've known her for nearly twenty years.

No, this—this isn't her. Not any longer. This is barely human.

"Devon, please—"

Your mother flashes before your eyes. You remember her hips grinding against you.

"Stop!"

You don't want to feel that way again.

"Please—"

You have a pizza slicer in your hand, I can't help but remind you. *So. Fucking. Use. It.*

"STOP!"

You reel your arm back and slice again, this time bringing the circular blade down Devon's face at a forty-five-degree angle. She merely freezes in place, blinking through the blood as it cascades down her cheek. She can't see you bring the pizza slicer down for a second slice, this time in the opposite direction, for symmetry's sake, opening up an X of flesh across her face.

Who in the hell do you think you are? Fucking Zorro?

Devon blinks.

And blinks.

Blood flutters through her eyelids. She looks perplexed by the trickling sensation. Confused. She keeps on blinking, as if she's caught in some autonomic mechanical glitch.

Then she stops. Reboots. Now she looks mad. Real mad. At you.

"Devon?"

She lunges forward, dropping all her weight on you at once. The only thing between you and all one hundred and thirty-odd pounds of her barreling down is a dull circular blade on a wooden handle. You hold it up horizontally, brandishing it with both hands, like a dagger.

The angle of the spinning blade combined with her weight com-

bined with her descent all equates to a bloody calculus that you'll
never quite comprehend. Math was never your thing.

But you slit your sister-in-law's throat. The blade sinks in and
simply . . . *rolls*.

A little to the left, at first.

Then to the right.

You maneuver the slicer along the fleshy hemisphere of Devon's
neck, back and forth, back and forth, until the blade meanders right
on over her jugular and cuts through the artery.

That's when you discover the human body truly is an endless
reservoir for blood. Blood pours down your wrist, your arm, all the
way down your face. You are now bathing in blood.

You will never eat pizza again for as long as you live.

Yeah, but . . . how long is that, pal?

"I'm sorry," you say—which is a really stupid thing to do, apologizing for slicing someone's throat while you're still at it, sawing even
deeper into their neck. "I'm sorry, I'm—"

Devon's eyes widen. Her jaw does this strange thing, you think,
where it sort of just plops open. She's gawking—at you, maybe—like
she's shocked that you actually had it in you.

Everybody recognizes your insufficiency at survival, even her.
This is just dumb luck.

You lucky, lucky son of a gun, I say, and for once you agree with
good ol' Coop.

Devon's body flops to the floor. You let go of the slicer, still embedded in her neck. You're just going to leave it there. You remain
on your back, blinking the blood out of your eyes as best you can.
It stings. Everything is blurry, but your eyes come back into focus
to find Marcus hovering above you, staring down with the placid
remove of a seven-year-old boy who has just witnessed his uncle
practically decapitating his possessed mother with a pizza slicer.

He's still gripping the tablet in one hand. He won't let the iPad
go.

The two of you keep pretty calm for a moment, taking it all in. Should you apologize?

Gee, Marcus, I didn't mean to saw your ma's head off. Sorry, big guy . . . No hard feelings?

Marcus holds one hand out for you to take, to help you up from the floor. It's the most tender gesture you've received in thirty-six hours. Maybe more. It's a balm for your soul.

So you take it.

VIDEO #12: 12/20 at 3:27 p.m. EST/Richmond, Virginia

(Cell footage recorded by Tamra Mehta [14], freshman at Greenfield High.)

MEHTA: Mommy . . . I'm in the library. The school is under lockdown but nobody's heard any gunshots. This doesn't feel like a . . . like a shooting or a . . . I'm so scared.

(Long pause.)

MEHTA: They're telling us to stay under the tables. I can hear other students crying. I think there's . . . I don't know . . . maybe ten of us. Nobody knows what's going on . . . Nobody is telling us anything. Nobody's getting any cell service . . .

(Pause.)

MEHTA: I was in sixth period. Mr. Kim—he heard something in the hall. He told us to stay seated while he stepped out to see what it was. We all just sat there, looking at each other. Somebody made a joke about it being a bomb . . . But then we heard screaming and . . . and . . .

(Pause.)

MEHTA: A few decided to run. They didn't make it far. We've been hiding in the—

MALE #1: Shut up. They'll hear you. You're supposed to stay quiet.

(Pause.)

MEHTA: *(Whispering.)* They're . . . in the halls . . . shouting or laughing or I don't know. I saw one of them and I . . . I knew him. His . . . his name was . . . is . . . Cam. Cameron. We were in English together, but that was like . . . Fifth grade? He was running down the hall and . . . he was laughing. He had a cap on. He's always wearing this baseball cap turned backward, even though the teachers tell him not to. He ran his head right into a row of lockers so hard he knocked his cap off . . . He fell to the floor. On his back. He was bleeding. I think he broke his nose. He was on his back . . . laughing . . . bleeding all over . . . in his mouth . . . laughing so loud.

(Pause.)

MEHTA: Cam just . . . just gets up and rams his head into the same locker again.

(Pause.)

MEHTA: There are others. Other students. I . . . I don't know how many. They're just running through the halls. They're still out there. We can hear them.

MALE #1: Quiet. I think I—

MEHTA: Mommy. Mommy . . . I'm scared. I'm so scared.

MALE #1: Oh shit, they're coming back!

MEHTA: I don't want to go out there, Mommy. I don't—

MALE #1: Shut up. Shut up, they're coming—

(Indeterminate sounds.)

MEHTA: Mommy. Mommy, they're here. Mommy, Mommy, they're here—

ASSAILANT #1 (UNKNOWN): You ready to wake up?

MEHTA: Please, Mommy, please—

ASSAILANT #2 (UNKNOWN): Open your eyes?

MEHTA: No no no no—

(Recording ends.)

HIT THE ROAD
Day One. 74 miles.

There are 301 miles between you and your Brooklyn brownstone, your handy-dandy map app says. Now you simply have to figure out how in the hell you're getting to Park Slope.

301 miles between you and Alicia. Before you reach Kelsey.

That's when it really hits.

Hard.

What if this is happening to them, too? You're here, trapped in Virginia, and they are . . .

They're . . .

You need to reach out and see if Alicia and Kelsey are okay. See if they're still alive—

Don't. Don't think like that.

It takes a few too many swipes to open your phone. You don't know whose blood is on your fingers—yours, Devon's, Mom's—but it keeps smearing, fingerpainting the screen red.

"Come on, come on, come on," you mutter under your breath.

Finally your phone unlocks and you speed-dial your wife.

All lines are busy right now. If you would like to try to make a—

You try again.

All lines are busy—

The internet still works, so you try texting Alicia.

No reply. Alicia has never been a texter, but still . . . *Maybe she just powered down her phone.* Better to think this—to believe this—than the alternative. Any other alternative.

Keep believing she's still alive, bud. It's all you've got motivating you to move.

Get your ass back to Brooklyn.

Consider your sister-in-law's car, still parked in the driveway. She won't be needing it anytime soon. Clearly. You've abandoned what's left of her bleeding body on her kitchen floor, scooping Marcus up from the pantry and carrying him out of the house. The boy is still holding that tablet. There is a pair of foam-padded headphones connected to the iPad that drag across the kitchen floor behind you, the wire snaking through the rotten food at your feet.

"Okay, okay," you repeat as you hoist him into your arms, wrapping one hand against the back of his tiny head and pressing his face down into your shoulder. "Okay, okay, okay . . ."

Certain realities are starting to sink in.

First one is: you're fucked.

So utterly fucked.

You don't need me to tell you that. You already know this—only now you've got this catatonic tag-along—your nephew, for shit's sake—so you find yourself suddenly struggling through the motions of survival. If it were just you, all alone in this nightmare, you'd probably curl up into a trembling ball and wait for the next slavering conservative to attack. Simply collapse into some submissive position and let them tear you to pieces, just like the good corporate overlord Rupert Murdoch intended.

But now you're on the hook, aren't you? Suddenly someone much smaller than you is relying on you to survive. Just look at this poor kid. Completely shell-shocked.

"It's okay," you manage to say to Marcus. "Let's, uh . . . let's get out of here." You're saying stuff just to say stuff. Even you can hear the uncertainty, the outright lie, in your voice.

You need to say something, right? Just to fill the air? To comfort this kid? Bring him back from whatever PTSD loophole his mind is spiraling in?

Devon's Subaru Outback is waiting for you. That means getting the keys.

Fuck.

You manage to untangle Marcus from your body and plop him down on the front porch.

You give a quick glance around the sherbet neighborhood to make sure nobody's coming.

Coast is clear.

"Wait here."

Not a peep from Marcus. He's giving off some major traumatized vibes, lost in that million-mile stare. Wherever his thoughts are, they are not here. With you. He's on his own little mental walkabout. You don't know if you're ever going to reach this kid ever again.

God, who would ever want to come back to this world anyway? Wherever his head's at, maybe it's better than here. Anything would be better than this fucking place.

"I'll be right back, okay?"

Can he even hear you?

The best thing to do is give the kid a little screen time. He's already got the goddamn tablet in his hands. Might as well plug him in. *Turn on, tune in, and drop out* . . .

So you slip the padded headphones over his ears.

You're already an afterthought to this child, who swipes at the screen and unlocks it, opening up an animated video with a dancing ghost or something.

Now . . . Let's get those keys, shall we?

After you, Anderson, you think.

Don't get saucy with me, young man . . . I'm only here because your mind needs company.

Fine. Let's go.

You take a deep breath before slipping back inside the house, as if you're plunging your head below water. You're submerging yourself in the cold, the dark. A Pottery Barn grotto.

Your plan? Hold your breath the whole time you're inside and sift through the murk for a set of car keys. Where would Devon put them?

Please don't be in the kitchen.

Anywhere but the kitchen.

Sure enough, settled on the center island is a fruit bowl full of miscellaneous debris—loose change, money clips, paper clips, pens, Post-it notepads, potato chip clips.

Car keys.

You do your best not to look at the bloody mess you've created. All you have to do is make a beeline for the marble counter, look straight ahead, keep your eyes on the—

Devon's gone.

Her body was there, *right there*, bleeding out over the floor in a radiating pool of Technicolor red, but now she's no longer where she used to be.

You step up to the puddle. You see your own blurry silhouette reflected in the blood.

That's you. Now where is she?

There's no way, absolutely no possible fucking goddamn way she could've gotten up.

Where the hell could she—

Devon embraces you from behind. Her arms weave their way around your waist, pulling you back against her chest in a wet lover's embrace. Her chin plops against your shoulder and you can feel how loose her neck is, the flesh around her throat open and gurgling up bubbles.

All you can do is stare down at the reflection of you two in the puddle of her blood.

"NOOOMAMAAADRAAAMAAA . . ." Her lips are at your ear. Her voice. There's a tinniness to it, a vibrato. Metallic, almost. Like electricity buzzing. Humming. Her words are made up of a hundred oscillating insect wings. Her decrepit breath spreads down your neck as she goes in for the lick, running her tongue along the slope of your spine.

Let that settle in for a nanosecond: Devon is licking you, sucking each vertebra along the back of your neck, one nodule at a time, and *you're letting her.*

You're not moving, frozen in place like some goddamn simpering idiot. Run already!

She's not letting go. Her hands tighten their grip around your shoulders.

You sense her reeling her head back to take a bite.

You just know it's coming. So you reverse course at the fastest speed your trembling legs can manage until you both slam against the inside of the open refrigerator door.

Impact untangles Devon. She falls into the fridge.

You don't know what happens. You'll never know. You're not thinking anymore. Your mind simply switches off and you shift into some animalistic autopilot—survival mode, at last—and you kick and kick and kick what is left of Devon. You grab hold of the fridge, for leverage, then stomp your heel down on her face. You don't stop stomping. It's safe to say Devon won't be bothering you or anyone else in this world ever again. She won't be picking herself up from the chilled coffin that once was a refrigerator. You have laid Devon to rest. Paid your respects.

You will never tell anyone what you did in this house—not Marcus, not Alicia, and most certainly not Kelsey. Never ever. What hell you have experienced under this roof is for you and your soul alone to contend with, if souls are even a thing you believe in anymore.

What exactly do you believe in, Noah Fairchild?

What's left?

<hr />

Your Chuck Taylors are drenched red. You remember them being white once upon a time. When you stumble onto the porch, every step is punctuated with a soggy *shlop-shlop* . . .

Marcus doesn't acknowledge the fresh blood.

You hold the keys out to Marcus and rattle them like the fucking goober you are—*ta-da*—actually believing the boy will be giddy to see you found them.

Nothing.

Marcus is more focused on the gang of charging children. There's three of them. No—four. All around Marcus's age. Maybe older? Younger? Who knows? Who cares?

What matters is these preadolescent Boob-Tube Charlies are all heading your way. *Fast.*

They're singing something. You can't tell what. Yet. You hear the lilt of their voices lifting—

up

and

down

and

up

and

down

—even before the lyrics sink in, whatever the words may be.

"Okay, okay," you begin again, a broken record, "into the car, let's go, let's go, let's go."

You two climb into Devon's Outback. You have to do all of the opening and closing and cramming in for Marcus, who seems to have lost most if not all of his basic motor functions.

Some kind of discordant tune drifts out of these kids as they come closer. Chanting, almost. Those Boob-Tubes are singing, aren't they? What the fuck is it?

"Baby Ghost, boo-boo, boo-boo . . . Baby Ghost, boo-boo-boo."

You know this song! Christ, there isn't a kid alive who hasn't sung it. Talk about a fucking earworm. "Baby Ghost" is a South Korean jingle designed to insinuate itself into the minds of children and parents everywhere. The song mysteriously popped up on YouTube not too long ago, its cheaply animated video racking up an astonishing ten billion views. You don't need to listen to the song to hear it, if you know what we mean. It is everywhere, and we mean *everywhere,* a ubiquitous tune that has reprogrammed the nation's preadolescent brains.

Kelsey loves this song. What kid doesn't? Of course these Boob Tubes are singing it.

"Baby Ghost, boo-boo, boo-boo. Baby Ghost, boo-boo, boo-boo. Baby Ghost!"

You slam the driver's door shut just in time to watch the Boob-Tube up front—a girl in pigtails—full-on face-plant against the glass. There's a boy pressing his face against the opposite window, too. He smears his cheeks and nose across the barrier, peering in, pressing hard. His lips split open and now you can hear the *tink-tink* of his braces against the glass.

"Mommy Ghost, boo-boo, boo-boo . . ."

He reels his head back and slams his forehead flat against the window.

"Boo-boo, boo-boo—"

He does it again—

"—boo—"

—and again—

"—boo—"

—smashing his forehead against the glass. You must take a moment to marvel at the tenacity of this child, like a fish attempting a painful escape from its own aquarium.

"Daddy Ghost—"

You only snap out of it once the window cracks.

"—boo-boo—"

A quick flinch and—*oh, shit, let's get moving*—you're back online, Noah. It takes far too many attempts to slip the keys into the ignition. You are not in control of your own body. The adrenaline and panic have turned you into a tuning fork, your bones reverberating with anxiety.

A scream erupts from the speakers.

Not a scream. A song. Some pop country tune blasts out from the car stereo—*Hey, ladies, the honky-tonk is all talky-talk, so why don't we cut the crap and take the night back . . .*

Devon really must crank the music up when she's driving. You can't tell if the female singer is crooning about empowerment or Jesus Christ or Ladies' Night or—or—or—

You switch the stereo off.

"Grandma Ghost—"

SMASH.

"—boo—"

SMASH.

"—boo—"

SMASH.

"—boo—"

Less than half a tank of gas. You can't help but curse Devon for not topping off.

Kids are climbing all over the car now. Tiny feet fumble up the hood and onto the roof. You're intimately familiar with the rubber skid of tennis shoes. They scuffle and slip all around.

You put the car in drive and *aaawaaaaaaay we go . . .*

The muffled sound of tiny bodies tumbling off the roof and into the street fills your ears.

It's very upsetting.

You take a glance into the rearview mirror, just to catch a look at the children now rolling around in the middle of the road, nursing their little boo-boos while you—

CRASH!

Fire hydrant. Everything halts. You're no longer in motion, suspended in place while the momentum within your body continues to plow forward. Your head hits the wheel and—

WHOMP!

—there's the air bag, punching your face, crunching the cartilage in your nose, a dusty blast of talcum powder filling your nostrils, eyes, even the roof of your mouth.

Eyes on the road, Noah . . .

You slowly come to, blinking back to this plane of existence. There's a tinkling of the engine, rain hissing on heated metal. Your eyes flutter open, dragging your consciousness back to the land of the living. You struggle to crane your neck to glance into the seat behind you.

There's Marcus, awake, headphones still cupping his ears. Staring at the screen, not saying a word.

"You—" You cough. "—okay?"

The kid blinks back.

═══

You promised Kelsey you'd be home by Christmas. You gave your word, Noah . . .

Four days, seventeen hours. That's what your handy-dandy map app says.

You can hike that. You've been training for this your whole adult life. Just think about the Brooklyn Marathon you ran back in—well, when exactly was that? 2017?

So you're no longer in tip-top physical condition, fine, but we can work with this.

What other choice is there?

Hoofing it home permits a certain view of the Eastern Seaboard you won't be able to see otherwise. This is how you spin it: *We're just going for a hike! Take in the view! See the sights!*

Whether it's for you or Marcus, you're not quite sure, but your persistence in putting a positive twist on just about every fucking mishap is really getting annoying, even to you.

Your handy-dandy map app draws a slender thread between you and Park Slope, but the traffic line goes from blissfully blue to blood red in seconds, letting you know that's where everybody else is. Well, at least the satellites are still working. You switch to "alternate route" and it's blue all the way up. The highways are better avoided. Let's stick to the back roads.

Route 17. Then 301. Then the Baltimore tunnel. Then the Jersey turnpike. The Goethals. The Verrazzano. Then 278 all the way to Exit 23, where you'll turn onto 23rd Street aaaand . . .

Home again, home again, jiggety jig.

Easy peasy, right?

Right?

VIDEO #676: *Newsday* reporter Andrew Strickler's personal YouTube channel

Nobody knows anything. This is all noise. People are sowing so much disinformation right now, it's unbelievable. Don't trust anything you read online.

Just trust me.

Do not—I repeat, do not—get your intel from Twitter. Or Facebook. Or any social media platforms, for that matter. There's just too many of them now, anyway.

Trust the source. Verify. Verify. Verify. If your news only comes from one outlet, and they're the only ones reporting it, well, then . . . chances are it's not true. News doesn't exist in a vacuum. It lives and breathes and . . . spreads. Other outlets will catch it. Pick it up. Cover it. But it's got to start somewhere. Begin somewhere.

So. What do we know? Absolutely nothing. Absolute fuck-all. We're . . . what? Only a few hours into the shit officially hitting the fan? I know everybody on my news desk is dead. Everyone I work with stopped answering their phones an hour ago.

So I guess I'm freelancing now.

This is not a zombie outbreak. Get all those goddamn movies out of your mind. This is not an infection. It is not viral. Not in a COVID cough-cough kind of way.

This is like some . . . some . . . I don't know. Some sort of social plague.

Large groups of people throughout the United States are banding together in some messed-up mob mentality. They have collectively lost their goddamn minds.

We're covering it like it's some kind of riot. Just another round of protests that have gotten out of hand. Whose lives matter now? But the stories I'm hearing on the wire talk about riots in . . . weird places. Small towns, miles away from the city. Boone's Mill, Virginia. Reading, Minnesota. One-stoplight towns that never in a million years would host a protest . . . Then those riots got violent. Really violent.

There's a kind of groupthink going on here. A thought or an idea has spread from one person to the next. A meme for the mind. Once that thought locks in, these people . . . they can't unthink it. It just keeps looping around their brain, repeating itself. It's like their mind is on autopilot while this thought hijacks their body.

A switch. That's what it feels like. Somebody flipped a switch in America and now all these people are going batshit. Men, women, young, old . . . I've seen elderly women and little kids and just about everybody in between lose their sense of self in the blink of an eye. Clustering together. Tearing the shit out of everything. They seem to be coming primarily from affluent areas. Suburbs. I don't have anything to corroborate this with yet, nobody's confirmed this, but . . . well, it seems like the people primarily affected by whatever are . . . are . . . Caucasian.

Fax News Brain. That's what we're—I'm—calling it. Literal brain rot.

VIDEO #354: Reverend Billie Gray's Temple Hill Baptist YouTube channel

This day has been foretold. Anyone who's been paying attention knows. Those taken aback by today's attacks have not been flipping through the Good Book.

For those just now tuning in to the end times—surprise, surprise—they're here. Did you pack a bag for the Rapture? Forget your passport? Were you left behind?

Look about you. Look around. Look who's still here. Notice that our world leaders have gone silent. Notice that our candidates and our politicians have all slipped into hiding—or joined the fray. Notice that the people sworn to protect us are powerless.

Why? Because the pillars of society have always been faulty. They hold up our ivory towers but they do not reach down deep. Now those pillars are crumbling.

Where has this attack come from?

From below. The gates of hell have opened. Look what has poured forth, people.

Demons.

Our loved ones have succumbed to demonic possession. Your mother, your father, your sisters and brothers. Your own children. Husbands and wives. Their bodies are now host to the most vile entities. They have been slowly corrupting the souls of our friends and neighbors for so long. They prayed to a false prophet they found on their television, their cell phones. They let them in . . .

Now it's up to us to cast them back out.

VIDEO #521: Sarah Leland's "Mad Mama's America" TikTok channel

False advertising. That's all. A lot of so-called "professional people" in charge are going to start telling us a bunch of horseshit. Pardon my French. Just because some guy in a white lab coat stands behind a podium and talks into a microphone doesn't mean he knows what the hell he's talking about. It doesn't matter how many twenty-five-cent words he can throw my way. I'm not buying it. Who put that fella in charge? What corporate interests does he serve? Is he really speaking for the people of the United States? Is it you or is it the oil companies?

You can't trust a word these people say . . . Don't listen to them. Don't believe them.

HUNTING PARTY
Day Two. 79 miles.

Kelsey loves to play road games. Whenever you cram the fam in the car and head down to Virginia, you play I Spy or Twenty Questions or the out-of-state license plate game.

What can you and Marcus play? What will pull him out of his shell?

I spy with my little eye . . .

A burning corpse by the side of the road. Make that two corpses. A couple clinging to each other, their singed limbs smoldering to the bones.

I spy with my little eye . . .

A man bleeding out behind the wheel of his crushed SUV, the shattered glass digging into his neck.

I spy with my little eye . . .

You know what? Maybe a road game isn't the best call.

Riding on your shoulders is Marcus's preferred mode of travel. Your nephew has been saddled on your back for the last few miles and it's wreaking havoc on your spine.

But what's the alternative? When Marcus walks on his own, he slows down, dragging his heels. Constantly complaining about his feet. The cold. The endless stretch of road ahead.

Or—you can simply keep him on his tablet and let him zone the fuck out.

Screen time it is! We'll worry about the batteries running out later . . .

I spy with my little eye . . .

A blazing school bus barreling down the road before you. At first, you think it's orange and yellow banners flickering out from each and every window, but no, now you realize the glass has shattered and those are flames pouring forth, whipping about the roof as the vehicle veers drunkenly along the street, smashing through whatever barrier of automobiles lies before it. You know there are children still onboard because you can hear them shrieking.

I spy with my little eye . . .

Every house is its own horror show in Northern Virginia. Behind each closed door is a family that's been pumped full of possession, an infection that's been slowly growing worse.

Now those doors are opening wide.

I spy with my little eye . . .

A couple in their sixties, standing on their lawn. He's in a blue shirt, she's in pink. Both train their semi-automatic rifles—his and hers—right at you. Take one step on their manicured lawn and you know they'll be perfectly within their so-called rights to start firing.

"Please," you start. "We need help. Can we just—"

"Keep moving, friendo," he says.

"Please," you try again. "We just need some water—"

"Just keep moving," the fellow says.

No one is going to help you in NoVa. Not anymore. The time for solidarity seems to have come and gone, if it was ever there to begin with. Most folks only protect what's theirs.

Stand their ground.

You tap Marcus on his knee. He pulls down his padded headphones from his ears.

"What." So the kid can still talk. Chalk that up to progress.

"How about we take a little screen break? Rest your eyes for a bit."

"You're not my father."

"Yeah, well, I'm the closest thing you've got."

Ouch. That came out more forcefully than you wanted. Marcus doesn't respond. He slowly sinks on your shoulders, his rear end sliding down the back of your neck.

You tighten your grip around his ankles and pull, lifting him upright again.

"Hey," you try again, not knowing how to start a conversation like this. "I'm sorry. That was . . . shitty. You okay?"

Of course the kid is not *okay.* Who the hell would be okay after all that's happened?

"You want to talk about . . . this?"

"No."

Kelsey never quite knew how to interact with Marcus during holiday visits. And neither did you, for that matter. He was always so desperate for attention. *Just play with your cousin,* you'd insist, but you knew if you were in her shoes, you would have acted the same way.

Marcus has some strong homeschool vibes.

"Where are we going?" Marcus asks.

"Home. Brooklyn."

"What's it like?"

"Just like life down here, I guess, only with eight million more people . . ."

"Dad says it's dirty," he says.

Sounds like Asher. You halfheartedly invited him and his fam up to visit a few times over the years, perfectly content with the fact that your brother never liked New York City.

"Doesn't it get loud? With all the shootings and stuff?"

You get used to it, you almost say. "It's not like that. Wanna hear something funny? It's actually harder for me to fall asleep when it's too quiet."

"Isn't it dangerous?"

"Where in the hell are you getting all this?"

Asher, obviously. His parents. You hear your own brother's voice in this conversation.

"I think you'll like it there," you say. "You can get ice cream whenever you want."

"Nuh-uh."

"Twenty-four-seven. We have shops called bodegas. They stay open all day, every day."

"You're lying."

"Hand to God. If you ever get a craving for rocky road at three in the morning, all you gotta do is slip on some shoes and head down to the corner store and *boom*, it's yours."

I spy with my little eye a . . .

Shopping cart.

You walk by a burnt grocery store cart left in the middle of the road. Crammed inside is a charred skeleton, cindered limbs dangling out both sides. The skull is bent back, staring at the black sky with empty sockets, jaw swung open to the chest cavity, gawking.

Marcus doesn't even notice. He's beyond the trauma the world repeatedly presents him now. These fresh bits of hell are no longer jarring to him. Or you. You want them to be, simply to cling on to some scrap of humanity that means witnessing a charred corpse crammed into a shopping cart would startle you, but . . . yeah. Not anymore. That feeling is long gone by now.

"Bodega," Marcus repeats, trying the word on for size. "*Boooh-day-gaaah.*"

"First round of Ben & Jerry's is on me." You smile, but it fades just as quickly.

There probably aren't any bodegas open anymore.

What's left?

"Bodega-bodega-booodaaaaaygaaaaaaa . . ." He shifts his weight across the back of your neck. Feels like you've got a sixty-pound grain sack on your shoulders, pressing into your spine.

"Why did you leave Virginia?"

"I went to college." *That expensive liberal arts college,* Asher would say. *What's that degree done for you lately, big guy?*

"Why didn't you come home?"

"Well, I . . . I just liked it better in New York." Better food. Better bars. Better bands. Better movie theaters. Better pizza. Better girls. Better shawarma. Better bookstores. Better—

"Why?"

"I just liked it, so I decided to stay."

"Why?"

"Because life is better in New York."

"Why?"

"Because it was just more my style."

"Why?"

"Because."

"Why?"

"*Because.* That's why."

"Dad said you're a leetiss."

"He called me a what now?"

"Leetiss. He said you're a leetiss. He said you think you're better than everybody else."

"Oooh . . . *Elitist.* Is that what your dad called me?"

"That's what I said." It may be Marcus doing the talking, but it's Asher's words finding their way out of your nephew's mouth. He's parroting his parents. How long before Marcus starts to rehash their half-baked conspiracy theories?

You really don't feel like explaining your dead brother's favorite insult for you to his son right now, so you change the subject. "Hungry? Wanna hit up a BK? Wendy's? Hardee's? Take your pick."

"Mom says that fast food is bad for you."

"Yeah, well . . . I won't tell if you won't tell."

"Can we go to a McDonald's?"

When you first climb through the drive-thru window, it smells—you can't overstate this—*glorious*. Good God, those golden arches open up like the gates of heaven.

Welcome, St. Peter says. *What'll it be?*

"Stay here," you say to your nephew. "Call out if you see anything, okay?"

Marcus nods.

Your mouth is watering by the time you find the head in the fryer vat. The crispened cranium has been crammed into a wire-mesh strainer, submerged within the bubbling tub of oil. The uniform still smolders at the shoulders, a breath away from bursting into flames, so you grab the handle and gingerly tug the poor teen out from their boiling sarcophagus and let them fall to the floor. What flesh is still clinging to their skull has a crispy texture to it, a deep-fat fried head. Their teeth gleam white, lips gone.

The head is sticking out its tongue at you. The shriveled muscle looks like a fried pickle.

So you won't be ordering any fries today.

You come across a coupling—*tripling? quarteting? quintupling? just how many are there?*—of McDonald's employees humping away in a giant fleshy pile in the dining area. They've knocked over every last table and chair and are now on the floor, grinding their pelvises into whatever nook and cranny their flesh has to offer. Their torn uniforms are covered in condiments—*please let that be ketchup*—as they suckle the sauce from each other's wriggling digits. It's enough to make you lose your appetite. Thank God Marcus isn't here to see this.

The young woman who'd been on drive-thru duty still wears her headset. The adjustable microphone pokes her sexual partner in his eye as she pecks at his face.

You can't tell if they're kissing or devouring one another. Maybe a little bit of both.

It's time to pick up your order and go. You're able to raid the drive-thru without interrupting the fast-food orgy. You find a congealing Happy Meal for Marcus, but he tosses the toy out. The boy has no use for happiness anymore. Not in this new world.

"Let's hit the road."

Your feet ache but you have to keep walking. You haven't made nearly enough progress along these back roads. At the rate you two are going, it'll be New Year's before you reach home.

You need to keep walking. *Just think of Kelsey*, you say to yourself. *Kelsey is waiting for you at home . . . Kelsey is one step closer with every step you take . . . Kelsey is still alive.*

Which means you've got to stay alive. You need to survive.

"What happened to Dad?" Marcus asks in between bites of his hamburger. He's walking now, to give your neck a break.

"He got sick."

"Mom, too?"

Opening Devon's throat with a pizza slicer flashes across your thoughts. "Mom, too."

"Will they get better?"

"I don't think so." Like you have any answers. You don't know what the hell is going on. You're the worst kind of liberal, Noah. An *uninformed* liberal. Not knowing what the hell you're talking about doesn't appear to preclude you from having your own opinion. But when push comes to shove, the truth is you don't have a clue. You can't mansplain yourself out of slaughter. A cursory Wikipedia search isn't going to save you now. Siri isn't going to rescue you.

You're on your own.

The skyline is braided in columns of smoke. Black threads unravel into the atmosphere above D.C., just ahead on the horizon. What about the cities you can't see?

The whole country is on fire.

You're barricaded by a cluster of strip malls on either side of the road. Shattered storefronts. The highway narrows. Abandoned cars corral you into a bottleneck.

You feel guided. Herded forward. You shouldn't be here. Something feels wrong.

You're not alone.

You slow down. Something up ahead seizes your attention. You instinctively bring your hand up to Marcus's face and cover his eyes. You don't want him to see this. Any of this.

There is a pileup of bodies straight ahead, a pyramid of limbs in the center lane.

Heads at awkward angles. Severe cricks in their necks. Whatever happened to these people, they dropped dead fast . . . and here you are, walking in the exact same direction.

Are you next?

You hear wheels. Plastic scraping against asphalt. Something's rolling your way.

Now you see her: a mother pushing a dual-purpose car seat/stroller combo, where the seat pops out and you can put it in the car. You had something similar for Kelsey when she was just a baby. You don't need to look for long before you realize there's something, well, *off* about the woman pushing the stroller. She's got Fax News Brain.

What about the baby?

This mommy spots you and Marcus. Bad call. You should've hid when you still had the chance. Now that she's locked eyes onto you, she's picking up her pace. Still pushing that stroller, mind you.

She's full-on trotting down the lane, gripping the stroller and forging ahead, as if she's going to batter both of you with the baby seat. She's grunting, shrieking.

You step back. You reach for Marcus, trying to grab his shoulder and tug him away with you, but there's a few too many inches between the two of you to take hold.

That mother is running now. The stroller hits a rock and wobbles. For a held breath, you think it's going to topple to the side. You're waiting for that baby to roll over into the road, but Mama keeps her grip, holding the stroller upright, plowing straight ahead. Her panting picks up.

"Just—"

Only a few yards between you now.

"—the—"

You can see how bloodshot her eyes are.

"—faaaaaaax!"

It's strange. You see her neck crick to her left shoulder before you hear the thunder crack. The sound of a rifle firing—*KEERAAK*—is slower than the bullet grazing Mama's forehead.

Mama doesn't seem to mind. It looks as if someone simply drew a red slash across her temple with a red Sharpie marker. She blinks out the blood now dribbling into her eyes, her lids fluttering faster, before continuing on her charge.

CRACK! This time you hear it first—the report—a rending of the air.

A rifle. Someone just fired at her.

And they *missed.*

Mama's still charging, furious now. She's close. Right there in front of you. You reach out with both hands and grab her stroller as it collides into you. She wants to mow you down.

CRACK!

You see the bullet entering, passing through, and exiting her skull.

SPPLCK!

Pink mist fogs up the air. A blossom of brain matter rolls over her shoulder. Proximity to the exit wound sends blood over your face. You feel its faint spatter wetting your cheeks.

Mama's knees soften and she drops to the ground.

You peer into the stroller. You just have to, you need to know if there's a—

No baby, thank god.

No—*thank God*. Go ahead and say it with a capital G, Noah.

You scan the surrounding area, behind cars, behind trees, searching for the clumsy sharpshooter. They could be anywhere.

More Boob-Tube Charlies pour forth from the storefronts. The rifle fire was enough to draw them out. You and Marcus are sitting ducks. You shouldn't have walked this way. Too many wrecked cars on either side, barricading you in, almost as if they've been set up this way.

You see them coming. There's not enough time to run. To escape.

What can you do?

Give up. *Welp, we gave it our best . . .* You wrap your arms around Marcus and cower down, creating a shell with your body, and squeeze your eyes tight, praying it's all over quick.

CRACK! CRACK! CRACK!

Rifle fire all around. Not just one rifle, but several. A semi-automatic pitter-pat, like a summer storm on a tin roof. You hear the dull impact of flesh against pavement, grain sacks hitting asphalt.

"Almost got you, there, didn't they?"

You open your eyes, slowly, looking upward. Who said that? Where are they?

"Up here!"

There. On the roof of the Hardee's. The markswoman is easy to make out. She's wearing designer-brand hunting gear—brand new, from the looks of it, straight off the rack. Fluorescent pink. The butt of her rifle is perched on her outturned hip. She's waving at you. How neighborly.

"You okay down there?"

More women rise. Dudes, too. All wearing designer sports gear. Not a trace of mud or blood on them—pristine neon pink and blaze orange. Vests that say *I'm visible and vivacious.*

How many? Five? Ten, tops, looming on the rooftops of various fast-food shops.

You just wandered into some bottleneck booby trap. *Let the bodies hit the pavement.* Instinctively, you raise your hands. A surrenderer's salutation.

"Who'd you vote for?" Mrs. Sharpshooter asks.

"Excuse me?"

"The last election. Which candidate?"

You take a closer look and almost immediately you can sense it. The awkwardness in the way they hold their weapons. These people never picked up a gun before today. They probably don't even have the safety on. They're swinging them around, aiming at one another as they chat without realizing they could accidentally take each other's heads off with an errant sneeze.

It's a miracle they didn't shoot you.

Democrats.

VIDEO #2310: Paul Morrison's personal YouTube channel

Do not attempt to adjust your screen. The revolution will now be livestreamed!

When we talk about the internet, we speak of "trolls" or "bots" feeding us misinformation . . . but what if they're demons? Actual demons?

What if this is their way into our world? Hear me out . . . Demons have been slowly insinuating themselves into our daily lives without us even realizing it . . .

Yeah—until now. If you paid attention to the message boards like

I have, you would've seen this coming. People have been talking about this for months. Years! Any time you caught wind of it, you'd laugh it off. "That'll never happen . . ."

Surprise! While half the country was laughing about the Great Reawakening, the other half was getting themselves buttered up for a big ol' demonic fuckfest.

They are all over the place. Fucking legion, you know? Elzegan. Xaphan. Promakos. Zainael. The list goes on and on. Most users know Elzegan, but everybody calls him—or it—"E." E is their top recruiter. He is an evil meme. A demonic virus that spreads through social media. E hops from one post to the next, shared by users, until he delivers his payload. People repeat it. Believe it. The more people push E on others, sharing posts or videos about it, the more powerful he becomes, infecting your friends, your family, everyone.

Ever opened an email you shouldn't have? Ever been spammed? It begins with a click. What if it was a demon on the other side of that phishing scheme?

What if by clicking you gave evil permission to infiltrate your life? Just like any computer virus, it spreads and spreads . . . Now they have control over the images on your screen. The talking heads on your TV. The pundits. The health food gurus. The TikTokers. YouTubers. Every face onscreen is theirs to manipulate.

A virus needs to infect as many people as possible. Your body, your very soul, is weakened through constant exposure to all this awful stuff online. The daily bath of BS eventually rewires your brain until you welcome your own demon inside.

They isolate you from your loved ones. Tell you what to do. Prepare your body by performing meme challenges. Change your diet. Juice cleanses with mysterious ingredients. You're not thinking for yourself anymore, regurgitating all these half-baked conspiracy theories. Sounds a lot like incantations to me.

Used to be a Ouija board that brought these devils in . . . Now all we do is click. By accepting the terms of service, we submit ourselves to these demonic forces.

This is a possession epidemic. A plague of possessions. It's consumed half the country. Your family has been weaponized by demons, lured into radicalization.

A demonic jihad.

VIDEO #612: Jessie Gettup's Twitch livestream channel

I heard all that talk about demons and shit. Really? You think a bunch of Reagans are running around with their heads all spinning, spouting that conservative claptrap? Nah, man. Nah . . . I think it's gotta be something that fried their brains all at once. Like a radio signal got sent through those 5G cell towers and whoever was flipping through their iPhone at—that—very—second—was all like, ZAP! You know what I'm saying? Microwaved their minds, dude. Now they're all just wailing away. Whatever they'd been watching or listening to is seared into their skulls and they're just loopholing that shit for the rest of their days . . .

Remember *The Exorcist*? That one scene with the old priest talking to the young priest? They're taking a smoke break from exorcising, just shooting the shit, and the young priest flat-out asks, *What the fuck, bro? Why a little girl?*

And the old priest, all solemn and shit, says: *To despair.*

But here's the rub: That shit was over forty, maybe fifty years ago now. One possessed girl doesn't cut it anymore. One demon doesn't do shit these days.

You want despair in this current cultural climate? You gotta crank up the volume. Turn that shit up to eleven, man! And how in the hell do you do that?

More demons. More possessions. Thousands of them. Fuck, man . . . millions.

I'd pay to see that shit on screen! It's true, though . . . We got a million little Reagans running around the streets now. Not just Reagan-Reagans, like little-girl Regans. Sorry, Linda Blair . . . I'm talking a shit ton of Reaganites. Ripe Ronnie Reagan republicans. Parents, grandparents, kids. Perfect vessels for possession.

Hell on earth, dude. That's all these demons want, I bet. Hell on motherfucking earth. Hell yeah. So . . . like, how do you give an exorcism to the whole country?

VIDEO #272: 12/20 at 4:12 p.m. EST/Duck, North Carolina
(Cell phone footage recorded by Natalie Gilman and Janelle Tompkins.)

GILMAN: Do you see this? Holy shit—look at them go! Oh my God!

TOMPKINS: Keep it down. They're going to hear you.

GILMAN: They're—uh, they're pretty occupied right now.

TOMPKINS: Don't watch!

GILMAN: You kidding me? I'm making my own sex tape—

TOMPKINS: Don't—

GILMAN: How many of them are there? Five, six, seven—

TOMPKINS: Come on, let's go—

GILMAN: Eight, nine, ten, eleven . . . I can't count them all!

TOMPKINS: Stop! I'm going to leave your ass here.

GILMAN: Fine. Go. I'm watching the show. I like that one. Over there. See him?

TOMPKINS: You're so fucking gross.

GILMAN: Eew, look at that nasty one over there! He's all old and shit.

TOMPKINS: Please, Nat, can we just go? I don't like this . . .

GILMAN: They ain't bothering you. They're just out here, living their lives, having some fun in the sun. Matter of fact, I might hop in. Join them.

TOMPKINS: Don't. Don't you fucking dare—

GILMAN: I'm just messing with you. There ain't no way I'm getting in the middle of that. Fucking senior citizen orgy. Look at them. All that pale skin. Whiter than a bunch of sheets on the clothesline. That shit—that shit is downright nasty. You can practically see the VD spreading . . .

VIDEO #437: *Newsday* **reporter Andrew Strickler's personal YouTube channel**

Half of the country is possessed. Just no other word for it, is there? Possessed by their televisions. Their screens. Attacking loved ones with their bare hands.

Riots. Violence. You know the drill. You've seen it on the news for months, years now. You've slowly grown accustomed to the chaos. It barely registers anymore.

Ironic, isn't it? The type of world Fax constantly warned your conservative mother and father about, night after night—pumping that paranoia into your parents—is now happening . . . Cities are full of violence, riots in the streets, rampant with crime and chaos. The right-wing prophesy actually came true, only . . . it's not Antifa in the streets. It's them, our parents, who are attacking.

What's been hidden behind closed doors, simmering beneath the veneer of friendly faces and sherbet-painted houses, is now spilling out into the streets . . .

Burning buildings. Burning bodies. Rome is burning, folks, and we are burning along with it . . .

So why hasn't the government swooped in to save the day? Why aren't there bombs getting dropped on all of this at this every second? On us?

You guessed it: Half—more than half—of the people in charge of the U.S. are possessed, too. This wasn't just your parents brainwashed by Fax News.

This is top brass. This is the president. This is everyone.

VIDEO #1008

(Cell phone footage recorded by Stuart Geismar [deceased].)

GEISMAR: This is as close as I think we can get . . . Here. I'll zoom in. There. Look. Just look at them all. I've never seen anything quite like it. They appear to be . . .

(Pause.)

GEISMAR: Roving. A pack. I've been following this particular herd for about an hour. As long as I keep a safe distance, they don't seem to notice. It appears as if they are heading westward. More members gather the longer they roam. The pack continues to expand!

(Pause.)

GEISMAR: Marvelous, isn't it? The sheer majesty of the pack. Let's see if we can pinpoint the alpha. Perhaps it's that woman there, at the front . . . See how graceful her moves are. How she—

(Pause.)

GEISMAR: Oh. Oh shit. Shit, shit, shit—

(Geismar begins to run.)

GEISMAR: Shit, shit, shit, shit, shit—

(Geismar trips.)

GEISMAR: NO—

(Clip ends.)

STRENGTH IN NUMBERS
Day Two. 86 miles.

The Beltway is choked with abandoned cars. The roads cutting through Washington are clearer than the highways around it.

It's safer sticking together, so you and Marcus glom onto this group of socially conscious survivors. You'll walk with them for the remaining few miles to D.C., at least.

The unofficial leader is Mrs. Sharpshooter herself—Martha. She is—*was*—the manager of a nearby Dick's Sporting Goods. There had been a clearance sale on fluorescent hunting gear when it all went down. Their hot-pink camo attire wasn't exactly flying off the shelves, so now you find yourself wandering along I-95 North with a roaming band of off-brand Barbie and Ken dolls, duck-hunting edition.

"Beggars can't be choosers." Martha's pleasant enough. Short cropped hair. Kind eyes. She smiles even when things aren't particularly pleasant, as if to say *Oh well, what can you do?*

Then there's Craig. He's been mansplaining the apocalypse while you've been hiking. He read online that this had been in the works for months. "A coordinated attack. I'm telling you, this is just the tip of the iceberg . . . When the truth comes out, it's gonna blow your mind."

Nobody likes Craig. Nobody listens to Craig. But Craig keeps talking anyway.

"We really got caught with our pants down, didn't we? This is just beginning, trust me."

A common conversation among the people you meet is *Who switched in your family?*

"My husband became one of them," Martha says. "You?"

"My mom," you say. "Dad. Sister-in-law."

"Welcome to the club." Martha smiles that warm smile. *Oh well, what can you do?*

People trade videos. Clips downloaded to their phones before cell service got all wonky. These snippets become a kind of currency. You barter for information, swapping cracked screens to share a TikTok video of a woman insisting you can cleanse the possession with bleach or a YouTube channel that purports that the possessed are actually human traffickers.

Suffice to say, there's a lot of conflicting intel.

You've watched dozens of mini horror movies in the last forty-eight hours, dozens of these no-budget, bite-sized *Blair Witch Projects*, capturing countless attacks across the country.

Craig starts in again. "I read this all started in a lab in China. They'd been working on some kind of supervirus that slipped out . . ."

"Can it, Craig," Martha says. She came prepared for the apocalypse, apparently. Disposable batteries. Portable solar-powered
charging decks. Bags of beef jerky that had passed its sell-by date. Still
chewy. Any random camping supply she could grab from the stock-
room and stuff in her backpack, she took it. Her plan? Make it to her
sister's house in Delaware. If she's still there. Everyone else is sort of
simply shuffling along, clinging together.

"Your boy all right?" Martha nods up to Marcus.

"He's my nephew. He lost his parents."

Folks have theories, lots and lots of theories, of what could possibly be causing all this. Everything from demonic possession to viral
infection to mass hysteria. Everybody believes something a little different: *My parents are possessed. My son lost his mind. My wife is infected.*

Where's the consensus? Jesus Christ, you just want the—

fax

—facts. Why is that so impossible nowadays? Where's the fucking
truth?

=

When was the last time you visited the Lincoln Memorial?

Fifth grade. Field trip. Mrs. Cook's class. You loaded up on a bus
so your class could wander the mall for the afternoon. You remember
the cherry blossoms on the trees, the delicious smell of them.

Now the air has a tinge of cinders to it.

You always wanted to take Kelsey to the Smithsonian: walk the
mall, visit the Lincoln Memorial. You thought it'd be fun to show her
the benchmarks of the country's foundation.

I spy with my little eye . . .

A mound of bodies on the Smithsonian.

I spy with my little eye . . .

A knot of bodies on the steps of the Kennedy Center.

I spy . . .

I . . .

Washington is burning. I'll keep reporting on the carnage, even though the real CNN cut their feed sixteen hours ago. Not that you know that. They're still broadcasting in your brain.

Thanks, you think.

Happy to help.

You're crossing over the Arlington Memorial Bridge. You spot a few bloated bodies bobbing along the Potomac. Before long, you'll reach the National Mall.

You're tired. So tired. You feel like you're about to collapse. One more breath and you'll pass out. Just think of Kelsey. *Kelsey is waiting for me. Kelsey is still alive . . . Kelsey is still safe . . .*

Kelsey is . . .

"Do you hear that?" Craig asks. "What the hell is that? Sounds like . . . grunting."

He's right. There's a repetitive roar in the air, like the cheering fans of a football game caught on a loop. It's been a couple hours since you saw any Boob-Tubes. You'd imagined D.C. would be teeming with them, but the streets have been relatively empty. It makes you nervous.

The grunts are growing louder now. More pronounced. There's a cadence to each pant, a rhythmic *heave-ho, heave-ho, heave-ho*, and suddenly you're not so sure if you want to know what's waiting for you around the bend. "Maybe we should turn around," you say.

"We're right there," Craig says. "I want to see what—"

"Stop." Martha halts. She's the first to see it, whatever this is. She's not smiling now.

"Holy shit," Craig says, eyes going wide.

There's an orgy along the National Mall.

There are bound to be hundreds—Jesus, *thousands*—of people humping away across the cherry tree–lined boulevard. There isn't a single inch of free space as far as you can see. They're on the lawn.

They're splashing around in the center pool's shallow waters. They're sprawled out across the steps of the Lincoln Memorial. Straddling Mr. Lincoln. They're crawling all over his statue, desperate to find a crevice to pound with their pelvises, grinding their hips against his massive marble shins. Giving the poor president a lap dance. Dry-humping his ear.

"What in the name of . . ."

In the name of *what*?

The exact same spot where Martin Luther King Jr. delivered his "I Have a Dream" speech . . . The very same location where the AIDS quilt covered the landscape . . .

They're all fucking on it.

You've never seen so many people screwing before, intertwined in one singular sexual act of depravity. No orifice goes untapped.

The long view displays a pale tapestry of interconnecting bodies. It ripples. Undulates. They don't look like people anymore, just a heinous mosaic of sexual wantonness, a live-action Caucasian Kama Sutra, every position represented in all its sweaty detail. So many grasping hands. Bouncing breasts. Flickering tongues. A roiling sea of naked flesh. The palest flesh. You're practically blinded by the whiteness of it all: a blanched landscape. You notice a pattern of bad tattoos: Dancing Grateful Dead bears. Celtic knots. Tramp stamps.

"Let's get it on," Craig says, doing his best Marvin Gaye, which isn't that good at all.

"Don't look," you say to Marcus. A little too late for that now, pal. The kid has been gawking at what amounts to the largest centerfold in history. This is bound to break whatever world record for biggest orgy Guinness had listed prior to today. The plateau of copulating bodies reaches—Jesus Christ—to the White House, fornicating all the way to the Capitol.

Now they're eating each other.

Kisses become nibbles become gnaws. One woman pulls the lips off her lover. If you can call him that. He returns the favor by biting at her breast. They're chewing chunks off each other, happily humping along as they swallow and go back for more.

All that white flesh . . . goes red. Wet. A Slip 'N Slide of skin.

You pull Marcus down from your shoulders and cover his eyes. This may be the first time he's more interested in seeing the tantalizing sights than the videos on his tablet, mesmerized by the mass intercourse stretching well on into the horizon. It's everywhere.

Everywhere.

"Keep your headphones on," you say, praying Marcus can't hear all the desperate groans. The sheer amount of moaning that rises into the sky is inescapable now, this ripple of exhales and sighs rising and falling over the copulating crowd. It washes over you. Overwhelms you. There is no pleasure in these panting sights. It's just flesh smacking against flesh, bodies grinding and humping and chomping and gnawing and oh my God you feel sick to your stomach.

The Washington Monument looms above it all, a massive erect penis poking at the cosmos, an ungodly cock throbbing above the mating masses, now a monument to debauchery.

Untold numbers of bodies swarm the base, fondling the balls of America. They stack up on top of each other, this mountain of flesh climbing up the monument's shaft, reaching its tip.

You have a hazy recollection of viewing a Fourth of July fireworks display right here along the National Mall. You watched the televised broadcast from home, kneeling next to your dad in his La-Z-Boy, softly singing along to "The Star-Spangled Banner," mesmerized by the colorful—

gaslights

—explosion in the sky. You can't help but picture the sky alive with bursts of color again.

You can nearly hear your father belting out the words he thinks he knows, while leaving out the rest—"*And the rockets' red glare, the bombs bursting through the air, that gave proof to the night that our flag was still there . . .*"—while the sky explodes, all the lights, the swirling colors.

"We need to leave," you say. "We need to get out of here. Now."

"Don't be such a prude," Craig chides.

The first possessed participant to notice you is a few yards up ahead. An older gent. Probably in his eighties. A pair of shredded arm bags dangle like pale flapping sheets, clothes drying on the line, stained red. He's between two men, tangled in their limbs, wrestling up for air, when suddenly he stops long enough to notice they have company. He continues to hump—and be humped—*pound-pound-pound*, chest heaving, wrinkled sheets of skin swaying, as he watches you. Stares at you. Not saying a word.

Then he barks. "Just! The! Fax!" It's all husk, a dry cough.

This draws the attention of his friends. The second they see you, their expressions tighten. Not that they stop humping, mind you. Their faces simply pucker as they pound.

They start barking now, too. "Just! The! Fax!" The sound is raspy—a donkey with colic. A trained seal snarfing for a fresh fish after performing a trick.

It sounds awful. So awful. And it's only getting louder. "Just! The! Fax!"

Before long, a tide of heads turns your way. It almost happens all at once. You can see this ripple pass through the crowd, everyone's necks craning and glancing at you.

You've interrupted their orgy. How rude.

"Go," Martha says. "Now. Go go go."

You don't look back. You just run. You hear the soft padding of bare feet—so many feet—behind you. You grab Marcus and press him against your chest, straining for breath under his weight.

But that barking, my God, it's just growing louder and louder. You can nearly feel the warm gusts of breath spreading down the back of your neck as those naked bodies gain on you.

The barking gets louder now . . .

"Just!"

They're getting closer now . . .

"The!"

They're gaining on you . . .

"Faaaaax!"

You don't see what happens to Martha but you hear her scream. Craig, too.

They're gone. Just like that. Swallowed by the naked crowd. It's every Democrat for themselves out here. Survival of the leftist. You know you're next if you don't keep running.

Faster, Noah. Faster. You're not going to make it.

Run. Run. RUN.

———

You hide in a gutted taco truck. The rear door had been left open, the remnants of salsa and chopped lettuce scattered across the pavement. You toss Marcus in first, and then you climb in, sealing the door shut behind you and praying that the naked horde doesn't notice.

You hear them. Bare feet on asphalt. The swell of people charges by so abruptly—

"just"

—the truck itself rocks on its wheels—

"the"

—and all you can do is hold on, hold your breath, hold on to your sanity—

"faaaaaax"

—until the sound dies down.

"Get out."

There is a man with a lead pipe pointed right at you. His face is covered with a blue paisley bandana, his unblinking eyes staring back. That's definitely the look of a man who has seen some shit. Whether that shit is relegated to the last seventy-two hours or longer is anybody's guess, but given that you're on the receiving end of that pipe, you definitely don't want to find out.

Your hands instinctively lift. "It's okay, we're okay, we're not—"

"You clean?"

"Yeah." You notice a chunk of scalp clinging to the hollow end of the man's pipe. A loose strand of auburn hair flickers in the wind, stuck to the metal with coagulating blood.

"Prove it."

"How?"

"Where do you get your news from?"

"The *Times* . . . We have a subscription to *The Atlantic.*"

"Digital or print?"

"Both?"

You notice movement behind him. Shifting limbs.

Children.

Two of them, huddled behind him. A boy and girl. Brother and sister. They look afraid.

Of you.

The man—a father, just like you—doesn't say anything at first. He simply stares you down, weighing his options. That pipe must be heavy in his hand. He tightens his grip around it.

The little girl leans over, just by an inch, and the man brings his hand up and scoots her back behind him. He's using his body as a shield. Against you.

"Their mother was one of them," he says. "Been stuck on that wellness crap. Saw her slip before our very eyes and didn't do a damn thing about it when I had a chance."

"Got the devil in her," the boy pipes up, then regrets it when his father shushes him.

He swallows something back, losing himself for a moment.

"Only choice I had was to . . ." He doesn't finish. You already know the rest of the story.

You feel the need to commiserate with this guy, man-to-man. Father-to-father. *Hey,* you want to say, *we're all just out here, trying to get by, you know? Make sure our kids get home safe and sound. Alive and in one piece, am I right?*

But he doesn't trust you. Doesn't know you from Adam. His fist tightens around the pipe again. Loosening, tightening, loosening, tightening. You see the strain in his knuckles.

"Where you heading?"

You swallow before answering. "North."

"How far?"

"New York."

This gets a laugh. "On *foot?*"

You nod.

"You think you two will survive that long?" Sure sounds like a challenge. A threat?

"Gonna try."

He's keeping his eyes on you, making sure you don't do something rash. But he lowers the pipe. Progress. "We just left Baltimore. Good luck getting through there. It's all messed up."

You two swap phones. Share videos. He has one where a guy explains that the possessed are heading to the heartland.

"Let 'em have it," the father says. His voice has an edge to it. "Keep it for all I care."

"I watched a video that says you can change them back."

"You believe everything you see on TV?"

"Maybe there's a chance," you say.

"And then everything goes back to the way it was? Before everything went to hell?"

He's baiting you.

"You think this happened overnight? You think this country just went bad *now?*" This father pulls down his bandana. He's chewing through his anger, ready to spit it out. "*Now* you're paying attention. Where the hell have you been the last ten years? Fifty years?"

"I didn't mean—"

"This ain't new. It's just new to *you*. Rest of us have been out here dealing with this shit for decades now. *Centuries.* It's only because life got all bad for you white folks that you're opening up your eyes to it all, but the rest of us have been faced with this shit since the day we were born . . ."

You open your mouth to say something, offer a retort, as if this were all some cocktail party debate and you're taking the opposing side. But you don't. Better keep your mouth shut.

"People's true colors sure are flying now," he says, then laughs. "Those evil feelings were in folks to begin with. All these demons did was simply tip the scales."

Marcus starts squirming. You can hear his breathing intensify.

"Marcus—"

He won't stop. He's having some sort of seizure, you think. "What's wrong, Marcus?"

"Better quiet your kid down," the man says. "They'll come back."

Marcus starts hitting you with his iPad, smashing the tablet against your shoulder.

"Marcus—"

"Get him to shut up or I'll—"

"Marcus, stop!" You grab the iPad just as he brings it back down. The two of you play tug-of-war until it slips from his grip. That only sends him further into his hissy fit. "Stop!"

The tablet won't turn on. Its batteries have finally died out. After nearly three full days of "Baby Ghost," the iPad has officially farted out on Marcus and it's sent him into paroxysms.

He's having a full-on temper tantrum—screaming, sobbing, but his eyes are dry. All you can do is wrap your arms around him from behind, cover his mouth with your hand and squeeze, hoping to subdue him.

But he won't stop. He bites your hand, wrestling against you.

"Get out," the other father says.

"It's okay," you lie. "I can get him to calm—"

The man doesn't say another word, only offering you the receiving end of his lead pipe. He holds it up, directly in your face, then points toward the rear door of the food truck.

This man won't risk losing his kids. Not for you. Not for Marcus. You can't blame him, can you?

"Good luck," he says.

VIDEO #1531: "Video Free America" YouTube channel, hosted by DemAnon

DEMANON: It's viral. When are you dumbasses going to understand that? This is not some religious uprising. This is a goddamn plague. What kind of virus is the real question we should all be asking ourselves here. Not whether this is the apocalypse. It's a man-made event. We did this. Not God. Not the Devil. Us.

China, to be more precise. I know you've seen the videos. Some lab tech risked his own life getting that recording out. Bats. Monkeys. Pigs. Birds. This started when some virus hopped species and some government bioweapons think tank forgot to tighten the lid on a particular vial of monkey bat pox and now look what we got . . .

VIDEO #2185: "Know Ur Enemy" TikTok page, hosted by RageAgainstU

RAGE: This is mass hysteria writ large. Mob rules now. Ever hear of dancing sickness? The dancing plague of 1518? Or what about those high school girls who all broke out into spontaneous epileptic fits in Le Roy, New York, back in 2011? Dozens of teenage girls suddenly erupt into seizures right there in the middle of their classroom. What was the cause of them all? It wasn't a virus or bacteria.

It was a thought. An idea. The notion—dancing! seizures!—was powerful enough to infect a group of susceptible people. These people just want to belong. Fit in.

So they pick a pandemic. Like it's all just another fucking clique.

We have always been a suggestible culture. We love trends. We love to belong. It doesn't take much to get people panicking. If one person goes crazy, spouting off about lord-knows-what, guess what? I want to lose my mind, too. It's the new jam.

This isn't a virus . . . It's a lemdemic. A lemming pandemic. It starts with one person and then they get another person buying into it and then another. Before long, you've got a full-on riot on your hands. It's the Middle Ages all over again.

We're just going to keep dancing, dancing, dancing . . . as the world burns down.

VIDEO #421: Ron Morrison's personal YouTube channel

What do they want? Simple question, right? What do these demons want?

They want out. To be free.

They've been cooped up in the underworld for millennia. Centuries under our feet. They see what mankind has and they're like "I'll have what she's having . . ."

They've been planning this. Biding their time before making their move. Waiting for the perfect confluence of events, dumbing us down, then . . . possession time!

Our bodies are theirs. Now they're free. All they want is total chaos. Hell on earth.

Remember back in high school? Your parents left you alone for the first time and what's the first thing you do? You throw a party. Invite all your friends over. But your pals invite their pals and they invite their pals and on and on and on . . . until you have no control over who comes into your home. And what do these hard partiers do? They wreck the fucking place. Destroy your home. Absolute chaos.

That's exactly what these demons are doing. They're in our house and now they're wrecking it. They don't care whose body it is. They'll just get a new one.

So for anyone out there still wailing away—"Why? Why is this happening?"—I mean, come on. "What do they want?" What kind of cockamamie question is that?

Demons don't have an agenda! They don't have a mission statement! They just want to fuck shit up! And that's exactly what they're doing. Fucking. Shit. Up.

VIDEO #731: Sarah Leland's "Mad Mama's America" TikTok channel

LELAND: Adrenochrome. That's what they're after . . . It makes perfect sense when you stop and think about it. Our adrenal glands create a potent chemical called adrenochrome. Its psychedelic properties hold the promise of immortality, but it has to be fresh. Straight from the glands. You can't synthesize it. The best way—the only way—to get the good stuff is from children. Frightened children.

You have to be terrified to produce a strong enough dose, so you have these people out there, kidnapping children in order to harvest their spiked blood.

What do they want? The answer's pretty clear. Our blood. They want our children's blood. We must protect our children against these demon-pedophiles.

VIDEO #1029: Charlie Clearing's personal YouTube channel

Whose horror story is this? Sure as shit ain't mine. It's every liberal's nightmare out here, isn't it? Just one big ol' NPR apocalypse.

Who are the possessed? It doesn't take some religious census taker to figure it out. Anyone with a pair of eyes can see whose bodies are hijacked . . .

Weak-willed wellness motherfuckers. Yeah, these demons knew who to dupe. Anybody looking to conspirituality got themselves overthrown from the inside out. These wheat-grass-drinking homeopaths got themselves radicalized. Catfished by a motherfucking demon. You believe that?

Do you think this just happened overnight? This was a planned attack. These motherfuckers have been priming our minds for yeeeeears. Look, just look, at your racist parents! When's the last time you were able to have a decent dinnertime conversation that didn't devolve into some complete conspiracy-laden clusterfuck? Months, right? Maybe years? Way, way back.

Talk about methodical. These motherfuckers have been planning this overthrow for a long time. That's some stone-cold shit. But you want to know what the real kicker is? It was easy. So fucking easy. Your family fell for it. They wanted, really wanted, to be taken over. Primed for possession. "Take me, take me!" Now they can't be held accountable for the shit they do. If there's any coming back from this, if the switch gets flipped and your racist, xenophobic, transphobic, Islamophobic, fucking-everything-phobic family snaps out of it, they're gonna be all like, "Oh, you can't hold me accountable for what happened . . . I was possessed."

Fuck that. And fuck you for letting it happen in the first place. This is on you, too. You better believe that. You made this happen. You. You're a part of the problem.

Don't think there isn't blood on your hands. You could've stopped this all from getting apocalyptic if you just talked to your parents.

Hope you're happy now.

So let's be clear on this salient point, okay? This is not everybody. This is not some worldwide takeover. Look. Just look at who's attacking who. This is—and I'm just going to say it here—this is some white people shit. There, I said it. Somebody had to. I'm sure your racist grandmother was a lovely person back in the day, baking her apple pies or whatever, but . . . I'm sorry. Look at her now. This is what happens when you let that shit fester. It's like a dam of shit. The levee ain't gonna hold forever. The dam is gonna break and when it does, guess what? You've got a flood of shit on your hands . . . and this shit is everywhere now. It's in our streets. In our cities. It's been hiding behind polite smiles and white picket fences for years, festering behind closed doors and gated communities . . . but all it took was some BS Malcolm Gladwell tipping point for it all to come spilling out.

You should have dealt with your fucked-up family when you had the chance. Now we've all got to deal with them. They're our problem now. I'm not holding back.

So yeah. This is not our horror story. This is *your* fucking horror story.

An *American* Horror Story . . .

But whose America, am I right?

BATHROOM BREAK
Day Two. 99 miles.

I spy with my little eye . . .

Storm clouds.

It's going to rain. For a while you thought it was merely smoke blocking out the sky, but you now realize those are thunderheads forming. You'll need to find cover before much longer.

Those clouds threaten to crack at any moment now. The sooty horizon has only blackened the farther north you've traveled, walking directly into the oncoming storm.

"We should look for cover."

Marcus hasn't spoken in hours. Maybe a day. Ever since his tablet lost its charge, he's been shaking. Shivering. Cold sweat. It's unnerving to see a seven-year-old slip into withdrawal.

The first few drops of rain strike your dry skin. Fat pellets against parched flesh. When was the last time you took a shower?

The drizzle picks up and quickly breaks out into a downpour. You close your eyes and tilt your head back. It feels like such a relief, rinsing the soot and grit from your face.

The relief doesn't last long.

Marcus shifts on your shoulders, the weight of him straining your lower back.

I spy with my little eye a . . .

Rest area.

You've almost forgotten what an honest-to-God rest stop is like. How crappy they are. You've grown accustomed to the service areas along I-95, glitzy shopping mall food courts.

This place is little more than a cinder-block outhouse and a wooden gazebo for picnicking families. A few abandoned cars sit in the parking lot, doors left open. The place is all yours from the looks of it.

I spy with my little eye a . . .

Community board. A wall for maps and flyers. Local businesses staple their ads here. But the entire expanse of corkboard has been overtaken with fresh missing-person flyers.

Their black-and-white photocopies draw you in.

LISA LOVE. Sixty-three years old. Went mad just three days ago and attacked her own grandkids. Last seen heading west on foot with a pack of rabid neighbors.

HARLAN REBELEIN. Forty-seven. Killed his wife with his bare hands and now his kids are looking for him. Last seen heading west on foot in his boxers and T-shirt, no shoes.

SUZANNE HARRISON. Ate her own son's face before hitting the road.

CARLA WEHUNT. PEG TURLEY. NATHANIEL CASSIDY.

So many. Too many to count. It's not their bodies that are missing, it's their souls. Each and every one of the people in these photocopied flyers is a family member who snapped. Same time, same date as everyone else. A communal cracking. Just like your parents. Now their surviving members have made a shrine out of some podunk rest stop community board.

"Let's set you down," you say.

The moment Marcus slips from your shoulders and you get your spine back, you can't help but let out a sigh of relief. The two of you rush for cover under the gazebo as the rain picks up. The downpour pounds against the wooden roof, spilling down in tinsel streamers.

It's downright biblical.

Here comes the flood . . .

What if there's some truth to that? Could this be the end? Is everything going to wash away, the two of you included?

"You hungry?" You spot a pair of vending machines. "Lunch is on me . . ."

The plate-glass window is shattered, the racks pecked clean. You peer in and see if someone might've left behind a candy bar or bag of potato chips.

The best you can find is a packet of gum.

You'll take it.

"One for you." You hand a stick of gum to Marcus, take another for yourself. "One for me."

The gum summons saliva in the arid desert of your mouth for the first time in forever and, *my God*, it tastes amazing. The best stick of gum you've ever had. You hope it lasts forever.

Juicy Fruit. What flavor even is that?

You want another stick. Mom always told you not to swallow gum, but you're so delirious with hunger. Maybe you can trick your stomach into believing you're actually eating something.

"Thirsty?"

Marcus nods.

"Watch this . . ." You kneel before the soda machine and slip your hand through the bottom reservoir. After some snaking around, you're able to pull out a can of Coca-Cola.

Marcus's eyes widen.

"Ta-daaaa."

You two hunker down in the gazebo and share a can of warm Coke. The electricity must've cut out at some point. Still tastes amazing. You've never been one for soda—all that processed sugar—but you'd sell your soul for another saccharine sip. You have to pace yourself.

"Don't hog it all . . ."

Marcus starts performing a jig. He shifts his weight from one foot to the other. At first, you laugh a little and start clapping your hands, as if this were a sugar rush hoedown. *Yeeehaw!*

Marcus grimaces and—*wait a sec*—you've seen this two-step before.

It's the pee-pee dance.

"You need to go?"

Marcus nods, *yeah, yeah, yeah . . .*

"Why didn't you say so . . . Number one or number two?"

"One."

"It's your lucky day." As fate would have it, you've come to the right place. You have been relieving yourselves out in the open for days now, so having a chance to use an actual toilet feels like such a luxury. Even in a run-down, piss-stained, graffiti-laced back-road rest stop.

"Let's do it," you offer, leading the way.

Marcus doesn't follow. You turn and notice he's still doing his two-step, frantic now.

"What's wrong?"

"I need privacy." He grits his teeth, hissing a bit, as if it's hurting.

"There's no one here."

"I can't go when someone's watching . . ."

"Got it."

You double-check to make sure the men's room is empty. Poking your head in, you're met with the smell. These bathrooms never have proper ventilation, sealing in the suffocating stench of urine. Sure seems like a design flaw. Nothing but breeding grounds for bacteria.

"Hello? Anyone?"

Coast is clear.

"All yours." You step back, holding the door for Marcus. "I'll be waiting out here."

Marcus hops in on his tippy-toes, hissing louder with each step, as if he's walking barefoot across hot coals. You can't help but see just a bit of yourself in this kid now and then.

"Call out if you need anything, okay? I'll be right here."

Even though you instantly regret it the moment the words leave your lips, you also say:

"You're safe."

———

This is not for you to see, Noah. To know. But I'll report on it anyway. Ol' Coop will bear witness to this exclusive, providing eyewitness testimony while you're ostensibly standing guard at the door, wondering if you should start building an ark.

The lights aren't on, so the poor boy is left with what little illumination seeps through the thin slit of windows along the upper wall. Too small to crawl through, too high to reach.

The downpour outside casts its gray haze over the tawny tile walls.

There is a row of standup urinals to Marcus's left, just below the windows. Porcelain monoliths, like a piss-stained Stonehenge.

But there's no time to take in the surrounding darkness. He has to go go gooooooo. *Now.* He's already unfastening the button of his pants, making a wobbly beeline for the urinals when he notices—

Someone is behind him.

Following him.

A shadow at his shoulder. Same height. Same speed. A doppel-gänger in every way.

Marcus nearly pees in his pants when he skids to a halt, turning to discover—

His reflection.

It's just him, staring back, as startled as he is. A set of mirrors mounted on the wall facing the urinals. They've been scratched into. Words are scraped against the glass. What do they say?

WAKE UP

Poor Marcus can't hold it in any longer. He's about to explode. He needs to pee now now noooooooow before his bladder bursts. Go goooo goooooooooooo.

But the mirrors. He doesn't trust them.

He can't turn his back on his own reflection, for fear it might reach out and grab him while he's peeing and pull him back into the mirror until they're both trapped behind glass.

That leaves the bathroom stalls: three toilets barricaded behind wooden booths. The doors for the first two are open. The third is closed. This should've been a red flag for the boy.

Obviously.

But Marcus isn't thinking about that final stall being occupied. All he's thinking of is—

PEE PEE PEEEEEEEEE

—his mind flashing yellow warning lights, sirens sounding in his skull. Uncle Noah already peeked in. He checked out the place. *Coast is clear,* he said. *All yours,* he said.

He's safe in here.

Marcus rushes for the middle stall. He slams the door shut, latch-ing the lock.

There. Safe, at last.

This toilet is all his. The walls of the stall are laced with indeci-pherable words. Marcus has mastered his second-grade reading levels, but he's not sure if the flowing cursive scribbled onto the walls is even the English language. But there are a few words he can make out:

OPEN YOUR

Open *what?*

The pictures are easier to comprehend. An illustration of a whale-sized wiener on the cartoon body of a ghost. How can that guy float? His weenie is three times the size of the rest of him. He's smiling at Marcus. Winking. *Thumbs up!* He's pointing with his other hand to—

A mouth. No, not a mouth.

A hole.

The wood has been carved—*chewed?*—open, a tiny portal open-ing between stalls. The wood seems to've been sanded down. Worn down with the oil of a million fingers.

There's duct tape around the edges.

Someone took a Sharpie marker and drew a mouth around the hole. Teeth rim the circumference. Lips line the crooked teeth. There are no eyes. No nose. Just a floating mouth.

Is there someone on the other side of the . . . ?

Marcus now notices another layer of sticky graffiti. Slender strips of mother-of-pearl reach out from the hole, stretching in every di-rection across the bathroom stall walls.

Glistening snail trails.

There have to be a dozen—more—slimy threads branching out in every direction. The trails are even on the ceiling, lacing the entire men's bathroom in a shimmering knot of slime.

What kind of slug could make that many trails? Where are they all now?

No time. Marcus needs to—

PEEEEEEEEEEEE

—so bad he thinks he might need to poo now, too. He's been holding his bladder back for so long, his body begins to rack with involuntary spasms. He pulls his pants down and plops onto the toilet, even though his mother always instructed him to take a strip of toilet paper and wipe the seat down first, cautioning him to double-check for loose dribbles of pee on the seats.

Unsanitary, she'd say.

Disease, she'd say.

Hep C, she'd say.

No time to dwell now. *Here it comes . . . Watch out below!*

Marcus barely makes it to the seat before he's peeing everywhere. The relief is instantaneous. There's a sense of accomplishment, a small victory. He made it! Into the toilet!

Yay!

No number two. False alarm.

Even after Marcus is done, he decides to sit there. Just for a little while.

Nothing in him wants to get up.

To move.

He can simply sit here and relax on this stinky toilet with his empty bladder for—

"Psst."

Marcus's entire body seizes at the sound.

Did he . . . ? Was that . . . ?

No. No, it couldn't be. He's alone. His uncle checked. Made sure the coast was—

"Pssst."

Marcus feels the need to pee again, even though there's nothing left in his bladder.

The muffled voice is coming from the neighboring stall.

Marcus hasn't exhaled, holding it in.

Marcus turns toward the wooden partition between him and the neighboring stall.

Toward the hole.

There is an eye on the other side.

A human eye.

Bloodshot.

Staring back.

Bloodshot might not be the right word. There are threads of red, sure, but there are other colors as well. Pretty colors. Pink and purple and green. An oily, slithery shimmer.

The colors start to swirl. They—

gas

—light up. Widen.

It winks.

"Baby Ghost, boo-boo, boo-boo . . ."

Marcus lunges to the side, tilting away from the hole—the eye— his shoulder striking the opposite wall. He topples off the toilet and hits the cool cement floor with a wet slap.

"Baby Ghost, boo-boo, boo-boo . . ."

Marcus wants to scream, to shout out for his uncle, but nothing comes. He wants to pick himself up and run, but realizes he can't. All he can do is stare back at that eye.

"Baby Ghost, boo-boo, boo-boo . . ."

They're singing to him. Whoever it is. His favorite song.

So he sings along.

What else can he do? Call out to Uncle Noah? That's probably the right answer. The smart call. But . . . but that eye. Those swirling colors. The stunningly wonderful—

gaslights

—shimmering hues. It makes him want to sing.

"Baby Ghost, boo-boo, boo-boo . . . Baby Ghost."

There's a chill in the tune. Singing this song has always given him strength, like hugging a teddy bear in the dark, but singing it now, the words feel flimsy. Paper thin. Soggy in this other person's voice. They don't sound like a person at all, to be honest. Not a healthy one, at least.

It sounds like there's something else in this person's poor throat. Trying to get out.

To crawl.

"Boo!"

Marcus glances down and realizes there is a gap between the floor and the wooden barrier between stalls. Less than a foot's worth of open space.

Marcus doesn't see feet. Whoever's on the other side of the stall doesn't have feet.

Is that possible?

"Your mommy wanted you to have thissss," the voice on the other side of the wall says.

Just then, a hand lowers into view from beneath the neighboring stall. Not to grab Marcus.

To offer something. A gift . . .

What is it?

A shiny new tablet. Fully charged.

"Want some screeeen time?" the voice asks. The tablet is turned on, even now, casting its oily colors across the cement floor, shimmering in pinks and purples and marvelous—

gaslights

—greens. The glow pulses and swirls, sparkling and spiraling bright, and Marcus wants to take it, take hold of the tablet with both hands, to bring it up to his eyes and—

dive in

head

first

—down, down, down the rabbit hole the boy goes.

VIDEO #861: "Hunting with Hank!" YouTube channel, hosted by Hank Maddock

Hey, everybody! Welcome to Hunting with Hank. I'm your host, Hank Maddock, and with me as always is my wife, Loraine. Say hi, Loraine!

Today we're checking out Chesterfield Towne Center to see if we can find any infected folks and put them out of their misery.

Your family is not your family anymore. Unless you know how to perform a nondenominational exorcism, I'd say your next best bet is to shoot them on sight.

Locking them up only exacerbates the problem. They're not coming back. Your loved ones are gone. Elvis has left the building. Your mom, your pop—they relinquished their bodies to these demons. Like handing over the keys to Dad's fancy Cadillac, they simply tossed their bodies to some hell-bent incubus itching to go for a joyride . . . and now they're going to run their flesh and bones right into the ground. These demons don't care what condition they leave their bodies in.

Best advice I can give—that I always give—is to shoot them. Shoot them all.

Oh! Lookie here. See who we've got . . . Female. Probably in her sixties. Seventies. Rummaging around the food court. She's separated from her pack, poor gal.

Just take aim, focus your breathing, aaaand . . . There! Bullseye!

VIDEO #3210: "Know Ur Enemy" TikTok page, hosted by RageAgainstU

RAGE: Yeah, I crossed paths with a possessed pack. They're making a pilgrimage. Those motherfuckers are migrating. Where in the hell are they all going?

To the middle of the country, that's where. These demons *seced-ed* from the underworld. You believe that? Only in motherfucking America... These possessed assholes are turning our country into their own personal playground.

The US of A is just more fun than hell. *Fact.* Don't act surprised when half of the country is huddled in the middle of America, erecting their temples or whatever, while all us survivors sequester ourselves along the coastal cities.

This is gonna be the new normal: half of the country's population hosts a demon while the other half has to figure out how to live without them.

VIDEO #941: "Living Well" YouTube channel, hosted by Sarah Leland

What the pharmaceutical companies don't want you to know is that the best way to get rid of this bug is in your own home. All you all got to do is look under your kitchen sink. If you've got a bottle of bleach in your basement... you're covered.

My husband had the bug. My kids had the bug, all three of them. Know what I did? A Clorox detox is all it took. They're right as rain now, the whole family.

I'm here to tell you it works—bleach works—no matter what these so-called scientists say. They'll say they have the cure, then they'll charge you up the wazoo... Who has the medical insurance to cover this kind of sickness anymore?

Why waste your hard-earned money when the cure's right here in your own home? You want to pad their pockets or do you want to cleanse your family?

You don't believe me? Here. I'll prove it. Watch me. I've never lied to you, people.

Down the hatch...

VIDEO #950: 12/21 at 1 p.m. EST/New Orleans, Louisiana
(Personal cell phone footage recorded by Cal Perkins.)

PERKINS: Welcome to the burning party, bitches! We're going around, rounding up and dousing our pals with gasoline and lighting the motherfuckers up!

(Assailant #1 charges.)

PERKINS: Here he comes! Hey, over here! That's right! You got me, come on—

(Perkins tosses accelerant onto Assailant #1.)

PERKINS: Ooooh! Bath time!

(Perkins lights Zippo, steps back, and tosses it onto Assailant #1, igniting him.)

PERKINS: Holy shit, look at him go up . . . Somebody brought the marshmallows?

(Perkins circles around Assailant #1 as he falls to his knees, then collapses.)

PERKINS: *(Singing)* "The roof, the roof, the roof is on—"

(Video ends.)

BABY GHOST
Day Three. 129 miles.

I spy with my little eye a . . .

A . . . Oh.

There's a kid on the interstate. A little girl by the side of the road. Blond hair. Overalls. OshKosh B'gosh. There's a square of cardboard tied around her neck. Someone—a parent, presumably—tore off a flap from an Amazon package and used a shoestring for a necklace.

Written in Sharpie, it reads: *NOT POSSESSED. HELP.*

You don't stop. You keep walking.

The girl turns her head, following you and Marcus as you go on your way. You feel her eyes on your back, the boy shifting on your shoulders, but neither of you says a word about her.

No more I Spy for you today. You don't want to see any more.

You've seen enough.

———

Marcus is uncommonly quiet. All through D.C., he wouldn't stop grilling you, but the boy's been keeping to himself this morning. Could he be backsliding into catatonia?

All the things you've seen these last couple days. The corpses on the street. The smell they left behind. You're going to be untangling this kid's trauma for the rest of his life.

The boy's still wearing his padded headphones. You think it's to block out the sounds all around you. Every so often you hear a scream. Better to block it all out, if you can.

At some point you catch him humming. You think it's humming.

Is he . . . *singing?*

When you ask, "What's the tune?" he clams up. It's been radio silence for miles now. The walk drags on without having someone to talk to. Except for me. Still got your ol' pal Coop.

Your mind wanders up to Brooklyn while your body barely budges through Maryland. Slouching toward Baltimore. The ache in your feet is unbearable, but you keep walking. No time to rest. You're losing track of time. What day is it?

Got to get home. Got to find your family. Alicia. Kelsey. You pray they're—

still alive

—okay. Your texts and calls have gone unanswered. Your emails bounce back.

Baltimore is burning. A skyline of smoke. Someone sketched the city in charcoal, then rubbed their palm upward, smearing their picture in a blackened smudge.

The harbor is to your right as you hike up the overpass.

You spot an adrift cruise liner. Pastel flowers and seashells are painted on its side. When you squint, taking the ship in, you realize the deck is splattered with red. A flock of seagulls swarms the bodies cluttering the shuffleboard court. There's a pool on the top deck— used to be a pool. Now it's a mass grave. The surface of the water is carpeted with bodies, bobbing along.

You always wanted to go on a cruise. Take Kelsey to Hawaii. You could take this ship all for yourself. Nobody would say no. All yours. Rechristen it in your name: *Noah's Ark*.

The highway snakes around the city, so you can avoid the fires, but the acrid smell of melted rubber and—*what is that*—meat—*but what kind*—drifts over whenever the wind shifts.

You want to get your mind off that smell. Change the subject for yourself.

"You doing okay up there?"

Nothing from Marcus. Just the subtle hum of a song you still can't pinpoint.

What's he singing?

"You hungry?"

Marcus makes some sort of grunt, acknowledging he's heard you, but that's about it.

"Bathroom break?"

Marcus shifts his weight over your shoulders, and you can feel him tremble. You think so, at least. His whole body spasms every so often, racked with these intense shivers.

"Cold?" When you get no response, you add, "Let's go shopping."

You pilfer a few items of clothing from an abandoned car. You have the pick of the litter. So many abandoned suitcases. So many dashed hopes of escape. All it takes is opening a car door and sifting around. Sneaking a peek. If a door is locked, a brick does the trick.

Look at you. Learning how to survive. I'm impressed, Noah . . .

From the looks of it, a family had packed as many of their belongings as they could before hitting the road, only to stall before reaching the Baltimore Harbor Tunnel.

Your clothes now.

There's a puffy coat that just about fits Marcus. It's a bit long in the sleeves, but it'll do.

Anything to keep warm.

You add an extra sports jacket to your layers, looking more and more like some sort of boho hobo. A modern day Fagin. You dig it. The twelve o'clock shadow. Survivalist hipster.

"How do I look?"

Marcus doesn't say much, lost in his thoughts. His song.

"What is that?" Of course the kid doesn't answer. He merely stares back at you, receding from the present tense, the world around him, lost in phantasmal music.

You turn toward the Fort McHenry Tunnel.

"Well, shit." You scan the surrounding area, looking for an alternative route.

There's nothing. No other option.

You're fucked, my friend.

"Let's get this over with." You don't want to be on I-95 but there are fewer choices when it comes to crossing rivers. You've clung to the coast as much as possible, but once you hit Baltimore—*halfway home!*—you are forced to maneuver through the choked tunnel.

Four tubes. Eight lanes burrow beneath the water and nearly all of them are blocked. Over one and a half meandering miles. That's a lot of darkness. Whole lot of shadows . . .

Sure you wanna do this?

Is there another choice?

The posted speed limit is fifty-five miles an hour and you're about to hoof it on foot. Usually, you can get from one end of the tunnel to the other in less than a minute.

Two, tops.

You remember this particular road game you used to play with Kelsey: everybody in the car holds their breath the second they slip into the tunnel, keeping their lips sealed to see who can make it to the other end without gasping. Kelsey looked like a bloated blowfish, cheeks bulging. Eventually someone's lips split and air sputters out, making everybody laugh.

Can you hold your breath the whole way on foot? Probably not.

"Pick a lane, any lane."

Marcus isn't any help.

"Okay. Suit yourself." You can't decide between the north- or southbound tunnel. The sheer number of cars makes it nearly impossible to navigate.

You'll have to crawl around them. Maybe climb over.

But it's the dark that worries you the most. The fact that you'll be trapped with one of two ways to go, forward or back. Not stellar choices.

What about a boat? Couldn't you just hop on a dinghy and cross the river? Or how about that Carnival cruise ship? Hijack it. Set sail! Ferry all the way up to NYC! *I am the captain now* . . .

No, this is the clearest shot.

"After you." You mean it as a joke, but Marcus doesn't laugh.

Doesn't say a word. Just walks into the darkness without you, leading the charge without batting an eye.

What the hell's wrong with him?

The natural light recedes the farther into the tunnel you go. You're surrounded by avocado-green tile. You've driven through this exact same tunnel countless times, but you've never really had a chance to take the space in. It looks like the walls of a mental hospital. A madman's bathroom in sore need of some grouting. Thin rivulets of water dribble down from invisible cracks and now you can't help but wonder if the whole thing is about to spring a leak.

Wouldn't that be a kicker? Drowning down here? After everything you've survived thus far, the thing to finally take you and the kid down is a collapsed tunnel . . .

You can't help but laugh at the thought, but then your laugh bounces back, echoing through the cavernous tunnel, and the flaccid sound of your own voice chills you.

So you walk in silence, following Marcus.

You almost ask: *Are we there yet?*

"You doing okay?"

Nothing. If the kid is afraid, he sure isn't showing it. When did he become such a cool cucumber? "You know if there's something on your mind, you can talk to me about it. Okay?"

Crickets. The only sound is your footsteps, rubber treads echoing through the vast chasm of the tunnel.

The sodium lights are off up ahead. You're willfully plunging yourself into darkness. You've made some bad choices these last couple of days, but you've learned from them, and now your inner Anderson Cooper is screaming to *turn around, go back, don't go there, DON'T.*

Are you listening to me? Your most trusted name in news?

Of course not.

What a pileup. You can tell this is where people panicked, where the laws of the road were thrown right out the window and people just gunned it, speeding through the tunnel until they crashed into the car ahead of them.

Why are you not turning around? Going back the way you came?

Why are you doing this, Noah?

"Hey. Take my hand, okay?" You have to bring your other hand up in front of you and feel your way forward, blindly guiding you and Marcus along. "Stay close. Don't let go of me."

His hand is clammy. Cold, wet skin.

"You feeling okay, pal?"

Nothing. Just humming.

"You're not coming down with anything, are you?"

His humming grows louder.

He's clinging on to a tune to protect himself, you think. This is merely a mental defensive measure. You know it well: hum along to some song to keep the trauma at bay.

You did it plenty of times yourself as a kid. Maybe it's time you do it as an adult. Couldn't hurt, could it? What song should you pick? There's bound to be an indie rock anthem you could wrap your mind around while you two creep deeper and deeper into the tunnel.

Come on. What Arcade Fire song fits the mood? Where's your vast recall of every last Neutral Milk Hotel banger when you need it? Surely you can select something. There's a whole jukebox in your brain crammed full of Modest Mouse tunes. You've probably made an apocalypse playlist in your mind already, haven't you? The track listing is nearly complete . . .

It's not until you've reached the absolute heart of darkness, winding between cars and stepping over the wreckage, where the black is at its blackest, where you swear you see shadows within shadows, that Marcus finally finds his voice.

"*Baby Ghost, boo-boo, boo-boo . . .*" His off-pitch singsongy lilt seeps out from the darkness. *Mommy Ghost, boo-boo, boo-boo . . .*"

It's out of tune, but you know the song straightaway. How you hadn't caught it earlier is anybody's guess, but now you recognize that this earworm has been in Marcus's head for miles.

He's been singing it over and over again, just under his breath.

Why? To comfort himself? You certainly don't feel comforted. You hated the tune before, but now, down here, with the Baltimore harbor pressing down over your head, the pressure of the Chesapeake Bay ready to crush the walls of this tunnel and you along with it, this song feels downright diabolical.

"Can we sing something else? Please?"

He's not listening to you. As a matter of fact, he sings even louder. Did this kid just crank up the volume on you? Is he fucking with you? He is! Holy shit, that son of a—

Wait.

It's only then, in total darkness, that you notice the glow. A blue-green murk seeps out from his shirt. That familiar aquamarine sheen of a screen, lit up and casting its oily colors.

Another goddamn tablet. "Where did you get that?"

"Daddy Ghost, boo-boo, boo-boo . . ."

"Hey. Answer me." You halt right there, in the middle of the tunnel, surrounded by cars and darkness. You kneel before Marcus and grab him by the arms. "Marcus—stop it. *Stop.*"

"Grandma Ghost, boo-boo, boo-boo . . ."

You peel back as many layers of clothes as you can, like skinning an onion. The further you go, the louder the song becomes. Marcus has been singing along to the song as it plays on repeat against his bare tummy. You finally reach the tablet tucked into his pants and pull it out.

"Give it to me." The screen peels away from his skin. Warm with the boy's body heat.

Welts. There's an angry red rash where the screen rubbed against his skin.

"Marcus—"

The boy squeals, hissing at you. He tries to grab the tablet back, but you won't let him.

"Marcus, stop!"

You lift your elbow and block the boy from seizing the tablet, while you simply stare at the screen. An animated ghost bobs up and down on-screen, swirling and twisting and flipping like a dolphin, smiling and waving its shrouded hand. The screen casts its oily—

gaslights

—glow over your body, across Marcus's face, the only light for a mile in either direction.

"*Grandpa Ghost, boo-boo, boo-boo . . .*"

"Stop it, Marcus!" You give the boy a shake, firm and steady, as if to rattle the song out of his skull. But it doesn't stop him from singing along. He's looped into the tune, synced up with the video, as if they're sharing some sort of mental wavelength. Psychic Wi-Fi.

You glance up. The glow of the screen casts a murky band of light along the rest of the tunnel. You notice for the first time that the entirety of the tiles are laced in shimmering strips of mother-of-pearl. Snail trails. Phosphorescent ivy. Hundreds, thousands, fucking *millions* of thin slug lines leading in every which direction. What the hell could have done that?

"*Boo-boo, boo-boo, boo—*"

"STOP IT!"

The boy's caught in a loop, a mental record skipping, repeating the lyrics over and over. "*Boo-boo-booboobooboobooboobooboobooboo-booooobooooooooo—*"

"SHUT UP!" You raise the tablet over your head and—

CRAAACK

—smash it against the pavement. The screen doesn't break, so you bring it down—

CRAAAACK

—again, then a third time—

CRAAACK

—until the glass shatters into a black web. The oily light sparks out and you are plunged into darkness once more, as if that's preferable. Somehow you feel safer in pitch-black than looking into those awful colored lights, listening to that vile song for the fifty-millionth time.

"*Baby Ghost, boo-boo . . .*"

You hear the song start up again, but this time it's not coming from the tablet. Or from Marcus, for that matter. It's coming from all around. Echoing faintly off the tiles, an exhale.

In the tunnel.

Somewhere close, deeper in the dark, near enough that you know you're not alone.

Someone else is here. With you.

In the tunnel.

And they're singing along, now, too: "*Mommy Ghost, boo-boo . . .*"

Make that several someones.

"*Daddy Ghost, boo-boo . . .*"

"M . . . Marcus?" Suddenly, there's a chorus creeping up from every abandoned car. Adults, maybe even a few children, too, sing along to the song Marcus brought forth.

"*Grandma Ghost, boo-boo . . .*"

Jesus Christ, it's everywhere. *They* are everywhere. They've been in the tunnel all along, hiding inside the cars, just sitting and stewing behind their wheels, fogging up the windows.

Now that stupid goddamn song has woken them all up.

They're moving now. Coming for you now.

Singing—"*Grandpa Ghost, boo-boo . . .*"

You grab Marcus by the arm and pull, breaking out into a run. You're not going to sit here and wait for them to pounce on you.

You keep colliding with cars. You feel like a human pinball bouncing back and forth between automobiles. They're too tightly packed together for their occupants to crawl out.

Marcus tugs in the opposite direction, singing that stupid goddamn evil song, he just won't stop singing, and you've got to drag him along whether he wants to follow you or not.

There. There's light up ahead.

Sunlight warms the tiles.

The end of the tunnel.

It's close.

So close.

You just have to keep—

The door to the car directly in front of you opens and you collide with it, sending both you and Marcus to the pavement.

"Let's go haunt, boo-boo . . ."

The driver—a woman—leans out from behind the wheel and peers at you, smiling.

"Time to wake, boo-boo . . ."

Drool snakes out from her mouth and strikes the pavement at your feet. She seems to have forgotten she's still wearing her seat belt, strapped back, the nylon sawing at her raw neck.

"We're all around, boo-boo . . ."

You crab-walk backward until there's enough distance to pick yourself back up onto your feet. Marcus wants to stay. That much is clear. He wants to sing with these people.

He's possessed. Somehow they got to him. Found him.

A tablet. He's been hiding a new iPad this whole time. Where in the hell did it come from? How did this kid get it without you knowing? While you've been carrying him on your shoulders, crossing state lines, walking for days, he's been slowly indoctrinated by YouTube videos . . . and you didn't have a fucking clue. That's the insidious thing with YouTube, isn't it? One video always leads to another, to another, to another, guiding you down a rabbit hole of interconnected clips. It's not long until a kid stumbles upon a video they're too young to watch, luring them into lord knows what, all on account of some goddamn demonic algorithm.

"Let us in, boo-boo boo-boo . . ."

You won't let the boy go. Absolutely won't. You've come this far, brought him this far. You're not abandoning him, possessed or not.

Maybe it's not too late. Maybe there's still time?

Can you bring him back?

You pick him up, hoisting him onto your shoulders. He thrashes and squeezes your neck with his thighs, but you grip onto his shins and start power-walking out of this fucking tunnel.

The voices are at your back now. The song is behind you.

"Let us in, boo-boo . . ."

Sunlight hits your face, warm against your cheeks. It's blinding, the sun, but you practically bask in it, hoping it burns you to a crisp. Anything is better than what's at your back.

Marcus bites and scratches at your neck, your arms, whatever he can grab hold of.

The boy has lost his mind.

Not his mind.

His soul. Lost his humanity to some fucking YouTube video. Some memetic earworm that burrows into your brain and takes you over from the inside out and now he's one of them.

One of *them*.

You've come this far. You're not about to give up on this kid. You absolutely refuse.

How do you stop this?

How?

There's no time to figure it out. You have to keep going. Running. Keep on your feet.

You unbuckle your belt. Reach up and wrap it around Marcus's chest, strapping both arms down. You flip him around so his back is pressed against yours and you cinch your belt around your own chest and buckle it. It's tight and hurts to breathe, but you're able to tether the boy to your back, facing away from you. His legs pinwheel through the air, kicking at nothing. Anytime he reaches for you, you simply bat his hands away. The angle is far too awkward for him to grab anything but your hips, which he does—repeatedly—but you keep smacking at his hands until he lets go.

"Quit it. Stop."

Your balance is off.

Way off.

But you wobble, regain control over your legs, stumble a few steps, then start moving.

"Okay," you say to yourself. "Okay, we got this. One foot in front of the other."

There. That's it. You got this. You can do this. You're halfway there already.

"Halfway home," you tell yourself. Words of encouragement, that's what you need. A little positive reinforcement. Anything to drown out the fucking song just at your shoulder.

"*Baby Ghost, boo-boo . . .*"

VIDEO #1201: Footage taken from Josh Wearing's personal TikTok account

JOSH WEARING: It's been three days? Maybe four. Four days since my wife . . .

(Wearing turns his phone on Paula Wearing, her limbs tied to a bed.)

JW: As you can see, I've secured her . . . after she hurt our son. Paula?

PAULA WEARING: *(Unintelligible.)*

JW: Paula, can you hear—

JW: I've been giving her water and that's—that's about it. The rest she spits up.

PW: *(Unintelligible.)*

JW: That's right, hon. I'm here. I want you to know I'm not giving up on you. I'll be here with you every step of the way. We're going to get through this together.

PW: *(Unintelligible.)*

(Wearing rests next to his restrained wife, holding his phone on them both.)

JW: I love you. I love you so much. You're stronger than this. You can beat this, I know you can. You just have to—to keep trying. I'm here, hon. I'm not leaving you. You just have to—you have to fight this. Please, honey. Please. Keep fighting.

PW: *(Unintelligible.)*

JW: You and me. We're fighting this together. Hear that, everybody? Together.

VIDEO #962: "DIY Exorcisms!" YouTube channel, hosted by Hank Maddock

So you wanna perform your own exorcism! Folks, have I got good news for you . . .

You can bring your loved ones back from the demonic brink with these three easy steps. Cast out those unwanted haints with this quick and easy cure-all.

It's simple! Don't you worry one bit over what denomination you or your family fall under. This works for Jews and Hindus, Catholics and Wiccans alike.

Don't sweat the details. Let's get to exorcising, what do you say? Follow me!

First, you got to get all that movie bullshit out of your mind. It's not like that Catholic crap. These demons don't give a hoot which god you pray to. They're like . . . parasites who dabble in politics. They attach themselves to the weak-willed, the most vulnerable among us, those who lower their guard and invite them in.

Why would anyone want them to come in? Look around. They've been pumping their paranoia into people for lord knows how long. They flipped the switch and—

BAM! They're in.

So . . . how do we cast them out? None of that "power of Christ" crapola cuts the mustard. You need to lure them out. Think of them more like spiritual home-wreckers. You invited them into your house and now they don't want to leave . . .

They'll eat you out of house and home. They'll wreck your house. Unless . . . well.

You need to show them a better home. A better vessel. A different body.

Regardless of your religious affiliation, there is a biblical precedence for this procedure. The Good Book makes reference to swine-swapping as the best process for exorcising demons around. Jesus got a demon to hop into some swine.

WWJD, am I right?

First: Find yourself a pig. Any pig. Pork is the preferred vessel for body swapping. You got to trick it. Trap it. Get something else to contain it. A dummy possession.

I can hear you asking yourself right now: Where in the hell am I gonna find a pig?

Look around! Plenty of swine out there. Those dirty little buggers are probably rutting not too far from where you are right now. You just got to get out and look.

Second . . . You got to secure your loved one. I know this ain't pretty. It can probably get downright uncomfortable. But for this to work, you need to make sure your family member is tied down tightly enough that they won't worm away.

Third . . . and this is the big one now: You got to tempt that little devil. You got to show it that plump pig and let it know how much nicer it is inside that swine.

Come on out now. Lookie what we got here . . . Mmmm! Fresh piggie! Everything's better with bacon! Come on, you know you want it. Come on, get it! Get it, get it!

VIDEO #1321: 12/20 at 3:30 p.m. EST

(Raw footage from Reverend Billie Gray's Temple Hill Baptist You-Tube channel.)

GRAY: Frame the shot. Be sure to get us both in when I say so, okay? We good?

(Gray clears his throat, addresses the camera.)

GRAY: We're taking our fight to the streets. Bringing the mountain to Muhammad.

(Pause.)

GRAY: The possessed walk among us. Our cities, our streets, are now overrun with those who have succumbed. This country is rife with these heathens. Our church has taken it upon themselves to perform roadside exorcisms for those in need. We can bring them back to the loving grace of God. Here. We'll show you . . .

(Gray steps back. Assailant #1 is gagged and restrained with zip ties.)

GRAY: You got her? Yeah? Okay.

(Pause.)

GRAY: Before you is a lost lamb. She has strayed, but we're bringing her back.

(Unintelligible chatter from Assailant #1.)

GRAY: That's right. That's right. Look who's quaking now. Let's do this . . .

(Unintelligible chatter from Assailant #1.)

GRAY: Out! I cast thee out! You can't stay in there forever! Out, you vile thing! In the name of the Father, the Son, and the Holy Spirit, I cast thee out!

(Unintelligible chatter from Assailant #1.)

GRAY: Look who's quaking now, yeah. That's right. Look who's quaking now . . .

(Unintelligible chatter from Assailant #1.)

GRAY: Out! Go back to the pit from which you came! Out, goddammit! Out!

(Pause.)

UNKNOWN: (Off camera.) Did it work?

GRAY: Just give it a second.

UNKNOWN: *(Off camera.)* Are you sure . . . ?

GRAY: Just wait. I think she—

(Unintelligible chatter from Assailant #1.)

GRAY: Jesus!

UNKNOWN: Holy shit—

GRAY: Oh, this is a slippery son of a bitch. That's okay. We got all day. You keep filming . . . We're about to go for another round. Just you and me, you hear? Just—

(Internal edit. Unknown time jump.)

GRAY: —so why in the hell did you turn it off? I didn't tell you to stop recording.

UNKNOWN: But it's not working.

GRAY: You don't know that. You don't know nothing. You're just recording. You can't even do that right. Now hold the phone up and film me, okay? Okay?

UNKNOWN: Okay, okay . . .

GRAY: Hour three. This one's stubborn, but that's okay. We've got the Lord on our side. We've got all the time in the world. All it takes is a little faith, patience, and—

(Unintelligible chatter from Assailant #1.)

GRAY: Shut up.

(Unintelligible chatter from Assailant #1.)

GRAY: I said shut the hell up—

(Unintelligible chatter from Assailant #1.)

GRAY: You're not winning today, goddammit! Get behind me, Satan! Get behind—

(Unintelligible chatter from Assailant #1.)

GRAY: Shut up, shut up, shut up!

(Gray's back is to the camera, eclipsing Assailant #1.)

GRAY: OUT! I CAST THEE OUT! GET OUT! OUT, OUT, OUT, YOU—

(Gray steps back. Silence.)

UNKNOWN: Is . . . is she? Is she breathing?

(Silence.)

UNKNOWN: She's . . . she's not . . .

(Gray turns to camera.)

GRAY: Get that thing off me—

(Recording ends.)

DEPROGRAMMING
Day Four. 211 miles.

Pick a pig, any pig . . .

You finally find a farm in Hopewell, New Jersey, not far from the turnpike. You hear the squeals about a mile before you reach them, shrill cries of hunger guiding you along.

You picked up a Bible along the way.

Funny how easy it is to find a Bible lying around. The Good Book certainly isn't in short supply around here. You grabbed one at an abandoned gas station in Delaware. You needed a snack and there it was, conveniently stacked on a spinner rack just next to the register.

You flipped through until you found the passage: *A large herd of pigs was feeding on the nearby hillside. The demons begged Jesus, "Send us among the pigs; allow us to go into them."*

Mark 5:11.

You're certainly no Bible expert, but you've had a few miles to think this one through.

Here's what you think Mark is getting at:

These demons begged Jesus to allow them to hop into a few pigs, then kamikazed off a cliff.

Now you're no Jesus, but maybe there's still a way to entice whatever's slithering inside Marcus to come on out. Swap bodies with some swine. If demons prefer pigs . . . give them pigs.

Easy peasy.

It'd be so much easier if Marcus would just shut the hell up. He's been singing that fucking goddamn song, strapped to your back, ever since Baltimore. You're losing your mind.

Losing? You're about to perform some roadside exorcism. Just make a quick pit stop on your way back home and see if you can't get rid of this demonic stowaway.

Dude, I'd say your mind is already *long* gone by now . . .

You found a phone charger at that last gas station. *Do your homework, Noah . . .* You watched a few YouTube tutorials for performing your very own exorcisms at home. A couple how-to videos have popped up in the last couple days. They run the gamut from being fun and informative to not very helpful at all, but it's better than nothing. It's brought you here.

The cold has reached your bones by now. It's a dull ache that weighs your whole body down. A dampness soaked into your skin. You feel bloated. Moist, a mildewed sponge.

You haven't been outside for this long in . . . in . . .

Well, never.

You haven't slept in a bed in days. Haven't felt warmth in just as long. Heat simply doesn't exist outside. It's December, for Christ's sake. *Thank God for global warming, right?* Part of you—just a sliver—finds this amusing. *If it weren't for climate change, it'd probably be a lot colder.* You realize you're laughing from the puffs of air fogging your face: *huh-huh-huh.*

Wait. Is it Christmas? How long have you been walking? You've lost count of the days . . .

Who knows? Maybe there's a manger around here. Got any gifts? Myrrh?

You follow the squeals.

You pass through an alfalfa field. Maybe it's soybean. All bare now. Marcus throws your balance out of whack as you stumble through the plowed terrain, your ratty Chuck Taylors slipping and fumbling across the runnels in the mud.

"Baby Ghost, boo-boo—"

"Shut the fuck up."

"Mommy Ghost, boo-boo—"

"Shut it."

How long has it been since these pigs were last fed? Days, from the sound of it. A week by now? How long has it been? They must be in pain. Starving. The entire farm cries out with the lonesome moan of famine. It's not just pigs. The bleating of sheep. Chickens. Cattle.

But it's the pigs that really get under your skin. Their cries are the most unnerving of all.

The most human.

You've grown attuned to the misery of humankind this last week of your life, hearing more screams than you'll ever want to remember. But there's something to these squeals. The sound of it, the downright intensity to its misery, that awful octave, reaching higher and higher . . .

It's more human than human. Childlike.

You're probably expecting something pink, aren't you? Cute and cuddly? Babe, or Wilbur from *Charlotte's Web*? Miss Piggy, perhaps?

Not these feral-looking Ossabaws. These Iberian pigs were shipped to our shores by Spanish explorers over four hundred years ago. You don't know why you know that. Even I didn't know that. Ugly sons of bitches. More boar than pig. Wild-looking. Long snouts. Dime-sized eyes. Massive, to boot. Their mangy coats are covered in shit-spackled patches of fur.

Those few along the outer perimeter of the herd lift their heads as you slowly approach, halting their squeals long enough to take you and Marcus in. His song halts, caught in his throat.

Can the boy sense the swine?

Hard to say. His thrashing at your back takes a bit of a pause, though. Maybe it's the smell of the place. The pungent aroma of manure hangs thick. The entire farm is shrouded in it.

"Hello?" You call out, just to be sure. The last thing you need is a shotgun to the chest.

No response.

"Anyone here?" Better safe than sorry. "Hello?"

All yours.

Your feet sink farther into the sodden soil the closer to the corralled herd you get. The last few rains are soaked in the earth. Everything's ruddy mud. The added weight at your back is pressing your shoes deeper down. You have to trudge forward, lifting your knees simply to pry your feet back out from the gunk. You're out of breath by the time you reach the wooden fence barricading those Ossabaws in. You need to take a moment, gripping the fence post. Breathe.

As soon as you begin to heft yourself and Marcus over, the pigs all scatter.

Listen to them squeal. The downright wail of it.

Just kids. So afraid.

What have you brought us? they all whine. *What is that ungodly thing?*

One leg over. Now the next. You suddenly lose your balance and—

Timberrrr.

—you hit the mud, shoulder first. It's so soft, the soil. The side of your head hits next, smacking your ear with pig shit. Marcus, too. You'd feel bad if you weren't so damn exhausted.

Impact smacks the air out of your lungs. You watch your breath exit your mouth, fogging into the atmosphere in front of your face, an exhaust pipe panting out one last puff of fumes.

You simply lie there. There's no breath to catch. Not anymore. You just need to rest. To gather what little strength your muscles can muster before unbuckling the belt at your chest.

The slack sends Marcus rolling over into the mud.

There's relief in this release, letting the boy go.

Funny that he doesn't run. Doesn't attack. The boy must be spent, too. You've been walking for days, carrying this kid while he gnashes at the air, singing that fucking song over and over and over again, a skipping record, nothing but an earworm burrowing into your brain.

You never want to hear Baby Ghost for as long as you fucking live.

Marcus's eyes have sunk back into their sockets. His lips peel over his teeth. Even his gums have receded, as if all the soft tissues of his body are shrink-wrapped against his bones.

The Ossabaws circle around, now curious. Why they're not running is anybody's guess. If they were smart, they'd keep their distance. Maybe they're so hungry, they'll give these two humans a try. Do pigs eat people? You feel like you read a book or saw a movie where they do.

You can't think straight anymore. Your head is full of cotton. Every thought is sluggish. Muted. But it doesn't matter anymore. You're on autopilot now. Someone typed in a command and the rest of yourself is simply going through the motions, your body functioning on its own.

Let's do this. Let's get it over with.

Easy-peasy.

You sense the swine surrounding you, forming a ring in the mud, snorting at your shoulders. Prodding you with their snouts.

You pick yourself up to your knees, wobbling from the sudden elevation, then grab Marcus. You roll the boy so he's on his back, staring up at you. Half of his face is painted in a crescent of shit. He looks up at you and snarls—grins?—beginning another rousing round.

"Baby Ghost, boo-boo, boo-boo . . ."

Fuck this. Fuck this so much.

"Shut up," you manage.

Marcus keeps singing.

How do you perform a social media exorcism? How can you cast a meme out from your mind? The only exorcisms you've ever seen are in the movies. How in the hell are you supposed to do this, Noah? You don't even know the right rituals, the correct pronunciation of the Latin.

You're not even Catholic, for Christ's sake. None of this makes sense. How in the hell are you supposed to drag your nephew back from the demonic brink? How do you stop it?

"Mommy Ghost, boo-boo, boo-boo . . ."

"Look. Look at what I've brought you. Take your pick." You have to lure the demon out. Tempt it into hopping from Marcus's body into one of these Ossabaws. How is anybody's guess.

"Daddy Ghost, boo-boo, boo-boo . . ."

"Fresh pig, *mmmmmm* . . . Don't they look good? *Mmmm . . ."*

"Grandma Ghost, boo-boo, boo-boo . . ."

"I cast thee out, unclean spirit!"

Jesus, just listen to yourself . . . Where's ol' Coop when you need him, am I right? You probably think I know how to perform an exorcism. I've performed a hundred exorcisms.

The power of Cooper compels you!

The power of Cooper compels you!

The power of—

"Grandpa Ghost, boo-boo, boo-boo . . ."

"Here piggy, piggy, piggy . . ."

What're you supposed to do? To say?

Laughing. You hear it.

"Go on!"

Marcus is laughing. Laughing at you.

"Hop on in!"

Your hands tighten into fists, mud squeezing between your knuckles.

"Go!"

He's laughing and laughing and laughing as he sings.

"Get out!"

You strike Marcus in the chest, just once, a halfhearted buffet, but he keeps laughing.

"Out!"

You're pounding Marcus's chest now. What kind of spiritual CPR is this?

"What do you want? What do you want from me?! WHAT DO YOU WANT?"

Your voice dies out.

"What . . . what do you . . ."

Wait. Time out. Hold on a sec . . .

Let's get this straight: you think—actually think—*demons* did this?

"What . . ."

You truly believed that people were . . . *possessed*?

Actually possessed?

Where in the world did that idea come from?

"What . . ."

Where are the empirical facts? The scientific data? Who cares what the pope has to say? Just because some guy—on YouTube of all places—says it's true doesn't fucking make it so.

There are no demons. No devils.

This is just you.

You.

Humanity at its worst. The hate in all of your hearts. The bitterness just finally boiled over and look what spilled out.

You did this to yourselves.

Demons don't belong to political parties. They don't register to vote. They're not even affiliated with any one religion. The Catholics all glommed on to the idea of demonic possession because of their own sense of guilt and ran with it, but that's just some Pazuzu-style bullshit.

Yeah, but . . . Even now you're trying to find a retort.

But?

But . . . *what*, Noah Fairchild? *What?* Just because some voice in your head purporting to be the prime-time anchor of a major news network said it's happening doesn't make it so.

Anderson Cooper, you fucking Judas.

You slump in the mud, mouth open. It's dawning on you now.

"No . . ."

Here it comes . . .

"No."

Sorry, Charlie . . .

"It's not real."

None of it.

Heartbreaker, I know.

It takes a moment for you to realize you're crying. The tears mix with the mud.

You wail.

It fills the field.

The void.

You don't notice it at first, but slowly, gradually, the ring of pigs pick up their pitch. It's impossible, but somehow they're squealing along with Marcus's song.

Jesus Christ, they're joining in. A chorus of grunts and squalls coming from all around.

They know the song. Of course they know the song.

Who doesn't at this point? Baby Ghost is everywhere.

It's ubiquitous.

Legion.

"Let's go haunt, boo-boo, boo-boo . . . Let's go haunt, boo-boo, boo-boo . . . Let's go haunt, boo-boo, boo-boo . . . Let's go haunt . . . Boo!"

You glance down at Marcus. That shit-eating grin of his, rimmed in literal shit. Pig shit.

Almost had you there, that grin says.

You motherfucker.

What's that old saying?

How's it go again?

The greatest trick the devil ever pulled was to convince people he didn't even exist? The devil is the ultimate gaslighter. He almost tricked you. He nearly had you convinced.

The ultimate—

gaslights

—fib. You see it in the boy's eyes. The swirling colors. The dull—

glorious

glorious

gaslights

—electricity within each pupil.

"Take me," you say.

Marcus keeps singing, laughing, the pigs wailing right along. The corner of his right lip pulls back and you know for a goddamn fact that this sniveling little devil is laughing at you.

"*Time to wake, boo-boo . . . Time to wake, boo-boo, boo-boo . . . Time—*"

"Take me!" You shout it as loud as you can, hoping to overpower the chorus of pigs.

"*Open your eyes, boo-boo, boo-boo . . . Open your eyes, boo-boo, boo-boo . . .*"

"Take me, dammit!" You pound your fist into the mud just next to your nephew's head.

"*Let us in, boo-boo, boo-boo . . .*"

"Come into me! Take me!"

"*Let us in, boo-boo, boo-boo . . .*"

"Leave the fucking boy alone!"

"*Let us in, boo-boo, boo-boo . . .*"

Something in you snaps. Whatever that last straw is, your civility, your decency, the thing that you believe makes you so *you*, it's just . . . gone.

But let's be honest with ourselves here, okay? The civility never really existed, Noah.

This is who you truly are.

Underneath it all.

Under the skin.

"You stupid little miserable fuck. You're just like your dad, know that? Your whole fucking family is what's wrong with this country. You're the ones pissing it all away. You and your guns, you pro-life, book-banning, trans-hating, body-shaming fucking twats! YOU!"

You're the worst kind of liberal. A self-loathing liberal. Who else would have the voice of Anderson Fucking Cooper chastising them in their head?

Your liberal values were a façade. A flimsy barrier between you and your own baseness.

You are no better.

You are worse.

Know why?

Because you *believed* you were better. You *believed* you were somehow superior to your brother, to your parents, to half of the country. You never *believed* the shit you preached.

You don't believe in anything.

You have nothing, no values, no belief system beyond your own selfishness. You don't believe in God or the Devil or any higher power, and you look down on those who do.

You laugh at them. Mock them.

In your snooty-pants superiority complex, you never had anything to call your own. No belief beyond what's right there in front of you. You have always been selfish. Empty. Craven.

You are a perfect vessel, ripe and ready.

You know it, the pigs know it, squealing with joy as you wrap your mud-covered hands around Marcus's throat and start to choke the life out of him, your ruddy-colored fingers slithering and constricting across his skin like snakes, serpents noosing his neck and cinching . . .

Squeezing the life right out of him . . .

So you begin to sing along: *"Baby Ghost, boo-boo, boo-boo . . ."*

Squeeeeeezing . . .

The words feel so good slipping out from your mouth.

Squeeeeeze . . .

You know the words. Have always known.

"Baby Ghost, boo-boo, boo-boo . . ."

Something soft nudges your shoulder. You turn to notice that an Ossabaw has approached you, nuzzling its mud-caked snout against your arm. Prodding you along. To keep singing.

"Baby Ghost, boo-boo, boo-boo . . ."

Now more pigs close in. The ring of swine tightens. It's no longer a circle. They're all there, tightening around in a football huddle. You can feel the heat of their exhales blasting out of their snouts, snorting along with the song as it picks up its pace, faster now, faster, faster—

"*Baby Ghost, boo-boo, boo-boo . . . Baby Ghost, boo-boo, boo-boo . . .*"

It's like a dam cracking. Or maybe it's your rib cage. All you know is that it feels *so good*. So fucking good to be singing, finally.

At long last. The words have been trapped inside your heart for far too fucking long.

Now you can sing. Sing with the swine. Sing with your choking nephew, his face turning purple. Sing with the country, all of the possessed, the chorus lifting up into the air and spreading across the nation, everyone, every last fucking one, joining in to sing along together.

"*Boo-boo-boo-boo-boooboooboooboooooboooobooooooooboooooo . . .*"

You can't help but laugh, absolutely cackle, at the sad fact that it's a goddamn kid's song, this fucking earworm designed in South Korea, that ultimately does you in, that pulls at your very soul and rips it to pieces right here in the mud, possessing your body like all the rest . . .

You'd like to teach the world to sing in perfect harmony. You'd like to wake up and open your eyes and keep good company. It's the real thing, isn't it?

It's just so goddamn laughable, isn't it?

You're a believer now. *You see.*

So you sing even louder.

Louder now.

Louder.

HOME AGAIN, HOME AGAIN
Day Six. 353 miles.

It's Christmas.

We don't feel any different when we ring our doorbell. We lost our keys somewhere along the way, so it is necessary to stand on our own front stoop and wait for someone to—

open the door

—answer. It's unclear what we feel, if anything, at this point, beyond bone-deep fatigue. Our body might fall apart on us at any point. We are barely standing on our own two feet.

At least we are not alone.

The boy is still with us. He walks by our side now, quiet. Afraid of us. Let him be.

We wait. Breath held.

We bring up our hand and rap our knuckles against the wood, gentle but persistent.

We wait for someone, this Alicia, to answer—

let us in

—the door.

We suddenly sense someone else's presence on the other side. They are trying to be quiet, but we can feel their warmth, their very essence, a candle flame in the dark, as they lean into the wooden paneling to peer through the peephole and take us in with their hazel eyes.

We hear them gasp. Their cries seep through the wood.

There is a sudden metallic slide of the chain lock drifting on its runners.

The hollow pop of a deadbolt, like bones.

The twist of a handle.

The air shifts as the door swings open. We see her—this Alicia—and we relish the shock in her eyes. Tears rim her lashes, plump and succulent, ready to burst.

"Noah?"

We nod. Smile. Smile so wide. Our arms are open now, ready to take her in.

"Honey . . . I'm home." We returned just in time to celebrate the birth of the begotten.

Deeper in the hall, we spy her. The girl. *Kelsey.* Peering from behind her mother's hip.

"Daddy?" Yes. *Daddy.* That's it. That's what we are. "You made it back for Christmas."

You kneel down. Face to face with the child. Arms ready to receive. To hold her.

Smile. Smile for her. Let her know she's safe. Safe inside your arms.

Before you *squeeeeeeeeeze.*

"Daddy's home, baby."

ACKNOWLEDGMENTS

Bless Trevor Henderson. You were the first person I spoke to about this story and your words of encouragement were just what I needed to begin.

Bless editors Andrew Cull and Gabino Iglesias for including the original short story "the spew of the news" in their collection *FOUND: An Anthology of Found Footage Horror Stories*.

Bless the beta readers Rachel Harrison and Nat Cassidy. Saints, both of you.

Bless—and apologies—to Max Booth III, who wrote it better. Please read *We Need to Do Something*. Josh Malerman, too, but in my defense I read *Incidents Around the House* after.

Bless Quirk Books. Bless the editors Jhanteigh Kupihea and Rebecca Gyllenhaal. Bless Nicole De Jackmo, Gaby Iori, and Christina Tatulli. Bless Jane Morley, Andie Reid, Mandy Sampson, Amy J. Schneider, David Borgenicht, Kassie Andreadis, Julie Ehlers, Kate McGuire, Kate Brown, Shaquona Crews, Scott MacLean, and Kim Ismael. Bless you for giving my stories a home.

Bless Daniel Carpenter and the whole UK crew over at Titan Books.

Bless my brother-in-arms Nick McCabe and everyone at The Gotham Group.

Bless Judith Karfiol. Bless Michael Hartman at Ziffren Brittenham LLP.

Bless Indrani. Bless Jasper. Bless Cormac.

Bless my family.

Bless you.

The following books proved invaluable in the research and inspiration for this novel: *The Dictionary of Demons* by M. Belanger. *United States of Jihad: Investigating America's Homegrown Terrorists* by Peter Bergen. *Pastels and Pedophiles: Inside the Mind of QAnon* by Mia Bloom and Sophia Moskalenko. *We Need to Do Something* by Max Booth III.

The Bewdley Mayhem Omnibus by Tony Burgess. *Pontypool* (the play) by Tony Burgess. *The Violence* by Delilah Dawson. *And Then I Woke Up* by Malcolm Devlin. *The Passage* by Justin Cronin. *Dark Persuasion: A History of Brainwashing from Pavlov to Social Media* by Joel E. Dimsdale. *Meme Wars: The Untold Story of the Online Battles Upending Democracy in America* by Joan Donovan, Emily Dreyfuss, and Brian Friedberg. *In the Skin of a Jihadist* by Anna Erelle. *A Good and Happy Child* by Justin Evans. *Domestic Darkness: An Insider's Account of the January 6th Insurrection, and the Future of Right-Wing Extremism* by Julie Farnam. *Boys in the Valley* by Philip Fracassi. *Come Closer* by Sara Gran. *Pandemonium* by Daryl Gregory. *Slenderman: Online Obsession, Mental Illness, and the Violent Crime of Two Midwestern Girls* by Kathleen Hale. *All These Subtle Deceits* by C. S. Humble. *The Plague Cycle: The Unending War Between Humanity and Infectious Disease* by Charles Kenny. *Cell* by Stephen King. *Doppelgänger* by Naomi Klein. *The Night Guest* by Hildur Knutsdottir, translated by Mary Robinette Kowal. "Hyphae" by John Langan, featured in the anthology *Fungi*. *The Many Hauntings of the Manning Family* by Lorien Lawrence. *The Penguin Book of Exorcisms*, edited by Joseph P. Laycock. *Spirit Possession Around the World*, edited by Joseph P. Laycock. *Extraordinary Popular Delusions and the Madness of Crowds* by Charles Mackay. *Daphne* and *Incidents Around the House* by Josh Malerman. *Demon Possession: A Medical, Historical, Anthropological, and Theological Symposium*, edited by John Warwick Montgomery. *The Demonism of the Ages, Spirit Obsessions, Oriental and Occidental Occultism* by J. M. Peebles. *American Girls: One Woman's Journey into the Islamic State and Her Sister's Fight to Bring Her Home* by Jessica Roy. *Tell Me I'm Worthless* by Alison Rumfitt. *Deliver Us from Evil: A New York City Cop Investigates the Supernatural* by Ralph Sarchie and Lisa Collier Cool. *A Head Full of Ghosts* by Paul Tremblay. *Escaping the Rabbit Hole: How to Debunk Conspiracy Theories Using Facts, Logic and Respect* by Mick West.